CANYON SECRET

Paddy Lee

CANYON SECRET

 A NOVEL

BY PATRICK LEE

Patrick C. Lee, Inc. Publishing
2716 Foothill Road
Kalispell, MT 59901
patrickleeinc@usamontana.com

Cover photos from *Hungry Horse Newspaper* Collection by Mel Ruder
Cover design by Rachel Jones of Wink Designs Studio
Text designed and formatted by Michael Dougherty

This is a work of fiction based on factual events. Names, characters, places and incidents are either the product of the author's imagination or are used fictitiously. Any resemblance to actual persons, living or dead, is entirely coincidental.

Published by: Patrick C. Lee, Inc. Publishing
                  2716 Foothill Road
                  Kalispell, MT 59901
                  patrickleeinc@usamontana.com

ISBN: 0-9712542-1-4
Printed in Canada

Quantity discounts are available on bulk purchases of this book for educational purposes or fund raising. For information, please contact the publisher.

Dedication

To all the men who built Hungry Horse Dam and to those brave men who died while working on the project.

Acknowledgements

I would like to thank all those men who graciously shared their personal stories with me. Bud Cheff, Emmett Myrhe, Bob Higson, Al Sparr, and Glen Kartheiser provided invaluable first-hand knowledge about working on the Hungry Horse Dam project. Bob Emerson, who worked as an electrician on the Dam, also provided me with important photographs and stories.

I would like to thank the women whose stories of life in Hungry Horse, Martin City, and Coram during the construction days helped me inject color and personality into the lives of the characters in the canyon towns. I am grateful to Edna Foley, Irene Schaffer, Judy Johnson, Frieda Ostby, Judy Rabadue and her mother for all the information they shared.

The History of the Canyon Area, produced in 1994 by the Canyon Citizen Initiated Zoning Group was a valuable historical resource. Reading this publication helped me understand the growth and development of each of the canyon towns.

The Hungry Horse News in Columbia Falls, Montana provided me with volumes of newspaper articles written about the construction of the Dam. The late Mel Ruder, the owner, publisher, editor, and photographer of the *News*, published a comprehensive series of articles and photographs detailing this period.

Butte, Montana's Jim Michelotti and his *Montana Standard Newpaper* article entitled "The Lost Neighborhoods," and Steve Luft's Master's thesis on the same subject, provided historical information, which I used to foreshadow the encroachment of the Berkley Open Pit Mine on the neighborhoods of Meaderville, East Butte, and McQueen.

I also wish to thank three retired Flathead High School English teachers for reading, editing, and discussing the early drafts of my manuscript. Harry Mular, Lynn Scalf, and Tom Antonovich applied the tools of their trade and made the final editing much easier.

Finally, I would like to thank my close friend Ken Siderius for planting the seed for this story several years ago when he shared exciting memories of his days in the canyon towns when he was young and somewhat impressionable.

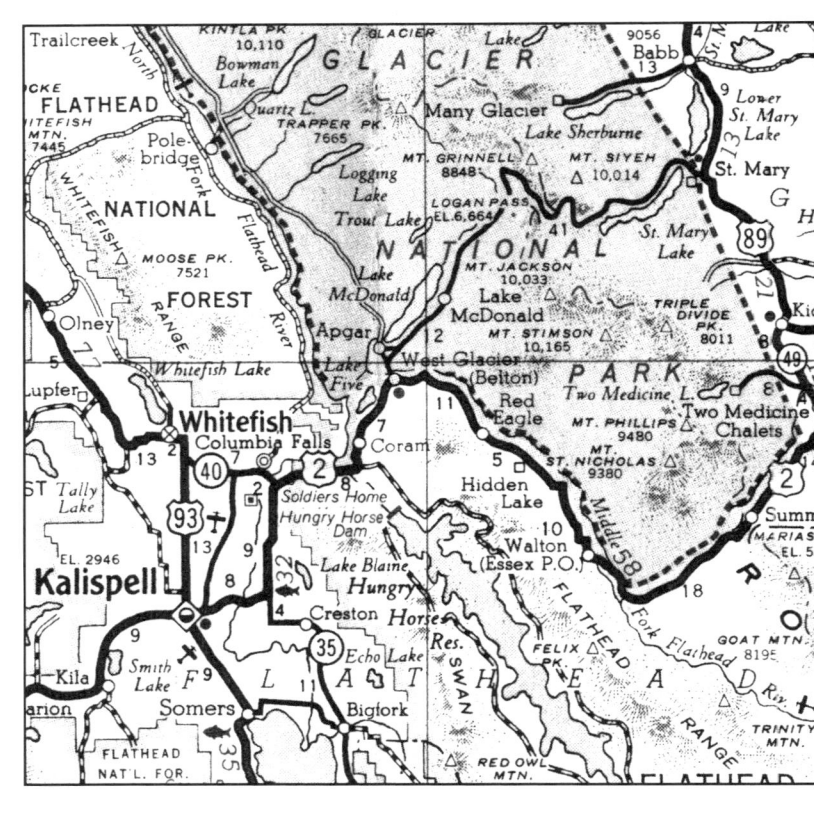

❧ CHAPTER ONE ❧

September 10,2007
Montana Veteran's Home
Columbia Falls, Montana

With a raspy voice the elderly man whispered to his morning personal care attendant at the Veterans Home. "Steve, talked to Doc Carr last night. Told me the cancer's gone wild. I ain't ate nothin' in two days. Can't keep it down." He struggled and managed to inhale two shallow breaths. His shaky hands slowly tugged his throw blanket up beneath his neck.

Steve carefully backed up to the exit door and guided the wheelchair out through the six-foot wide double pane glass door. He moved closer to the man in order to hear as the failing man continued to whisper, "Told my niece school's out for me. That's the long and the short of it, I expect."

His attendant lovingly ushered the man outside to the concrete pad in the picnic area. He carefully guided the chair as tears started down the cheeks of his tan face. The man in the chair meant so much to him. More than once Steve found an envelope stuffed with money in his employee mailbox. With the money he continued classes at the local community college. The young man wiped his eyes and runny nose with the upper part of his white short sleeve shirt. Steve struggled as he attempted to speak to the seventy-four year old man who now slumped down in the wheelchair. They stopped next to a table in front of the clump birch trees. Steve rearranged his patient comfortably in the chair. "Here we are Mr. A, right at your spot. Are you sure I can't get you anything?"

In a barely audible and weak gasping voice, he answered, "No thanks, Steve. I'll wait for the police right out here. After I die, make sure you read my will. I left a little something for you. You finish school and become a nurse." Steve disappeared back into the building and dried a new set of tears from his face.

The old man listened and heard the door close behind his devoted attendant. Now alone, he considered how he'd tell his story to the police. "After fifty-five years of feeling guilty, I'll get this weight off my chest. Just to be done with the secret will be worth it. They can't do much to me now; I'm circling the drain."

The September sun filtered through the wilting leaves of the birch tree and warmed the back of his wrinkled neck. He coaxed the down throw blanket from his shoulders and covered his legs. His circulation problems now chilled his legs most of the time. He slowly raised his head as his tired eyes wandered toward the east. Through his thick, scratched trifocals, he found Badrock Canyon. Teakettle Mountain guarded Badrock to the north and Columbia Mountain protected it to the south. Looking toward Bad Rock Canyon, he focused his mind back to the task at hand.

"With the cops, I best get right to the beginning. Right to where it all started. I won't leave nothin' out. The police won't care much about what happened back then, but it'll clear my conscience. I need to do it." He lost the battle with sleep and blinked his eyes closed. His mind sleepily traveled back through time to 1952, to the streets of the McQueen Addition in Butte, Montana.

⌐ CHAPTER TWO ⌐

McQueen Addition
Butte, Montana
May 9, 1952

Mikhail Anzich slowly walked down the concrete steps of Holy Savior Church after the 10:30 Mass. Most of the church congregation emptied ahead of him and stood outside in small groups laughing and talking. He took some extra time after Mass and prayed for the strength and courage to do what he knew was the right thing to do. It had to be done. Life sent him down a course that he couldn't control. He anguished over his decision and the negative effects it would have on his family, his neighbors, and his labor union brothers. His thoughts abruptly ended as his close friend John Nolan yelled up to him. "Hey, you thick-headed Bohunk. Get your head up."

Mikhail angrily approached Nolan and the two other men who leaned against the handrail at the bottom of the stairs. In his deep and gruff voice he whispered, "Nolan, I told you not to call me that in front of people. Especially when there's women around."

"I keep forgettin'. I'm just so jealous of your big-"

"Don't say it! I mean it."

The men with Nolan stepped back and joined their wives. It wasn't safe to be close when Nolan pushed the limits with Mikhail. Neither man wanted Mikhail to think they were part of Nolan's teasing.

John Nolan laughed and nodded his head to Mikhail to start walking toward the side of the church. As they walked by women leaving the church front, Mikhail tipped the corner of his newsboy cap with his right index finger. He imitated this sign of respect and courtesy that he learned from his father when they walked home from this same church many years earlier. He bristled from Nolan's teasing, but his real anger originated from other pressing issues.

Again Nolan interrupted his thoughts, "When you tellin' all these people that you're leavin'?"

Mikhail stopped near the front of Holy Savior School and looked southward toward his neighborhood of McQueen. He continued to recognize people as they walked by. "I'm tellin' the officers of the McQueen Club tomorrow afternoon. They'll tell everybody else. I'll tell the men at the union meetin' tomorrow night."

"And when you tellin' my nephew?"

"Tomas ain't your nephew! He's your godson!"

Nolan laughed again, "I adopted him last week when you were in takin' a dump. He likes me better'n you anyways."

Mikhail shook his head and managed a weak smile as he looked away from his long-time tormentor and confidante. Nolan brought a lighter side to the problems Mikhail faced. "Someday Nolan, I'm goin' to-"

"Yeah, yeah. I've heard that one a thousand times. You're too big and slow. That empty bucket on the top of your shoulders weighs you down."

The two friends resumed their walk again, "I'm tellin' Tomas tonight after supper."

"Call him Thomas, or Tom, or Tommy. You don't live in Serbia or Croatia or wherever the hell you're born. You're the only one who cares about that shit anymore."

"It's Slovenia. We're Slovene."

"It don't matter. You're all the same. You're all Bohunks to me."

The men walked down Leatherwood Street toward their homes on Garfield Street. Nolan managed to temporarily chase away Mikhail's anxiety about his situation. He grinned and without looking at Nolan, he answered, "It's worth leavin' Butte, just to get away from the likes of you."

They continued their bantering until they passed in front of Nolan's home on the corner of Garfield and Leatherwood. As they had done for the forty years they knew one another, the two old friends said good-bye and made plans to meet in a couple of hours to walk over to the McQueen Athletic Club for the afternoon.

Once alone, Mikhail quickened his pace. He again faced his decision to leave McQueen and everything he loved. The labor strike of 1952 entered its fifth month with no possibility of settling in sight. The business agents from the six unions just returned from Washington, D.C. with the disappointing news that Senator Mansfield wouldn't interfere and pressure the Anaconda Company to sit at the table to negotiate. The main issue to resolve was the Company's demand for cross-productivity whereby officials insisted that two out of every eight-hour shift, men could be assigned to work outside of their craft or local union. It was a tactic to break the strong union hold on employment. The union movement gained strength following the labor strike in 1946. Solidarity was at its all time high in Butte labor history. The unions stood strong against the Company's plan.

Mikhail filled the role as shop steward for the Iron Workers Union. He and his son picketed every day of the strike. His commitment and example focused the strikers during the painful months of the strike. Now he planned to leave to go work on the final months of construction of the Hungry Horse Dam in northwest Montana. He had to pay the medical costs for his granddaughter, Anna. The expenses for the iron lung and the months of no paychecks drained the family's small savings. His son-in-law brought in enough to pay for the day to day house bills and his fancy new pickup. With the strike and no money coming in for over five months, the hospital planned to move Anna to the County Hospital with other polio and tuberculosis patients.

Rumors of the Anaconda Company beginning open-pit mining instead of underground mining threatened the McQueen Addition and its sister neighborhoods, Meaderville and East Butte. The Company planned the open-pit mine right where these historic neighborhoods thrived. The nearby hillsides and the neighborhoods would be destroyed once the Company dug the open-pit mine. The Company already approached two neighbors to sell their homes and property. Mikhail's stomach turned each time he thought of losing his beloved home and neighborhood McQueen. Most likely he'd never return to Butte following his work at Hungry Horse. He couldn't tolerate the thought of the changes to come. His neighbors didn't believe the Company about the pit. The handwriting was on the wall, and Mikhail knew it.

The most painful problem for Mikhail was still the loss of his wife to the owner of the National Bank where she worked. For months after their divorce, he still thought she would come to her senses and return to him and their home in McQueen. This hope ended a week earlier when he read her marriage announcement in the *Montana Standard*. Mikhail snapped out of his torturing self-talk when he heard the front door close as his son Tomas walked into the kitchen.

— · —

The next evening, Mikhail and Tomas drove in silence. As he pulled away from the curb in front of his house he recalled the days of the streetcar. Until 1937 when the buses came, he and his family caught *The Dinky* in front of his house and rode it over to the Pittsmont Mine. From there they transferred and rode out to the Columbia Gardens or to uptown Butte. The crowded streetcar ran continually up to midnight.

He looked straight ahead as he steered his black 1949 Chevy sedan around the corner of Front Street and headed north up Main Street. The windshield wipers kept time with the radio and Hank Williams and his new hit song, "*Your Cheating Heart*." With one quick motion, he turned the volume knob down. She was on his mind all day long and this song pushed the pain to the front of his troubled brain. Two years seemed like yesterday; it still made him crazy to think about her. The sudden silence in the radio caused his son to turn and look at him. "Don't like that song, Dad?"

He didn't answer and stared straight ahead. His mind now shifted and focused on the upcoming union meeting. Union leaders promised a quick week or two and the Company would beg to have them back at work. That was five months ago. No end in sight. Tension grew at home between the strikers and their families. Wives grew impatient and more frightened as the meals became smaller and the bills piled higher. Some strikers wasted what little money available from maintenance shifts at their favorite beer joints. The lack of money affected the gas stations, bars, and clothing stores. Grocery storeowners no longer carried the men. The men on strike feuded with one another. His announcement tonight promised to be very unexpected and unpopular.

His son spoke again. "Dad, will any of the men get mad enough to want to pick a fight with us? I guess they'll be unhappy with us leaving."

Mikhail stopped for the red traffic light at the corner of Main and Granite. He cleared his throat and spoke, "We might. Most likely we'll have to fight more than one if it gets goin'."

"But who'd be crazy enough to choose you?"

"John Navarro might."

"Is he as tough as everyone says? He ain't close to your size."

Mikhail directed his car left onto Granite Street and shifted into second gear. "He is. I seen him fight two men at once."

Tomas shifted nervously in his seat as his stomach somersaulted. "Who'll most likely come for me?"

"Nelson. Or maybe O'Leary." He slowed and angle parked in front of the Union Hall. A good crowd of men wearing bib overalls and yellow slicker raincoats stood outside of the Iron Workers Union Hall door. Some of the men passed a bottle of cheap whiskey and wiped off the bottle lip before and after they took long swigs. Tomas noticed that many of the men wore white carpenter caps like his father.

As Tomas and Mikhail joined the men, Tomas sized up Jimmy Nelson and Dick O'Leary. He told himself that he might have a chance with Jimmy, but O'Leary probably would knock him out. His stomach continued to churn as Dick O'Leary welcomed the father and son to the crowd. "Take a pull Mik, it'll cure what ails ya."

Mikhail shook his head no. Everyone knew he was on the wagon since he hit his wife's new lover. His powerful backhand slap broke the man's nose and eyeglasses. The man didn't press charges, and Mikhail swore off liquor following that incident.

The front door opened and the men trudged down the hallway toward the meeting room. Nineteen-year-old Tomas glanced at the photo of his father on the wall along with the photos of the other trustees and officers. Again nerves engulfed his stomach. "This is gonna be bad. Dad's been one of the leaders at the picket line and I been there with him. Now we're leavin'. I wish it was over."

Mikhail sat in a wooden chair near a table on the small stage in front of the rows of collapsible wooden chairs. Chairman Vic Pollard called the meeting to order, "Brothers, welcome. We got two or three things to talk about before I open it up to floor. First, we're shy on pickets Sunday morning in front of the Mountain Con Mine. I need three more men. Sign up with Ducky Kelly before you leave tonight. Number two-"

Dick O'Leary interrupted the chairman as he accidentally dropped the empty whiskey bottle on the wooden floor. "Sorry, Vic." The other men threw impatient stares at the red-faced O'Leary as Chairman Pollard prepared to continue. Pollard cleared his throat and used his gravely voice to gain the attention of the men, "As I was saying there, number two, Mother's Day is this here Sunday, and it would be a good idea if we shortened up the picket time for the married men. Some of you single guys need to take longer turns at the gates. Sign up with Duckey on that too."

He coughed and sipped from his water glass, "Another thing. You probably heard Senator Mansfield ain't about to help us force the bastards to the table. We might be needing a vote in a week or so to see if we want to keep goin'. Be thinking about it. Now I open it up to the floor." A slight pause followed as Mikhail slowly raised his hand. "Chair recognizes Brother Mik Anzich."

Mikhail clumsily pushed back the undersized chair and he stood up to speak. His six-foot-seven frame and two hundred and fifty pounds rose from the table as he prepared to talk. Some of the men in the front two rows cranked their necks to make eye contact with him. "I got somethin' to say. So I'll say it right out. Don't want any of yous' to hear it second hand. Me and my boy leave Monday for Hungry Horse to work. My little Anna has the polio. We got to work to pay the bills. Ain't nothing we planned to do. Family comes first. We'll be out in back after the meetin'. If you've got a problem, that'll be the time to speak up."

He sat down and stared straight ahead toward the back of the room. The silence roared and deafened the room. No one made a sound. Chairman Pollard cleared his throat. "The floor's open." Still silence. Only hushed grumbling by O'Leary and Nelson. "Well, I guess this meeting's over." He slammed the gavel down and looked across as Mikhail walked down the three stairs toward the back door. Tomas followed him out the door and into the dimly lit gravel alley behind Union Hall.

Mikhail walked to the edge of the alley where it met a wooden picket fence. He slowly took off his gray sweatshirt and hooked it on an exposed nail on the fence. Pulling out a pair of worn leather gloves from his pocket, he slipped them on his giant calloused hands. Tomas took off his black horned rimmed glasses and placed them in the pocket of his jean jacket, which now hung on the fence. He slipped on his yellow leather gloves and pulled them tight over his fingers. "I'm scared Dad. Most scared I've been in my life."

"Me too, Tomas. It got'a be done this way."

"Any tips for me?"

"Stay on your feet. Both men'll put the boots to you if you go down. Stay up and box like Nolan learned you." The back door of the Union Hall exploded open. Dick O'Leary led the group toward the two men standing in the alley. A large circle of men choked off the alley as they surrounded Mikhail and Tomas. Mikhail spoke first, "Do you chose me, John Navarro?"

The short, stocky Mexican made his way into the circle and faced Mikhail. He spoke broken English through his wide smiling lips, "You're wrong to leave, Mik. I don't fight you. I owe you one favor. You got me and my brother our jobs. I fight on your side this time. He took off his white dress shirt and handed it to his brother. Tomas stared at Navarro's huge dark chest, biceps and neck. The men standing near him took a couple of steps backward. Navarro walked over and stood alongside Mikhail.

Dick O'Leary stepped into the circle. "I can't take you, Mikhail, and I'm sure as hell not going to try Navarro. But I chose your pup there. Nelson gets to finish him off if I don't git the job done."

"Now hold on there lads." Tim Nolan pushed his way from the back of the crowd and entered the circle. "I can't miss all of this fun now can I? It's not goin' to work for the Kid to fight the both of you, now will it? I'll go a few rounds with you, O'Leary. My nephew can have it out with Pee Pee Pants Nelson."

Mikhail spoke up, "Butt out, Nolan. Not your fight. Tomas'll handle his own."

Nolan took off his gray sweater and tossed it to Mikhail. He laughed as he answered Mikhail. "My fight now you big ugly Bohunk. I'll be goin' up to Hungry Horse with you and my nephew."

Mikhail bristled after hearing the words of his close friend. "He ain't your nephew."

"Ya, he is. I adopted him. Ya can't remember shit can ya?" Some of the men laughed. "Now let's go here, O'Leary. Let's show the boys what a couple of Micks can do with their dukes." He shadow boxed a few steps and came within inches of O'Leary's face. Then he danced backwards as he circled his fists. "Come on, Big Dog, let's see what ya got."

O'Leary lumbered toward Nolan and led with some fierce left jabs that Nolan easily dodged. The big man fired a circling right hand that flew just above Nolan's head. Nolan unleashed five jabs that accurately found the O'Leary's whiskey-redden face. Blood exploded from the nose of the stunned man. Nolan danced backwards again and bowed to the crowd of men. One of the men yelled, "Kick his ass O'Leary, teach the cocky little prick a lesson."

Dick O'Leary knew he had to get his opponent on the ground. He charged, missed with a clumsy tackle and skidded face first on the gravel. Again Nolan taunted him and the crowd with his dancing and shadow boxing. Jimmy Nelson lost control and Sunday punched Nolan in the right cheek and knocked him to the ground next to O'Leary. Nolan quickly rolled away from his enraged opponent and sprung back to his feet and danced toward Nelson.

Tomas jumped into the circle and stood in front of Nelson. Before Jimmy Nelson fired a punch, Tomas landed three lightning quick jabs to his chin and forehead, and followed with a strong right hand to his cheek. Nelson went down. Tomas danced back and waited. Nelson waved his hand. He had enough.

Dick O'Leary crouched on one knee and wiped the blood from his nose on his bare arm. "I've had enough for now Nolan. We ain't done. You gotta come back to Butte sometime. We'll finish it then. I had too much time in the bottle tonight."

"That'll be fine Big Dog. I'll look you up for sure. Anybody else wanta go a couple of rounds?"

The crowd dispersed. Mikhail watched as O'Leary helped Jimmy Nelson stagger through the door. He also watched John Navarro flip his white shirt over his shoulder and saunter back into the building behind the grumbling crowd. It saddened Mikhail to think that he lost such good friends and co-workers. He didn't tell Tomas, but he knew they'd never return to Butte. His family came first. The doctor bills had to be paid. They'd come back for his daughter and little Anna later. He joined his son and Nolan as they took the long way around to his Chevy. Nolan rehashed the fight with Tomas and praised him for his footwork. "You learn good, Kid. You remind me of myself as a young buck."

Tomas didn't respond to Nolan's comments. It was done. That's all he cared about. Nolan interrupted his thoughts, "What time we'll be leavin'?"

Mikhail held the door open and looked at Nolan. "Why you goin', Nolan?"

"Christ Almighty, somebody gots to take care of a big ugly Bohunk like you. That nose might scare up a bear or two. Maybe one of them grizzly bears might think you're a mate and mount ya. I'm surprised they even allow your type to work outside of Butte." He laughed and winked at Tomas.

Mikhail replied, "Eleven on Monday."

----·•·----

In 1952, more than 57,500 Americans contracted polio. As children got older and played with others, swam in public pools, and went to school, they were exposed to the poliovirus, which then caused paralytic poliomyelitis. The poliovirus lived in water and was transmitted from feces. When it entered the stomach it attacked cells in the central nervous system, which controlled muscle function. Polio paralyzed its victims by killing off the spinal cord's motor-nerve cells, which control various muscles.

In the cases of respiratory paralysis, the chest loses its muscle action and the patients were in danger of suffocation when they could not get enough air into their lungs.

Five-year old Anna Sednick woke up three weeks earlier with a headache, fever, and a sore throat. She swam the afternoon before at the YMCA pool. After suffering from breathing problems, her mother rushed her to the hospital where the doctor placed her in an iron lung. The iron lung pumped air into lungs through a tracheotomy tube in the windpipe. Mikhail withdrew the remainder of his savings to keep his granddaughter breathing using this machine.

She looked up at him from her machine. The bellows motor pushed air in and out of the tank and made a whooshing sound. Anna timed the whooshing sounds and talked in between the whooshes, and said, "Papa, I'll miss you. Who'll read me stories?"

Mikhail leaned over the iron lung and softly looked at her beautiful face. He couldn't remember ever crying before. The sensation overwhelmed him as he tried to answer her. It didn't seem real that this mountain of a man who so many feared and respected was reduced to such a state of helplessness. His daughter Katya answered for him, "Mommy'll read to you while Papa is away. You know some of the words yourself, and you'll read to Papa when he comes home. OK."

"OK, Mommy. Papa can read to Uncle."

Tomas walked out of the hospital room into the hallway and sat in one of the chairs. He placed his hands over his face as he wept and mumbled to himself. "Why did all of this happen to us? What did little Anna do to deserve this terrible disease? And now we're leavin' Anna and Katya when they need us most."

Mikhail came to the door and called Tomas into the room. "We're goin' Son. Time to say goodbye."

Tomas walked around to the other side of Anna's bed. He bent down and kissed her cheek. "Get better, Butterfly. We'll ride the roller coaster at The Gardens when I get back. Understand?"

With a breathy quiet voice, Anna replied, "You're a big chicken, Uncle. You get scared on the hills."

"I'll just have to close my eyes and hold your hand when we go down the hills." Tomas faked a forced smile and walked over to his sister.

Katya burst into tears as she firmly hugged her brother. Through her tears she whispered, "Be good to my husband. He's a good man. Tell him how much Anna and I love him."

"I will, big sister. Can't promise what our dad'll do. But I will, I promise."

Anna looked up at her grandfather and said, "Papa, why is everybody crying?"

Nothing in his life prepared him for this moment. Not even his rough childhood after his dad died. Not even this horrible strike and the scene at the union hall prepared him to leave his beautiful little granddaughter lying in a mechanical tube. "We cry cause we're sad to leave."

"I'll get better Papa. Okay?"

Mikhail Anzich embraced and kissed his daughter and walked out of the room. His life totally flipped upside down. He walked by the nurse's station and hurried down the stairs to the parking lot.

Tomas read aloud the May 6, 1952 edition of the *Hungry Horse Newspaper* that his brother-in-law David mailed to him. Mikhail drove as Tim Nolan slept in the back seat with his mouth wide open.

The Hungry Horse Project is a combination power and flood control project that was contemplated as a result of a survey of the area by the United States Geological Survey in 1934-35. The name of the project came from Hungry Horse Creek, a small tributary that entered the river about two miles upstream from the dam. This creek obtained the name when several half-starved horses were found in the snow-filled valley during the early days of the region.

Hungry Horse Dam is on the South Fork of the Flathead River, fifteen miles south of the west entrance to Glacier National Park and twenty miles northeast of Kalispell, Montana. The dam site is in a deep, narrow canyon approximately five miles southeast of the Fork's confluence with the main stem of the Flathead River. The dam will play an important role in the program for meeting the growing need for power in the Pacific Northwest and a storage system for controlling devastating floods.

The South Fork River is diverted through a thirty-six foot diameter horseshoe shaped tunnel about one thousand feet long through the right abutment during the construction of the dam.

Tomas stopped reading as Nolan passed some foul gas. Nolan opened the fly window in the back. "Sorry boys, too much chili at the Chili King last night. Throw that in with the ton of Butte Special Beer I drank, a man's gonna have some gas."

Mikhail shook his head as he looked over at his son. Tomas laughed and rolled down his window to let out the rotten odor.

"Can't imagine what the dam looks like, Dad. It's almost finished. About five months or so to go."

"Can't neither." His thoughts quickly changed to his son-in-law, David. It was a lot to ask to accept a job from him. "David most likely won't let us forget what he's done for us. Even though we're working to help his daughter. I don't trust him, but we got no other choice. He comes from good people. Don't make sense how he turned out. We just got to make the best of it. Five months ain't too bad a time."

The rustling of the wax paper in the backseat caused Tomas to turn around and Mikhail to look into the rear-view mirror. Nolan dug into the tuna sandwiches on homemade bread that Katya prepared for them. Mikhail couldn't pass up the opportunity to kid Nolan, "We only gone hundred miles. Food's to last us until tomorrow, go easy on it."

Between mouthfuls, Nolan came back, "I'm all in from all the back seat driving I'm doin'. Maybe you could keep it on the road some so a man wouldn't have to work so hard. Then I wouldn't have to eat just to keep up my strength."

Tomas laughed again as he folded the newspaper and slid it under the front seat. "Once we get past Missoula up there, it'll be the farthest I ever been away from Butte. Isn't that something?"

Through a mouthful of sandwich, Nolan jumped back into the conversation, "Oh it's something alright, Kid. Maybe your dad over there could get up off his big, brown Slovene ass once in awhile and take you someplace."

Tomas wondered how Tim Nolan teased his father and got away with it. No one else ever said a harsh or teasing word to his father. Yet Nolan said anything he wanted and his father just smiled and shook his head. They must be real close friends all right. It's a good thing for me and my father that Tim Nolan is along. He makes it a lot easier. I can take my mind off Katya and Anna once in awhile when he's around.

CHAPTER THREE

Named for its shape of the number five, Lake Five was well known for its incredible color of blue, the beautiful variety of pine trees, and the spectacular backdrop of the peaks in Glacier National Park. A small town nearby, known as Egan, consisted of a boxcar depot, a sawmill, a company store, and housing for the railroad workers. The Western Fruit Express Company operated the Lake Five ice harvesting business during the winter. At times, as many as eighty men harvested ice from the lake. Ice was loaded into railroad cars and shipped to the division point in nearby Whitefish, Montana. Tourist cabins that opened in the 1920's hosted train travelers from east of the Rocky Mountains who came to tour Glacier National Park and vacation at Lake Five.

Standing barefoot and wrapped snugly in her grandmother's patch quilt, she stood on the back porch and waved goodbye to him as he drove away in his new Ford pickup. Warm sunny afternoons and rainy evenings of spring greened up everything nature allowed to live following the harsh winter of 1951-52. Cottonwood and birch trees sprung new branches and leaves almost overnight. The early evening smell of the red ocher dogwood and the fresh breeze off the lake permeated her senses as she deeply inhaled. A mating pair of loons swam gracefully through the still water in the bay in front of her long, sloping yard that led to the gravel shoreline.

This was her favorite time of the year. The dark, cruel winter finally left. A fresh start. A new beginning. Her thoughts shifted from the beauty of Lake Five to the complicated man who drove away from her log cabin. "What in the world am I doin' with this married man? My husband'll be home tonight. He'll come driving up as soon as the train from Havre drops him off after his twenty-four hour shift. I hope and pray he's so tired he goes right to bed. I don't think I could stand it if he demands sex."

Her thoughts of the last four hours and the incredible love making that she came to need and treasure burst into her mind. "Damn him, he's so irresistible. I never knew it could be like this. But we can't continue like this. Now, his in-laws are coming to work the dam. I can barely keep track of my husband's schedule, run this string of cabins, volunteer for everything in Martin City and carry on with David. Now, I need to wait around until his in-laws go to work so he can call and set something up. I'll go nuts keeping track of everything."

As she walked back into her bedroom, she continued her self-talk. "Why can't I just let him go? He's no good. I know he pays for it with the girls at Mabels whenever he wants. He gambles, drinks, and spends too much money. He has a family in Butte. When did I lose my nerve? How did he take me over? Goddamn you David! Let me off the hook." She burst into tears and returned to her bedroom.

———◆◆———

By August 1946, two-hundred thirty-five business lots were leased, a park and playground had been platted, and water mains were laid. Over the next six years, twenty-five hundred residents settled down in Martin City. A third-class post office was built along with a four-room school and a jail. A forty-seat movie theater built of logs opened in 1947.

A women's dress shop, two drug stores, a taxi, gas stations, grocery stores, cafés and bars, a variety store, hardware stores, apartments, a pool hall, a sporting goods store, a barber shop, barracks for the dam workers, an electric shop, a car garage, a lumber company, a rooming house, a confectionary store, and a butcher shop opened their doors for business in less than one year. All fifty-six businesses opened to accommodate the workers for Hungry Horse Dam.

As planned, David stopped his pickup in the parking lot of Bill's Texaco Gas Station at the entrance to Martin City. He arrived an hour and a half late. David expected his father-in-law to make something of him being late. If it wasn't this, it'd be something else. Mikhail leaned against his black Chevy with his arms folded. A patented scowl on his face greeted David as he approached. "Long ways to drive for you?"

"Good to see you too, Mikhail. Where's Tommy?"

Mikhail straightened up and stretched his neck and shoulder muscles. He spoke in a low, deep voice, "Tomas's usin' the can in the station."

He looked at Mikhail's powerful arms and huge hands. David's stomach nerves jumped. He visualized what Mikhail would do to him if he knew what he did for the last few hours. David mentally shifted gears and chased leftover thoughts of Lila standing on her porch. "You eat yet, Mikhail?"

"Your wife made us sandwiches."

David's stomach turned even more. "Kat is a beauty alright. I sure miss her cookin'."

Mikhail winced every time David called his daughter Kat instead of Katya. He disliked everything about David, but when he called her Kat, Mikhail boiled inside. "Katya said to tell you, she and Anna love you." He walked into the Texaco gas station and waited outside of the men's room for his son.

Badrock Canyon is located in the northeast corner of Flathead County, along the southern boundary of Glacier National Park. The Canyon area follows the course of the Middle Fork of the Flathead River for approximately thirty-six miles. Early towns sprung up near the railroad. The towns of Hungry Horse and Martin City developed with the building of Hungry Horse Dam.

The locals in Martin City called it the most scenic boomtown in America. It was situated fifteen miles from Glacier Park and four miles from the Hungry Horse dam site. The canyon boomed in the summer of 1948. A wild west character of the canyon boomtowns soon became evident. Gambling, prostitution and liquor came with the big influx of dam workers. Thirteen bars gave the town of Martin City an old Montana look of gold rush days.

The Deerlick Saloon was one of the first buildings in Martin City. Mikhail disliked going into bars and being around men while they drank. He noticed Tim Nolan standing at the far end of the bar talking and laughing with the bartender and another man. Two ten-cent beers lined up side by side in front of him. He approached the three men but only looked at Nolan. "Time to check into the barracks. Let's go."

Nolan finished off the beer in his hand and picked up another. "Whoa there. Do ya know who I'm talking to here? This here is Billy Socolich."

"You're on your own." Mikhail turned his back and walked out the door. His head throbbed, and he desperately wanted to get into bed. He slept poorly the night before. Thoughts of leaving his daughter and granddaughter punished his mind and robbed him of sleep. Visions of the men at the union meeting penetrated the insides of his eyes. He hated any indebtedness to David, and now Nolan complicated things. Nolan didn't have a job waiting for him or a place reserved at the barracks.

Mikhail saw Tomas sitting in the front seat of the pickup talking to David. His son hadn't learned to hate, distrust, or despise anyone, let alone David. Tomas trusted and liked everyone. Many people told Mikhail that his son was the most peaceful man they ever met. "If Tomas spends much time with David, he'll learn how to distrust and hate in a hurry." Mikhail climbed into his car and fired up the engine. He started to pull away, but stopped suddenly as Nolan banged on the backseat window. Mikhail didn't acknowledge him as he took his place in the front seat.

"You've a good-size bug up your ass, Mikhail. Couldn't be that you need a stiff drink and a good screw to clear your head, could it?" He laughed and drank from the glass of beer he stole from the Deerlick.

Mikhail ignored Nolan and followed David's truck up the Martin City Hill toward the barracks. As he approached the top of the hill, Nolan enthusiastically pointed out his window at a house with two smaller buildings a few feet away. "There's Mabel's. Right at the top of Sugar Hill, just like Billy told me. I'll be takin' my nephew there on payday to lose his silver bullet."

Mikhail swirled his head, "No, you won't!"

"Ya, I will. Only three bucks. I might lay down a ten and let one of those nasty little girls take him 'round the world. It'd be good for him. He's nineteen now. It's time."

Mikhail slammed on the brakes, glared and then growled at his childhood friend. "He don't get it that way! He'll find somebody good, and that's soon enough."

Nolan yawned before he took his final swig of the beer. "We'd better get goin'. Davey boy took a left up there."

David and Tomas stood outside of the truck and waited for the black Chevy to join them. David lit a Camel and leaned against a post attached to the porch of the barracks. Nolan walked up to him and said, "So, Davey, you still screwing good people over every chance you get?"

David hated being called Davey. He knew Nolan called him that just to get his goat. "I've jobs for my family, but not you. You might be out of luck, Timmy."

"Oh, I don't know. They made a chickenshit Croat into a boss. Can't be too tough to get along up here. I'll probably be runnin' the place before the week's out."

Tomas looked back and forth between his father, his brother-in-law, and Nolan. He hoped they were kidding, but nobody laughed. Nolan held a smirk on his face, and David showed red from the neck up as they stared at each other. Mikhail interrupted the tense scene, "Show us where we stay."

The barracks were built to house three-hundred workers without families. Each man lived in a room that had a single bed, a chair, and a bench in the small room. Showers and bathroom were military style located down the hall. There was a mess hall, a bakery, and a bowling alley attached. Mikhail and his son took rooms across the hall from one another. Nolan found an empty room near the end of the opposite end of the building.

As they unloaded their duffle bags from the Chevy, David approached Mikhail. "You need to be at the Union Hall at 9:00 tomorrow morning. It's set up for you and Tommy. You'll be able to go out on afternoon shift tomorrow at 4:00 o'clock. They'll fix you a lunch next door and keep a tab until payday. I'm staying in a trailer in Hungry Horse behind the Dam Town Bar if you need anything. I'm on day shift. Probably won't see you for a while. Good luck."

Mikhail never said a word. He slung the large army bag over his shoulder and went into his room.

----•◆•----

Tomas nervously read the April summary sheet as he waited for the bus to take him up to the worksite at the top of Hungry Horse Dam. He stood close to the posted newssheet and squinted through his dark rimmed glasses as he read.

Concrete placing and payrolls soared to new levels for 1952. Concrete placing on the dam averaged 5,500 cubic yards a day during April. Contractors report employment at the 1,600 mark. Total employment on the project including the Bureau of reclamation is at 2,000. Mid-April payrolls exceed the $2,400,000 a month level. Minimum rate of pay at the dam for seven-day week is $114.56 for laborers. Currently, there are 525 laborers, 411 carpenters, 100 steamfitters, 70 mechanics, 61 truck drivers, 54 electricians as well as other crafts and trades.

At present, the major part of the dam runs up to 454 feet above bedrock, and is 81 feet thick and 1,680 feet across. At the bottom the concrete is 321 feet thick. Cement car shipments to Coram, Montana are currently 71 bulk cars a week.

Water storage in the reservoir now totals 282,000 acre-feet. Visitors at the project Vista point overlooking dam construction are averaging about 2,500 each Sunday with about 150 visitors on the weekdays. Last year 260,000 visitors saw the dam being built.

Mikhail joined his son. "Anything good there?"

"Ya, as laborers, we're going to make over a hundred dollars a week. That'll really help Kat with the doctor bills."

Mikhail loosened the snaps on his extra large jean coat, "We work seven days a week."

Tomas looked up at his father, "Nothing else to do but work I expect. Do ya think Tim Nolan will land a job?"

The bus pulled up outside of the quonset hut and the men climbed the stairs to the bus. Mikhail nodded his head toward Tomas. They walked out of the building and up the stairs into the bus. Finally he said in a low tone of voice, "Probably. Nolan's a good electrician. They'll put him on."

Tomas sat near the window on the trip up the hauling road to the top of the dam. As they passed the tiny lake on the left, he noticed a small aluminum boat anchored in the middle of the lake. He spoke as he saw the person in the boat reading a book. "Look at that, fish jumpin' all around the lake, and that woman out there's readin' a book. I'd be fishin' instead of readin' if I was her."

Mikhail glanced briefly at the boat and then at his son. He imagined just how nervous Tomas must be on his first day of work. The union assigned Tomas to a cement crew using a vibrator to tamp down the cement as it was poured. "Tomas'll work hard. He's going be dog-tired when he gets back to the barracks. Probably won't be able to lift his arms in the mornings for a week or so. He'll do a good job for em'."

The first view of the partially completed dam intimidated Tomas. "Look at the size of that thing! And it's not even finished yet. I can't wait to see the water it's holdin' back. Wonder where I'll be workin'?"

The stocky, bearded man across the aisle gave a stilted laugh, "You'll find out soon enough, Kid. Just follow me; you're on my crew."

Tomas spoke nervously, "Thanks, sir. I, I appreciate it." The men sitting around them laughed. Mikhail smiled and nodded his head.

The man stuck out his hand, "Don't call me sir, I'm Shorty Davis."

He removed the glove from his hand and shook the man's

rough, bony hand. "I'm Tom Anzich, glad to meet ya."

Mikhail gave a short wave of his hand in the man's direction, "I'd be his father, Mikhail Anzich." He wondered why his son introduced himself as Tom. Maybe Nolan was right. *Even Tomas wants to be called by his American name.*

Johnny "Shorty" Davis waved back and faced forward as the bus came to a stop in front of the concrete mixing plant. "This is it Kid. Let's go."

The other men on the cement crews gathered their lunch bucket, coats, and hardhats and started for the bus door. Tomas followed suit and quickly turned back to his dad, "I guess I'll see you down below around midnight, huh Dad?"

"Ya. Pay attention."

Shorty Davis stepped inside the cement mixing plant and stopped to sip his thermos cup of black coffee. Tomas looked at the glory hole below the mixing plant and walked into the back of Shorty Davis. Hot coffee spilled down the front of Shorty's black canvas work pants. "Jesus Christ, Kid! I said stay with me, not on the top of me."

The other men laughed as they made their way toward the bank of lockers near the west wall of the shack. One of the men called over to Shorty Davis, "You'd better not decide to take a crap anytime soon, Shorty. God knows what you do with the Kid."

Davis laughed and flipped the man the finger. He walked over to his six-foot locker with Tomas following him but at a distance. Davis smiled at his new young partner and said, "Come on over here, Kid, and park your slicker in my locker. We'll find you a locker later on."

—•◦•—

Climatic conditions were such that concrete placement was stopped during the winter months. From about the middle of November to the middle of March each year, all construction activities were reduced to a minimum with only drilling, repair, and maintenance, and other incidental work carried on. Four power skylines were used to haul cement across the dam with use of cable. Each bucket held eight cubic yards of concrete. One set of cables opened the buckets, one set held the buckets. The bucket would be opened and the concrete dropped onto the pour area. There was a portable tower on one side of the dam to accommodate the locating of the buckets for the pour.

Three shacks that housed men directed the cables for the buckets. The fourth shack housed the bellman or spotter. The bellman signaled the operator with a bell system alerting him when to drop the load of cement. Each pour area was a five-foot wide area. Men used vibrators and tamped the dropped cement into the area. Two men operated each vibrator. These pneumatic vibrators operated by the laborers removed the bubbles in the pour and had to be done carefully to keep the integrity of the cement.

Floodlights hung from a pulley that expanded the length of the dam and put off enough light at night that a person could read a newspaper at the base of the dam. Cement pouring went on twenty-four hours per day, seven days per week.

Cooling pipes were installed within each pour to bleed off the heat from the concrete. The water came up from pipes and hoses that stretched the length of the dam. The water originated upstream two miles and traveled on red wooden pipes down to the Dam.

Tomas stood and watched the men go through their daily routine of getting ready to begin their shift. Most of the men drank coffee, talked, and smoked Camels or Lucky Strikes. He waited to hear instructions from his new friend and co-worker, Shorty. Tomas nervously waited to get started. He wanted to see the dam and the water behind the dam. I can't wait to get going. We're getting paid so we should be working. He twisted his shiny new brass GSM identification badge so that it hung straight on his shirt pocket. Number GSM 3170. I think that's a lucky number. I'll like it better after it gets worn like Shorty's.

A shrill whistle blew and startled Tomas. The men laughed as he exhaled a "What's that?"

"Time to hit the bricks, Kid. Let's go." Shorty exchanged some final parting remarks and walked outside toward the tracks leading out to the center of the dam. "We'll be pouring in the middle today. Don't go at it like we're beating snakes. Me and you are on one vibrator. Go at my pace and we'll get along good."

Four other men joined them as they climbed down into the five-foot deep area. The day shift laid the cooling pipes, rebar, and encased the area with the footings. The three pneumatic vibrators sat in the corner of the pour area. Shorty pointed up toward the power lines that hauled the bucket of concrete. "Watch this Kid. The bucket'll come our way and stop above us on the signal of the bellman. His operator will then drop the load. Stand against this wall; cause when that load empties that bucket's goin' go skyward-fast. It'll scare the shit out of you the first time."

As predicted, the concrete flowed out of the bucket and covered the prepared area. The emptied bucket shot upward. Tomas jerked and belted Shorty with his forearm. Again the men laughed and enjoyed the young man's embarrassment. "Now the fun starts Kid. Get on the purchase end of this big prick and let's start tamping. Get on the stick and stay on it."

CHAPTER FOUR

Four women sat and talked at the large round table facing Main Street in Martin City. This coveted corner in the Club Café was reserved every Friday morning at 8:00 for the four women. Between cups of free coffee, they eagerly discussed the upcoming fundraiser. The Canyon town dance was less than two months away. Funds raised would be used to purchase a resuscitator for the volunteer fire department.

She sat quietly and listened to the update on money raised so far. What a unique group we are, she thought. "How in the world did we ever find each other? Come on now, how many times do you see a Madam of a cathouse, a housewife of an accountant, a widowed theater and women's clothing store owner, and the wife of a railroad worker who rents and cares for cabins on a lake together. And here we are, organizing one more fundraiser. People just look at us and shake their heads. But somebody has to run these two towns. It sure isn't going to be any of the men around here. They're working or drinking all of the time. Hungry Horse and Martin City would dry up and blow away without us."

"Maybe you'd join us here, huh Hannah?" Mabel looked at her dear friend as she spoke. "Where did you go anyway?"

Hannah Holley lowered the white coffee cup from her lips as

her face reddened. "Sorry ladies, I just drifted off there for a minute or two. I wondered how the four of us ever landed here at the same time and then found each other."

For two years now the Care Less Group as they called themselves met regularly and organized the Martin City and Hungry Horse citizens to provide assistance to families in need, sponsor youth organizations, schedule social activities, and raise funds to advance the growing community needs. Mabel tapped Hannah on the forearm as she spoke, "Hannah, the Lord works in mysterious ways. We found each other so the men around here wouldn't screw everything up."

Coffee erupted from Hannah's mouth in mid-drink and she coughed violently and struggled to catch her breath. Not quite finished coughing she answered, "You know a lot about men screwing up Mabel. In fact, you probably know a lot about men screwing down too."

The group erupted into loud, uncontrollable laughter. Normally very reserved, well-dressed, and made up perfectly, Betty Hansen seemed out of character as she joined in the free-fall activity, "In fact, I bet Mabel knows every direction men screw. Up, down, sideways, on their heads."

Mabel wiped the tears from her cheeks and attempted to talk, but she laughed again so hard that she passed gas. The laughing then reached high notes of squealing and gasping for breath. "Oh dear God in heaven, make them stop. I can't believe you, Betty, saying that. Wouldn't your husband have a cow if he heard you." Lila reached for another table napkin to dry her eyes one more time. The other three ladies drew breaths and rubbed their fatigued cheek muscles.

The waitress poured fresh coffee into their cups. Hannah thanked her and then asked, "What'll we do if ticket sales come up short of the $563 needed for the resuscitator? God knows, if we keep laughing this hard, we'll be the first ones to need that damn machine."

The three ladies subtly looked at Mabel as she stirred the two sugar cubes into her coffee. Her eyes burrowed deep into the steaming cup as she responded, "I believe I can part with some of my hard-earned cash if we need a few bucks."

More than once Mabel made up the difference of what was needed for the various fundraisers. The fire truck, Boy Scout uniforms, the children's Christmas party, and the money for the Little League team equipment and new uniforms all were made possible by Mabel's generosity. The community didn't seem to mind that the money came from the dam workers playtime with Mabel's girls on Sugar Hill. Her girls were welcomed anywhere in town as long as they minded their manners and didn't solicit on their own. Mabel had escorted several girls to the bus depot in Columbia Falls for not following her strict rules of public behavior.

CHAPTER FIVE

Rain streaked his office window that faced the front of the dam construction site. David Sednick stared out at the massive concrete project partly shrouded by the dense clouds and pelting rain. He finished signing the time cards for the two-week period for the day shift and rested before tabulating the individual hours for each of the two-hundred and fifty men on his shift. The image of the one-hundred and twenty-five acres on the North Fork of the Flathead River that he bought burst into his mind. Five more payments of eight hundred dollars each remained before he owned the title. Only the realtor and the previous owner knew of his special purchase.

David looked away from the window and down to the stack of timecards in front of him. Six more months he thought. Six more months. I'm done in October. Then I'll build my log home up the North Fork. Kat won't like it up there. Too bad. It'll be great for weekends with some woman and for hunting season. The phone rang and interrupted his daydreaming. "Hey David, it's Tommy."

"Hi, Tom. What's up?"

"I got the long change to day shift startin' Saturday, and I was wonderin' if you wanted to do somethin'."

David searched his mind for his schedule for the weekend. "Ya. Sounds good to me. How about lookin' around Glacier?"

The excitement in Tomas's voice came through the receiver as he answered, "That sounds great David. What day?"

"Let's meet Sunday morning around ten. We can drive to the end of Lake McDonald and eat our lunch there. I'll pick you up at the bunkhouse." After he hung up the phone, he smiled and relished the thought of how his plans with Tommy would irritate his father-in-law. "Maybe I'll start to do a lot with Tommy. We can stop at a few bars along the Trapline and end up at Mabels. That'll really piss off his old man."

☞ Chapter Six ☜

The forty-seat Royal Theater stood on the south side of Main Street in Martin City. The locals and Dam workers who worked the project for a few years spoke for most of the seats. There was unspoken assigned seating and new customers to the one story, log movie house soon learned which seats were available and which seats were reserved. On opening night of a new movie, only one row of seats remained open to first time customers.

Mikhail and John Nolan lumbered up the three stairs to the front door of the theater. Friday night and the first paycheck for the two drove them to the Royal to watch Abbott and Costello in *Meet The Invisible Man*. Mikhail loved to go to shows and hadn't been in a theater for over a year. Nolan teased Mikhail the entire half a mile walk from the barracks to the Royal about their lousy choice to go to a show instead of to one of the thirteen bars in Martin city. "Our first night off and payday and we go to a goddamn show. We should be drinking and getting primed for Mabels."

Mikhail managed a grin before he answered, "You don't need no more primin'. You already had a six pack."

Nolan entered first and slapped down a silver dollar on the table in front of the girl selling tickets. "I'll be paying for the both of us, honey. The bohunk is too cheap. I get stuck for paying his way. You probably should charge him double because of his big ass."

The teenage girl giggled and handed a ticket to each of the men. Mikhail shook his head as he passed the red-faced girl. He walked over to the concession table and bought a big box of popcorn and a Hershey candy bar. "You want anything, Nolan."

"Ya, I'd like a can of Great Falls Select and a shot of Seagrams. And then I'd like a good-"

Mikhail gave him a slight push that broke his thought. "Get us a seat Nolan." The two men walked down toward the front of the theater and sat on the right side near the exit door. Mikhail sat near the aisle and Nolan left a seat between them. Mikhail ate his popcorn and stretched out his long legs, "Perfect seats he thought. No seats in front of me for once."

Three women visited as they walked up the aisle and stopped next to Mikhail. The taller, well-dressed lady whispered to him, "Sir. I believe you're sitting in my seat and the man next to you is sitting in my friend's seat. You'll have to move."

Before Mikhail could respond, Nolan leaned toward the women and quietly said, "Ma'am, I believe you should go shit in your hat. Find a different seat your own self."

The women stomped back up the aisle and returned quickly with the owner of the theater. Hannah Holley owned the theater for over a year and managed to breath life into the building with the latest movies and a clean, modern appearing decor. The Royal was a focal point of the community for the locals and a peaceful distraction for the dam workers. She stopped in front of Mikhail and Nolan. A kind smile introduced her well-practiced speech about reserved seating and the location of other seats for new customers. "Gentlemen, welcome to the Royal Theater. You're new and don't know about the seating rules we have here. One of you needs to follow me and I will show you to your seat."

Mikhail stood up and towered over the four women standing in the aisle. The women slowly moved their eyes from his toes up to his head. Without saying a word he walked back up the aisle and sat in the aisle seat in the last row of the theater.

Nolan motioned the women to join him as he slid down to the seat near the wall. "Now join me ladies. This is a big night for you's. I'm John Michael Nolan. This is your lucky night. The three women moved into their seats and glared at Nolan.

Hannah spoke to several of the other seated customers and attempted to make eye contact with Mikhail as she walked by. He ignored her and stared straight ahead. She thought, "My god, he's the biggest man I've ever seen in my life. I'm glad he decided to move on his own. Not bad looking neither. And he's clean shaved, Lifebuoy soap too. Interesting. I'll have to find out his name." She waved her hand to the man in the camera booth, and the lights in the theater went out.

Two *Tom and Jerry* cartoons erased the tense memories of the seating discussion with the women. Mikhail laughed freely and set his empty popcorn box on the floor in front of him. His right leg stretched into the aisle, but his other knee pushed hard on the back of the seat in front of him. He relaxed and awaited the start of *Abbott and Costello.* The worrisome thoughts of his granddaughter, his son-in-law, and his ex-wife drifted away as the comical story of *The Invisible Man* flashed in front of him on the screen. He didn't notice Hannah watching him as he laughed at the slapstick antics of his favorite actors, Bud Abbott and Lou Costello.

———— ·•· ————

The movie ended and Nolan walked and talked to the ladies who chased Mikhail out of his seat. They tried to ignore Nolan as he reviewed the funny part of the show. The tall, well-dressed woman was still unhappy with his comment to her and walked in front of him toward the lobby. Mikhail stretched as he waited for Nolan. Together they walked out into the lobby in the direction of the front door. Hannah chatted with each of the customers as they left the show house. As Mikhail walked by her, she spoke, "You seemed to like Abbott and Costello."

Mikhail stopped and looked in her direction before he answered, "Ya, I do." Mikhail shrugged his huge shoulders and strolled out the door into the cool evening air. Nolan mocked him as they walked down the stairs to the boardwalk, "Ya, I do. That's it. You thick-headed bohunk. She tried to strike up a conversation with you. Christ Almighty, I ain't learned you nothing. She probably wants to get a look at that monster between your legs."

Mikhail forced a laugh and said, "See you tomorrow, Nolan. I'm going to bed."

"Well, I'm going to Whitey's for a few before I go up to Mabels to share my short steel with one of those lily white little maidens."

As they crossed the dirt street, the three women and an older man wearing a blue suit approached them. The man stopped in front of Nolan and spoke, "My wife told me you swore at her in the theater."

Nolan shook his head and pointed toward Mikhail, "Not me. It was my friend here. He gots a terrible mouth on him. He just can't control his tongue around flat-chested, big hipped, hawk-nosed witches like your wife. It's just a problem he's got."

Mikhail paused as the man stepped right in front of Nolan. "What's your name, fella?"

"I'm Mick Powers and I'm proud of it. What's yours?

"It doesn't matter who I am. You can plan on having a pink slip on Monday. You're done working at Hungry Horse Dam and that's the way it's going to be."

Nolan laughed in his face before talking, "I was lookin' for a job when I found this one. Old Mikhail Powers will make out just fine."

The man stepped back, adjusted his suit coat, and left with the three women at his side. He strutted along after he set things straight in front of his wife and her friends.

Nolan and Mikhail continued across the street stopped, and stepped up onto the boardwalk. Mikhail spoke first, "You just cost Powers his job."

"I know. I've had a belly full of Powers. He brags too much. Besides I want his job. He's a prick and the rest of us will be the happier without him."

Mikhail looked up the street, "You better hope he don't find out about you."

"You gonna tell him?"

"Only if ya keep it up about that woman runnin' the show house."

Nolan laughed and headed toward the door to Whitey's Bar.

Mikhail started toward the barracks. About a block from the barracks, he leaned against a streetlight post and laughed louder than he had in years. His thoughts of Nolan with the man in the suit roared into his mind.

Other thoughts of his friend surfaced from their childhood days living in McQueen. Nolan moved into the neighborhood a year after his father died in a mining accident at the Leonard Mine. His mother later married an Italian man who lived in Meaderville. Nolan was the only Irish kid in the entire neighborhood of McQueen. He learned to fight well as the Italians challenged him on a regular basis. But his quick sense of humor and smart answers made him irresistible to the girls and most of the boys. He met Mikhail in the fifth grade at Holy Savior School. From there they were inseparable and spent the next forty years living side by side.

As Mikhail turned the doorknob to the barracks, he realized he left his cap back at the show house. He hurried down the road to the Royal Theater and walked up the three stairs to the front door of the log building. Hannah talked to the girl who worked the concession stand. They turned and faced him as he entered the front door. "Ma'am, I left my cap. I'd like to get it now."

Hannah motioned with her hand to help himself. He brushed the curtain aside and retrieved the worn newsboy hat that his granddaughter gave to him the previous Christmas.

As he walked out the door, he nodded and said, "Goodnight."

Hannah closed the cash register door before speaking, "I'm goin' over to the Club Café for coffee and pie if ya want to join me."

He looked at the clock above the concession stand. Nine o'clock, he thought. Not too late. He planned to call Katya and Anna the next morning. "Well, okay. I'll meet ya over there."

Hannah Holley sat in the booth in the corner of the café and talked to Judy, the waitress, about the man she invited for coffee. They didn't notice Mikhail enter the door and walk over to the booth. Hannah saw him first and glanced over Judy's shoulder. Judy looked back and reacted like most people who stood that close to Mikhail. She managed a weak smile, turned red, and slowly moved toward the kitchen.

Hannah motioned for Mikhail to sit down across from her.

After he wrangled his huge body into the tight quarters of the bright blue booth, Hannah said, "I didn't think you'd come."

He felt awkward but forced a comment, "Good pie, you said."

She relaxed against the back of the booth seat before talking again, "And I intend on keepin' my promise. Would you like apple or peach?"

"Apple."

"Okay then." She excused herself and walked through the swinging door into the kitchen. Judy talked with the cook as Hannah entered. "Isn't he as big as I said?"

Judy giggled, "Oh he's big alright. I wonder if he's that big all over." The cook turned away from the two women and flipped a hamburger over. The two women covered their mouths to hide their laughter.

Hannah gained control and ordered two pieces of apple pie and more coffee. She joined Mikhail back at their seats and said, "Apple pie comin' right up. By the way, what's your name?"

He replied, "Mikhail. But you can call me Mik."

She slowly stirred the cream into her steaming hot coffee, "Well Mikhail, my name is Hannah. But you can call me Hannah."

He smiled and enjoyed her joke. "Hannah what?"

"Holley. And what's your last name?"

"Anzich."

"Where you from, Mikhail Anzich?"

"Butte."

She shook her head slightly and caught his dark brown eyes looking at her, "Are you always so talkative? Or is it just because that's all the energy you have left from laughin' so hard at the cartoons and Abbott and Costello?"

It occurred to Mikhail that she watched him at the movie. He felt the blood rush to his face at the thought of her noticing him. Judy saved him as she brought the pie and coffee to them. "Well here you go you two. Enjoy your pie."

Mikhail placed his paper napkin on his lap. He picked up his fork and waited for Hannah to take a bite. The pie tasted delicious. He watched her dab her napkin on the corner of her mouth after each bite of pie. They didn't talk until the final flaky crust crumbs disappeared from Mikhail's plate. Hannah folded her used napkin and set it onto her plate. "Would you like another piece?"

"No thanks. That's plenty."

"Do you have to work on this Saturday, Mikhail?"

"No. Umm, I'm on the long change. I'm off."

She hesitated, then looked at Mikhail, "If you aren't busy, would you like to fish with me at North Lion Lake?"

"Ah, ah I think so."

"Try to hold in your excitement a little."

Mikhail shrugged his shoulders, smiled, and spoke again, "I'd like to go on Saturday. I don't have no fishing gear with me."

"I've everything you'll need. How about meetin' me out in front of the Royal around 10:00, and you can follow me up to the lake."

"Okay. Thanks." He awkwardly slid out from the booth and stood not knowing what to do next. "10:00 o'clock Saturday, then."

She smiled and answered, "10:00 o'clock Saturday." Her light blue eyes watched him walk to the door. He stopped before leaving, looked back at her, and gave a short wave with his index finger. Mikhail quietly let the door close behind him and then disappeared into the dark gravel street.

CHAPTER SEVEN

After he finished his bacon and eggs breakfast at the Club Café, Mikhail walked down the board sidewalk to the Texaco station. As far as he knew, this was the only pay phone in Martin City. It was Saturday and his day to call his daughter. He carefully inserted the dime and waited for the operator. She placed his collect call to his daughter, Katya. It had been two weeks since he talked to her and he looked forward to hearing how she and Anna were doin'. He waited until after Katya accepted the call before talking. "Hi, it's your dad."

Katya laughed to herself at his greeting. He greeted her the same for as long as she remembered. "Hi, Dad. How you and my brother gettin' along?"

"We're fine. Workin' hard and stayin' out of trouble."

Katya gathered her strength before asking her next question. "How's David doin'? Have you seen much of him?"

"No, we're on different shifts. I guess he's takin' Tomas up to Glacier Park later today."

She sighed and held back her excitement; at least David and her brother were doin' things together. It's a start; maybe Tommy can convince dad how wonderful David can be. "Oh, that'll be fun for both of them. I bet Tommy is excited to see the Park."

Mikhail thought about telling her about his upcoming fishing trip with Hannah but decided it could wait until another time. His mind changed to thoughts of his granddaughter, "How's Anna doin'?"

"Oh, she's about the same, Dad. Some days I think she's gettin' stronger, and then the next day she acts weak. She asks about you about every twenty minutes or so. She can't figure out why you can't come to see her. I try to explain, but she's just too young, I guess."

Mikhail swallowed hard. "Can I talk to her?"

"Sure. I'll walk the phone over to her. Hey Anna, it's your Papa."

Anna fumbled with the phone as she slowly moved the black receiver up to her mouth. "Papa. I miss you. When you coming to see me?"

He wiped the tears with his huge left forearm, "Soon Anna. Me and Tomas are workin' hard. I'm comin' home in a few weeks."

"Are you goin' to bring me a present?"

"Ya. It's in the Chevy."

Katya whispered that time was about up. "Say goodbye to your papa."

Anna smiled before speaking. Her left hand held the small teddy bear that Mikhail mailed to her a week earlier. "Papa Mik. Goodbye."

"Bye, Anna."

Katya took the phone from Anna and walked back to the table where she kept the phone. "Dad, are you able to come in a few weeks?"

"Yeah. I've another long change then."

"Better let you go. I love you Dad. Say hi to Tommy and David. I miss all of you so much." Tears welled up in her eyes as she looked away from her daughter.

"OK now. That's it on that. We'll be together soon. Hang tough. Goodbye now." Mikhail hung up the phone and bumped the cluttered desk as he walked into the men's room.

On Saturday morning, Tomas sat on the front step of the barracks and waited for David to pick him up. He didn't sleep very much the night before. He felt anxious as he waited. He couldn't wait to see Glacier Park. I've seen lots of pictures, but this will be different. He also planned to fix things up between his brother-in-law and his father. "It might take me awhile," he thought "but I can do it. It'll mean a lot to Kat and Anna. If Dad hears what a good guy David is, he'll change his mind about him." Tomas spoke to various other workers who walked up and down the barrack steps. Finally after waiting for an hour, he spotted David's black pickup make the turn toward the barracks.

David stepped out of the pickup and walked toward Tomas. "Sorry for being so late, Tom. I had to help some volunteers with setting up for their picnic." David had just left Lila at her Lake Five cabin. He spent the night. Lila insisted on fixing breakfast before he left. After breakfast, David made it to the porch to leave. As he looked through the screen door he saw Lila drop her robe to the floor. She stood naked and smiled at him. He went back into the kitchen and they made love one more time on the couch near the bay window.

Tomas picked up his lunch bucket and smiled at David. "Oh, that's fine, David, I sat here and enjoyed the sunny morning. It's quite a day out, ain't it?"

"That it is. That it is. Well, let's go see Glacier Park." David turned on the radio as they pulled out onto Highway 2 East. Frankie Laine just started singing *Do Not Forsake Me*. The words rushed images of his wife and daughter into David's mind. Guilt only followed once in awhile after he spent time with another woman. It must be because I'm with Tom. He quickly brushed the thoughts aside and sang along with Frankie Laine. "Do not forsake me oh my darling-"

Tomas interrupted as he asked, "David have you seen *High Noon*? It goes along with this here song."

"No. I ain't seen a show for a couple of months now. Did you see it?"

It felt good for Tomas to be talking like this to David. He focused back to the question, "Yeah, I did see *High Noon*. It was good. Maybe my favorite show so far. Dad really liked it too. He likes cowboy shows." Again he thought how his father and John

Nolan would like David if they'd just give him a chance. After all, he helped out some people already this morning. He's doin' something pretty nice for me right now, too.

David broke in on Tomas' thoughts. "Do you know much about Glacier, Tom?"

He shook his head as he answered, "I read somewhere where the Park started in 1931, but other than that, I don't know much."

"Take a look at that book there on the seat next to ya. It'll tell ya all you need to know about the Park."

Tomas turned to the introduction and started to read about the foundation of Glacier Park.

David put on his right turn signal and pulled into the parking lot of the Dew Drop Inn. "I know it's only 11:00 in the morning, but I need some beer. Com'on in. Ya can meet a friend of mine."

His stomach turned a little. He knew his father didn't want him in any bars. Besides he was only nineteen. The only beer he ever tasted was the short drink John Nolan gave him when Tomas graduated from Butte High School last year. His father found out and chewed out Nolan pretty good and told Tomas that every dumb thing he did in his life was when he drank. He told Tomas not to drink—now he walked into his first bar.

As David entered the bar, the bartender looked away from the sink and wiped her hands on the bar towel wrapped around her waist. "Well. I'll be go to hell. If it ain't the man of my dreams. Where've you been hidin' out? I heard you got yerself a girlfriend-"

David put his finger up to his lips and slightly threw his head to the side. Jackie Johnson picked up on his signal to change the subject as she noticed the young man following close behind David. She came around the bar and gave David a big hug. She whispered in his ear, "I need a little lovin' from you one of these nights. I ain't had nothin' like it for a couple of months. So get yer ass up here without yer little buddy. Follow."

David laughed and slowly broke the embrace. He managed one arm still around Jackie's tight waist. "Jackie, this here is my brother-in-law, Tom Anzich. How about a couple of Great Falls Selects for a couple of hard workin' guys from Butte."

Tomas spoke up, "I'd like a Nesbitts Orange please. No beer for me."

She extended her large, tan hand and waited for Tomas to shake hands with her. He slowly shook her hands, but his eyes focused right at her noticeable cleavage. As usual, she left the top two buttons of her white shirt undone. "My eyes are up here, Tom. Not down there."

His embarrassment disturbed his speech as he attempted to cover the mistake of his wandering eyes. "I, I, I'm happy to meet you Madam." He had not seen a woman like this before.

Jackie and David laughed at hearing 'Madam'. She spoke through the laughter, "Call me Jackie." David laughed even louder and sat down on one of the stools at the bar. He patted the top of the seat next to him to tell Tomas to sit down. Tomas sat down and David playfully tussled his hair with his hand. Tomas shrugged his shoulders. David's sign of acceptance relaxed him even though he wanted to be a long ways from this bar.

David quickly finished two beers. Tomas drained his soda in between looks at the other bar patrons. The two men said goodbye to Jackie and drove up the highway to West Glacier and entered Glacier National Park.

The town of West Glacier was once known as Belton. It came about as part of the Great Northern Railroad expansion and Glacier Park. The resident population increased in 1915 as three hotels for Belton were constructed. Most residents worked at either Glacier Park, for the Great Northern Railroad, or were hotel employees of the Belton Chalets and Lake McDonald Lodge inside of Glacier Park. It was during this time that the first car and bus transportation, Glacier Park Transportation Company, began to transport visitors from Belton to Apgar and Lake McDonald Lodge in the Park.

In 1949, the name Belton was changed to West Glacier, and the residents were employees of the U.S. Forest Service and Glacier National Park. By 1951, the population increased to three hundred, and it later declined through the 1950s. Hungry Horse dam workers on their days off kept the stores and bars open during the off-season from the Glacier Park visitors.

—•••—

The early summer day dawned much like the ones before it. Temperatures, warmer winds, and sunshine erased the traces and memories of the hard winter experienced by the locals in the Canyon and its foothills. Hannah worked in her usual way, mind racing with the same questions. "What day is it? What do I have to get accomplished today?" She temporarily relaxed. It was Saturday. The time didn't matter. The Royal was closed until the matinee at 2:00.

Her contentment with these ideas long with the knowledge that a perfect day spent on Lion Lake lazily passing the time was quickly replaced with the vision and memory of inviting Mikhail to join her. She had single-handedly compromised an often repeated, routine, and most enjoyable outing. It was now a planned, anxiety-ridden excursion with decisions to be made. For some strange reason she wanted to get to know this man from Butte.

How would she explain her tackle box? The idea of trying to look more feminine was ridiculous. Comfortably filling hours with this man seemed insurmountable. Her standard of fare would have to be adjusted other than Maggie's homemade brew. Hannah knew enough about the world and Butte. Any man from those parts certainly had downed a few beers in his lifetime. She knew Mikhail was worth getting to know and her own reactions to him were intriguing even if she couldn't explain it.

She gulped her morning coffee and looked across the back alley for Maggie's signal that all was well. Maggie aged well, but Hannah continued to have concerns for her well-being. Neither of the women had room for two in their cabins. Neither could have survived the loss of privacy either. Seeing the metal blind one-quarter raised set Hannah's mind back to the matter at hand. Changing her mind wasn't a trait she had developed. Moving forward was.

Mikhail arrived right on time. It was still morning and quite cool. He was puzzled by Hannah's invitation to go fishing with her. What did it mean to accompany her to Lion Lake? Was it to be a hike, a picnic, a car ride, fishing, or just floating around in her boat? He silently chastised himself for his inability to feel comfortable enough to even ask. He had only shrugged and agreed to come along. His experiences were few, not very successful, and altogether rather disastrous. He didn't think this would turn out much better.

When Hannah came out of the Royal Theater, Mikhail immediately knew the outing was to be one involving fishing. She struggled with a bulky, cumbersome tackle box, a vintage looking rod, and an oval, cane woven picnic basket. Mikhail wished he had his own fishing equipment.

Instead of following her in his car, Mikhail accepted Hannah's invitation to ride with her. The ride to Lion Lake was not exactly filled with conversation. They measured each other up and tried to get a sense of how this day was going to turn out. "You don't talk much, Mikhail."

"I spend a lot of time thinkin' about talkin'. Then just decide not to say anything."

"I could probably take a lesson there," she answered. "I never mull over what's on my mind. Weighing my words seems like such a waste of time."

They arrived on the north shore of Lion Lake, away from the traffic and construction of the dam. It delighted Mikhail to see a stout rowboat tied off to a log on the shore. Somehow he felt the playing field would be leveled if he were on the water. Fishing was a skill he had acquired and felt a sense of relief that he could do something with his hands and show off a skill.

Hannah tugged the picnic basket, tackle box, and rod that had seen better days down to the boat. She reached under the bench of the boat seat and removed an old mesh bag. Her hand slid into the picnic basket, grabbed some brown bottles and stacked them into the opening of the mesh bag. "These are my good friend Maggie's homemade brew," she stated while securing them to the side of the boat. "We'll be needin' these soldiers to be cool when we want them. Sippin' on Maggie's milk is just the ticket when the sun crests those hills."

Mikhail pondered. He took time to physically notice his partner for the day. Most items were freshly laundered denim that had turned a softened pale blue from repeated washings. The denim jacket was cut short with sleeves that needed to be rolled so her hands were unencumbered. Hands. Mikhail stared at her hands. They looked like the hands of a woman who did little physical work. The pedal pushers rode low on her hips. Hips. Where did those come from? She wore freshly bleached Keds on her rather large feet. Her hair was loosely tucked neatly behind her ears. No baseball cap or ponytail for today. Hannah owned little jewelry, costume or otherwise, and her only adornment was a gold choke chain around her thin neck with a cross dangling down. The piece of jewelry looked like something she never removed. Most men would ask just to make conversation. Mikhail decided not to. She pulled out a floppy straw hat and tucked it into her tackle box while she marched back to the truck to retrieve her cigarettes.

Mikhail stood by the boat and waited for her to return. He didn't want to put anything in until she identified the location for everything piled on the shore. His breath caught in his throat and speech was next to impossible. Apparently, the temperature was warming up. She cruised down the path while simultaneously removing her well-worn blue jean jacket. Underneath, Hannah casually wore a paisley patterned, pale yellow halter-top that she had fashioned from one of her late uncle's oversized bandanas. Her breasts were small without a hint of having suffered from the hands of gravity.

Her soothing-looking skin had obviously seen past summers on just this lake. The pale yellow material of the skimpy halter-top and dark brown sunspots blended beautifully into a pattern that Mikhail wanted to play 'connect the dots on' with his hands. She reached into the boat and exchanged her Keds for single strapped, brown leather sandals. This Pygmalion-like transformation from a lady running a show house to an irresistible temptation left Mikhail backing up and bumping into the log that held the rowboat fast.

Mikhail needed to think fast or he was going to fall into the lake. He avoided looking at her, any part of her, and hurriedly piled the gear wherever there was room. The hell with where she wanted it. She wasn't playing fair. He headed full bore into unfamiliar territory for him. Hannah sensed his urgency and attempt to hide his feelings of male wantonness. She had intended on a reaction, but this was greater than anticipated. "I'll row," he briefly gruffed.

"Great, I'll have a beer," she nonchalantly answered. "There's an anchor of sorts up there by you when you've decided on a good spot. It's just an old coffee can filled with cement, but it's always done the trick before." Again she grinned to herself thinking that

Mikhail was probably engrossed in her other 'tricks'.

His thoughts humored him and calmed him at the same time. A beer sounded just like what the doctor ordered and he wanted one. "No thanks. I don't drink. But you go right ahead and I'll fish." He found a semi-sunny spot, gently placed the anchor over the side, and prepared to fish.

Hannah popped the top of the brown beer bottle with a metal opener she kept tied to her belt loop. She opened her tackle box and revealed the contents. Books and magazines filled the tackle box. "This is what I do when I come here on weekends to be alone, all alone. Are you interested in hearing about this or should I shut up and let you bait that hook you've been holding for twenty minutes?"

"No, no go ahead," he encouraged. He was left speechless anyway and as long as she talked, he didn't have to say a word.

"There's basically three kinds of reading material here. I have hundreds of old *National Geographic* magazines that my uncle saved. When I want to travel around the world to all parts beautiful and mysterious, I read them. When I want to improve my mind, challenge my thinking, and expand my circle of thinking, I read the Classics using my library card in Kalispell. *Catcher In The Rye* and *Les Miserbles* are a couple of my all-time favorites. I've read each of them several times. When I'm horny and just into a good quick read, I choose these trashy novels written by unknowns but a hell of good time regardless."

He looked at her and back down to the worm in his left hand and the waiting hook in his right. "Well, well okay then. I'll just fish and let you read." This was the first time he ever heard a woman use the word horny. He thought how this last hour with her was the first time for a lot of things.

CHAPTER EIGHT

On Monday morning, Mikhail and Tomas walked into the quonset hut and waited for the bus to take them up to the dam site. The predicted June rain started during the night. The mood in the hut matched the dreary weather outside. A large group of men sat on benches and read the June 19th *Hungry Horse News.* Tomas picked up a discarded copy of the local newspaper and started to read the weekly Dam progress page.

To facilitate the rapid clearing of the dense forest area, the clearing contractors used a method which involved using a two inch steel cable dragged by two heavy tractors to snap and uproot brush and small trees on the steep sides of the reservoir. A four and a half ton hollow steel ball, eight feet in diameter, weighed down the cable and supported it at the most effective height. The balls are constructed of one-inch boilerplate with a steel shaft in the center that connects to the heavy cable. The cable is kept about four feet off the ground. Contractors cleared dense forest with trees up to twelve inches in diameter as fast as a man could walk. Two hundred acres were cleared last Tuesday in four hours.

As the reservoir filled with water, contractors constructed a ferry made of four pontoon boats lashed together that hauled men and equipment across the South Fork River. Logging and clearing crews worked seven days per week and ten hours per day and earned as much as $1,000 per month.

Mikhail interrupted Tomas and handed him the bulletin regarding a worker who accidentally died late Sunday afternoon. The man was killed just fifteen minutes before quitting time while working with a logging and clearing crew in the reservoir area. He worked as a signalman and a choker setter. The crew worked in a swampy area near Graves creek on the west side of the reservoir when a tree fell on him crushing his shoulder and breaking his back and leg and several ribs, and puncturing a lung. He died about forty-five minutes later. Mikhail spoke quietly, "We'll each be giving one days pay for the man's family. I signed us both up. It'll come out of your next check. Your brother-in-law will take the money over to the widow."

"Oh Dad, I can't imagine what it will be like for that family. I don't know what we'd do if anything ever-"

"Just pay attention. Watch what you're doin' all the time." The bus honked outside and the men paraded out the door. Their heads were down and no one spoke a word the entire ride up the road to the dam site. Mikhail took a brief glance at Lion Lake as the bus passed by. A brief thought of Hannah entered his mind but quickly disappeared as he thought about the young man killed yesterday in the logging accident. He also thought about Tomas' comment about what the family would do if anything happened to him. He glanced at Tomas and treasured the closeness of him.

ᔐ CHAPTER NINE ᔐ

W.R. Scalf, General Superintendent of Contractors GSM reviewed the final draft of his memorandum for the craft department heads, shift foreman, and walking bosses the June 27, 1952 payroll information for the Hungry Horse Dam Project.

Payrolls reached their 1952 peaks with 1,834 jobs or about 150 more jobs than last year's peak. Payrolls are now about $2,480,000 a month.

Included in the GSM employment total are 525 laborers, 345 carpenters, 100 steamfitters, 70 mechanics, 68 truck drivers, 60 electricians as well as other crafts and trades. Our employment pattern at Hungry Horse actually calls for a large crew working through the middle of September.

Other items of interest are as follows:

First of all, the federal auditor will be here next Tuesday to begin his month-long audit of the books. Make sure your payroll, timecards, overtime, everything is up to snuff. Our office people only give what you tell them.

Number two; I'll meet with two FBI agents here on Friday. I don't know what's that all about, but I'll fill you in after I meet with them.

Number three; Hungry Horse will operate before October 20th of this year. President Truman will be here to throw the switch on the first two turbines. We can expect lots of newspaper, magazine, radio, and secret service people starting to show up on site. It will be wild around here in late September.

Scalf signed the memo and took it to his secretary and said, "Mary, please run copies and get them distributed today. Also, send a copy to Al Sutter at the Hungry Horse News." He walked back to his office and put on his rain slicker. Before leaving he stopped by Mary's office again. "Oh, and Mary, I'm goin' into Columbia Falls to give my respect to the Dick Curtain family. Dick was the man who died yesterday in the logging accident. I'll stop and pick up some groceries for them first."

———•·•———

The next morning David Sednick scanned the memo from Superintendent Scalf. His eyes stopped on the item about the federal auditor coming next week.

The telephone on the wall in the foreman's shack rang and shook David from his deep concentration on the Superintendent's September 27th memo. He picked up the phone. "Hey Dave, how about a beer after shift tonight at the Blue Moon? We need to sit down and talk about Scalf's memo and the auditor's visit next week."

David's stomach turned as he answered, "Ya, ya that'll work. How about 5:00?"

"Great. We don't have anything to worry about, do we?"

"No. Everything's fine. See you then." He hung up the black wall phone and walked out to the back porch of the shack. From there he stared toward the backside of the partially cloud-clad Columbia Mountain. He took a deep breath as he thought.

The reality of his extra source of income frightened him in the beginning, but after two years of stockpiling thousands of dollars from his commission, the scheme no longer frightened him. Now the fear roared back into his mind. Every two weeks, he deposited two-thousand dollars into savings accounts in various banks around the Flathead Valley. David didn't know the source of the laundered money, and he didn't want to know. He followed instructions and collected his commission.

The man on the other end of the telephone recruited David two years ago to become part of his fraudulent scheme. David also received a walking boss job in addition to his commission for processing the checks.

David devised his own scheme for making additional money. He processed five bogus, fictitious workers with employee records, timecards, employee numbers, and non-existent payroll deductions. Each pay period he handled all of the paychecks for his shift. Now the whole thing might surface with the auditor reviewing the payroll records.

Panic stricken, David mulled over his mistake. "I just had to do it, didn't I. How in the hell will I account for five extra men on the payroll for May and June? I need time to think. He'll have my ass if he finds out. I just have to find a way to cover the last two months."

≈ CHAPTER TEN ≈

It was Tuesday morning and the Care Less Group broke with their Friday morning tradition for breakfast at the Club Café. The fundraiser dance to purchase the resuscitator for the volunteer fire department was only five days away. The four women sat around the corner table cluttered with lists and bags of decorations. Betty Hansen tapped her water glass as she attempted to bring the group back to the tasks at hand. The other three women talked at the same time. No one seemed to be listening to the other one talking. "Ladies. We've lots to do. July 2nd is only a few days away. Where are we with everything?"

Hannah picked up her list that contained large checkmarks. "Well, I got the decorations, lined up the music, picked up the beer and whiskey, and I got a crew of kids to help me clean and set up at Rocco's. I still need to get a couple of door prizes and three bartenders. Other'n that, I'm set."

In each of their minds, the four ladies separately looked forward to the event with some trepidation and with some excitement. Hannah wondered if Mikhail would attend, and if he did, would he show her any attention. She still wondered how their day on Lion Lake went. She hadn't seen or heard from him since they parted late Saturday afternoon.

Lila worried about David showing up. She wanted to see him, and at the same time hoped he wouldn't attend. Her husband was on the road for the weekend, and David was off work Saturday and Sunday. If he was drinking, he might make a scene and their secret might be exposed. Oh, I wish he'd call and let me know what his plans are. That man drives me crazy.

Betty Hansen experienced a terrible argument with her husband before he left for work at the Dam that morning. In her mind, she reviewed their argument. He told her he wasn't going to any ridiculous dance with a bunch of drunks and worn-out old women. Instead, he was going to Kalispell with a lawyer friend of his to see the movie *Singing in the Rain*. "Sometimes I wish he'd drown in the rain. He's so boring and self-centered. We do nothing fun together. Maybe I'll just have more than a few drinks and dance up a storm with some rowdy Dam workers. That would serve Mr. Hansen right," she said to herself.

She sat and looked at her friends as they reviewed their lists and made final plans for the dance on Saturday night. Mabel Simons smiled and enjoyed the friendship and banter of her three close friends. They accepted her for just who she was. Her Madam job really never mattered to any of them. She cleared her throat before she joined in the exciting planning discussion for their big event. "I talked to Mary Curtain today after her husband's funeral. I asked her about comin' with me Saturday night. She said it's too soon after her husband's accidental death on Sunday. But I told her I need her to help me with the raffle ticket sales. At any rate, I think we'll give her whatever money we make over the cost of the resuscitator."

Hannah wiped the tears from her eyes as she spoke, "You're a great lady, Mabel. We're so lucky you live here. Thank you."

The other ladies echoed Hannah's sentiment and wrapped up their meeting. They planned to get together Saturday afternoon at 2:00 to decorate and get Rocco's Super Club ready for the July 2nd fundraiser dance.

CHAPTER ELEVEN

Each year since the beginning of the Dam construction, the Ironworkers Union sponsored the Ironworkers Ball. The celebration began and ended at the Blue Moon. The wooden building took up a double lot at the intersection of Highway 40 and LaSalle. Traffic from Kalispell and Whitefish intersected at the front door of the Blue Moon. The past winter at the Ironworkers Ball, a fight broke out inside the bar near the front door. A fierce winter storm raged outside but paled in comparison to the intensity of the two men fighting. The heavy wooden door didn't hold the force of the two men as they exploded through the door and out into the parking lot. Two other men held the door in place and the driving snow out. No one knew who won the fight as the crowd quickly came back inside as the fight and the storm raged on.

The mounted deer, mountain goats, fish, and elk crowded the walls of the Blue Moon and brought the flavor of hunting and fishing in Montana inside the famous watering hole. David Sednick opened the door to the Blue Moon Bar. Four men sat at the bar and quietly talked and drank their tap beers. They made a passing glance at him as he entered. A young man and woman stood off to the left of the bar and played eight ball.

David stopped by the bar and ordered a double shot of Jim Beam and quickly drained it. He picked up his can of Great Falls

Select beer and walked over to the corner table near the west wall of the bar. He faced the door. His plan was simple. He'd tell the truth about the additional two months of fraudulent time cards and ask him for a way out.

The large wooden door opened slowly and the late afternoon light from the outside poured into the dimly lit Blue Moon. The man in the expensive blue suit looked out of place as he stopped at the bar and ordered a bottle of Pepsi Cola. He acknowledged David's wave and walked over and sat down at his table. "Thanks for coming, Dave. How's your family in Butte doing?"

David nervously took a long drink of his beer before he answered, "My little Anna is doin' a lot better. I talked to my wife yesterday. The strike's getting worse, and she's worried about it getting rough. She'd like to move up here, but until Anna gets strong enough to get off the iron lung, she's goin' to have to hang tough in Butte. I'm goin' down in three weeks or so."

"That's good news, Dave. How's it working out with your father-in-law working here?"

"I ain't seen him in a couple of weeks. I see my brother-in-law some and that's been fun. He's a good kid."

The man across from David calmly lit his Chesterfield and blew a large, perfect circle of smoke. He admired it as it disappeared into the air and then he looked at David. "We need to be sure of everything before the auditor digs into payroll. Accounts payable matches perfectly. Make sure-"

"I, I have it taken care of. We're in great shape."

The man systematically rubbed out the remains of his cigarette in the glass ashtray. His entire mood and demeanor changed and his pasted smile turned into a scowl. Without looking up from the ashtray he spoke, "Now with our other project, Dave. Everything is ship shape, right."

Perspiration rolled down David's armpit and blood rushed to his face and neck, "Ya. We're in great shape."

"You're repeating yourself David. That concerns me a little bit. For your sake, we better be in great shape. As I was saying, Dave, make sure your records match mine. Bring them around Friday afternoon and we'll compare. I want to see my deposits on our other project too. Follow." He stood up, straightened his tie in the reflection of the mirror above the beer sign, and left through the side door.

David sat motionless. His brain went numb while his stomach hinted at emptying his baloney sandwich lunch. He walked into the men's room and splashed some cold water in his face. His pale face stared back at him in the cracked wall mirror. Oh shit! I'm in it up to my eyeballs. What the hell am I going to do with May and June? It's all written in ink. The paymaster's records will show I paid out five more checks than there are men for two months.

———•✦•———

Back in Martin City, Tim Nolan sat across from Tomas in the Club Café. He enjoyed watching the young man devour his cheese-burger deluxe and fries. It was obvious Tomas was in the middle of a growth spurt. Just in a matter of a month, his biceps and shoulders showed muscular definition. He ate like a man who faced his last meal. Tomas looked like he grew several inches just since his high school graduation a year earlier. His voice even seemed deeper and more man-like. Nolan guessed Tomas put on ten to fifteen pounds in the last couple of months.

His thoughts came to an abrupt end as Tomas wiped the corner of his mouth with his paper napkin and their eyes met. "I think you and Dad are wrong about David. He's really a good man. I'm gettin' to know him, and-"

"Bullshit, Kid. He's a first class prick. Stay away from him. He'll take you down the wrong road."

Tomas sat back in the booth. "You're wrong. I know you're wrong." His voice quivered as he finished his words. It was the first time he ever spoke like this to his godfather. The words came out before he measured what he said. "I, I'm sorry. Please just give David a chance. That's all I mean. You'll see."

Nolan's face reddened as he waived his finger at Tomas. He stammered as he spoke, "Don't you never talk to me like that again, Kid. Where was he when you made your First Communion? I was there. Where was he when that Stosich kid kicked your ass after school and you came to me cryin'? Who taught you how to box so you gave that kid his own asskickin'? And I don't remember seeing him at your graduation from Butte High. Where was he when your mother moved out on you and your dad? Goddamn you! You listen to me. Stay away from that crooked, worthless son of a bitch! He's no earthly good I tell ya." The other customers looked over toward their booth, but no one said a word.

Tomas watched and heard the café door slam as Tim Nolan disappeared into the street. He had never seen his godfather so mad. Oh God, what've I done? He walked over to the cash register and paid his bill. The young girl working there smiled at him as he fumbled for his wallet. "Your father's pretty made at you ain't he."

"He ain't my father." Tomas shrugged his broadening shoulders, forced a polite smile, and walked outside to look to see if he could track down John Nolan.

———•·•———

For the first day in two weeks it didn't rain. Friday, he thought as he set his coffee cup down on his office desk. "Today I get to meet with two FBI agents. I wonder what the hell they want with me?"

His secretary Mary knocked on the doorframe to his makeshift shack of an office. "W.R., the two gentlemen from the FBI are here to see you."

"Thanks Mary, send them on in."

Two men in dark blue suits walked into his office. They introduced themselves as Agents Hughes and Moore. "Mr. Scalf, we're here to talk to you about something confidential. It's imperative that this conversation remains here between us only. Is that understood?"

"I understand. What's going on?"

Hughes went ahead first, "We have good reason to believe that there is a murderer here on the Hungry Horse Dam site. There were identical unsolved murders at the Hoover and Grand Coulee Dam building sites. Both murders occurred during the last months of completion. Both murders were execution style with single gunshots to the head. Both were from the same rifle."

Scalf walked toward the coffee pot and filled his white clay cup. "Can I get either one of you a cup?"

Moore motioned yes with his finger. Scalf filled a cup and brought it to him at his chair near the window. Agent Moore picked up where his partner left off. "Both men killed were shift bosses and had been with the projects for at least two years."

His partner cleared his throat and continued, "We need a list of every man employed here now who worked on either or both Hoover or Grand Coulee. We also want a list of your walking bosses. We'd like those lists before five o'clock today."

W.R. Scalf wasn't used to being instructed what to do. He normally was the one barking out the orders. "Why do you need the list of those men?"

Moore answered, "If they worked on the other two projects, they might be good suspects in those other murders. Or they may be planning to kill someone else here. I think it's obvious why we want a list of your walking bosses."

Scalf nodded his head before he replied, "I'll get those lists to you before five. Come back then and pick up the list from my secretary."

"No, you compile the lists and you keep the lists with you. No one else is to have any idea what we're doing here. Not even your secretary."

His lip curled and he rubbed his right ear as he normally did when his temper flared. Scalf organized the papers in front of him "Pick up the lists from me later."

Before Al Sutter became the owner, publisher, editor, and photographer for the *Columbian News,* four previous publishers in the area saw their newspaper company fail. All he had when he founded *The Hungry Horse News* was the $4,000 he saved from his career in the United States Navy, a desk, a portable typewriter, and his trademark Speed Graphic camera. Sutter was thirty-one years old in 1946 when he founded his newspaper. In the beginning, he distributed the first editions of his news for free in an effort to attract businesses interested in becoming advertisers. Much of his early advertising arose from the many bars and taverns that catered to the Hungry Horse Dam workers.

The *Hungry Horse News* featured black and white photographs mixed in with local news articles and controversial editorial written by Sutter. His newspaper depended heavily on photographs. Breaking news events became a large part of his repertoire. His nose for late breaking news allowed him to be first on the scene of a car accident, a burning building, or important event like the first photographs of the building of Hungry Horse Dam. He used the unwieldy Speed Graphic to insure high quality photographs. His photographs allowed for short, concise stories. These photographs portrayed the story.

Superintendent Scalf kept Sutter informed of all progress in the building of Hungry Horse Dam as he chronicled each phase of construction. He was the only person allowed to see Scalf without an appointment. Sutter greeted the Superintendent's secretary as he entered her office. "Hello there, Mary. You got any news for me?"

"No, Al. Pretty quiet as far as I know. But then I don't know much about what goes on around here."

He dressed in a checkered shirt, weathered sport coat, a white hat with a colored band around the rim, and he toted his oversized camera, clipboard, and a light meter. "Is the Supt busy?"

"I imagine he is, but he seems anxious to see you all the time. Just go ahead and knock on his door as you always do."

Scalf motioned him in and managed a smile. "I see you got a copy of my latest memo."

"I did. What's the FBI want?"

Scalf shook his head slightly as he shuffled the papers on his desk into his briefcase on the floor. "I can't tell you much at this point, Al. Maybe I'll have somethin' for you in a week or two."

The young newsman rested his camera on the floor and lifted his clipboard to the desk as he sat down across from the Superintendent. "Did they ask you about the unsolved murders on the Grand Coulee and Hoover Projects?"

Coffee blurted out of Scalf's mouth. "How in the hell did you hear about that? The FBI left only twenty minutes ago. Do you have my office bugged?"

He tilted his head to the left as he measured the light in the room using his light meter. "My old Navy friend in Coulee called me yesterday and asked if anyone had been murdered at Hungry Horse. He filled me in on the unsolved murders."

"You gotta keep this quiet, Al. The FBI is all over it and not in the mood for anybody butting in. You'll get the first crack at a story once they nail it down. Right now, nobody knows nothin' about nothin'."

"I'll lay low for awhile. But I might snoop around just a little bit."

"Shit no, Al! You never just snoop a little bit. Let them do their jobs. We got secret service men and magazine people comin' around soon in makin' plans for Truman in early October. We can't have some high profile murder investigation going on too."

Sutter picked up his camera and prepared to take a photo out the front window in the direction of the Dam. Looking through the lens of his camera he said, "First crack at the story, right?"

"First crack."

———————

David drank the lukewarm coffee. He drank enough coffee during the night to last a lifetime. The lack of sleep and the overdose of caffeine dulled his thoughts and emotions. He just wanted to get it over with and get to bed. The shift hours for the past two months were now rewritten in his financial record book. The five fictitious employees and their hours worked were now erased in the fire in the garbage can outside of his trailer. Now he had only one more bit of work to do. He waited outside of the office of the bookkeeper, Fred Winters.

The thin man with the rounded eyeglasses quietly shut the door to his 1949 Ford Sedan. Everything about his car was perfect. Just like his suit. Just like his bookwork. Just like everything about him and his life. This wasn't going to be an easy task David thought. Fred Winters spoke to David as he placed the silver skeleton key into the worn door latch to his office. "What brings you here so early, Dave?"

David struggled to gain some clarity in his thoughts and a bit of motivation to even answer Winters, "I need to temporarily borrow the timecards from the men on my shifts for all of May and

June up to yesterday. The Federal Auditor is comin' next week and I need to compare my records with the timecards."

"Well, Dave, I'm sure my figures are accurate. There's no need to compare. I copied my figures directly from the timecards you tendered."

He really didn't have the energy to argue with this man. "I'm sure your figures are right on the money, Fred. I just got to be sure. Alright."

After he set his lunch bucket in the small fridge near the window, he continued, "It's unusual. I hate to mess with my-"

"I need to compare your goddamn timecards with my record book! So do I get them, or do I have to go to the building next door and have Hansen come and get them for me?"

Fred Winters nervously pulled out a ring of smaller keys from his desk drawer. He fingered the keys until he rested upon the key for his file drawer. The ring of keys clanged on the gray concrete floor. After he picked up the keys, Winters slipped on a rubber thumb grip and fingered the stack of the 1952 May and June time cards. "Here are your shift time cards. Bring them back to me in an hour! One hour, you understand. One hour."

Without making any eye contact, David took the rubber banded timecards and left. Once back at his trailer he banged around his bathroom cabinets for aspirin. None. He went to the kitchen and looked above the sink and found a near-empty bottle of aspirin. He swallowed the remaining three pills and washed them down with a dirty mason jar of water. "I got to get rid of this pounding headache so I can take care of these goddamn timecards."

He spread the timecards on the kitchen table. One by one he removed the bogus timecards for each week. He placed them into a stack. Then he discarded the stack into the garbage can outside. He spilled some fuel oil on the cards and dropped a wooden match.

Back in his kitchen he organized the remaining timecards back in alphabetical order just like Winters had them arranged. "I'm sure my figures won't work out exactly, but the auditor won't be able to figure out why. My books'll match the bookkeeper's timecards and that's all I have to worry about."

CHAPTER TWELVE

The development of a road through Badrock Canyon naturally coincided with the construction of the Great Northern Railroad. Known originally as the tote road, this route was used to transport materials to the railroad building sites. At first, the road was so low that it flooded during high water, but it was later improved. In 1929, the South Fork Bridge was built and the highway surfaced.

Until the completion of Transcontinental Highway 2 in 1930, no automobiles could pass through the upper part of the Canyon. Throughout the 1920's, vehicles were loaded on railroad flatcars at either the East or West Glacier stations, with their owners following in passenger coaches, for a fee of $12.50.

U.S. Highway 2 was completed in July of 1930, with the last barrier, a large outcropping of rock, removed about a mile west of the summit. Traffic was first allowed over the pass on July 20, 1930. As this segment of the highway had been named the Theodore Roosevelt Memorial highway, the Roosevelt monument was built in October of 1931 at Marias Pass.

The development of the highway greatly increased traffic not only through Badrock Canyon but also into Glacier National Park. With the completion of the Going-to-the-Sun Road in 1933, this area of the country became a new national destination for transcontinental automobile travel.

He stared aimlessly out of the caboose window of the Great Northern Railroad freight train as it picked up speed twenty minutes out of the station in West Glacier. The cars on Highway 2 traveled faster than the train as it headed east for Havre. This normally was a good time for him to think and appreciate the beauty of the Middle Fork River and the backdrop of Glacier National Park. But not today. It was Saturday morning and he'd be gone until late Sunday night.

As he looked at the cars zooming by alongside the train, Rich Toma reviewed the ugly argument he had with his wife, Lila. He told her that things had changed between them. He relived his words again. "You're different, Lila. I found two cigarette butts outside the back porch and you don't smoke. The truck tire tracks in the mud near our car don't make no sense neither. Whose truck do they belong to? You don't come to me in our bed during the night like you used to. You act like you don't want me to even touch you."

His mind temporarily left their argument as the train entered the quarter mile tunnel when the train track followed the wide sweeping bend in the Middle Fork River. In the darkness of the tunnel, he angrily flashed back to the big thing on his mind. The sickening smell of Old Spice on his pillowcase as he lay down to sleep Wednesday night haunted him. He hated the smell of Old Spice. "There's somebody else, I know it. I'll talk to her again Sunday night. She don't know it, but I got somebody keeping an eye on her tonight at her dance. I'll kill the son of a bitch once I find out who he is."

At 2:15 Saturday afternoon, Hannah Holley walked into Rocco's Club and escorted three teenagers loaded down with decorations and cases of beer and liquor. The boys joked with each other about what a great party they'd have drinking all of this free booze. Hannah took the bait and engaged in a conversation about the drinking age and the evils of drinking. "The only thing you three juvenile delinquents will be drinking is the Pepsi I have in my cooler. Don't you dare let me catch any of you sneaking any beer."

The boys laughed and enjoyed the company of the lady who

operated the Royal Theater. She seemed to find a way for them to work at small jobs around town earning money. They cleaned her show house on the weekends in exchange for watching the movies for free.

The other members of the Care Less Group already rearranged tables and chairs and sang off-tune to the record player as it belted out Guy Mitchell's hit song, "Pittsburgh, Pennsylvania." It was the fifth time the song filled the near-empty Supper Club, and the women circled the boys as they sang.

Hannah pretended to mouth the words but didn't know more than a couple of words. She picked up one of the floor mops leaning against a table and used it as a floor microphone as she imitated a singer in the band. Her giddy friends joined her arm in arm and moved in a disorganized group and sang as loud as they possibly could. The song ended and the group broke into laughter that echoed around the walls of the empty supper club.

Betty Hansen composed herself and suggested that they perform that act tonight when the band took their first break. "Seriously, we should do this tonight. Can you imagine the look on everybody's faces? It'll be fun. Let's do it!"

Mabel joined in, "I'd have to have a few high balls first, before I'd try anything like that." She then realized what she said, but it was too late. The other ladies erupted again into out of control laughter.

"I bet you've had more than one set of high balls, Mabel. I bet Hannah's new friend from Butte has a pretty-"

Hannah interrupted Betty before she finished her words. "Don't say another word, Betty Hansen. I'll wet my pants for sure. Stop."

The reward for the ladies in volunteering so much time and energy into the various activities of Hungry Horse and Martin City was the feelings and fun they experienced by working together. Each woman battled their own form of loneliness and sometimes frustrating relationships with the men in their lives. But only positive feelings came from being together with one another at times like this. It was easy to find the energy and buried senses of humor when they got together. Only small pieces of who they really were came out in their personal lives away from the group.

Lila still stung from the morning verbal attack from her husband Rich. Her stomach turned and her head throbbed at the thought of being caught cheating with David. She needed to be with her friends right now, and this fundraiser was a perfect distraction from the seriousness of Rich's words. He was a good man when they were younger. Patient, fun, loving. He still was a great provider. But now they passed like ships in the night, barely talking. They only went through the motions of what they once were. If only I'd gotten pregnant and had children. That's what we both really wanted. If only...What a terrible time to get involved with David. My life's a mess. Oh God, please keep him away from me tonight. I can't be with him again. I just can't.

Hannah placed her arm around her as they walked toward the kitchen. "Is everything alright, Lila?"

"I'm okay Hannah. I just have a headache. That's all."

"Have you taken anything for it yet?"

Lila forced a smile as she fought back the tears. "No, do you got anything?"

Hannah walked back to her brown leather purse on the table near the stack of decorations. She returned with a bottle of aspirin and offered it to Hannah. "Thanks Hannah. This'll take care of it."

"What do you think you'll wear tonight? I'm not so sure now that we're going to do an imitation of Guy Mitchell and his band." Secretly, Hannah was torn as to what she would wear just in case Mikhail dropped by the dance. She really never had anything nice to wear. Besides, he probably wouldn't show up anyway. She told herself to quit acting like a kid anyway.

"Well Hannah, I'm thinking of wearing my yellow spring dress and white flats. Nothin' fancy or anything. How about you?"

Betty Hansen interrupted them as she sauntered into the kitchen with the boys right behind her carrying the beer and liquor. "How do you want to set up the booze, Hannah? I need to know that because I plan to have a few drinks myself tonight."

Hannah smiled and replied, "Just set the beer in the ice box back there boys. And set the Whiskey and Vodka on the back shelves. The bartenders will arrange how they want things when they get here at 5:00. You kids haul the ice from the bar out front back here into these ice chests. We need to keep our liquor separate from the main bar."

Mabel's feet pained her most of the time. They really ached after she stood too long. She limped slightly as she walked toward the other women. "I think I'll set up the cash box and raffle ticket basket near the front door. I need to borrow these three gorgeous young bucks for awhile." The three boys benefited from Mabel's generosity two years earlier when she bought their baseball uniforms for them so they could play in the Columbia Falls league. Two of the boys also treasured the Boys Scouts uniforms that she paid for last spring. They eagerly followed and talked to her as she led them to the storage area to pick up her supplies.

———•◦•———

Rocco's Supper Club thrived as the restaurant, bar, and dance hall of choice in the Canyon. The one story white building stood across from the entrance of the main haul road to the top of Hungry Horse Dam. Couples depended on the excellent service, clean facilities, and great food. Special occasions with fine dining called for a night at Rocco's. Weddings, anniversaries, holiday dinners, birthdays, and Saturday night dances highlighted the reputation of Rocco's. It also provided the best dance floor and bandstand in the valley.

The gravel parking lot in front of Roccos' held seventy-five cars if everyone parked correctly. Latecomers lined their cars along the highway as people rolled into the supper club for the fundraiser. The Hungry Horse fire truck parked outside the front door advertising the event. Tomas read the sign as he and his father slowly walked toward the steps to the front door. "What's a resuscitator dad?"

Mikhail paused as his right foot touched down on the bottom step. "I'm not sure. But they must need one if they have this big a goings on to buy one." A new pair of Can't Bust Em black pants was the closest thing Mikhail had that resembled something a little dressier. He and Tomas changed into what good clothes they had after they showered at the barracks after work. Mikhail's dark thick hair held an excess of Wild Root Cream Oil. The hair laid close to his scalp and never moved one hair in the wind. Tomas wanted to tell him he looked funny, but knew better. He thought John Nolan would take care of that once he saw him.

Mabel greeted the father and son as they entered the Supper Club. "Good evening gentlemen. Welcome to our little party." She sat on a wooden chair behind the small table. "There's no charge to come in, but we hope you might buy a couple of raffle tickets. They're four bits a piece or three for a dollar. How many would you like?"

Mikhail handed her a silver dollar. "Tomas, you can fill out tickets. Put Anna's name on all three tickets. You can buy your own." He looked toward the bar where he spotted Nolan. "I'm goin' over to say hello to Nolan."

Betty Hansen and an older woman stood drinking with Nolan. He just finished telling them his latest farmer's daughter joke. The little group was laughing as Mikhail approached them. Nolan was in mid-drink when he spotted his friend, "What the hell you got on your hair?" It looks like the hairdo you had when we made our first communion and your mother plastered your hair with sugar and water." Betty Hansen erupted with laughter and enjoyed the feeling of her second highball. Nolan appreciated her recognition of his fine sense of humor.

Mikhail shook his head and bluffed a punch at Nolan. "Hello, Nolan."

Betty introduced herself and the lady standing with them. She moved back to the bar and set her empty glass down on the makeshift bar counter. Her friend followed her and left Nolan and Mikhail talking. "Maggie. Hannah has a little crush on that big fella there. Don't tell her I told you though. But keep an eye on those two tonight. Maybe-"

"Two highballs ladies."

Betty responded to the bartender, "Correct Jack. You're my hero." She handed one of the drinks to her friend Maggie and they returned to Mikhail and Nolan.

Across the floor, Lila made small talk with several locals. Her concentration focused on the door in the event David came to the fundraiser. She once again rehearsed her plan in her mind as she pretended to listen to the conversation about the rain and muddy streets. She was going to avoid a scene with David but make sure he knew their affair was over. As difficult as it would be to live without his exciting ways, she'd break it off tonight or at the latest, tomorrow. Her stomach flipped over as she heard his laugh bellow outside. He was here and most likely not feeling any pain.

David and his bartender lady friend, Jackie, entered the front door of Rocco's. People turned and looked as David stumbled to the floor. He and his friend laughed, and she fell over on top of him in her vain attempt to help him stand up. Mikhail sent a menacing stare at David while Tomas hurried to his side and helped him.

He brushed himself off and continued his uncontrollable laughter. "Thanks, Tommy Boy. Pretty slippery floor for the middle of summer. Maybe your dad over there put a banana peel down for me to fall on."

Tomas laughed and helped Jackie up to the chair placed near the door. She hugged him and kissed him on the cheek. "Thanks Kid. You're a doll. Me and Dave had a few too many at the Dew Drop before coming down. After I get my bearings, you and me are going to dance up a storm, you understand."

Tomas smiled at her and intentionally avoided staring at her abundant cleavage. "Oh, I ain't much of a dancer, but I'll give it a try. I think I have two left feet."

"When you're as good looking as you are Kid, it don't matter if you can dance or not. Just flash those big browns and you'll probably get yourself laid tonight."

He felt his face redden from the embarrassment. "Oh, not me. I, I, I'm goin' to go get some punch. Talk to ya later, okay?" Tomas walked toward the bar and thought of what she said to him. "Boy, I wonder what that is like havin' sex. Maybe before the summer is out I might find out."

David noticed Lila and started walking toward her. She went outside through the side door. He went to the bar and ordered a whiskey seven and went out the same side door to talk to Lila. She stood near the edge of Rocco's and looked back to see David walking toward her.

He smiled as he approached her. "You look great. Let's get out of here and go have some real fun. I'd like-"

Tears rolled down her cheeks, "David listen to me. It's over. I can't do it anymore. I am-"

"Whoa there, Nellie. You know you can't do that. We'll talk

about it in bed. Let's go." He reached for her and spilled his drink as he bumped into her arm. "Goddamn it! I never even got to take a drink out of it."

"David. Don't call me again. Don't follow me back inside. You're family is in there. Your date can make her own way home. Stay away from me. I mean it. My husband is on to us. There ain't no tellin' what he'll do." She dried her tears with her blouse sleeve and started to walk away.

David grabbed her by the arm. "You won't last without me. You will come beggin' by the end of next week. It will be too late for you. I'll have a new whore by then."

Lila pulled away from his grip and hurried back into the building and into the ladies room. She closed the stall door and cried uncontrollably. The restroom door opened and she covered her mouth with the soaked blouse sleeve. "Lila. Are you alright?"

She managed to answer between sobs. "Hannah, I'll be okay in a few minutes. Can you give me some privacy?"

Hannah removed her hand from the stall door handle and backed away. "Sure, I, I'll be near the bar if you want to talk." Lila heard the restroom door close. She sat on the stool and breathed deep as she realized she did it. It was over as suddenly as it started. It would be horrible whenever she'd see him, but she'd face her husband without the guilt. "Thank God summer season's here. The tourists would keep her busy with the cabins. The Dam was going to be finished in a couple of months, and David would be gone. Hell with him. He's such a selfish bastard."

———•◦•———

The McCartan Trio cranked up the loud speakers as they started to sing out the words to Guy Mitchell's hit tune, *Pittsburgh Pennsylvania*. Each man wore the same red-checkered yolk shirt and black suspenders, and the Trio consisted of a piano, a trap drum set, and a country guitar. Mikhail watched as Hannah sprinted away from him in mid-sentence and joined her friends in front of the bandstand. He watched as they held arms and screamed out the words to the song. Those who weren't yet dancing grabbed the nearest person to them and moved out onto the floor flinging their arms and singing whatever words to the song that they knew. It looked to him like everyone in the hall was laughing and singing.

Mikhail set his Pepsi down on the table once he spotted Tomas dancing with the blonde-haired lady with her shirt half open. It felt good to see Tomas enjoying himself like this. How he has changed in such a short time. As tough as it was to leave Butte, maybe it was a good thing for the family. All we need now is to get Anna well and move up here with Katya. His pleasant thoughts dimmed as he remembered seeing David drunk and falling on the floor with the lady that was dancing with Tomas. He sipped on his Pepsi as he wondered what would become of David.

Nolan danced with two older ladies at the same time. He cast a silly glance at Mikhail and mocked him, as he stood alone. Mikhail couldn't make out the words Nolan was yelling at him because his attention shifted to Hannah. It pleased him that they were becoming friends even if he wasn't sure what to do with her.

She waved at him as she danced with the ladies in her group.

After the song ended, Mikhail noticed some of the people went outside to catch some fresh air. Hannah and her friends wiped their eyes from tears of laughter as they walked toward the bar. She approached Mikhail and picked up her Great Falls Select can that she left on the table near him. He watched her gulp down a drink and smiled as he looked at the beads of sweat coming down the side of her face. He looked in her eyes and spoke, "You sing good."

Hannah sighed deeply as she set her drink back on the table. "There you go again, talking up a storm. Talk, talk, talk. How about a dance so you don't talk so much?"

"Oh, I don't dance."

"You mean, not until now." She set his Pepsi on the table, grabbed his hand, and led him out towards the middle of the floor.

"I'll show you how to do it. Trust me."

He stopped and forced a nervous laugh, "No. I don't dance. Let's walk outside."

"Okay. Have it your way. You're too big to argue with anyways." She held his hand tighter as they joined the others outside.

They walked up and stood near Nolan and listened to him tell his dance partners that he once set a record for dancing with five ladies at once at the Columbia Gardens in Butte when he was a young lad. He turned to Mikhail and Hannah and said, "Ask the big Bohunk here if that ain't the honest to God's truth. Just ask him, but speak really slow because he has some problems following along."

"They were his nieces."

One of the gray-haired ladies laughed as she playfully slapped Nolan on the shoulder. "You're such a bull-shitter, John. But we still like you. Let's go get a drink."

"Oh, I can't keep up with you two. I better see what's going on with the big Bohunk here."

Hannah let loose of Mikhail's hand and turned toward the door, "I need to go to the Powder Room. I'll meet you back inside in a little bit. Maybe I can convince you to try a dance or two."

Mikhail watched her disappear back into Rocco's before he spoke to Nolan. "Did you see David?"

"Christ, you'd have to be blind and deaf not to see him. He was drunk on his ass. I don't know how long I can take it before I punch him in the chops. I think Tommy's half listenin' to him."

Mikhail wrinkled his face as he listened to Nolan, "Tommy told me Davey was a good guy and we should give him half a chance. I got pissed and told him Davey was a prick and to stay away from him."

"Oh."

"That's it! Oh! Wake up for Christ's sake. Don't you worry about Tommy falling for that worthless prick's happy horse-shit?"

"He'll be okay."

Nolan walked away between two parked cars and then stomped back to face Mikhail. They had done this sort of thing a hundred times before when Nolan went on one tirade or another. Mikhail learned to let Nolan rant and rave and sooner or later he'd calm down. Nolan looked up at him, "I'm telling ya we got' a keep an eye on him. You can't let him take Tommy down the wrong road with him. If you don't, I will."

"We'll keep a eye out."

Mikhail watched as Nolan stalked away toward the alley waving his hands and arms in the air. He thought about following him but decided to go in and visit with Hannah. As he returned inside, he made a plan to talk to Tomas the next day about David.

CHAPTER THIRTEEN

The small community of Polebridge lies at the northwestern edge of Glacier National Park. It is nestled between the Continental Divide and the Whitefish Range of mountains. Polebridge consists of a scattering of houses, cabins, trailers, and small ranches up and down the North Fork of the Flathead River Road. At the center of the community is the Polebridge Mercantile.

This point of contact is a combination store, post office, and gas station. The Northern Lights Saloon serves beer and meals a few days per week. Polebridge has no traffic lights, no electricity, and guards the northern entrance to Glacier National Park and the North Fork Valley. It is home to wolves, elk, black and grizzly bears, eagles, mountain lions, deer, and moose.

The afternoon after the fundraiser at Rocco's, Hannah carefully guided her 1949 Ford up the North Fork Road. She recently battled the reoccurring memories of the day she heard her husband died in a work accident. He plunged his bulldozer off the road into the North Fork of the Flathead River three-hundred feet below the construction site of the road. Hannah slowly pulled her car off to the side of the road near the spot where her husband slid off the embankment seven years earlier.

The pain that once shot through her heart each time she parked here in the past subsided with each passing month. She stepped out of the car and walked over to the edge of the embankment. The bouquet of lilacs she gathered that morning flew gently from her hand, and in slow motion, separated as they disappeared under the ledge of the cliff. Hannah thought of how much Ken loved the smell of lilacs and how he cut them fresh for their kitchen table most days in June. She whispered between her cupped hands, "Oh Ken, why did you have to leave me so early? We had our whole life ahead of us. We-" Small tears seeped from her brown eyes. She walked back and braced herself against the hood of her car.

A forest service pickup sped by her and the thick dust forced her to cover her mouth and nose using the side of her arm. "Bastard," she yelled without looking up. She walked around to the car door, slid into the driver's seat, and closed the door behind her. She pounded the steering wheel as she yelled, "I got to move on Ken, this is getting me nowhere! I can't keep doin' this to myself! I know you'd want me to get on with my life!" Tears again blurted out as she covered her face with her hands.

She started her car and continued the drive up the dusty, potholed road. As Hannah pulled into the empty parking lot of the Polebridge Mercantile, she took a quick look into the rear view mirror. She laughed at herself as she noticed dusty-like creases below her eyes and her lipstick smeared like a clown. "Oh, my mother is really going to think I lost my mind." She laughed again at the thought of her talking to herself. A three-legged black and white dog limped across the porch of the Mercantile and carried a man's work boot in his mouth. "There's no place like home. This is just what the doctor ordered."

The boards of the porch creaked as Hannah walked toward the door to the Mercantile. She stooped down and scratched the dog behind the ear before she entered the store. The over-sized wedge of cheese on the glass counter called her name. She grabbed the cheese slicer and popped a chunk of the cheddar into her mouth.

From the kitchen in the back came the static noise of her mother's radio. Hannah quietly strolled back to surprise her seventy-year-old mother. Memories of doin' the same thing as a little girl flashed by in her mind. Her mother acted surprised and swore at her for frightening the hell out of her.

June Holley rolled out the bread dough with the well-used

rolling pin. Flour dotted her old overalls and gray sweatshirt. Splattered white flour covered the right side of her face. She listened to the radio and hummed along with Rosemary Clooney on the radio as she worked. The aroma of the fresh hot-crossed buns cooling on the rack above the wood stove filled Hannah's nostrils as she stood in silence and stared at every move her mother made.

Again the cherished childhood memories sprinted across her memory and triggered thoughts of a much younger, much trimmer woman. Her hair turned completely gray, but the long ponytail reached well below her broad shoulders.

"Hi Mom, what's cooking?" June Holley dropped the rolling pin, swung around, and barked at her smiling youngest daughter, "Goddamn you Hannah. You scared the living hell out of me. What in the world?"

Hannah didn't let her finish her sentence and wrapped her arms around her and kissed her on the unfloured cheek. She laughed and said, "I heard you baked today and since I was in the neighborhood, I decided to stop by and make a pig out of myself."

"I bake bread everyday but Sunday, so what brings you home?" She picked up her rolling pin and continued her work. "It don't really matter. It nice anytime you come. Can you stay for the night or more?"

Hannah nibbled at a corner of one of the hot cross buns, "Ya, Mom I'd sure like to. It's been a couple of months since I saw you."

Without looking up from her dough, June spoke again, "You look like shit warmed over. Couple a days with me and I'll have you up and runnin' like you did when you raced all them neighbor kids on the Fourth of July."

Hannah took a bigger chunk of the bun and talked as she chewed, "I did kick their butts, didn't I. Don't think I could now. I got ten or twelve pounds on me."

"Keep eatin' them buns like that and you'll have lots more on ya." She balled up the dough and kneaded it with her strong fingers. "How the show house doin' these days. I imagine the dam workers and the kids out of school keep you hoppin'."

"I been busy with lots of stuff. We had a fundraiser last night for the fire department. It went good and we cleared three hundred fifty bucks. Everybody had a good time too."

June cut the dough in half and filled two baking dishes and covered them with a damp dishtowel. She placed them on the side of the stove and motioned Hannah out the side door. Hannah helped herself to a bottle of pop from the Pepsi icebox near the doorway. Once outside her mother placed her hands on her hips and breathed in the clean air of the North Fork. "You act like ya got somethin' to tell me honey. What's up?"

Hannah offered her mom the Pepsi bottle and inhaled the sweet air herself, "I might have met someone, Mom."

"What ya mean? You either met somebody or ya didn't. Which is it?"

"I met a fella from Butte who works at the Dam. Don't know what to think of it though. Today on the way up, I stopped where Ken died and had some strange thoughts about everything. I mean-"

She moved closer to Hannah and returned the pop bottle after she swallowed her drink. "Honey. Kenny's been gone for pert near seven years now. It's time to think about movin' on for your own self. It's time."

Hannah walked out into the tall grass facing one of the meadows in front of the North Fork River. She slowly turned toward her mother, "Mom, I know you're right and I'm interested in gettin' to know this new guy. Is that selfish of me to want to do it?"

She wiped her hands on her apron as she walked to meet her daughter, "No. It ain't one bit selfish. See where it goes. You're forty-three years old. None of us need a man around, but once in awhile on them cold winter nights, it ain't too bad to snuggle up against their big bare asses and hold on tight."

Hannah spit out the dark, sweet liquid as she sipped and laughed at the same time, "Oh Mom, you kill me sometimes with what you say." They both laughed out loud and hugged each other one more time.

⸻

Mikhail shifted into third as he slowly passed Holy Savior Church after the five-hour drive from Hungry Horse to Butte. The hours flew by as he spent the trip recalling his days as a teenager following the accidental death of his father in the mine accident at the Mountain Con Mine. He quit school and worked for a glass company installing windows and glass doors just so his brother and mother could survive. The pain and loneliness of the months after his dad died roared into his mind as if it happened last week. He could see the school principal enter his math classroom and talk to the teacher. They both threw a glance toward Mikhail as the principal whispered to the teacher.

Mikhail witnessed this in years gone by as other boys lost their dad to a mining accident. After the principal left the classroom, the teacher walked to Mikhail's desk and asked him to follow him outside. He vividly remembered how the teacher walked in front of him down the hall to the principal's office without saying a word. They walked into the office, and the principal closed the door behind them. Mikhail saw this scene in his mind a hundred times before as the principal reached up and placed his hands on Mikhail's shoulders. "Mikhail, I've some bad news for you. Your father died today at the mine."

He shook his head in an attempt to erase the painful and all too real memory. Since that time, he never recalled a time when he didn't have a great deal of responsibility on his shoulders. The past two months working in Hungry Horse passed by quickly and the encouraging news about Anna's health getting better offered some hope in the upsetting circumstances of his life. His new friendship with Hannah also made Mikhail think that his life was going to get easier. The possibility for he and Tomas working at the Anaconda Aluminum Plant project after the Hungry Horse Dam work finished, excited him. Starting a new life for himself and his family injected a new hope for the future. Mikhail pulled his Chevy to a stop a block away from his house. He blubbered some words as he stepped on the gas and released the clutch, "Come on now. Be strong when you go in. Anna and Katya are countin' on you. Let's go!"

The Labor Strike in Butte turned violent as the morning *Montana Standard Newspaper* reported the headline news of July 2nd.

Butte was tensely quiet Sunday night as residents fearfully awaited a possible third night of lawlessness, but up to a late hour there had been no reports of the kind of wanton destruction that terrorized the community during a weekend of unchecked vandalism and looting. As the city grimly viewed the results of mob destruction at more than a dozen homes, ravaged by roving gangs of hoodlums armed with axes and bludgeons, there was no recurrence of the depredations that went on Friday and Saturday night.

The weekend of terrorism which started Friday, reached a peak during the weekend when gangs of teenage youths and women swooped down on the home of men employed protecting Anaconda company property from damage in the strike-bound city. Practically every home damaged by the wanton mobs was occupied by wives and children of salaried employees of the Anaconda Company, not affiliated with any union and who are manning pumps and mine hoists which must be kept going to save the copper mines from irreparable damage.

Butte Miners Union refused to further provide maintenance crews during the strike until the Company agreed to sit at the bargaining table. The men, whose homes were targets of the vicious attacks, make up the maintenance crews who are protecting the mining property.

The Butte Miner's Union issued a statement condemning the violence. "The Butte Miner's Union and its members are not responsible for, nor do they condone acts of vandalism such as has occurred recently. On the contrary, we strongly condemn such acts and urgently request all our members and the general public to assist us in maintaining an orderly strike so that a settlement can be effected."

The heroic battle of a Butte mother to save her home and protect her two girls from the wrath of a frenzied mob was related here Saturday by Mrs. D.P. Lowney of 2210

East Summit. Mrs. Lowney defended her home and children for two days before being overwhelmed by superior numbers and the fact that she was unable to obtain help from the county's peace officers. Although Mrs. Lowney and her daughters, one fourteen, the other five, were terror-stricken by hoodlums, armed with axes, clubs and sledge hammers, she withstood a two-day siege by the riot-bound vandals, bent on destruction of her home.

Katya raced out to the curb and embraced her father as he fumbled to close the car door behind him. "Oh Daddy, thank God you're here. Did you hear what's goin' on here in Butte with the riotin'and everything? Oh Daddy, I'm so scared it might happen here in McQueen. And-"

"Whoa there Katya! Whoa. Easy does it. Let's go inside now." He placed his powerful arm around her back and gently guided her toward the front door.

Mikhail drew a deep breath as he opened the screen door and allowed his daughter to walk in first. He visualized this moment for weeks now as he prepared to see his granddaughter Anna and his daughter. Once inside, he paused, smiled, and cried again as he looked at Anna sitting in his big rocking chair with the breathing mask on her face and the electrical cord plugged into the wall behind her. The iron lung was nowhere in sight. He worried that his legs wouldn't hold the rest of his body upright.

Anna held out her arms and motioned for her grandfather to come to her. Her smile forged its way through the plastic mask covering her face. Her hair hung in two pigtails, and her favorite blanket covered the rest of her frail body.

Mikhail managed to get to his knees in front of her and held one hand behind his back with the Indian doll he bought in Hungry Horse before he left. He bent forward and Anna wrapped her arms around his neck. After the embrace she slid the mask up to her forehead, kissed him, and then in a breathy voice, she said, "Papa Mik, what's that behind your back?"

He sat back on his heels and brought the Indian doll in front of him and handed it to Anna. "You mean this?"

"Oh yes, Papa, yes." She hugged the doll to her face. "She's pretty like me."

Katya wiped the tears from her cheeks and moved closer and spoke to Anna, "Okay Anna, you need to put your mask back on. You can talk to Grandpa later, okay."

"Okay, Mom." She slid the mask down over her mouth and hugged the doll one more time. Katya and Mikhail stood arm in arm and smiled as Anna introduced the new doll to the crowd of other dolls and stuffed animals lying on the table next to her chair.

⚬━•┄•━⚬

That evening after Anna went to sleep, Katya joined Mikhail at the kitchen table where he sat and read the last two days editions of the *Montana Standard*. He never looked up as she sat next to him with her cup of tea. "Daddy, what's come over the strikers?"

Mikhail looked up from the newspaper and sipped from his coffee cup, "The strike's gone on now for eight months. Don't know who's behind the mobs, but it ain't the men on strike. The union's got good men at the head."

"But then who'd do this sort of thing. The pictures in the paper scare me, Daddy. And them two innocent boys getting shot for no good reason. The cops ain't doin' nothin' about it. I- "

He took another drink of coffee and put his hand on her shoulder. He sighed and said, "Katya, when can you and Anna move up to Columbia Falls? There's plenty of work and a good place to start over for all of us."

She picked up an Oreo cookie from the dish and dunked it into her tea. She knew when a conversation ended with her father. He changed the subject and that was it. "Doctor says Anna might be strong enough to travel come September or October. She's only been on the oxygen mask setup for a week. We still got to try the battery for a bit instead of the electricity. Once that gets worked out, we can start to move her around a little more. Doctor says it's all new stuff and we got to go slow and work out the bugs."

After he folded the newspaper, Mikhail stood up and stretched his huge body. "I'm shot. I worked a double shift yesterday. I need to hit the sack. We can talk more in the morning."

Katya stood up and hugged her father and kissed his cheek. "I feel safe with you her, Daddy. Just like when I was little. Tomorrow we can talk about everything. David, Tomas. Everything, okay." He nodded his head and walked down the hallway to the comfort of his bedroom.

The next morning Mikhail rose out of bed after a solid six hours of sleep and quietly slipped out the back door of the house. He tried not to disturb Katya or Anna as he walked across the alley and opened the gate to his neighbor's yard. George Maletta sat on his porch and smiled as he recognized Mikhail enter his manicured yard. Mikhail lumbered toward the elderly man and quietly spoke, "Any coffee left, George?"

"I always got coffee for you. Come on up and sit down." He slowly rose to his feet and opened the screen door to his kitchen and went inside. In a few minutes he returned and handed Mikhail a steaming cup of coffee. "When did ya get home, Mikhail?"

"Yesterday afternoon."

George muffled a laugh and shook his head, "I see you still are a man of few words. How's things up North?"

"Goin' pretty good." Mikhail took another large gulp of his coffee. "Tomas is doin' good. So's Nolan."

"How about your son-in-law? Ya see him much?"

"No."

George stood up, grabbed Mikhail's empty coffee cup, and walked back into the kitchen. He picked up the notice he received from the Anaconda Company's man about selling his property and walked back out to join Mikhail. "Take a look at this. The god-damn Company wants to buy up all the houses in Meaderville and McQueen for their goddamn open-pit mine. I told the guy to stick it up his copper collar ass."

"When did this happen?"

"The skinny little prick walked door to door about two weeks ago and handed us this paper and wanted to make us an offer. All of McQueen is upset about it. They wanna start breakin' ground west of Meaderville once the strike ends."

Mikhail tugged at the skin on his neck as he welcomed the effect of the strong coffee, but coiled at the thought of McQueen actually giving way to an open-pit. "Any way to stop it?"

"Don't know yet. We got people lookin' into it. All of us met couple of times at the McQueen Club. Nobody wants to move. The Company plans on just burying the school and the church. Can you imagine that shit?"

Mikhail knew it was time to change the subject as his neighbor's face grew redder and his hands started to shake, "My little Anna is getting better."

George shook his head and forced a smile. "I know. I go over everyday and talk to her. Your daughter's a beauty. Too good for that husband of hers." He sipped on his coffee and composed himself with deep sighs through his nostrils. "Is he ever goin' to come down and see the girl?"

"Next week, I think." Mikhail continued to pull at his neck and wanted to change the subject again. "What's goin' on with the mobs wreckin' the homes?"

"Jesus Christ, Mikhail, how many things we gonna talk about? You keep changin' subjects on me. Shit, I don't know! It's time for the strike to get over. Somebody's gonna get hurt. You stayin' up in the Flathead?"

He hesitated after taking a drink of coffee, "Ya. I'm movin' Katya and Anna soon as she's well enough."

The air blew out of his lungs at the news. "When?"

"September or October."

"Oh." The old man pushed off the arm on the chair and groaned as he stood up. Mikhail watched as the elderly friend walked to the edge of his porch. He gazed toward his neighbor's yard. Maletta paused before he spoke again, "It'll be hard to lose your family, Mikhail. We been neighbors since you was a boy."

Mikhail walked over and stood next to George, "It'll be hard to leave you, George. You took over for my dad after he died. I-"

Without moving, he raised his voice and interrupted Mikhail, "That's enough for now. I'm gonna go get some breakfast. I'll see you later."

As he limped back to his house, Mikhail scolded himself for

being so abrupt with his dear friend. I should've broke it to him different. I don't think sometimes. He walked into the house and heard the water running in the tub. Soon he'd need to talk to Katya about David. And now the Company is gonna destroy McQueen. Oh this is goin' be a great Fourth of July alright.

———•—••—•———

Back in Hungry Horse, Tomas boarded the bus down from the Dam after he worked a double shift on the third of July. The ninety-two degree weather and the torturing work pace of tamping the concrete provided the workers with an exhausting day of work.

Tomas removed his sweat-soaked tee shirt and silver hardhat. He put on a dry shirt that he carried with him. He checked his pocketwatch-4:30. He looked over at his partner Shorty Davis and said, "The first thing I'm goin' do is take a long shower and then a nap for an hour or so.

Shorty Davis answered "Hit the sack early tonight, Kid. We got the same kind of day tomorrow, but we get time and a half cause' it's the Fourth."

"Oh, okay Shorty." He then remembered David told him that they were running the Canyon starting at six. As the bus neared the bottom of the Dam Road, he cleared his throat and said, "Shorty. What does running the Canyon mean?"

Shorty looked back from the window, "It means you start up at the West Glacier Bar and you have a drink in every beer joint between there and the Blue Moon. How come ya ask about that?"

"Well my brother-in-law David told me I'm runnin' the canyon with him tonight."

"What's your old man think bout' that?"

Tomas straightened his lean body up and cleared his throat again, "He's in Butte for a couple of days. He probably won't like it."

"I don't like it either, Kid. Some men have got themselves hurt workin' when they're hung over. You best stay clear of him and the bars."

"Ya, you're probably right Shorty. I'll tell David I ain't goin'."

He scratched his stubble beard and puffed on his Camel,

"Just be ready to go at 8:00 tomorrow mornin', Kid. I don't work with drunks or anybody who might get me hurt. Ya follow?"

"Yes, sir, I follow."

The bus stopped in front of the quonset hut and the men slowly climbed down the stairs of the bus. Tomas started to walk away, but Shorty called him back, "Kid, if ya need any help in tellin' your brother-in-law, let me know. I'll put it in words he can understand. Follow?"

He smiled and replied, "I'll be fine, Shorty. Thanks, see ya in the mornin'."

After a long shower, Tomas stood in his room drying his hair when the door opened and David rushed into his room. "Let's go Tommy Boy. Drop your cock, and grab your socks. We're goin' drinkin'."

He slipped on his underwear and set the wet towel on his bed. "I ain't goin', David. I got to work tomorrow. And I-"

"We all gotta work tomorrow for Christ's sake. But tonight we're drinkin'. Hurry up!"

In order to take his mind off the grueling work, Tomas spent a lot of time imagining how to please David and get his dad and Nolan to start over with David. "Oh what the heck, I won't get another chance like this when my dad's gone. I'm doin' man's work and need time with the guys. Well, I can go for a while, David. But not too long, I have to -"

David tossed the clean tee shirt from the back of the chair and hit Tomas in the face, "Right. I'll have ya back here by 7:30. Let's hit it!"

Once inside of the truck, Tomas shook his head and smiled as he snapped the church key on the can of ice cold Great Falls Select. "I just opened a can of beer for the first time in my life. I can't believe it."

John Nolan tucked in his white tee shirt and zippered up his pants. He put his arm around the girl Mabel picked out for him that night. They walked out together and stopped at the door to the outside, "You're a fine girl. Maybe I'll be back tomorrow and we can shoot off some more Fourth of July fireworks together."

The skimpy clad girl laughed and swatted him on the butt. "I'll be here waitin' just for-" She stopped talking as the expression on Nolan's face changed. He glared at the two men staggering out of their black truck. She sensed trouble and hurried across the parking lot to Mabel's house.

Tomas weaved back and forth and David totted him along arm in arm. "You're gonna get your first piece of ass right now, Tommy Boy."

Nolan stepped in front of David. "Well, if it ain't Nolan the little prick. Out of our way, this boy is gettin' his ashes hauled. I already arranged it with Mabel."

Nolan pulled Tomas away from the clutch of David. "He's coming with me asshole! You and me'll settle this later. And if you ever pull a stunt like this again with this kid, I'll kill you, you son-of-a-bitch."

"I'll be here little man. Anytime, anywhere."

"Oh, I'm, I'm gettin' sick." Tomas turned and staggered behind the truck and vomited.

Mabel limped as she and her bouncer walked over to David and Nolan. "Boys. You can settle your beef someplace else. It ain't happenin' here. Hit the road."

Nolan walked toward Mabel and Tomas. "I'll take care of him, Mabel. Here's three bucks for the girl you lined up for him." He guided Tomas across the road and down the path to the barracks. They stopped one more time as Tomas threw up again.

"Goddamn you. I told you to stay away from him. The best part of him ran down his mother's leg."

"Tomas wiped his mouth with his forearm and mumbled, "I know. I know. I didn't listen. I love you John. You are the-"

"Just shut up. Did you eat anything?"

"Just some beer nuts."

"I'm goin' to have to kill that worthless-"

Tomas stopped and waved his hand, "It was my fault. Not David's. Don't do anything to-"

"I told you to shut up." They got to the stairs of the barracks and started up. Tomas lost his balance, and in slow motion rolled over the railing onto the gravel. Nolan looked down at him and said, "It's a good thing it's early. You gotta get up and go. I'm waking you up at 5:00 and you're gonna have the coldest shower and toughest walk of your life."

The two men stumbled into Tomas' room. Nolan flipped the young man onto the bed. He passed out before Nolan turned out the light.

CHAPTER FOURTEEN

It was the Fourth of July and the mercantile would be hopping with business. This was the biggest business day of the year for Polebridge and for her mother. Hannah woke up and slowly pushed back the blankets with a full body stretch. She felt the blood rush to her toes and fingertips giving her that welcomed warm feeling. As she made two fists to gently rub the sleep from her eyes like a contented feline, she thanked her lucky stars that she always had a list of activities to tick off mentally in the morning. She couldn't imagine what it felt like to get up with a blank slate on her brain. The only thought better than knowing that the day was waiting for her was sipping those first drops of very hot coffee. That, too, was a gift.

Hannah dressed in the semi-darkness; it was 5:30 and her mother had been up for an hour. The kitchen was warm from the baking of the bread and pastries. Her mother greeted her with a cup of coffee. "Mornin' Sunshine. It's about time you rolled out. Probably thinkin' about that big boy from Butte."

"How did you know that?" She hugged her flour-covered mother on her way out the door. "I'll be back in about twenty minutes and you can put me to work. That's right after I devour some of that bread coolin' on the counter."

As she walked to the bridge over the North Fork of the Flathead River, Hannah laughed as she did have a nasty dream about Mikhail. "It's been awhile since I've done that." She sipped her coffee and continued with her thoughts. "Hmmm. I wonder what he dreamt about last night. I might have to ask him sometime."

She stood on the bridge and looked north toward Canada. The river still ran high and the water reached the reeds on the shoreline. She looked over at the Ranger's station and smelled the wood smoke coming from the chimney of the log house. The Ranger manned the north entrance to Glacier National Park and was up getting ready for the busy day ahead. He stepped out onto the porch and emptied a basin full of wash water. He waved to Hannah before going back inside to eat his waiting breakfast.

The Fourth of July in Polebridge featured a parade that went from the Mercantile down the half-mile to the North Fork Road and back. Locals wore patriotic costumes, rode horses, and walked in the parade. The tourists visiting Glacier National Park crowded in front of the Mercantile and the Northern Lights Saloon next door. The volleyball and horseshoe games continued all day long. Most of the tourists had their own beer, but the Northern Lights sold out all of their extra supply before dark every year.

Once Hannah returned from her walk, she stopped by the outhouse, left the door open, sat down, and gazed out over the field in front of the river. "I never get tired of the scenery around here. Maybe if things work out, I'd bring Mikhail and his son up here sometime to see this with me." She giggled as she thought that it probably wouldn't be from the inside of this outhouse.

———•••———

Before and during breakfast on July Fourth, Mikhail daydreamed about his father telling him the history of McQueen. He vividly recalled his father's voice as he looked out the front porch toward the East Ridge. Many times in school Mikhail wished that he could have recalled historical facts like he did about those of McQueen. Mikhail told the same stories many times to Tomas and Katya when they were younger.

In 1891, a small community began life on Sunflower Hill named for the yellow flower that covered the hill. This newly formed community was named McQueen after the McQueen placer mining claim. In 1901 McQueen had grown to approximately fifteen homes. People moved to McQueen from primarily two locations, mining camps from around the United States and from fast growing Meaderville, its neighbor to the west.

The ethnic makeup of McQueen was largely Slovenians, Austrians, and Croatians. It had a small makeup of Italians, English, Swedes, Norwegians, Germans, Scots, and Finns. Many of the residents of McQueen spent their days raising chickens and hogs. As time passed and more mines opened up and became the predominate employer, many of the men turned in their hayforks for picks and shovels. Many of the "old country" traditions and recipes made their way to McQueen. Foods like kielbasa, blood sausage, cheese strudel, and homemade smoke dam were proudly served in the McQueen households.

The isolated location of McQueen kept it from having the same type of infrastructure as Butte city had. The streetcar system finally was brought to McQueen in 1909. McQueen also did not have a running water system in the early years; the residents used a community well at the northwest corner of the community. McQueen was one of the first neighborhoods to put in sanitary sewer and streetlights.

The first grocery store was built in 1907. Other businesses soon popped up such as Cesarini's Grocery, Lutey Brothers Grocery, Grosso Meats, Tipperary Candy Store, Petritz Shoes Repair, Merlak's Grocery, Tomich Barbershop and the kid's favorite, Nettie's Super Ice Cream. The Crystal Theater, which later became known as the McQueen Club in 1944, offered entertainment to the area.

Jesuit missionaries started the Holy Savior Catholic Church in 1901 and the elementary school in 1904. The McQueen Athletic Club and the McQueen Firehouse were the center of activities for many of the residents. The McQueen Club, the firehouse, Holy Savior Church, and the school were the heart and the people were the soul of the community.

After breakfast, Mikhail helped Katya with the dishes. As he dried the last cereal bowl, he asked, "No parade this year, huh?"

She wiped the splashed water from the sink counter and answered, "No. Nobody's got money to build a float this year. Nobody feels like celebratin' much anyways."

He set the bowl in the cupboard and looked in the living room to see Anna napping in his big chair. "No, I don't suppose so. Anything doin' at the McQueen Club?"

"Ya. They're having a potluck around 4:00. You wanna go over, Daddy? I'll fix something and then I can stay with Anna. It might do you some good to see your friends. Everybody still asks about you."

Mikhail shrugged his shoulders, "Oh. I don't know. George most likely has talked to most people by now. They'll know we're moving to Columbia Falls."

"Daddy. Let's sit down on the porch and talk about it."

Once they got seated on the small wooden bench on the porch, Katya began the conversation she rehearsed during her sleepless night. "How'll this all work? Me and David are still legally separated. I miss him like crazy. But soon as we're together, we start to fight. I don't know if-"

"You and Anna can live with me and Tomas. We'll have a big enough house for the four of us."

She stood up and walked to the edge of the porch and leaned her elbows on the rail. "Me and David need to work it out. Anna'll need a mother and dad to help-"

"He ain't come down once since March to see her. And even that didn't work. He got drunk, remember."

She promised herself she would not cry. Fighting tears, she managed to turn and face her father. "He's under a lot of pressure with his job. The poor man works seven days a week so we can get the best care for Anna."

"So do me and your brother."

Her voice cracked as her temper flared, "I know, I know. But he's a boss and the men depend-"

Mikhail felt his own anger build as he flashed on David falling drunk into Rocco's Club two nights earlier. "Katya. He plans to come down soon and you can talk it over. If it don't work out at first, you can live with us. Then-"

Her self-control vanished. "Why does it always have to be what you want?" Tears gushed. She slammed the gate after she ran down the steps of the porch and then disappeared into the alley.

Mikhail started to go after her but stopped as he heard the muffled voice of Anna from the living room through the screen door. He composed himself the best he could and went into the living room. Anna had her mask up on her forehead and struggled to catch her breath. "Put your mask back on, Anna."

The harsh tone of his voice frightened her and she struggled even more to catch her breath. He gently slid the oxygen mask over her face and knelt down by her chair. "Easy now. Easy now. Take slow breaths." He forced a reassuring smile and kissed her on the forehead. "It's gonna be all right now."

Mikhail stroked her hair with his hand. "Shhh, now. Shhh." Anna caught her breath and the color came back into her face. Her little chest slowed down from the earlier heaving. He handed her the Indian doll that fell off her chair. A smile came across her face and she pressed the doll against her shoulder.

He changed his position to sitting on the floor. "Did I hear you snorin' last night?"

She shook her head and gave him a harmless slap on his arm. Anna pointed at him and imitated him snoring. He laughed and softly rubbed her tiny arm. Talking was easier with Anna than with adults. This puzzled him and wondered why he was so short with adults and yet he talked easily with her, "Happy Fourth of July. Would you like a story about your mom when she was a little girl like you?"

Enthusiastically she nodded her head and squeezed her doll even tighter.

Mikhail rearranged his legs and arms and began. "One time on the Fourth, we took your mom up to Park Street to watch the parade. She wore this little red cowboy hat with the string under her chin." The memory of seeing Katya as a child with the little hat triggered a similar memory of his wife as a young woman. For the first ten years of their marriage, Mikhail and Barbara lived a good life together. He felt she did everything right as she raised Katya and Tomas as little kids. They were happy together and shared the marriage in all ways. He flashed on seeing Barbara as a twenty-five year old women holding Tomas in her arms while Mikhail stood and watched his daughter wave at the ladies riding on the beautiful floats.

Barbara's long brown hair draped below her shoulders and the smile on her face beamed as he made eye contact with her as he looked up from the parade. They made love that night after the kids went to sleep and she promised she'd love him forever.

He felt Anna's hand tapping him on the arm. Mikhail realized he drifted off in the middle of the story. "Sorry, Anna. Anyway. Your mother waved at the pretty lady riding on the truck. The parade stopped for a minute in front of us. The lady waved your mother over to her. I took her over there, and the lady asked if your mother could ride up on the truck with her for the rest of the parade. I said okay. She hopped up and sat next to the pretty lady and waved to the people as the truck went by. I walked alongside on the sidewalk and picked her up at the end of the parade."

Anna drifted off to sleep before he finished telling her the entire story. He slid the blanket up snuggly and covered her and her little doll. Mikhail drifted off back to the memory of seeing he and Barbara lying in their bed vowing to love each other until the end of time. An angry memory swiftly replaced that one as he flashed on the night fifteen years later when she asked him for a divorce so she could live with another man.

The screen door closed and snapped Mikhail from his trip back to Barbara. Katya walked into the living room and stared at her father still sitting on the floor with his hands on his lap. "Sorry, Daddy. Poor sleep last night and I took it out on you. Can we try it again?"

"Only if I can get up." They both managed weak laughs as he struggled over to the couch and climbed up to his feet. They hugged and he whispered, "We'll work it out."

"I know we will. Let's go fix something for you to take over to the McQueen Club this afternoon. I ran into George in the alley and he wants you to drive him over there. He can't be too mad at you. I told him you would, so you're stuck."

He nodded his tentative approval and placed his hands in front of him in surrender. "Do you remember that time when you rode in the float on the Fourth?"

"How could I ever forget? You caught up with me at the Civic Center and nearly collapsed from exhaustion from walking that far. And then you had to carry me all the way back up to St. Joseph's Church on your shoulders when mom met us with the car."

"I told Anna that story today. She sure looks like you sometimes."

Katya opened the cupboard door and pulled out some bowls. "People that visit her tell me that all the time. When I look in the mirror sometimes, I think I look like Grandmother Moses. The extra weight and my scraggly hair don't help me none."

He shook his head one more time and headed to the bathroom for a shower.

———•••———

At five in the morning of the Fourth of July, John Nolan stood over the sprawled body of Tomas as he lay sleeping in the under-sized single bed of his room in the barracks. His mind soared back to the beautiful spring morning that Tomas was born. One of the nurses brought Tomas over to him as he stood by Mikhail in the hallway outside of the delivery room. He recalled her words to him, "You have a beautiful son, Mr. Anzich, and he even looks a little like you. You can go and see your wife now." Nolan shook his head as he vividly remembered the look of surprise on Mikhail's face. Nolan wished that Tomas was his son. He watched him grow from that baby in the hospital through his years in school.

And now he stood over a boy turned man. He wanted to kiss him on the head like he did when he was a little boy. Instead he reached down and firmly grabbed him by the shoulders and yelled, "Alright, time to get up and face the music. If you're goin' to dance, you're goin' to pay the fiddler."

Tomas jerked up and sat with his eyes scanning the room for

his bearing. "What? What do-"

"Never mind. You're goin' to work that big head of yours off before you go to work. Get on your clothes! You're goin' for a long walk. Hurry up!"

Tomas slid around in the bed and placed his feet down on the floor. He still wore his socks and clothes to bed. He searched for his shoes. And then it hit. His head pounded and his stomach heaved. Tomas bent to reach his right shoe and stopped. He jumped up and ran for the bathroom. Nolan heard him vomit. One of Tomas's shoes lay upside down in the hallway leading to the bathroom. Nolan picked it up and walked slowly down to join Tomas who wrapped his arms around the toilet. Dry heaves tortured his body and nothing remained in his stomach from the night before.

Nolan placed an arm on Tomas's shoulder and said, "Let's walk. You'll feel better." He remembered from his own experience of dealing with severe hangovers. "Come on, Nephew. Let's go."

Tomas gathered himself and pushed himself up from the toilet. They stopped and got his other shoe and went outside. The sun came up over the ridge as they walked down the road leading to the east side of the Hungry Horse Reservoir. After walking about half a mile, Tomas stopped and blazed through another bout of dry heaves. He wiped his mouth with his forearm, and with Nolan's encouragement, they continued walking. An hour and a half later and having endured Nolan's constant barrage of stories of his hangovers, Tomas walked up the stairs to the barracks. Nolan walked fast and never slowed down except to stand and watch Tomas attempt to clear his stomach. Sweat poured down his face as he walked in. He took off his clothes and wrapped a towel around his waist. He went in and with Nolan's constant haranguing, he tolerated a long, ice cold shower.

After he managed to eat some scrambled eggs, toast, and drink several cups of coffee and tomato juice, Tomas boarded the bus to the top of the Dam. He climbed into the back and avoided the eyes of his partner, Shorty Davis who sat in the front row. Tomas berated himself about getting drunk with David and vowed to never drink again. He knew Shorty would question him about last night. Shorty made it real clear yesterday afternoon about not working with drunks. Tomas promised himself to put on a good act and work non-stop until the whistle blew at 4:30.

Shorty waited for him at the side of the bus. He liked Shorty but tolerated some bad moods that included ranting and raving. The look on Shorty's face looked to Tomas like it was going to be one of those kinds of days. "Did ya get drunk with your asshole brother-in-law last night?"

Tomas stood his distance and answered, "No Shorty. I drank three beers with him and was in bed by 9:00. I feel great today."

Shorty walked away and mumbled, "Ya, you betcha."

He jogged up alongside Shorty and walked together. They set their buckets and jackets down on the bench in the shack. Without looking up Shorty growled at Tomas, "You'd better be feelin' great. We're short-handed as hell and they are stickin' a new guy in with us. Besides we been challenged to more pours by next block over. It's gonna be hotter than yesterday. So you'd better be feeling great." He looked right in Tomas's eyes and continued, "You follow, Kid?"

Tomas swallowed hard as the smell of the Copenhagen on Shorty's breath filled his nostrils. His stomach moved but held. He also fought the dull throb of the headache and said, "Yes, sir, I follow."

Shorty nodded a slight approval, spit out his snoose, and poured a cup of coffee from his thermos. They stood there and watched their boss Fred Spear and a young Indian man walk toward them. "Hey, Shorty, this here is Cliff Buckless. He'll be workin' with ya today. He'll be the third and will spell you and your partner. Heard ya been challenged. You start in block number six. Hope you kick Buck's ass."

Shorty nodded and introduced himself to the new man. "Have you run a vibrator before there, Cliff?"

After a short pause, Cliff answered, "Yes."

Shorty shook his head as Tomas walked the new man toward block six. He thought how it was bad enough working with a hung over partner, now he had to put up with a Blackfeet Indian who was probably hung over too. Shorty worked with lots of Blackfeet Indians and liked how steady most of them worked. He just wished it hadn't happened on a day when Buck Morris and his crew challenged them to a pour. Maybe this young guy'll work out. I don't want to listen to big mouth Morris bragging on and on for weeks.

The bellboy signaled the operator and he guided the bucket of concrete over to block six. The men stood in the corner and watched the contents enter the five-foot block. Tomas gave himself another pep talk, "Work harder than you ever had before. Shorty'll tan your hide if you don't." Shorty picked up his end of the vibrator and signaled Tomas with a slight nod of his head. Every nerve in his head reacted as the vibration rolled through his arms and up through his neck. He rejoined his private thoughts, "Oh God, I promise to never drink again. Please help me make it through today."

During lunch, Tomas listened to every word Cliff told him about the Going to The Sun Highway and the eastern side of Glacier Park. "Cliff, would you take me up there sometime? I'd help pay for gas and everything. I'd really like to see it."

"I will take you there on our day off sometime. I can show you my home in Heart Butte. You can then see the Mountains from the other side."

"I'd like to do that, Cliff." Tomas remembered looking up towards the area of the Going To The Sun Highway on his first trip to Glacier with David. "I'd like-"

"It's time to hit the bricks. You can talk about Glacier on your own time. Let's roll." As he did every day, Shorty handed his bucket to Tomas after eating. "Take this on up for me will you, Kid?"

Tomas sighed relief once he realized Shorty forgot about last night. Shorty's crew had finished tapping three pours before lunch and Shorty took the opportunity to razz Buck about them lagging behind.

John Nolan insisted that Tomas bring two extra jugs of water with him. Tomas drained his regular jug and worked on one of the extras as he walked back to block six to join his crew. He felt strong and realized what Nolan told him was right. "Kid, the one thing about a good hangover is that sometime during the day you will start to feel better. It'll feel as good as a good shit." Tomas felt warm inside as he thought of how good care Nolan took of him that morning. He now understood how Nolan and his dad were such good friends. After his father, John Nolan was the greatest man he ever knew. I am so lucky to have him as my godfather and step-uncle.

The bus ride down to the bottom was loud and Shorty and his crew celebrated the victory over his rival Buck Morris. Shorty loudly bragged how he beat Morris with a snotty-nose kid and a first-time Blackfeet Indian kid. "I whooped your ass Morris with a couple of young greenhorns. And one of 'em was even hung over, but don't tell his old man. He'll get his ass kicked." The bus erupted into loud laughing and others joined in teasing Morris and the men in his crew.

Shorty continued, "We're meetin' down at Whitey's and the drinks are on Buck. I think I might try a martini tonight or some other fancy drink. Oh ya, Morris. My young pups will have Shirley Temples too." Again the raucous group of men roared their approval.

Cliff quietly whispered to Tomas, "What is a Shirley Temple?"

He remembered back to his senior year prom dance and the dinner at the Arrow Club in Meaderville after the dance. "Oh it's a real sweet drink that doesn't have any booze in it. I bought one for my date after the prom once."

He nodded his understanding but couldn't imagine any of the bars in Hungry Horse serving a girl's drink. Cliff Buckless watched many of his friends and family members get drunk and behave badly when he lived on the Blackfeet Reservation. After basketball season of his senior year, he packed a small suitcase and hitchhiked over to Hungry Horse and started working on the Dam.

He walked by many of the bars in the Canyon as a way of reminding him that he would never drink. Cliff flashed on that cold night in February when he was twelve years old. The tribal police car pulled in front of their house at two o'clock in the morning. He still remembered the red light swirling around and around. He scratched the frost off the glass, and he and his little sister peeped out of the window. The greatest fear for him in life came through right at that moment. The knock on the door sounded like a giant pounded with a large rock. He and his sister opened the door and heard the news of the head on car crash on the bridge between East Glacier and Browning. His parents and his uncle were dead.

The noise of the screeching brakes from the dust snapped Cliff out of his reoccurring horrible memory. Tomas gave him a light elbow. "Are you okay, Cliff? It's time to get off."

"Yes, Yes. I am fine. It was good to meet you."

"Me too. You're a hard worker. I had trouble keeping up with you. Are you going to do anything tonight for the Fourth?"

Cliff sauntered down the steps of the bus. "I am going back to the barracks in Hungry Horse. After a shower, I'd like to get something good to eat. Maybe go bowling right there too. I don't want to go near the bars."

"Would you like me to join up with you?"

Cliff stood quietly for a few seconds. It was strange for him that a white worker wanted to do anything with him. He mostly spent the time alone or with other Indians who worked on the Dam. "Okay. At six, right here."

"Great, Cliff. I'll go shower, and then I have to track down my godfather for a bit; then I'll meet you right here."

After a great fried chicken and mashed potatoes dinner at Rocco's, the two young men walked toward the bowling alley at the quonset hut near Cliff's barracks. As Tomas and Cliff waited to cross the highway, three drunken men staggered out of the bar in Rocco's. One of the men cupped his hands and yelled, "Hey Blanket Ass, what you doin' off the Rez?"

Tomas suddenly turned around, "What did you say?"

The same man answered, "I wasn't talkin' to you dumbshit. I was talkin' to that Indian you're with."

Cliff didn't turn around and started to walk across the highway. Tomas walked to the three men and stopped right in front of the man who was yelling. "Why you being so mean to him? He's a good man, and a great worker. Leave him alone."

The man inched up right next to Tomas and got eyeball to eyeball, "Are you goin' make me, Indian lover? Because if you are, I'm gonna kick your ass too."

Tomas quietly repeated himself, "Cliff isn't botherin' nobody. We're just goin' bowling, mindin' our own business. Like I said, leave us alone."

The man pushed Tomas hard in the chest and his two friends closed in behind him, "Put the boots to him, Jim. Teach that Indian Lover a lesson."

Cliff jogged back across the highway and stood next to Tomas. He quietly spoke to Tomas, "Let's go bowling. Forget about them."

"Hey. Ya hear that? The card-carryin' blanket-ass can speak. Ugh!" The other men laughed and tightened the circle.

The sheriff pulled his black 1949 Ford sedan to a dusty stop behind the circle of men. He stepped out and waived his bully club in front of him. "What's goin' on here men?"

The drunken man doin' all of the talking said, "Nothin' Sheriff, we'd be just talkin' here. That's all."

Sheriff Patrick Schustrom's tough reputation in the Canyon prevented many fights from happening. He walked over and stood in front of Tomas and Cliff. "Is that what's goin' on here, men?"

Tomas nodded yes. Schustrom walked slowly backward toward his car. "That's good then. I'll just sit here for a while so's you good friends can talk some more. Maybe I'll learn a thing or two about a thing or two." He flashed a wry smile and closed the car door behind him.

The three men walked away and went inside the Bucket of Blood Bar just down from the parking lot of Rocco's. Tomas and Cliff crossed the highway and entered the bowling alley to celebrate the Fourth of July.

CHAPTER FIFTEEN

Three weeks after the Fourth of July, Mikhail's boss stood with another man and greeted Mikhail as he stepped down from the bus. "Hey Mikhail. Want you to meet somebody. This here is Dick Kearney. He's the shift superintendent for the iron workers." Mikhail shook hands and didn't say anything. His boss continued, "Dick needs another hook tender and I know you had your iron worker card from Butte. Wonder if you'd like to give it a try?"

Mikhail looked at Kearney and answered, "Don't know nothin' about that work."

Kearney stretched his sore back before he spoke. "Each shift at Hungry Horse Dam uses four hook tenders per shift. These men transport every piece of material used on the dam back and forth from one location to the next. Everything from sand and gravel to equipment such as the large northwest shovel. Tenders also tie and untie the buckets and larger skips that go back and forth across the canyon. They use a signal system as many times the operator can't see the bucket or his bell man."

He stopped and pointed up to the four cableways that hung high above the Dam. "Them cableways haul the buckets. It's an endless cable. That there cable is five inches thick in diameter. We called it gut. The cable gets sent through the main tower and then through one of the four towers. Our tenders sometimes ride the buckets and guide the material to its location." He pointed over to the operator shack. "The operator follows signals from his bell man. When he can't see the bellman, the tender uses a paddle to signal. You'd learn what the signals mean. Up, down, left, right."

Mikhail's boss laughed and said, "Did you get all that, Mik? Old Kearney there usually talks faster. You're lucky this time."

Mikhail slowly removed his hard hat and ran his fingers through his thick, black hair. "What do I do when I ain't ridin' the buckets?"

"You'd be unloadin' the buckets. Non-stop and it's dangerous work. But you'd be making about a buck more an hour."

"Who'd show me the ropes?"

Kearney nodded his head at a man walking by them. "You'd be workin' with that fella right there. That's Bud Reynolds. He's the best hook tender we got on the project. You'd learn from him I expect."

Mikhail looked at Kearney and stuck out his hand, "Okay."

Kearney shook his hand and walked over and caught up with Bud Reynolds. "Hey, Bud, hold up there a minute."

The short stocky man stopped and greeted Kearney, "Mornin', Dick. Is this my new partner?"

"Ya, it is. Meet Mikhail Anzich."

During lunch, Mikhail listened to his new partner talk about himself. Mikhail thought how this man loved his work. He gave Mikhail a short history of how he started working at the Dam in 1947. His first job was digging the diversion tunnel. He was an ironworker and laid reinforcement steel in the tunnel too. Bud Reynolds virtually worked on the construction of every phase of the project. He helped build the towers, the cement mixing plant, and the overhead cableways. His longest lasting job was that of a hook tender.

Mikhail enjoyed listening to the stories and planned to share them with Tomas. "Where did ya come from, Bud?"

"I was raised in the Ronan area, and as a young guy I worked for the U.S. Surveying crew. I climbed every peak in the Mission Mountains and placed markers on the peaks for their flyovers to base their locations. I later moved to Martin City and started a butcher plan and meat shop. My brother-in-law owned the grocery store attached, and once the work here on the dam started, I sold the business to my brother-in-law."

Mikhail checked his pocket watch as Bud closed his lunch bucket. "Time to go I guess."

"Ya Mik, time to go."

———————

Later that day, Bud Reynolds sat in his old rocker on the front porch and drank ice tea with his wife. He set his cup down on the weathered picnic table and said, "I got a new partner today. He caught right on and worked steady all day. I enjoyed talkin' to him and I was wonderin' how you'd feel about havin' him and his friend over for supper sometime."

Sara Reynolds looked up from her novel. "What's his name, honey?"

"Mikhail Anzich. He's from Butte and workin' to get money for his granddaughter who has polio. He's the first guy in a long time who I think might work out to be a good friend."

She set her novel in her lap, sipped her tea, and then continued, "How old is he? And is his friend a woman or a man? And one more thing, how-"

Bud's robust laugh interrupted his wife, "Holy cow, Sara. I only worked with him for one day. I just thought it might be fun to have them over. We ain't had nobody over for awhile."

She walked over to him and kissed him on the head, "That'll be fine, honey. How about Saturday? I can pick up a couple of fresh chickens at Byrd's Meats. We can have potato salad with it. How's that sound?"

"Sounds great to me. I'll ask him tomorrow. Oh, by the way. You know his friend. She's the lady who runs the Royal Show house."

"Hannah?"

"Ya, I'm pretty sure that's what he told me. They're just friends at this point, but he seemed to think a lot about her. That was the most he talked all day. Otherwise, he didn't have much to say."

Sara knelt down in front of her husband, "I really like Hannah.

She's fun and interesting. I haven't talked to her for a while and it will be great to see her. Good. I'm glad you wanta do this." She went inside and pulled out her recipe box and looked for a dessert idea for Saturday. She hummed as she thought how it would be nice to have a good friend besides her family. "Hmmm. It would be different having a new friend to talk to about my ideas and worries."

Down in Hungry Horse in the Dam Town Tavern, John Nolan ordered another round of beers for himself and the other three men at his table. He held court with the other electricians and waved his hands as he told stories. "Now, you men think you know tough guys. Why I know that the bartender over there is a better fighter than any of them men you talked about. Billy Socolich was a middleweight contender before he got hurt in that car wreck back in 1948."

The bearded man to Nolan's left jumped in, "You're so full of bullshit, Nolan. Johnny Linderman from Ronan only lost one fight here in Hungry Horse. He's gotta be the toughest man on the project."

Nolan gulped the remains of his beer and set the glass down hard on the table. "Tell me about the fight Johnny lost. Then I'll tell you if I think he's the toughest guy around here."

The man shook his head, smiled, and began his story. "Well, it happened a couple months back. There was a jam on one of the flows to turbine number two and things was gettin' pretty backed up. So the Navy flew in this skin diver to go down and work on the busted flow. It took him a couple of days and nights to get the job done, but he did it. He-"

"For Christ's sakes, get to the story," interrupted Nolan. The other men laughed and razzed the man to get on with his story.

"Anyways, as I was saying, this skin diver went down to the Dam Town Tavern to have a few after he finished the job. While he was tellin' about fixing the flow, it came out that he was a boxer in the Navy. He fought all over the world for the Navy. It was about that time when Johnny Linderman came over. Johnny asked the guy if he wanted to go out back and show him how tough he was.

The-"

Nolan interrupted him again, "Holy shit, are we ever goin' hear about the fight?"

"Nolan, if you interrupt me again, you'll see how tough I am. Shut up and listen." He winked at Nolan and started again. "The Navy guy told Johnny that he didn't want to fight while they both been drinkin'. So they made plans to meet behind The Dam Town on Friday afternoon at 5:00."

"Well, what happened?" Nolan stood up and waved his hands. "Finish the goddamn story before I die of old age."

After the men stopped laughing, the bearded man continued, "They met Friday night at 5:00. Big crowd. Guys bettin' all over the place. I bet on Johnny for sure. Most the bets were on Johnny. The two men stepped in the circle. Johnny was taller and bigger than the Navy skin diver. Away they went. Johnny never laid a hand on the guy. Fastest guy I ever seen. He hit Johnny twenty, twenty-five times at least. Johnny kept coming back for more until his brother stepped in and waved it off. That Navy skin diver never even sweated. Jesus he was fast. Johnny told me later that this kid also packed quite a punch too."

Nolan drank his beer in one gulp. "Oh, dear God in heaven. If that story went any longer I think I would'a died of cotton mouth disease." He slapped the bearded man on the shoulder and then faked a few jabs at the man. They both laughed and toasted their glasses.

Danny Fisher entered the story telling. "Well, let me tell you one about our bartender Billy Socolich. Me and him hanged over the front of the Dam on a lined scaffold repairin' a line wire for the telephone system. This practical joker up top held out his dick like he was peeing on us when he actually poured coffee on us. The coffee got on Billy's new Can't Bust Em pants. He thought the guy peed on him. So up he goes. He climbed the scaffolding hoist rope and just beat the shit out of the guy, right in front of a laborer walking boss and all. Nobody said a word, and Billy slid down the rope back to our platform."

Nolan asked, "What did he say when he got back down to ya?"

Fisher laughed and then answered, "He never said a word. He just picked up his pliers and finished splicin' the line. Not one single word I tell ya, and I wasn't about to ask em'."

Nolan went to the bar and picked up four more beers. After he set them on the table, he looked around a couple of times and then said, "Now men. I'm gonna tell you somethin' and it don't leave this here table. Understand? The other three men nodded their heads and Nolan continued, "There is one man on this entire job you never want to get on the wrong side of. I can tease the hell out of him, but I know when to stop. He'd take your head off with one back hand if he loses control."

The bearded man leaned forward toward Nolan, "Well tell us you dumb shit. Who is he?"

He looked around again and ducked his head in and out and lowered his voice, "Mikhail Anzich, my best friend."

Danny Fisher leaned in and asked, "Is he that big guy I see you with once in awhile waitin' for the bus?"

He nodded his head, smiled, and answered, "Yep. That's him. Don't never mess with him. He's a great friend, but in Butte he's got himself quite a reputation. He don't drink no more because of how bad he hurt a guy once. You most likely won't never see him in a bar."

Fisher sat back in his chair, "Is that his boy with him?"

"It sure is. He's my godson and I adopted him as my nephew."

The men laughed and the bearded man shouted at Nolan, "You can't adopt a kid for your own nephew. You're so full of shit, Nolan."

Nolan laughed and winked at the lady sitting at the bar. She winked back and seductively walked back to the ladies room. Nolan watched her behind all the way back. "See that little thing there. I'll be teaching her a few tricks later tonight."

Fisher slapped Nolan on the back, "And her old man over there will teach you a few tricks with that pool cue he has in his hand."

The men laughed and accepted free beers from Billy Socolich. "Have one on me, boys."

———•◦•———

He sat on her kitchen chair and read the sports page from the July 25th edition of the *Hungry Horse News*. Lila Toma poured him another cup of coffee and set it down next to David as he read the news. She pulled up a chair right next to him and kissed him softly below the left ear. He looked up from the paper and smiled before he spoke, "I'm so glad we talked it out and are back together. I really missed bein' with you."

Lila sat back in her chair and closed her robe over her bare legs. "I missed you too, David. That was very nice last night and this morning. But what are we going to do? We're both still married and it sounds like your family is moving up here in a couple of months."

"Oh we'll cross that bridge when we come to it. It'll all work out."

She stood up and walked to the kitchen sink. She rinsed out her coffee cup and looked out the window at Lake Five. Another beautiful summer morning. Where had the time gone? They were just here doin' about the same thing and the snow piled halfway up to the window with the temperature twenty-four below zero. "David, we have a big bridge to cross right now." She pivoted around and looked down at him. "My husband's still very suspicious of me. He told me that one of his friends might be keeping an eye on me when he goes over to Havre. I'd leave him for you, but I'm not sure he'd let me go."

David set the paper down on the kitchen table and confidently walked over to her. He wrapped his arms around her and moved in for a kiss. She pushed back. "David. What are we going to do? I'm scared and worried. If you don't have a plan, I can't go through with it any longer. I just can't."

He stepped back and sat back down on the chair. "Well, we know you can't stay broke up from me for very long. You only lasted-"

"You're such a bastard, David!" Lila cried and stormed away into the bedroom. She returned with his pants and shoes and flopped them on the floor in front of him. "You need to get out right now. I mean it. Don't contact me unless you plan to leave your wife and marry me. Get out!" She ran back into the bedroom and closed the door behind her.

David dressed, finished his coffee, and slowly walked to his truck. As he closed the door, he noticed a man sitting in an older

Ford pickup parked in between two of the cabins. The man looked away as David looked his way. David started his truck and backed out of the driveway. He drove slowly behind the parked pickup and stared into the truck. The man pulled his camera down from the dashboard and set it in the truck seat. David quickly released the clutch and kicked gravel as he sped away. "Shit!" He yelled as he left the Lake Five grounds and stopped at the stop sign that led to the highway. "Shit, shit, shit!"

———••———

The next morning David waited outside of Superintendent Scalf's office. He nervously talked to Scalf's secretary Mary about the heat wave and the lightning storm last night. Finally, anxiety overwhelmed him, "Mary, what's goin' on. Looks like he's talkin' to all the walkin' bosses."

"That's right. He is." She turned away and slid another piece of paper into the typewriter.

David moved around in front of her and put on his best flirting face, "Are you wearin' your hair different these days?"

Without looking up or stopping her quickly moving fingers on the keys, she answered, "No. Same as I have for the last fifteen years."

He walked back over and looked out the window at the cement crew in the last block as they vibrated the cement into every possible edge in the block. David looked more intensely and watched Tomas and his partner easily handle the powerful two-man vibrator. His interest quickly changed as he heard the door to Scalf's office open. The man in visiting the Superintendent thanked Mary for the coffee and spoke quietly to David.

Scalf waved him in and pointed to the chair in front of his desk. "Have a seat, Dave, I'll be right with you." He walked out and used the bathroom behind Mary's desk. While he stood there, he reviewed the instructions given to him by the two FBI agents. They told him to ask each walking boss the questions written on the typed sheets. He walked by Mary and into his office.

David nervously started the conversation, "What's goin' on Supt.?"

He picked up the sheet of paper with David's name on it and prepared to start with the FBI questions. "Dave, I can't tell you too much about this, so you just need to trust me. I'm askin' every one of the walkin' bosses these same questions. That's all I'm tellin' you right now. Later on I might be able to tell you more."

After he waved his hands that he understood, David flashed a sigh of relief from his anxiety all morning about why the Superintendent might want to talk to him. The adjusted timecards seemed to be the top reason for a meeting. But then he remembered that the auditor still planned to work here on the financial records for another few weeks.

Scalf began the questions and recorded David's answers on the sheet in front of him. David easily answered the questions until he got to question number ten. "Last question, Dave. Has anyone on the job contacted you about doin' anything illegal?"

David felt the effects of the lack of sleep from worrying about Lila's husband. Throughout the night he wrestled with the idea of the man in the old pickup taking pictures of him leaving Lila's cabin in the morning. "Maybe the guy just liked takin' pictures of the lake or somethin'? But then maybe he was Lila's old man's friend spyin' on her?" Scalf cleared his throat and snapped David back to the question. "What was the question again Supt.?"

Scalf repeated the question. David squirmed and unconsciously rolled his head several times. He moved his lower lip up tight against his upper lip. "Um, no. Um, not that I can think of." His eyes darted around the room and stopped on the photo of the early clearing of the trees from the canyon in preparation for the Dam. He read the handwriting on the black and white photo. "To W.R., from Al Sutter."

The Superintendent stopped writing and looked up. "You don't sound too sure of yourself there, Dave."

He struggled to gain his composure, "I'm sure, Supt. Nobody talked to me about nothin' like that there. I, I haven't done anythin' illegal."

"I never said you did."

He rubbed his brow and then felt the whiskers on his chin. "I'm fine. I just didn't understand you the first time." David faked a laugh and asked, "Anything else, Supt.?"

Scalf shook his head and finished writing David's answer to the last question. He made a mental note to remember how David acted but didn't put any notation on the list of FBI questions. David left and walked right by Mary without saying a word. He felt his stomach flip over as he replayed how poorly he reacted to the final question. I need a couple of drinks to settle me down. David walked over to his pickup and pulled out a half-empty bottle of Jim Beam. He swallowed the remaining whiskey in one drink.

CHAPTER SIXTEEN

The Care Less Group noisily chattered about the upcoming activity scheduled for August third. Hannah got the attention of the other women by clinking her spoon on her coffee cup. "Ladies, ladies. Let me read the article in the *Daily Inter Lake* about the upcoming copper liberty bell parade in Martin City. We have lots of work to do and less than two weeks to get it done."

Mabel wet the pencil on her tongue as she wrote down some of the jobs to be done. She listened to Hannah read the article from the newspaper.

The Montana copper liberty bell, symbol of the U.S. Savings Bond Independence drive, will be on display in Martin City the afternoon of August sixteenth. The bell, one of forty-nine Independence Day replicas cast at Annecy, France will arrive by truck at noon. The nation-wide U.S. Saving Bond Independence drive opened on July Fourth and will continue until Labor Day on September seventh. The Montana bell replica was officially dedicated on July Fourth in Butte. Six U.S. copper companies donated copper for the bell project.

Columbia Falls mayor Fred Keller today issued a proclamation declaring Wednesday as the start of the bond drive in the Flathead Valley. The mayor's proclamation follows: On Wednesday, August sixteenth, the U.S. Savings Bond Independence drive opens throughout the Flathead Valley. Its symbol is the liberty bell, encircled by the campaign theme: Save for your independence-Buy U.S. Savings Bonds.

The year-round savings bonds program, of which this annual campaign is an important part, fosters true spirit of self-reliance and the urge for self-betterment that, along with individual enterprise, inventiveness, productivity, and thrift have carried us steadily forward since the first settlers braced the wilderness to build a free America.

As your mayor, I urge all who are able to help the volunteer savings bonds committee of this Valley reach every possible bond buyer during the campaign. The more we exceed our Independence drive quota and the more we spread the habit of regular saving, through the payroll savings plan or purchase of bonds at banks and post offices, the more we shall have done for ourselves, our community, and our nation. I call upon the citizens of the Flathead Valley to signal the opening of this independence drive by the ringing of bells throughout the Valley and the displaying of flags of our nation during the parade through the five cities. The parade will begin in Martin City and continue through Hungry Horse, Columbia Falls, Whitefish, and finally end in Kalispell.

Hannah set the newspaper down and took a drink from her water glass. "So. What jobs do we need to do to pull this off? The parade starts here in Martin City."

All eyes shifted to Mabel as she adjusted her glasses and placed her pencil on the first item on her list. "Number one, we need to advertise here and in Hungry Horse so people will know what's going on. Number two, we need to get a hold of the sheriff to take care of traffic and lead the parade."

Betty Hansen interrupted Mabel, "I'd like to get a hold of the sheriff right by his-"

Hannah laughed and then said, "Don't say it, Betty Hansen. We'll never get back to Mabel's list."

"Okay. But you ruin all my fun. Sheriff just has such a cute bum." The ladies returned to their noisy string of laughs and snorts. Mabel released gas, and the group lost control.

Finally Mabel replaced her tear-stained eyeglasses and continued, "Number three, someone and not me, needs to hand out information on the savings bond drive. I think a couple of you could walk through the crowd giving out the sheets of paper. Number four, how about a little picnic or something down in Hungry Horse?"

Hannah noticed that Lila looked down at her hand and spun her wedding ring around in circles. She tilted her head as she looked at Lila. Lila shook her head and managed a slight smile. Hannah mouthed the words, "Are you okay?"

Lila looked at Hannah, shook her head no and mouthed back, "I'll tell you later."

The waitress refilled all of their coffee cups. After she walked away, Hannah volunteered to take Mabel's list and make assignments, "I'll plan this out and we can go over it Saturday here durin' lunch. I think Betty should contact the Sheriff. I'm sure he'd do whatever she says."

Betty slapped her on the arm. "I'd be happy to contact him. The sooner the better."

— • ◆ • —

After Betty and Mabel drove away from the Club Café, Hannah put her arm around Lila as they waved goodbye to their two friends. "What's going on Lila? You look like you're a thousand miles away."

Lila bent over and picked up an empty crushed pack of Camel cigarettes and dropped it in the trashcan near the door of the Café. She looked up through tears at Hannah and spoke in a low voice, "I'm in trouble, Hannah. Can we go somewhere private and talk? I, I really need a friend right now." She burst into tears and welcomed Hannah's embrace.

"Ya. Let's take a walk up to the Royal. I need to open it up anyway for tonight's movie. We can have all the privacy we need." Arm in arm the two women walked across the gravel road and entered the front door of the theater. Hannah guided Lila into a small office to the side of the concessions. The stale smell of popcorn from the night before lingered like a permanent resident.

Hannah cleared a messy stack of magazines from a wire-frame ice cream parlor chair and slapped it a couple of times. Lila formed a weak smile and sat down. She blew her nose with a well-used white handkerchief that she retrieved from her purse. After she inhaled deeply a couple of times, she quietly spoke, "I've been seeing a married man for a few months now. I'm pretty sure my husband knows something's up. He's accused me about it several times. God knows I've tried to break it off. But I keep going back. Oh I'm so stupid, I-"

"Take it easy, Lila. You're doin' fine. Get it all out. Start from the beginnin' if you have ta. I'm just here ta listen. Go ahead."

She set the drenched handkerchief back into her purse and continued, "He works at the Dam and his wife and little girl live in Butte. It just happened. I didn't see it coming at all. Next thing I know he was in my bed every time my husband left for Havre overnight. I broke it off the night of the fundraiser at Rocco's. Remember. You saw me crying in the bathroom." Hannah nodded her head forward, but didn't say a word. "I thought I ended it. But I ran into him in Columbia Falls at the Post Office and we spent last night together. I broke it off again this morning. But I don't know if I can stay away." She fought tears again.

Hannah slid her chair closer to her. She padded Lila's shoulder and handed her a clean handkerchief. "Did you say he's from Butte?"

"Yes. He's got a good job as a boss and everything. His little girl has polio. In fact, he and his brother-in-law are going to Butte this coming weekend to see her."

The words struck Hannah like lighting. She remembered Mikhail talking about his sick little granddaughter in Butte. Mikhail also told her that his son worked with him on the Dam. He even grumbled about his son-in-law living and working here. She slid her chair back and moved around to the door. Without looking back at Lila, she quietly talked to herself. "Oh shit. He has to be

Mikhail's son-in-law. What the hell do I do now?"

Lila interrupted her thoughts, "I'm fooling myself, Hannah. He ain't going to leave his family for me. Plus, my husband's bound to find out and then we'll really be in trouble. What should I do? What would you do?"

Hannah focused back to Lila. "I'm not sure. I need to think about it some. I'm here for you, Lila. But I'm just not sure what you should do."

There weren't any more tears left for the moment. Lila stood up and walked toward the theater door. "Thanks, Hannah. Please don't think poorly of me. It just happened."

Hannah wrapped her arms around her. "I don't think poorly of you. Why don't you come up and watch the movie tonight, and afterwards we can go over to my house and drink a couple of homemade beers. We'll work out somethin'. I know we will."

Lila thanked her again and told her she'd see her at 7:00. Hannah watched her as she slowly walked down to the Café and climbed into her car.

They sat outside of Mabel's and talked about the meeting with the Care Less Group. Mabel placed her hand on the door handle as she prepared to step out of Betty Hansen's 1952 Ford sedan. "Betty, do you have a crush on the Sheriff? You lit up when his name came up. It seems like -"

She turned and faced Mabel, "Oh, I was just carrying on a little bit. I think I have a crush on every twenty or thirty-year-old guy around that will give me the time of day. I'm thirty-eight years old, and my husband turns fifty in a month. We ain't lovers or even friends for that matter. I don't think he knows I'm alive. We pass like strangers in our house. The only thing important to Mr. Hansen is makin' money."

Mabel removed her hand from the door handle and set it on Betty's shoulder. "Have you tried to talk to him about it?"

"I've tried. I really have. He acts like everything is just fine. Mabel, we don't sleep in the same room, let alone the same bed. It's been two years since he touched me. The only time he acts like we're married is at his stupid parties or dinners with the other big shots who work at the Dam. Then he's friendly and very cozy to me. But soon as we're alone, he gets quiet and lost in his own world. I could walk around stark naked and he wouldn't know the difference. Maybe I'll try it tonight just to see." She faked a laugh and threw her hands in the air.

"Why do you stay with him if it's that bad? I mean, you're young, very good lookin', and have lots of money. Why not pack up and leave?"

"Oh believe me, Mabel, I think of that a hundred times a day. I married him when I was twenty years old and had nothing. He promised me the moon, and for a while I got it. But he changed at the Grand Coulee Dam job, and we continued to drift even more apart ever since he took this job. His mind's always somewhere else. I've cried, thrown tantrums, threatened to leave. Everything, and he ignores me."

"Maybe you should leave for a while and see if he changes."

Betty returned the key to the ignition. "I think I need to add a little spice to my life at least. Maybe I'll come and work for you a couple of nights a week." They both laughed as Betty turned the key and the engine fired right up. "I'll stick around for the summer and then I might head to Seattle and stay with my sister for a while. She knows what's goin' on here and says the same thing you're sayin'."

Mabel opened the car door and peeked back in before saying goodbye. "Maybe the Sheriff might add a little spice to your life. After all, he does have a cute bum." Betty erupted into laughter and watched Mabel limp toward her house.

CHAPTER SEVENTEEN

Shorty Davis finished his bacon and eggs breakfast with his wife Carol. As his daily routine demanded, he then used the bathroom, walked to the kitchen window, and wound his pocket watch. He carefully placed the antique silver watch in his lined Copenhagen can and twisted on the lid. The butterscotch mints waited by his packed lunch bucket. Shorty stuffed them into the pants pocket of his bib overall jeans. As he stared out of the window, he blessed himself and whispered the same prayers he said for the past twenty years. Carol laid his yellow rain slicker on the back of the chair near the front door. "It rained and snowed off and on all night long, Johnny. You'll be needin' your slicker today."

Shorty turned around and said, "August first and the thunderstorms and sticky snow are right on time. Did you hear that thunder last night? There were some beauties."

Carol closed the distance between them and kissed him on the cheek. "It might be worth your while to shave tonight after work Mr. Davis. After all, it's your fiftieth birthday and who knows what I might have in store for you tonight." She twisted her head away in a flirty motion and continued, "I just hope you ain't too old."

He laughed and replied, "You'll see how old I am when I get a hold of you tonight. Fifty ain't too old. You'd better take a good nap this afternoon 'cause you're goin' to need it."

The slap on his behind barely reached his skin. "Go to work and bring home the bacon. I'll be fresh as a daisy when you come through that door. Now get going old timer." Shorty picked up his lunch bucket and rain slicker, kissed his wife goodbye, and walked to join his waiting ride to Hungry Horse.

Carol picked up the breakfast dishes and smiled to herself at the thoughts of their bantering. She thought of how fast time had gone by since their wedding thirty years earlier. Now he's fifty. She flashed on how handsome he looked in his blue wedding suit that he borrowed from his older brother. Carol sat down at the kitchen table and finished her second cup of coffee. He's still cuter than hell, and I'll fix his wagon tonight with the surprise party.

The men slowly boarded the bus. Yellow rain slickers and silver hardhats trudged along as each man waited his turn to climb onto the bus. Tomas walked right behind Shorty just like he did every day. Shorty continued with a Navy story that he started while the men waited in the quonset hut. "We just finished pulling out of Frisco and cleared the Golden Gate Bridge when the Captain sounded general orders. I was a Seaman E-3 Gunners Mate and I bolted to the bow to join my gunner at our BMG-M2. I-"

Tomas listened carefully and interrupted Shorty's story, "What's a BMG?"

"It's short for a Browning Machine Gun. We used them against hostile small surface craft and commando-types. Shit, you interrupted me and I can't remember where I was goin' with that. Let's see-"

Buck Morris seized the opportunity to tease his nemesis Shorty Davis. "No wonder you can't remember where you was goin' with another one of them borin' Navy stories. You're fifty years old for Christ's sake. It's lucky you remembered to get on the bus this mornin'." Except for Tomas, most of the men within earshot of Buck's comment laughed. Over his right shoulder, Shorty flipped Morris the finger.

Tomas loved hearing about Shorty's Navy stories. He memorized all of the ports he visited, the people from other countries he met, and the women from the Asian countries that he spent time getting to know. Tomas started to entertain thoughts of joining the Navy himself. He even talked to Shorty about it. "What a jerk that Buck Morris is to Shorty. It's just that he's so jealous of all of Shorty's experiences." He faced his partner and said, "Go ahead, Shorty, what happened after you got to your machine gun?"

"I'll finish the story once we get to the block, Kid." He flipped Morris a dirty look and popped a butterscotch candy into his mouth. He silently looked out the window as the bus passed North Lion Lake, and he thought about how much he enjoyed telling Tomas his stories. "The Kid is the only one that's interested in my Navy stories. What a great kid he is. I hope he does join the Navy; he could go to any school he wants. I wonder what his old man thinks about it?"

The men walked slowly to block number four and climbed down the ladder. Tomas climbed down first and took Shorty's lunch bucket from him and set it in the corner with his bucket. He readied the powerful vibrator for the day as Shorty poured himself another cup of coffee. Clifford and the other two men joined them in the block. Shorty growled as he surveyed the condition of the block to be poured. "The rain and snow made a mess out of them steel forms. Be careful today, it's slicker'n hell in here today. Pay attention, Kid. We'll rotate out more often until this rain stops."

— • + • —

The operator shack hugged the east wall of the mountainside next to the cement mixing plant. After the full buckets left the cement mixing plant, the endless cable roared through the giant wheels housed in the operator shack. Buckets hung off a carriage attached to the cable. Each bucket held sixteen cubic yards of cement and measured ten-feet high, six-feet long, and six-feet wide. Each cubic yard of cement weighed about twenty-three hundred pounds.

Jiggs Quinn enjoyed his reputation as the top operator on the Hungry Horse project. His booming baritone voice matched his laugh. He reviewed the order of the bucket drops with his bellboy,

Frank Rodriquez. "We'll start out with drops on the six block. Then we'll catch four and finish up on the two block for the first run." Jiggs laid out the rest of the order of drops for the morning.

Rodriquez jotted the order down on his pad, looked up and asked, "Did the rain cause any problems last night?"

"Graveyard shift told me they had a couple of short-out electrical problems. They picked up the slack in time, so no big problems." Jiggs pinched a small chew from his Copenhagen can and slipped it behind his lip. "Give me plenty of time in between loads just in case. I'll tighten slack more often in case we get another power overload or short-out. Okay?"

His veteran bellboy smiled, gave a thumbs-up signal, and walked down the stairs of the shack. In his mind, he reviewed the order of the concrete drops and mapped out his points to stand and signal for each of the cement drops for the blocks.

———•·•———

After he finished telling his Navy story to Tomas, Shorty Davis barked out the rotation schedule for the day. He gathered the attention of his crew as the loaded bucket of cement headed their way. The crew hugged the corner as the bucket dropped its load into block number four. Each block was thirty-feet wide, ten-feet long, and five-feet high. The bucket soared skyward as the load emptied. Tomas and Clifford fired up their vibrator and started packing the concrete on their side of the block. The other two men followed and started pounding the concrete into the corners of the block right next to Tomas and Clifford. Shorty worked behind the crew and prepared the back-up vibrator. His eyes shifted up through the pounding rain as the bucket disappeared on its journey back to the mixing plant.

Jiggs Quinn watched the next bucket empty above the two block and sky for the trip back to him and the mixing plant. His bellboy walked back to his point to direct the next load back to block six.

Shorty's crew in block four moved through the cement and backed toward the west wall. The vibrators noisily forced the cement down into all possible crevices and small holes. Shorty set the back-up vibrator in the corner of the block. The rain pelted his hardhat and bounced off his slicker. Noise from the vibrators shut out the rest of the world from the five men working in blocks four.

Frank Rodriquez signaled from above the four block and Jiggs sent the loaded bucket out of the shack. The bucket glided over the first two blocks. Jiggs felt the electrical power shut off. "Shit! Oh no!" His voice roared out of the shack as he frantically reset the buttons and pushed the power buttons in front of him. No response. "OH my God. No!" He pounded on the red emergency shut off button several times and ripped the phone off the hook. No dial tone.

The endless cable went slack. A fully loaded bucket dropped from the skylines as it flew pass block three and continued its downward route toward the four block. Shorty casually glanced over his shoulder and saw the out of control bucket racing toward his crew. "Look out! Get over the side!" His crew kept working. In slow motion action, he lifted one boot at a time out of the heavy concrete and slipped as he attempted to close the distance between the oncoming bucket and his oblivious crew. The bucket doubled its speed as it entered the top of the block. The men seemed a mile away as each of Shorty's labored movements seemed slower than the one before. He yelled again. "Get out of the block!" No reaction from his crew. His voice pleaded in a slow motion action. The words lingered in the air. The men continued to work. "Get out! Get out!"

Shorty stepped up on a partially exposed crossbar in the rebar. And with the two by six board in his hands, he heaved his body into the backs of his four men. Tomas and Clifford bounced over the steel forms and landed on the front of the forms outside of the block. The other two men landed between the steel forms and the front part of the block. Their vibrators whipped over the front of the Dam. Both men hung on to the wooden supports.

The roar of the crashing bucket into the walls of the block caused men in nearby blocks to look up. They unconsciously shut down their vibrators and stood in confused disbelief. The east wall of the block collapsed. Red-hot cement poured over the face of the Dam like lava from an erupted volcano. Most of the reinforcement bar anchors in block four violently separated from the mangled steel forms. Excess cable continued to roll and tear at the walls of block three. And then it stopped. Deafening silence covered the east end of Hungry Horse Dam.

Mass confusion flooded the accident site. Stunned men stood frozen in time and struggled to believe what happened. Other men raced to the four block and peered into the area devastated by the run away concrete bucket. The first aid team came from all sections of the construction site and gathered as a group near the disaster area.

Word of the accident quickly spread to the west end where Mikhail and his partner talked and unloaded a stack of metal pipes used for cooling poured concrete. Bud Reynolds nodded his head and wrinkled his sun-tanned face as the walking boss filled him in. Mikhail set the final three pipes on the storage rack. He turned and faced Bud walking quickly toward him. Bud gathered his breath. "Mikhail. A full bucket of mud crashed into block four where your kid-"

In two steps Mikhail blew by Bud and disappeared around the bend of the Dam. He stumbled as he stepped over lumber, tools, makeshift stairs, and ironworker's materials. His mind raced and the same horrible memory of his childhood and the news of his father's accident ripped into his mind. His heart roared with pain. Men stepped aside as he trampled by them. Mikhail struggled to catch his breath and the nerves lit up every inch of his heaving stomach. Block number five stood ahead of him. Voices belted out instructions and men grabbed ropes, shovels, and boards as they sped toward the devastated four block. Mikhail bowled four men over makeshift stairs and handrails. Men set heavy boards across the surface of the block while other men pulled the tangled endless cable up and out of the block. Mikhail looked. Tomas was nowhere in sight. His heart sunk and his stomach heaved his breakfast.

One voice stood above all others. Jiggs Quinn shouted instructions, "Hook that goddamn come-along cable to that bucket. You over there, get to that pickup parked near the safety gate." His partner, Frank Rodriquez pushed the man out of the way and hooked the come along cable. He then raced to the Dodge Power Wagon pickup and jumped in the cab. He pushed the ignition button and the engine fired to life. Jiggs waved his hardhat, and Frank slowly backed up. What was left of the now empty bucket fought the pressure. The truck tires spun, and black smoke rose from the gravel road. Finally, the bucket eked away from the crushed west wall of block three.

Mikhail now stood next to Jiggs Quinn in the block. Both men gasped as the moved bucket partially revealed an arm and foot of a man. Another man carefully removed concrete and splintered wood and steel. The crushed man's body became exposed. Jiggs stepped back and whispered for the first time in his life. "Good God Almighty, it's Johnny Davis."

Mikhail also stepped back and tears flooded from his eyes. It wasn't Tomas. Relief and grief poured through his body. A quick prayer raced through his mind. Then grief roared. He knew how much Tomas respected and trusted Shorty Davis. But his attention reeled behind him as he heard Tomas scream, "NO! Not Shorty! It can't be. It's his birthday! He saved our lives. NOOOO!"

Two first aid men grabbed him by the arms and guided Tomas up and out of the block. Mikhail's legs struggled to hold up his weight as he followed Tomas. He reached his son and held him for the first time since he was ten years old. Tomas cried and called Shorty's name over and over. Mikhail patted his back and said nothing. There weren't any words. He saw through his own tears another team of men carrying Clifford out on a stretcher.

The other two other members of Shorty's crew walked arm in arm toward the first aid shack. Their yellow rain slickers now were splattered with cement. Silence roared back in as men continued to uncover the battered body of Shorty Davis. Dr. Green walked by Mikhail and Tomas after checking Shorty. He placed his hand on Tomas's shoulder and shook his head as he walked back to the first aid shack.

CHAPTER EIGHTEEN

After he visited his friend Clifford at Kalispell Regional Hospital, Tomas walked down the back stairs of the three-story brick building. Clifford suffered severe burns from the concrete that spilled over him in the accident that happened four days earlier. The doctor planned to release him the next day after his morning check-up. Clifford's neck burns posed the biggest health problem. The burns on his hands and right arm prevented him from returning to work for a week or two. Tomas felt relieved after hearing that his new friend beat any infection or serious skin damage.

He walked to David's pickup parked behind the hospital. As he reached to open the truck door, Tomas noticed David drank from a can of beer. He took a quick look at his pocket watch and saw that they had a half-hour before the 10:00 a.m. funeral service for Shorty Davis.

The beer in David's hand surprised Tomas as he looked up from his watch. It seemed like David drank more often now. But Tomas cast it off after David described the pressures he faced as a walking boss. His thoughts shifted quickly to the task of surviving the rigors of the upcoming funeral. Tomas climbed into the front seat and dusted off his dress black shoes with the cuff of his dress pants.

David didn't ask about Clifford. He started the truck and pulled out of the parking lot. They drove in silence over to the parking lot of St. Matthew's Church. After he shut off the engine, David popped another beer, took a drink, and said, "I hate funerals, Tommy. I think I'll sit out here in the truck and wait for you."

Tomas quickly snapped his head toward David, "You ain't goin' in?"

He shook his head and took another drink of his Great Falls Select. "Like I said. I hate funerals. You go ahead, I'll take a nap and wait. You'll be fine."

Tomas tried the door handle, but it didn't open.

David opened his own door and walked around the back of his truck and opened the passenger door from the outside. "Damn door. It sticks on me sometimes. I'll fix it when we're in Butte. Now you better get in there. It's pert near ten o'clock."

Only three years after the city of Kalispell had been surveyed and laid out, the first bishop of Montana in March of 1894 directed the building of St. Matthew's Church. Eventually parishioners outgrew the small wooden church structure. On April 2, 1910, the new church was built and in a copper box for the cornerstone a photograph of Bishop Shea, copies of local papers, a few coins, a small leather-bound bible, the parish calendar, and a small golden cross were placed.

St. Matthew's Church was extensively damaged in February of 1938 by a fire that started in the basement. The ornately sculptured wood altar was destroyed. As part of the reconstruction and repair, new altars were created and the church was completely redecorated.

Tomas slowly entered the vestibule of the church. His eyes surveyed the beauty of the church as he stopped and focused his attention on the full-length stained glass windows on the south side wall. Beads of sweat rolled from his armpits. He slowly glanced at the back of the heads of the people who came to show their respects to his partner. He wished David had come in with him.

Near the front of the church his eyes stopped as he recognized the heads of Jiggs Quinn and his partner, Frank Rodriquez. The walk down the south side aisle seemed to take forever. Tomas appreciated the stained glass windows as he walked below them. Once he got to their pew, he motioned to Frank to ask their permission to join them. Frank patted the space next to him, and Tomas sheepishly knelt down on the kneeler. He bowed his head and respectfully said a quick prayer for Shorty's family. After he sat down, Jiggs nodded his recognition and extended his hand across in front of his partner. His rough, calloused hand felt warm, and Tomas welcomed the touch of the older man. Tomas nodded his head in recognition back. A thousand words exchanged between them without uttering one single syllable.

From the choir loft the organist stepped down on the pedal and her fingers struck the opening notes. The congregation rose to their feet as the priest led the casket down the center aisle with the help of the six pallbearers. Shorty Davis' family followed the closed casket to the front pews of the church. Tomas swallowed hard at the thought of Shorty laid out in a suit, tie, and white shirt. He felt weak as he looked at Shorty's wife, Carol. Shorty talked constantly about his lady at home. She stood straight and tall. One of the family members with her held her arm securely and guided her into the front pew. "He must be their son," Tomas thought. The priest stood in front of the casket and opened the well-used book of prayers that he held.

For the first time in his life, Tomas experienced deep, punishing grief. Years earlier, he lost himself in his schoolwork and his friends to stuff the pain from his parent's divorce. Loss of Shorty Davis crushed him as tormenting grief overwhelmed him. Vivid memories of riding next to Shorty on the bus back and forth to work flashed in front of him like a movie on the big screen at the Rialto Theater in Butte. Flashbacks of working side by side in the hot sun on the Fourth of July roared to life. And now, nothing. He stared at the casket and vaguely heard the words of the priest. Tomas broke. Tears streaked down as he rushed his hands to his face. He felt the strong, reassuring arm of Frank Rodriquez around his quivering shoulder.

After the funeral, the congregation filed downstairs to the basement for lunch. Carol promised Shorty she would follow his wishes should anything happen to him. The ladies of the church prepared a potluck lunch. Each person there fixed a plate and sat at the tables normally used for bingo. Tomas sat with Jiggs and Frank and picked at his ham sandwich. The two men jumped to their feet as Carol Davis stopped and stood next to Tomas.

The entire crowd heard Jiggs, "Carol. I'm so sorry. I-I-"

She hugged him and whispered, "Jiggs. It wasn't your fault. It wasn't anybody's fault. He thought the world of you."

Jiggs stood and fought off tears. "I thought the world of Johnny too. He, he was a fine man. And he loved you and your boy there."

Tomas rose from his chair and in his typical quiet voice attempted to talk. Words failed him. Carol Davis embraced him and whispered in his ear, "You're his young partner, aren't you?"

He stood back from the hug and said, "Yes ma'am, I'm Tom Anzich."

"Shorty talked about you every night when he came home. He said you listened to his wild stories of his days in the Navy." She forced a smile and continued, "He said you were the best worker he ever worked with. And that's saying somethin' since he worked with a lot of good men."

Tears rolled down his cheeks, "Thank you, Mrs. Davis. Thanks a lot. He showed me the ropes. And he made me work as steady as I could. He called you lady." She embraced him once more and sobbed on his shoulder.

Carol Davis slowly withdrew and placed her tear soaked hands on Tomas' cheeks. Sometime in the next few weeks, please call me; I want to give you a picture of my Johnny with some of his Navy friends. I think he'd like for you to have it. Okay?"

"Yes, Mrs. Davis. I'd like that too. Thank you."

In the parking lot, Tomas shook hands with Jiggs and Frank. With his head down, he walked over to David's pickup. David slept with his head against the side of the door. The open window picked up his snoring as Tomas reached the door on the other side. He opened the door and jarred David awake. "What? What's goin' on?" He shook his head and spoke, "Oh. It's you Tom. Boy, I went out like a light. The nap helped. Now I can drive to Butte."

Without asking about the funeral, he drove away from the parking lot. Tomas noticed the five empty beer cans on the floor.

He considered asking David if he should drive but sat back, folded his arms, and closed his eyes. The events of the last hour and a half slowly rolled over and over in his mind. Sleep overtook him. He awoke fifty miles later as David pulled to a stop at the Oasis Bar in Polson.

— • • —

Back in Martin City, John Nolan sat on Mikhail's bed. He knew he had to make peace with Mikhail following their hour-long argument about Tomas going to Butte with David. Nolan chastised Mikhail for his lack of attention to Tomas. Earlier, Mikhail bristled at the insinuations Nolan made about his attitude toward his son. But like they did for thirty years, Nolan started the road back to forgive and forget. "You ain't gonna slick your hair down with that Vaseline again, are you? That Hannah woman will laugh her lovely little ass off."

Mikhail roughed up his wet hair with the towel after his shower. "I'll put whatever I want on my hair."

Sometimes Nolan laughed before he blurted out something very funny. He enjoyed his own sense of humor more than the person with him. "Ya, go ahead. Grease the shit out of it. That way when you hit your head on the doorframe into her kitchen, you'll naturally slide right on by without gettin' hung up." He laughed again as he visualized Mikhail sliding through a doorframe. "Then you can-"

Mikhail laughed and said, "Shut up, Nolan." He snapped the towel and stung Nolan's leg. "I don't know why I keep you around."

Nolan stood up and walked toward the door to the hallway. "You thick-headed Bohunk. You'd still not be able to tie your shoes if it wasn't for me. And you'd still leave a table with shit all over your mouth if I wasn't there to point to your big ass mouth. One more thing, you sure as hell wouldn't know what time it was because you was sixteen before you learned to tell time. Without me-"

The end of the wet towel zinged Nolan on the arm. "Go pester somebody else, Nolan. I'm gonna be late for pickin' her up the way it is." Mikhail smiled and like a thousand times before, stuck out his hand for Nolan to shake.

Nolan grabbed his hand and looked down to see his small right hand completely enveloped in Mikhail's monster size hand. "You better be sorry. Next time I'll kick yer big brown ass up and down this here bunkhouse." He released Mikhail's hand and continued, "Think about what I said about Tom. That's all I'm goin' say about it." Mikhail nodded his head forward and walked back to finish dressing.

———•·•———

He fixed the last button on the clean white shirt that he bought the afternoon that his new partner Bud invited he and Hannah over for supper. Mikhail noticed that the extra large shirt now fit snug. The hard work for the past months tightened his already muscular chest, back, and arms. He shook his head as he noticed the farmer's tan on his arms. As he reached for his pants, Nolan's angry words about needing to pay more attention to his son jumped to his mind. Nolan made good points about how tough it was on Tomas to lose his partner and that Mikhail needed to be more of a father during this tough time. Mikhail brushed the thought off as he recalled being there on the accident scene holding Tomas.

He laced his shined black shoes and reviewed more angry words from Nolan about allowing Tomas to go to Butte with his son-in-law. Mikhail felt it was a good time for Tomas to get away for a while and visit his sister and niece. He didn't bother to tell Nolan that he hugged Tomas before he left for Kalispell. His son thanked him for allowing him to go and for being so strong during those three days after the accident.

The short drive over to pick up Hannah allowed Mikhail to look at himself in the rearview mirror. He smiled as he viewed his very dry and out of control bush of hair. Nolan's advice stuck with him as earlier he set the Vaseline jar back on the small shelf above his mirror. He yawned and switched his thoughts from Nolan and Tomas to Hannah. Surprisingly, Mikhail felt relaxed and looked forward to spending time with her and Bud and his wife. The fried chicken planned for supper made his mouth water. He laughed as he thought about Nolan telling him he didn't know how to wipe food off his mouth.

———◦•◦———

Hannah sat on the top step of the four stairs that led to the porch in front of Maggie's cabin. She wore a cotton square top shirt. The background of her shirt was white and the pattern design held brown and yellow circles in rectangles. The large tan collar perfectly matched the Capri pants that she wore. Mikhail arrived ten minutes early and stopped in front of the two women. He lumbered out and walked around the front of the car toward the porch.

Hannah pushed up from her knees and slowly walked down to meet him. "Mikhail, I want you to meet my best friend in the world. This is Maggie. I'm pretty sure I mentioned her to you."

He reached up and held Maggie's extended hand, "Happy to meet you, Maggie."

She smiled and rolled his hand over and looked at the lines in his calloused hand. "I see many things in your hand. I believe you have suffered loss of loved ones in your life. The initial M shows through strong lines. Did you lose someone with that initial?"

Without letting loose of her hand, Mikhail searched his memory for people in his life who died. His father's name jumped forward. "My father's name was Marko. He died when I was young."

Maggie patted his hand as she spoke, "I see that. You also have a strong letter that comes across the middle of the M. I can't make it out. That person is a special friend and will bring you much happiness. Maybe it's Hannah."

"Well, we'd best be goin'. Our friends are expectin' us for supper." Mikhail moved back and stood by Hannah. She walked up and kissed Maggie on the cheek and joined Mikhail. He drove the five miles to Columbia Falls and listened to Hannah talk about Maggie and her palm reading experiences.

Mikhail finally saw an opportunity to speak, "You look real nice tonight, Hannah. I ain't never seen a shirt like that before."

"Well, I'll be go to hell. You just talked more right now than you did the rest of your life. Are you feelin' okay?"

His laugh freed any anxiety that she might have had about their time together. "I feel good. Maybe Maggie was right about you."

"Maybe. I look forward to meetin' your new partner. I know his wife Sara a little bit. This should be fun. And thank you for the compliment."

———•·•———

After eating supper with Bud and Sara, Mikhail drove Hannah home. He shut off the engine in front of her cabin. Stomach nerves tightened. He knew he'd struggle with the good night. Their last date ended with him standing on her porch like some fifteen-year old boy on his first date. He remembered searching for something clever to say to Hannah. It was times like this that Nolan told him he didn't know if to shit or go blind.

Tonight his confidence helped him make a decision. He'd kiss her tonight for the first time while they stood on her porch. Before he could get out of the car, Hannah slid over next to him and tilted his head toward her. In a very calm, slow motion, she parted her lips and moved up and kissed him.

Mikhail watched her lips close in and touch his own lips. He closed his eyes and savored the sweetness of her soft lips. She slowly pulled back a few inches and her eyes and smile joined his. He moved to her and matched how she kissed him. It was close to four years since he kissed his ex-wife. And these two kisses were the best in his life. He whispered in her ear. "Now I know Maggie was right. You do make me very happy."

Arm in arm they walked to her door. "Mikhail, I really enjoyed tonight. It was very nice. Your partner Bud and his Sara are fun people. I'm glad we're getting together with them next Friday night."

They kissed softly one more time and said good night. As he walked to his car, he noticed how good it felt to think about someone other than one of his family members. He also thought how the long lost erection scrunched in his pants felt pretty damn good too.

≈ CHAPTER NINETEEN ≈

The Oasis Bar in Polson stood as a main-stay for customers driving Montana Highway 93. Travelers stopped often and used the restrooms, drank a couple of beers, and usually toted along a six-pack or two for the road. David finished the second of his tap beers, and Tomas drained his ice-cold bottle of Pepsi Cola. He held true on his July 5th promise not to drink again. The bartender ignored David's attempt at friendly conversation and paid more attention to the baseball game over the static of the well-used radio. David ordered a six-pack of Great Falls Select, and handed them to Tomas to take to the truck. He sauntered back to the men's room and lit a ciga-rette as he walked.

Tomas regretted not eating the sandwich after the funeral. His stomach growled, and he planned to ask David to stop somewhere around Missoula to eat. He checked his pocket watch as he waited for his brother-in-law to join him in the truck. It was 1:30 and Tomas figured it would take about three to three and a half more hours to make the drive to Butte.

On the drive to Missoula, Tomas tried to talk to David about him joining the Navy. "David, what do you think about me joinin' up with the Navy? I really have-"

David interrupted him in mid-sentence, "I don't know. Hey,

what did you think about that bartender back in Polson? She sure was friendly to me. If I wasn't married, I'd probably take her up on her offer to stay the night."

His eyebrows felt the pressure of his eyes squinting. He hesitated before answering, "I, I didn't pay no attention. I was thinking about seeing Anna." Tomas looked in his side view mirror, signaled, and passed the slow-moving farm truck overloaded with hay.

David ignored the words about his daughter, Anna. He popped another beer and then asked, "I mean, did you notice how that lady bartender kept flirting with me? You must've seen the way she smiled and brushed me when she set my beer down."

He stepped on the gas pedal and hit sixty miles an hour. "Didn't notice nothin' about her." Tomas didn't care to talk about any bartender. He wanted to talk about his plans for the Navy. Or talk about Anna. "When did you see Anna last, David?"

"Jesus, it's hard to keep you on the subject. I'm talkin' about some good-lookin' woman, and you're talkin' about some other shit."

Tomas shook his head and decided to just drive and forget about talking to David. He noticed David slurred his words and only wanted to talk about some bartender. As they neared Missoula, David told him to pull over at Fred's Bar and Restaurant right outside the city limit of Missoula.

After a quick burger and fries, Tomas stood up to leave for the truck. David grabbed his arm hard. "Sit down for Christ's sake. I ain't ready to leave yet. I just ordered a boilermaker. What's your hurry anyway?"

Tomas looked down at David's hand locked onto his muscular forearm. Quietly he confronted David, "Let go of my arm, David." His hand loosened and Tomas continued, "I'm really anxious to see Kat and Anna. It's been about three and a half months. I can't wait. Besides, I told Kat we'd be home around five o'clock."

He mumbled something to himself as he stared into the back bar mirror." He awkwardly spun the barstool around and faced Tomas. "So you think you're gettin' pretty salty, huh? Maybe we should go out in back and see who's who."

The bartender tapped the nightstick on the bar. "Time for you to hit the road, pal. Pay up and leave."

David fell asleep in the truck about thirty miles outside of Missoula. Tomas experienced a form of relief. He didn't like being around David when he got drunk. Memories of July 3rd stood fresh in his mind. His stomach turned as he thought how cross his sister would be when David showed up drunk. He decided to remain as quiet as possible and hoped the two-hour drive to Butte would be enough time for David to sober up some.

The drive to Butte went by quickly and David slept soundly. He never moved a muscle. About five miles outside of town, Tomas gently nudged David and woke him up. David sat up straight and said, "You gotta pull over somewhere quick. I gotta piss right now." Tomas guided the truck to the turn off at Ramsey. David quickly ran over and relieved himself behind a parked car. Tomas needed to go too, but he decided to wait until he got to McQueen. After he zippered his pants, David walked around to the driver's side. "I'll take over from here. Push over."

The smoke from David's cigarette blew across the front seat and caused Tomas to cough. He quickly opened his window and stuck his head outside to catch some fresh air. David tapped the ashes off his cigarette into his pants cuff. The truck swerved into the middle of the highway. He looked up and corrected. Tomas quietly asked, "Are ya sure you're okay to drive, David?"

"Ya, I'm okay. I have a bad headache, but I'll be fine. Pick up those empties and stuff em' in that there bag for me. I don't want your sister seeing them. She'll go off shift on me." He laughed and patted Tomas on the thigh. "It'll be good to see them again. I ain't seen em' since about March or April." Tomas wondered how a father could stay away from his sick daughter for that long.

David stopped the truck in front of the McQueen Club. "Let's go in and have just one. It'll do my hangover some good. Just one, I promise you Tommy Boy."

"It's almost five right now. Knowing Kat, she has dinner waiting for us."

"Okay. Okay. You win. Let's go." David dreaded seeing his wife after such a long time. He knew that he didn't want to get back together. All the alcohol in Hungry Horse didn't drown the fact that he and Kat weren't any good for each other any more.

Divorce would be tough. And now he had to see his little girl sick and weak from polio. He wished he'd found the courage to come visit sooner. David wondered if he could even stand being here for two days.

Tomas snapped him from his thoughts. "There she is sittin' on the porch waitin'. She's wearin' her apron. Can only mean supper's waitin'." After the truck came to a stop, Tomas rushed out of the truck and lifted his sister up off the porch and into the air. "Oh Kat! It's so great to be home. You look real good. And you smell good too. Did you cook lasagna?"

She laughed and slapped his back urging him to put her down. "Put me down you wild man. Of course I made lasagna. Now go see your niece. She wouldn't take a nap she was so excited."

Tomas gently set his sister back down on the porch and kissed her firmly on the cheek. She hugged him and looked over his shoulder at her husband. David sheepishly stood at the head of the sidewalk and forced a smile. She walked down the porch steps toward him. He closed the distance between them as tears burst from her eyes. Kat Sednick embraced her husband for the first time in months. She smelled his stale beer breath and his cigarette smoke-drenched shirt. It didn't matter; they were together.

Tomas learned from a phone call two days earlier that his niece Anna showed some improvement. But she remained weak and remained totally dependent on the oxygen mask for breathing. Tomas flashed on the last time he saw her and how she looked trapped in the iron lung. He walked into the living room and made her favorite face. His fingers pulled hard on each side of his mouth and his eyes crossed and pointed downward.

Through the oxygen mask she giggled like he saw her do every time he made that face. Tomas walked over to her with his hands in front of his chest. He curled his fingers and wiggled them like a cat moves their claws. Anna moved her hands in front of her eyes and blocked his hands from her view. She giggled harder now and then started to cough. "Oh, I'm sorry Butterfly. Take it easy now. The monster is going to take a rest. Oops. He's gone now. Whew! That was close. All gone."

Anna regained her breath and reached out for her uncle. They hugged around the tubes. "You look like a million bucks my Little

Butterfly." Tears came easily for him as he whispered to himself a prayer of thanks. He visualized this moment for weeks and begged God to send her good health. Her improvement exceeded his expectations. She looked good. Tired, but good.

Anna cautiously lifted the mask up onto her forehead. She whispered in a wispy and breathy voice, "Is my daddy here too?"

Tomas broke into a big smile. "Yes, he is. He's out talkin' to your mom. He'll be right in."

The paper bag he laid on the floor caught Anna's attention. "What's in the bag, Uncle?"

He shook the bag. "What do think it is?"

"Don't tease."

He opened the bag and pulled out two cutout doll books. She opened her mouth and snorted in some air. Anna pulled the mask down over her mouth and nose. A big, open smile crossed her pale face as she fingered the pages of the first book, *Puss and Boots.* Anna slid the second book on top. *Raggedy Ann and Andy* contained a boy and a girl doll with several outfits. "What does it say? What does this one say?"

"It says Raggedy Ann and her friend Andy."

Anna turned the pages slowly. She pointed to Raggedy Ann. Her muffled voice cleared the oxygen mask, "Raggedy Anna?"

"That's what it says. It's about you."

The front door opened slowly and David and Katya walked in arm in arm. Anna looked up from her book. Her brown eyes focused on her father. He hesitated before going to her. Katya led him toward the big recliner chair. Words eluded him. Reluctantly, he knelt down in front of her and touched her arm. "I, I, I."

Anna raised her mask once again, "Hi, Daddy. I missed you."

Tomas excused himself and went outside to the porch. More tears rolled down his cheeks. He wondered how many more times he could cry. Shorty's death drained his bank of grief tears, and now Anna wrenched any remaining tears from somewhere. He didn't know where. But somewhere. "Maybe this visit is just what David needs to straighten up. Now maybe we can get back together as a family. Dad and John Nolan will learn what a good man he really is. We can all help him to stop drinking. That's his main problem anyway."

After they finished eating Katya's lasagna dinner, Tomas helped her clean up the dishes and the kitchen. He dried the last plate and placed it in the cabinet above the toaster. In the background he heard David talking with Anna. Katya dried her hands on the dishtowel he used. She folded the towel and carefully tucked it in the door handle of the refrigerator. She watched her brother walk outside onto the back porch. In her mind she flashed back to days when they were children. It seemed like yesterday. And now she watched a full-grown man stand on the porch. "When did he become a man? I've been so busy being a mother; I've missed his whole growing up. My brother, a man. Holy smokes."

She joined Tomas on the porch, stood next to him, and placed her arm around his waist. "How much do you weigh, Tom? You've really gotten huge."

He looked down at her and smiled, "I weighed on your scale in the bathroom before supper. If it's close at all, I'm right at two hundred fifteen. And after your supper, I'm right at two-hundred and forty."

His sister squeezed him and laughed like she did years ago before her life changed so much. "I really have missed you. You make things so much easier. Things are still real tough here with the strike and Anna and that. You look real good. So strong. The work up there's good for you. You must really like it."

Tomas nodded his head, but his mood changed. He looked out over the neighborhood and sucked in some air through his nose. "I lost my partner in a bad accident. He saved my life but got crushed in doin' it. He, he," Tomas gulped hard and resisted the overwhelming urge to cry.

Katya slid in front of him and placed her hands on his bulging biceps. "Oh, Tommy. I'm so sorry. It had to be awful on ya. Do ya want to talk about it?"

He shook his head and displayed a weak smile for her benefit. "No thanks, Kat. I need to deal with it alone. One of them things. Ya know what I mean?"

"Ya, I do know. Let me know, though. I'm all ears. You've always been there for me. So I owe ya some good listening too. Alright."

"Alright. I'll be fine. It'll just take some time." He walked down the stairs, turned on the hose, and took a drink.

His sister watched him and again flashed back to their days as children. Drinking out of the hose was a daily thing for him. Their mother scolded him and warned him of catching trench mouth. The warning never stopped Tomas, and he never caught trench mouth. Most times he ended up squirting his sister with the hose. In her mind's eye she reviewed wrestling over the hose and laughing until she almost got sick. The cold water snapped her from her trip through memory lane. She hopped off the porch and attempted to steal the hose from him. Things changed over the years as he held her off with one hand and drenched her with the other. Once again Katya laughed until she almost became sick.

The next morning David and Katya took a ride. Tomas stayed with Anna and played with the cutout dolls that he gave her. He purposely misplaced items of clothing on Raggedy Ann. Anna rolled her eyes and rearranged the clothes where they belonged. She slid the oxygen mask up. "Uncle. The dress goes here. Not up there. Silly."

He slapped his forehead and picked up the white apron cutout and attempted to place it on the legs of the doll.

A loud gasp of air flowed out of Anna's mouth. She placed her mask back in place. Her little fingers gingerly slipped the cutout apron from around the doll's legs and attached it over the dress. Anna shook her head and gently slapped Tomas on the forehead.

Tomas shrugged his shoulders and turned his hands upward, "I don't know where these clothes go. I thought this little white thing was Raggedy's pants."

Again Anna shook her head and pointed to the picture on the cover of the cutout book. "Oh, that's where it goes. It's a good thing I ain't no Raggedy Ann doll. Huh, Butterfly." He reached up and kissed her on the head. The smile she gave him made the long, difficult trip with David worth every minute of the drive from Hungry Horse.

On the drive back from Ceserani's Grocery store, Katya turned toward David, "I'm happy you and Tommy are here. It's like we're a family again. Do you think it'll work as well once we move up to Columbia Falls in October?"

"What? Did you say you're movin' up to Columbia Falls? That's the first I heard about that. When did this all happen?"

"Well David, didn't Daddy talk to you about it?"

A hundred thoughts ran through his mind with the thought of his wife and child living near him again. His freedom to come and go would end. It would be difficult to see other women. And dealing with her father all of the time. "No! He never told me a goddamn thing about it. We don't talk or see each other. We hate each other for Christ's sake!"

She regretted even mentioning it to him. A perfect visit's now ruined. "I'm sorry, David. I thought for sure Daddy would tell you about it. Please don't be angry. It's been a perfect visit. Let's talk about it some other time." She affectionately touched his shoulder. "Please, David. Forget about it for now."

"Okay. Okay. We'll talk about it later." He didn't speak another word all the way back to the house. His mind moved on to his date later on that day with his old girlfriend. Her husband worked on the docks in Seattle during the strike.

Katya interrupted, "Are you still goin' to the baseball game with Tommy?"

"Ya. Ya. We're goin' at 1:00. McQueen's playin' the Silver Bow Park team. Should be a good game. I promised Tom I'd take him."

"Good. Anna can rest and we'll have another nice supper and evening together."

They carried the groceries inside and for the time being called a truce to their argument about moving to Columbia Falls.

The Butte Copper Baseball League began in 1944. All of the games were played at Clark Park, the stadium built in 1921 by one of the Copper Kings, William Clark. Baseball and football games were played there during those seasons. In the winter, the field was flooded and ice-skating took place during the frigid months of December and January.

The ride to Clark Park took ten minutes and on the way David splashed on some Old Spice from a bottle he stashed beneath the front seat. He wiped the overflow from the white bottle on the thigh of his Wrangler Jeans. Tomas looked but didn't comment. Since breakfast, his fatigued mind battled the accident scene on the Dam. He relived the movement of the men in their frantic rescue efforts. Fatigue sent him a siege of irritation and crowded him with the thought of Shorty Davis. His daydreaming went unnoticed as David backed his pickup into a makeshift parking spot near the sidewalk on the right field side of the stadium.

Tomas struggled out of the seat, as the passenger door once again would not open from the inside. Calmly, David came around and opened the door for him. "The game's on me today, Tommy. My treat. It'll be worth it just to see some of my old friends and watch a ballgame on a beautiful day like this here one."

A tight-lipped smile faked its way across Tomas's mouth. Quietly he answered, "Yep. It's nice today. I hope McQueen wins. The Standard said Mulcahy pitchin' and he hasn't lost a game this year so far."

The old turnstile squeaked as the two men handed the elderly man their ticket stub and walked under the grandstand. David handed Tomas a silver dollar and said, "I need to use the John before going in. Buy us a couple of bottles of pop. Be sure and get a cup for me with some ice in it. I'll meet you at the bottom of the steps." He stepped in through the open door and went into the men's room.

He twirled the silver dollar between his fingers as he waited for the cute girl to fill his order. Tomas looked around at the people as they talked and moved toward the steps to the grandstands. He overheard two middle-aged men talk about the exciting news going around about the Anaconda Company making an offer that sounded pretty good. Tomas felt a twinge of hope for the town that the Strike of 1952 might be coming to an end.

David joined him and took the cup with the ice from Tomas. He motioned Tomas over to the space behind the men's room. From his back pocket he pulled out a pint of Jim Beam and poured half of it into the paper cup. He topped it off with a dab of Pepsi. Tomas grimaced as he stared at the whiskey bottle. Memories of David's previous actions while drinking bothered him. He turned away and walked toward the stairs.

It appeared that most of the McQueen community already took seats on the ancient wooden block seats. Tomas and David sat down on the last two seats in the front row near the aisle. It was perfect for Tomas as he stretched out his long legs into the front aisle and sat back against the bleacher type seat. David took a few long drinks from his pop cup. The first pitch came, and the crowd clapped as the batter popped up to the shortstop. David took advantage of the action and poured more from his whiskey bottle into his cup.

After the first inning, Tomas noticed a high school friend sitting a few rows over. She sat with her parents and casually sent a few looks his way. The last time he saw her he said goodnight after their date to the prom over a year ago. His family situation and the Strike prevented him from asking her out after that one and only date. David gently elbowed him, "Hey, Tommy. I gotta take off for just a little bit. Somethin' I gotta do. I'll be right back."

"Don't you want me to go with you, David?"

He stood up and waved his hand, "No. Stay here and enjoy the game. Like I said, I'll be right back." Before Tomas could answer, David disappeared down the steps. His patience with David grew shorter by the minute. Maybe his dad and Nolan were right about him. Last night was good, but he started drinking early today and now he just left.

Tomas and his friend both snuck a look at the same time and quietly snickered. Between the second and third innings, she came over and sat down next to him. "Hi, Tom Anzich. Long time no see."

"Hi, Susan. How's it goin'?"

The white peddle pushers she wore contrasted perfectly with her tan legs. Hours of delivering A & W Root Beer to customers in their cars provided her with a great opportunity to get tan. Her bare arms matched the dark brown skin on her legs. "You look good, Tom. I heard you worked on the Hungry Horse Dam. I-"

One of the three young men sitting two rows behind them interrupted her, "Hey, Anzich. How's it feel to be a scab?"

Tomas slowly turned away from his friend and looked in the direction of the high-pitched voice behind him. He recognized one of the men, but didn't know the other two with him. Susan placed her hand on his arm, "Don't listen to them, Tom. I broke up with the bigmouth a couple of months ago. He's jealous and still thinks we'll get back together."

The pitcher dropped the resin bag and bounced the ball a couple of times in his mitt. He approached the mound and looked in at the catcher for the signal. Tomas tried to ignore the remark from the guy behind him, but his irritation with David and his fatigue from not sleeping the night before shortened his patience. Again the man from behind belted out another barb loud enough for Tomas to hear, "I heard the Union is blackballing Anzich and his old man for scabbing."

Without saying a word, Tomas bounced out of his seat and leaped up to the row where the three men sat. He excused himself and crossed in front of the people who also sat in the row. Once he reached the three men, he squeezed between them and sat down. His voice cracked as he spoke, "Which one of you called me a scab?" Even sitting down he towered over all three of the young men. My dad and me ain't scabs. We're workin' the Dam so my niece can fight the polio."

Two of the men looked away from Tomas' deep-penetrating stare. Susan's ex-boyfriend glared at Tomas. "It was me, Anzich. So you wanna make somethin' of it."

"I don't want no trouble. Just wanna watch the game and go see my sister and little niece."

"You ain't only a scab. I think you're a chickenshit too."

Tomas looked at the field at the crack of the bat from McQueen's Kasun. He watched as the ball sailed over the right field fence. The crowd stood and cheered as McQueen took a three run lead. He looked down at the man in his Golden Glove gold sweater with the pair of boxing gloves on the side. "Like I said, I don't want to fight ya."

He walked toward the aisle. The man hit him in the back of the head with a half-full cup of soda pop. Tomas turned around, motioned his head, and said, "Let's go."

The three men noisily climbed out of their seats and followed Tomas down the stairs. A few others followed to see the fight. Under the grandstands, Tomas stopped and faced his opponent. Rage overcame him and matched the storming butterflies in his stomach. Everything that happened in the past week pushed him to an angry place he'd never been before. He glanced around to try and recognize one person he knew. Nobody. He looked toward the parking lot. No David in sight.

A tight ring circled him. The man put in a mouthpiece and fingered on tight gloves. He snorted a few times through his nose, bobbed his head back and forth, and mumbled through his mouthpiece, "Let's go, Scab. Tomas' hands hung by his side. The man snapped two quick jabs into Tomas's face. Before he could follow with a right hand, Tomas unleashed a right hand of his own. The loud snap of the man's jaw echoed around the rafters of the grandstands. The man staggered and attempted to launch another round of jabs. He dropped quickly to his knees. His jaw hung open. It was badly broken.

The speed and power of Tomas' punch frightened him. Hours and weeks of vibrating cement with Shorty developed his upper body to a muscular level he'd never known. With his fists clenched, he stared down at the man as his two friends hovered around him. The crowds disbursed as someone yelled the cops were coming. Tomas knelt down beside the injured man. "I told you I didn't want any trouble. You wouldn't stop. Now look. I'm sorry. I-I"

One of the man's friends said, "You gotta car to take him to the hospital?"

"No. I came with my brother-in-law. He left for a minute."

The police officer walked up to the scene. "Jesus Christ. His jaw's broken. You do this?"

Tomas nodded his head and helped the man to his feet. The stunned look on his face imprinted its ugly distortion into Tomas' memory. Another police car pulled up in front of the gate. The attending police officer waved the other police officer over. The two officers walked the injured man to the car. They placed him in the back seat. Tomas stood and watched as the police car turned the corner onto Texas Avenue in route to St. James Hospital. The other police officer stood with Tomas. "You and his pals need to come with me up to the station. We'll figure it out up there."

———•◦•———

Afterwards, on the trip from the police station to McQueen, the police officer asked Tomas questions about Hungry Horse Dam. As he stopped in front of their home, the police officer faced Tomas. "He deserved it. I'll give you that. His whole family would cause trouble in church. But you'd best get a hold of that temper of yours. You don't know your own power. Your share of fixing that broken jaw might be pretty stiff. Walk away next time. You'll hurt somebody sometime. Understand, Anzich?"

In his typical quiet voice, Tomas replied, "Yes, Sir. I understand. Thanks for the ride home." He stuck out his hand and the officer firmly shook it. Tomas walked to the door and wondered what he'd tell his sister about David.

The screen door squeaked as he opened it. Anna smiled at him as he entered. He turned quickly to see his sister approach from the kitchen. She dried her hands on her apron. She looked around him and outside and then asked, "Where's David?"

"Umm. I don't know for sure, Kat. It's a long story for being gone such a short time."

She gently reached up and touched his bruised right cheek. "What happened to your face? Did you get hit or something?"

"I got into a fight and-"

"Who with? Where's David?"

His hands rose in front of his face. "I need to use the bathroom first. Then I'll tell you all about it. And what smells so good out in the kitchen?"

Katya's voice turned irritable. "Just use the bathroom." She returned to the kitchen in her patented lightning quick, angry pace. Anna turned her head from her uncle to her mother and back to her uncle until he disappeared down the hall toward the bathroom. She lifted her oxygen mask and took a sip of her lemonade.

———•–•———

David said goodbye to her and tucked his white tee shirt into his jeans and clumsily closed his zipper. He puffed on his cigarette as he sat in his truck seat. "Holy shit! It's almost six o'clock. Can't believe I spent all day with her. Shit!" The steady diet of whiskey drinks clouded his mind. He dropped the keys as he attempted to start the engine. Another clumsy move knocked the cigarette out of his mouth onto his lap. His head pounded as he pushed the cigarette onto the floor and stomped it out with his boots. Then he remembered he left Tomas at Clark's Park. "Christ! I better go by there to see if he's standin' out there waitin' for me."

Katya's pork roast dinner with mashed potatoes and homemade applesauce sat on the table. The clean housecoat and make-up job she applied caught her brother's compliment, but it wasn't for him. David bounced the truck into the curb in front of the house. He talked to himself and convinced himself that he wasn't too drunk. The sidewalk embraced his fall ten feet from the front door. Katya stared at him through the bay window. She stormed into her bedroom and slammed the door.

David staggered into the living room. Anna poked at her dinner from the adjustable table in front of her. She watched in amazement at her brother as he devoured the large portion of gravy-covered food. They both looked up as David banged his knee against the coffee table. "Oopps! How's dinner?"

"Mommy's crying."

Tomas set his plate on the arm of the couch and stood up.

He took David under the arm and tried to lead him toward the door, "Let's go outside and talk, David."

"Screw yourself. I'm hungry. Where's my supper?" He pushed away from Tomas and staggered into the kitchen.

The bedroom door flew open and Katya stomped out. She stopped at the stove, picked up the tin foil covered dinner, and tossed it against the wall just barely missing David's head. "There's your supper you drunken son-of-a-bitch. Eat it off the floor like the dog that you are!"

Tomas hurried over to Anna who started to cry and fight to breathe. "Shhh. It'll be okay. Take a breath, Butterfly. Take a breath." He patted her arm as she struggled to fight the sobs and started to choke and cough.

Katya heard Anna struggling and rushed into the living room. "Tom, get him out of here! Get him the hell outside!"

This time Tomas applied his strength and got behind David. He placed both his arms through David's and locked his hands behind David's head. David struggled but couldn't break the powerful hold that restrained him. The screen door flew open. Once outside the two men rolled off the porch steps into the lawn. David yelled at the top of his lungs, "I'll kill you. Let me up. I'll kick your ass.

The same police officer that dropped off Tomas earlier responded to the domestic disturbance call in McQueen. When he arrived, a couple of neighbors held David down on the lawn in front of the Anzich home. Tomas knelt on David's back and talked quietly in an attempt to calm him down. David cried and continued his loud barrage of threats and curses.

The police officer stood over them and asked, "What's going on here?" He looked down at Tomas, "You been fightin' again? I just dropped you off less than three hours ago."

He faced the officer, "No, sir. I tried to calm my brother-in-law down, but he's too drunk. He won't listen and started swearing and swinging at me. Our neighbors here helped hold him down."

Another police car pulled up and stopped. This officer joined the crowd. "Need any help here, Eddy?"

The first officer unbuckled his handcuffs and moved closer to David, "Ya. Give me a hand putting this guy in the back seat of the car. He needs a night at the crowbar hotel to cool off."

Inside the house, Katya spoke softly to her crying daughter. Her breathing stabilized, and her mother comforted her. "Don't cry Anna. It'll be fine. Your daddy drank too much whiskey today. He's taking a ride with the police officer to sober up. You'll see him in the morning. Everything will be okay." Anna sniffled as she attempted to talk through the oxygen mask.

After the police cars left, Tomas thanked his neighbors, one-stepped to the porch, and entered the house. He walked to Anna and kissed her on the forehead. His smile and light arm patting tugged a smile onto her red face.

Katya sauntered into the kitchen and started to clean up the mess she made. The makeup she applied so carefully earlier smeared her face from crying. As she looked up into the mirror above the sink she noticed how her pale skin looked bleached and old. To herself she talked. She knew it was over with David. "I can't do this to Anna or myself. I just can't." No tears rolled from her eyes. She used all of them up in the bedroom.

⸻ ◦ ⸻

The next morning, Tomas got up early after another sleepless night. He made coffee, showered, and put on a fresh white tee shirt and jeans. The clock in the bathroom read 6:40. He walked outside and picked up the neatly rolled August 7th Sunday newspaper and sat on the bench on the porch. The aroma of the coffee saturated his senses as he prepared for the first taste. "I'm getting like my dad liking coffee so much. I never drank it until Shorty got me started." A rich memory of sharing a cup of Shorty's coffee on the bus ride up to the worksite blew gently before his mind's eye. He wondered if he'd ever be able to drink coffee again without thinking of his partner.

Tomas set his cup down and slipped the red rubberband off the rolled *Montana Standard* newspaper. His eyes widened as he scanned the two-inch headline, **Strike Offer Reached At Midnight**. A subtitle read, *Union To Vote On Tentative Agreement At Noon.*

The coffee cup met his lips as he read the story.

Union and Anaconda Company officials would not release the details of the agreement until after the membership votes today at noon. If accepted it will end the 181 day strike and the longest strike on record since the 1934 strike.

Tomas continued to read the entire article. He wanted to wake his sister and somehow let his dad in Hungry Horse know that the strike would end soon. But no way to get a hold of him. "I wonder if he'll want to come back home."

His thoughts ended as he heard the toilet flush in the bathroom. Kat poured a cup of coffee for herself and brought the pot out to the porch. Dark wrinkles under her eyes told Tomas she didn't sleep either. She sat next to him and sipped her coffee. Prior bad experiences taught him not to bother her until after she took at least three sips of coffee. And some times not until after she finished her first cup. By the looks of her today, he planned to wait until she spoke first.

She refilled his cup and then her own. After a long drink, she spoke, "David and me are done. Yesterday was the last straw. I gotta take care of Anna. We'll be gettin' divorced as soon as we get it worked out. I'll tell him before you go back today."

She leaned against him and tightened her white sweater around her. When convinced she was finished talking, Tomas said, "If he'd stop drinkin', would that make a difference? I mean if I could talk him into doin' somethin' about it, do-"

"Tommy, it's more than that. A lot more. The drinkin' is the big problem, but there's more. I ain't going to talk to you about it. We're through. He can go his way, and we'll go ours. It has to be that way."

Kat had many of her dad's habits. She finished conversations before the other person might be finished. For now it was over talking about she and David. He gently slapped the newspaper, "Well here's some good news. Looks like the strike's about over."

She pulled the paper from his lap. Quickly she read the headlines and a few sentences of the story and hugged Tomas. "Thank God. It's over. We got to tell Daddy somehow."

"Take it easy, Kat. It's only seven in the morning and he works day shift today. We plan to leave around 9:00 o'clock this morning. We'll be in Hungry Horse before he gets off shift. I can tell him then. Okay, Big Sister?"

Through the haze of the ugly events from the night before and the worthless night of sleep, Tomas and Katya shared the good news on the strike. "Do you think Daddy will change his mind about all of us livin' in Columbia Falls?"

Tomas finished his coffee and half-heartedly shrugged his shoulders, "I wondered that myself when I read the story. He's pretty set on workin' at building the Aluminum Plant and us gettin' into a nice house. He wants to start over."

"What do you want to do, Tom? Do you want to stay and live up there?"

He stood up, stretched, touched his toes, and held the position for a few seconds. He sat back down and quietly told his sister about his secret plans about the Navy.

Katya frowned and slid down a little bit in the bench, "What did Daddy say about you joinin' up with the Navy?"

"I ain't told him yet. Probably tell him next week sometime. I wanna finish the job on the Dam. If you move up, I'd like to stay around for a while until you and Anna got settled. That's what I'm thinkin' right now, anyways."

———•◦•———

Despite being told not to drive by the policeman who dropped him off at the house, David drove the entire two hundred fifty miles back to Hungry Horse. He and Tomas never exchanged more than a few words about the settlement of the strike. Tomas tried several times in the first fifty miles to talk about yesterday, but David made it very clear he didn't want to talk about it. They stopped in Missoula for gas and used the men's room. David never stopped again until he pulled up in front of the barracks in Martin City. Tomas went in and out of sleep during the five hours. After a terse goodbye, Tomas grabbed his travel bag, his pillow sack full of clean laundry, and walked into the barracks. David drove straight to Coram and the Dew Drop Inn. His friend Jackie set up a can of Great Falls Select for him and backed it up with a shot of Jim Beam.

ᴄ CHAPTER TWENTY ᴄ

W.R. Scalf removed his messy stack of bills and used blueprints from his corner table. As he walked the paper pile to his bookshelf behind his desk, he noticed his project bookkeeper and the federal auditor waiting in the outer office near his secretary, Mary Metcalf. The auditor called for this meeting to review his findings after completing his month-long audit.

Scalf waved the two men into his office and pointed his finger toward the small round table in the corner of his office. The three men sat down, and Mary sat at the superintendent's desk and prepared to take notes as instructed.

Scalf balked at the idea of a Monday morning meeting at 8:00 o'clock, but the auditor insisted. He arranged the white legal pad in front of him and looked at the auditor as he spoke, "It's your meeting. Let's hear what you got to say."

The auditor precisely laid the paper-clipped papers into three neat piles. His pressed white shirt brought out the deep green color of his tie. Scalf glanced at the man's lily-white hands and commented to himself that this man had never done a day of physical labor in his life. His eyes came up when the oral report started. "First of all, I have examined the daily, weekly, and monthly reports compiled by Mr. Winters here. He's done a fine job of putting everything in order. It made my job much easier." He released a smug smile in Winters' direction.

Scalf nodded his head and patted Winters on the shoulder. "That's my man Winters. Great work as usual."

The top stack of spreadsheets contained wage disbursements dating back to May of 1951 and stopped at March of 1952. "These figures match perfectly and the wages, benefits, hours worked, overtime, and holidays are perfectly tabulated." He meticulously set this stack to his right side and squared the edges of the papers so they sat perfectly square.

Scalf watched in amazement and reflected back to the previous auditor who came from pay offices in Anaconda prior to working at Hungry Horse. That man examined everything carefully, pointed out the problems and everybody went back to work. Now this new guy obsessed on how level his paper stacks sat. He shot a rolled eyes glance at Winters and came back to the auditor as he approached the second stack of spreadsheets.

He cleared his throat and covered his mouth with his partially fisted hand. "Now, I have discovered some problems with the wage and benefit spreadsheets from April of this year to the current month. There is a serious discrepancy between some of the wage earning sheets."

Fred Winters corrected his sitting posture and sat up even more erect. "I beg your pardon. That cannot be. I spent countless hours matching timecards, wages, and benefits expended. There-"

"The problem is not in your work, Mr. Winters. Please understand that. My problems noted occurred in inaccurate time sheet completion. For some reason, April through the first week in August 1952 presents a substantial amount of hours worked without corresponding benefits and taxes paid. I'm sure there is a logical explanation. It will require you to do a serious comparison of every time card against the benefits and taxes not paid for that time period."

Sweat rolled down from his armpits as he adjusted his black horn-rimmed glasses. Fred Winters nervously attempted to write down his assignment. The pencil point broke under the pressure of his fingers. "Damn it!" He quickly retrieved a newly sharpened pencil that rested next to his tablet. Again the lead snapped.

"Jesus Christ, Winters. We'll run out of pencils if you don't relax. Do you know what you have to do?"

"Yes, Superintendent Scalf. I, I need to compare time cards with taxes and benefits paid through the contractor's business manager."

"That's right. Take a walk for yourself and get to it. When you figure it out, give me a call and we'll take care of it." He gently waved his hand toward the office door, and Winters took his leave.

"Mary, that's all I need for now. Would you do me a favor? Call Al Sutter from the *Hungry Horse News* and ask him to drop by today or tomorrow? Thanks Mary."

After Scalf's secretary left the room and closed the door behind her, the auditor looked over his shoulder before he spoke, "Superintendent. I didn't want to say this in front of Mr. Winters, but I think someone is falsifying a huge number of hours worked. You just need to be prepared for that because I believe your bookkeeper will find the source of the problem."

"Holy shit! It takes you a long time to say something. Why all of a sudden does this happen? Things are Jake until April and then all hell breaks loose. You sure?"

Again he cleared his throat and adjusted the knot in his green tie. "I am positive. I paid an auditor in Kalispell to double-check my work. He concluded the same thing as me. Yes I'm quite sure."

Once the auditor walked down the stairs from his office, W.R. Scalf dialed the contractor's number. After the fourth ring he answered. "Hey Johnson, it's W.R. How's tricks?"

"Not bad W.R. What's goin' on up at the big house?"

He took a drink of his lukewarm coffee, made a face, and answered, "The federal auditor just paraded out of my office. He found some kind of a problem with wages, benefits, and taxes paid since April. I got my man Winters on it, and he's gonna get in touch with your business manager to figure things out."

"Thanks for the warning. I'll let my man Hansen know the call's coming. What did ya think of the auditor?"

Scalf blew some air through his smoke-stained teeth in disgust,

"Strange guy. He fussed with his stacks of paper all the damn time. And it took him a month to say what's on his mind. I think he knows the score all right. I'm generally happy when these guys come and go."

"I know what you mean. How about a beer some night? There's a new spot in Kalispell I'd like to try."

"Good enough, Johnson. Take it easy."

———

The roast beef sandwich and cherry pie his wife made from Sunday's leftovers hit the spot for Scalf. He snapped the metal buckles closed on his worn black lunch bucket. Al Sutter stood in his doorway. "Did you save any of it for me?"

Through his wooden toothpick, he answered, "Hey Al. How ya doin'? Come on in."

In typical Al Sutter fashion, he wore a blue-checkered short sleeve shirt. The patented white hat and red colored band covered his unruly mop of black hair. In his left hand he toted his speed graphic camera, and in his right hand he carried his well-used clipboard. Scalf noticed a freshly printed copy of the latest edition of the *Hungry Horse News* clipped to his board. Al Sutter enjoyed the ritual of handing Scalf one of the first copies of his latest newspaper.

"I see you brought me the latest copy of your rag. Anything of interest this time?"

In his very casual manner, Sutter gingerly unclipped the weekly newspaper, unfolded it, and took a final glance before handing it to the Dam Superintendent. "You'll be real interested in this edition W.R. You most likely will want to hang my hide up on the back of your door. Like I've told you before. I cover the news."

Scalf picked up his glasses from the white tablet on his gray metal desk. He accepted the newspaper and read the headlines and stared at the crystal clear photographs on the front page. In great detail, Al Sutter covered the accident that killed Shorty Davis. The chaos that unfolded that day a week earlier jumped to life before the Superintendent's eyes. He focused on the photograph of the destruction the full concrete bucket inflicted on the construction area and on Shorty Davis.

Al Sutter joined his hands in front of him in a pyramid shape. He moved his lips close to his fingers as he watched Scalf digest the content of his writing and photography. Sutter noticed a lone tear slowly roll down the face of the man across from him. Scalf's lips quivered slightly as he moved his eyes down the written page. Al Sutter knew he missed a golden opportunity for a special photograph, but he didn't move a muscle. He respected the man too much to disturb him at that emotional moment. So many times he watched warm smiles cross this man's mouth when he enjoyed a photograph that showed the Dam's building progress.

Once Scalf gently set the newspaper down on the desk, Al Sutter sat back in his chair. "You'll get calls on this one. People will want to know why the electrical system failed. I wanted you to have time to get ready for this. I'm sure the union people will want an answer and a solution."

Without saying a word, Scalf motioned his head forward and nodded his agreement. Again he glanced at the telling photographs. The reality of a good man losing his life struck home. This part of the job haunted Scalf. Each time he sat with the man's family after an accidental death tore at his heart. To most people the reality of accidents and death on the job sometimes got outmatched by the sheer size of the accomplishment of building a dam. W.R. Scalf struggled to speak. For him, reality had set in ten minutes after the accident occurred.

CHAPTER TWENTY ONE

As Mikhail waited for his son to join him for a late dinner at Rocco's Supper Club, he reread the *Hungry Horse Newspaper* for the third time that day. He anxiously awaited the opportunity to tell Tomas the great news. The newspaper was folded once to the second page. Mikhail read the article that he circled earlier.

On August 10th, 1952, C.F. Kelly, Chairman of the Board, Anaconda Copper Mining Company, announced that Anaconda would build its $45,000,000 aluminum reduction facility two miles northeast of Columbia Falls near Teakettle Mountain.

The Company plans to begin producing aluminum before September of 1955. Initial construction will consist of two potlines with an annual capacity of 67,000 tons. At full capacity with five potlines and 120 pots per line, 185,000 tons of aluminum ingot will be produced each year. Employment at full capacity is approximated to be 550 people. Clearing land for the reduction plant will begin this October as President Truman throws the switch at Hungry Horse Dam to begin producing power. The building process will create over five-hundred jobs.

> The Potline building will form the largest single building in Montana, covering 1,750,000 square feet or about forty acres.

Mikhail smiled and folded the paper. His partner Bud told him during lunch that he took a foreman job at the construction site for the Aluminum Plant. He'd agreed to begin once his work at the Dam was finished in early October. Bud invited he, Tomas, and Nolan to join him on his crew at the Aluminum Plant construction project.

It pleased Mikhail to know that at least for the next three years and probably longer, he and his family had solid work lined up. Now he could bring Katya and Anna up to Columbia Falls to join him and Tomas. They would finally be a family together again. He checked his watch and wondered what held up Tomas. The waitress filled his cup with fresh coffee. He looked up to see the front door swing wide open. Nolan and Tomas walked in laughing. Nolan just delivered the final line to his story from his days as a teenager in Butte.

Mikhail pretended not to notice and studied the menu even though he made up his mind about the fried chicken dinner. Nolan broke the quiet of the dining room, "Hey Bohunk, do you remember the name of that girl from East Butte who used to charge us a nickel to look up her dress. Then she'd charge us a dime to-"

Mikhail prevented him from going any further. He pointed to the seat next to him and barked, "Sit down Nolan! You're in a restaurant. Mind yer manners." He shook his head and rolled his eyes in Tomas' direction. The two men sat down, and Tomas fought hard not to burst into a loud laugh.

The waitress returned and greeted them, "Good evening men. Can I get you something to drink?"

Nolan smiled at her and spoke, "Ya, doll. John Nolan's having a brandy ditch tonight. And my nephew here'll have the same."

Mikhail slowly turned and glared at Nolan and answered for Tomas, "My son will be having coffee too."

Nolan laughed and winked at Tomas. "So Mikhail. What was her name?"

"Who?"

He leaned toward Mikhail and whispered, "The girl from East Butte who used to charge us to look at her snapper. You know. You paid her a quarter on the Fourth of July one time. You probably got to look all the way up to her tonsils for a quarter."

Tomas lost control. Coffee exploded from his mouth. He coughed and laughed uncontrollably. Nolan had a way of doin' that to him. He remembered being a little boy and starting to laugh before Nolan even spoke. Just his facial expressions and the way he moved his eyes and cheeks. Tomas tried to sit away from his godfather at serious settings like church. He couldn't help himself sometimes. Nolan made him laugh that easily.

Mikhail rubbed the space between his eyebrows with his fingers. More thoughts of Nolan from days earlier ran across the screen in his mind. "Nolan. Where does he come up with these things? I wouldn't play that game with him and that girl. Whatever her name was. I never paid her a cent. Not once." He backed his chair away from the table and said, "I have to go to the can. When the waitress comes back, get me the chicken dinner."

The waitress returned with another drink for Nolan. "I guess we're ready to order up, Doll. My big friend's back draining his weasel. He told me he wants the chicken dinner. I'm drinkin' tonight so nothing for me. How about you Tommy?"

The waitress threw a flirtatious smile at Tomas and adjusted her black ponytail with a flip of her head. "I'd like the ten-ounce t-bone with a baked potato, please."

She smiled at Tomas and said, "Comin' right up gentlemen." She wet her lips, twirled around, and shook her hips as she walked away. In her mind, she modeled women in the movies doing all of these feminine things to tease a cute man.

Nolan bent closer to Tomas. "Now I'd bet you pay a quarter to see her little snapper, wouldn't you Tommy Boy?"

Shaking his head, he coughed again. He set his coffee down in anticipation of something Nolan might say. "She seems like a nice girl. Probably cost more than a quarter."

Nolan burst out laughing. Tomas caught him by surprise with his quick comeback. "You're catchin' on. Stick with me, Kid. You'll have em' rollin' in the aisle."

After they finished dinner and Nolan drained his fourth brandy ditch, Mikhail retrieved the newspaper. He straightened it out and placed it neatly in front of him. "I got somethin' here to talk about to the both of ya."

Nolan interrupted, "Is it a want ad for a dog. My nephew could use a big old dog to keep them nasty waitresses away from him. Why just today-"

"Nolan. I'm serious here for a minute." He raised his hands in front of him and nodded in Nolan's direction. "The Company is beginning construction of their Aluminum Plant in October. Right about when we finish up here at the Dam. Bud's gonna foreman up there and he's offered all of us good jobs." He shifted his eyes back in forth between Nolan and Tomas. The painted smile on his face awaited their response.

He slid his chair back a little, stretched, and yawned. "I don't know about jumpin' right into more work. Old John Nolan might need a little vacation. All work and no play makes Johnny Nolan a dull boy."

"How about you, Tomas? We could live together with Anna and your sister. Probably have enough to buy a real nice house. Get our family back goin' again."

The look on his father's face didn't make what he had to say any easier. His stomach turned and butterflies rolled as he prepared to say what he rehearsed a thousand times. "Dad. I want to talk about somethin' too. I, I want to join the Navy. But I wouldn't go until after Kat and Anna got settled up here. I'd work until-"

Mikhail sunk six inches into his chair. He never saw it coming. All he could see was the family living together, and maybe, just maybe down the road bringing in Hannah. Slowly at first. Whatever she wanted to do. He visualized working side by side with Tomas in building the Aluminum Plant. Then later working together in some part of the Plant itself. Now this. The goddamn Navy. "Where did that come from?"

Tomas looked to Nolan to help him. He talked to Nolan about his plans for the Navy two days earlier. Nolan told him it would be a great idea. He blew some air between his teeth before he spoke. "What do you think, Dad? About me goin' into the Navy, I mean."

Mikhail straightened up in his chair and swallowed the last cold sip of his black coffee. "Well Tomas, I, I need some time to think on it. I thought you'd like the idea of us workin' together and that. What gots you thinkin' about the Navy?"

He gulped as he prepared to answer his father. "Shorty got me thinkin' about it. He told me of all his times in the service. I want to see all them places he told me about. I want to get trained in somethin' I can use when I git out."

"You'd get lots of iron workin' trainin' right here at the Plant. You could work and live a fine life right here. This Aluminum Plant is gonna give a good livin' for a lot of men."

Nolan saw his opening when the tormenting silence lingered between Mikhail and Tomas. "You gonna ask me what I think about this, Mik? Or do I just bust in anyway?"

Mikhail waved his hand a couple of times, and Nolan followed the cue. "Wouldn't hurt nothin' for the Kid to get out on his own for two years. That's what it sounds like anyway."

His face flushed red. He stood up, locked his lips, and slowly rolled his head forward and backwards. "Sounds to me that the two of yous already got your minds made up. No sense in me talkin' anymore. I don't know nothin'." Mikhail pushed back, and his chair crashed loudly on the linoleum floor. Other customers tried not to look at the scene developing at Mikhail's table. He bent over, sat the chair up straight, and prepared to leave.

Tomas stood and softly spoke, "Dad. Let's go back to the barracks and talk about it some more. I want you to be with me on this. Otherwise, I won't go." His words found the back of Mikhail's head as he made his way to the cash register. He mumbled something to the cashier and laid down a five-dollar bill. The front door swung open, and he was gone.

Tomas rubbed his hand over his mouth and shrugged his shoulders. His stomach heaved and his throat went dry. Now what, he thought. Nolan yawned one more time and flipped down a four-bit piece on the table as a tip. He put his arm around Tomas. "Don't worry about it Kid. He'll get the hang of it. Give him some room for a couple of days so's he can chew on it. It'll all work out in the end. It'll all work out."

Two days later, the ring of her doorbell jolted her as she finished icing the German chocolate cake. Since Shorty's death, sudden noises frightened Carol Davis as her deep thoughts and feelings of grief dominated her every moment. She jumped back from the kitchen counter, and the butter knife crashed to the linoleum floor. Carol looked out through the kitchen window and saw Tomas standing at her front door. After she picked up the knife, she wiped her hands in the dish towel and went to meet Tomas.

"I'm happy you called, Tom. I've been meanin' to track you down, but there's been a lot to do with final details. "She hugged him and led him into the kitchen. "You told me German Chocolate was your favorite, so that's what I made."

He cautiously entered her kitchen and experienced strange feelings as he quickly scanned the refrigerator photos and knick-knacks arranged on the shelves. Shorty lived everywhere in that kitchen. Now Tomas was in his kitchen. The same kitchen where he and Carol had coffee in the morning. The same kitchen where they ate all of her fabulous holiday dinners. "Sure smells good, Mrs. Davis."

Carol hung her apron on a hook behind the pantry door. "It should smell good. I'm the best baker in Flathead County."

"Shorty used to tell me that all the time. He even gave me some of your carrot muffins sometimes." He realized that he mentioned Shorty. "I'm, I'm sure sorry, Mrs. Davis-"

"That's okay Tom. It's good for all of us to talk about him."

Tomas chastised himself as he preached to Clifford on the drive over in Clifford's car that he would cheer her up and see if she needed anything. "Okay, Mrs. Davis. I'd like to talk if that's okay with you."

She sat down at her chair in the kitchen and invited Tomas to take a seat. "We can talk all you want as soon as you quit calling me Mrs. Davis. My friends call me Carol. So please, call me Carol."

His shoulders hunched as he talked. "Okay, Carol. I'll sure try, but it'll be tough to get the hang of it at first. I've been using Mrs. and ma'am for so long."

"What would like to talk about, Tom?"

"I think of Shorty all the time. Goin' to work just ain't the same without him. I just can't believe he's gone. All of us on his crew feel like that. We keep lookin' and listenin' for him." Tears welled up, but he managed to keep going. "He was just such a good man. I sure respected him. I didn't even mind him yellin' at me. Shorty looked out for me right from the beginning. I." Tears won the battle. He corralled them with his hands.

Her right hand touched his shoulder just like she'd done two days earlier with her son when he broke down in her kitchen. It broke her heart to see this beautiful young man cry so hard for her husband. This demonstration of strong emotion proved to her how much her husband affected people. Tom barely knew her husband. Yet here he was. A big strapping young man emotionally crushed over the death of his partner. She expected it from their son but not a fellow worker who he barely knew. "Let it out, Tom. Let it all out. It's the only way to begin getting over it."

Talking through his runny nose and gushing tears, he asked, "How can this be fair? What's God thinking? Shorty saved our life and lost his own. It's not fair I tell you!" Tomas wiped his face with his arm and fought to regain himself.

"I've wrestled with this same thing over the past weeks. One minute I'm fine. The next minute I'm yelling at God, at the people who brought in the Dam, the shitty weather. Everything. It's gonna take a long time. That damn man spoiled us. Then he had the nerve to up and die on us." Her slight laugh injected some relief into the difficult moment. "Keep talking about him, Tom. See me as much as you need to. In the end though, you got to go it alone."

"Okay, Mrs. Davis. I mean Carol. Thanks, you really helped. And you miss him more than all of us. Thanks."

She stood up and walked around to the counter near the sink and the waiting cake. A big smile found its way on her face as she picked up the cake knife. "How about some of this cake? It'll change your mood alright."

Tomas nodded, "I'd like some of that cake. I ain't had any since my mom fixed it for me a long time ago before she left."

After eating the cake and drinking coffee, Carol placed the dirty plates and silverware in the sink. She walked into the living room and returned with a small brown paper bag. One by one she gingerly picked out a photograph from the bag and placed it in front of Tomas. With her long index finger she pointed to a young Shorty Davis in his dress blue Navy uniform. "This here one was taken in Singapore with a couple of his buddies. It was that damn smile that stole my heart away. Look at them pearly whites. What a ham he was, even back then."

Tomas smiled and touched the edge of the well-worn black and white photograph. "I can see him in there alright. He looked good in that uniform."

"Oh yes he did. And he knew it too that little scamp. When he came home on leave, he'd show up with them dress blues on. He knew what he was doing all right. We got married six months after this picture was taken."

Tomas moved his wooden chair in closer to the table. Carol placed the next photograph down. "In this one here, he's in San Francisco on the deck of their battleship standing behind one of their machine guns. Look at the cigar in his mouth. Showing off again with his white hat cocked off to the side. The man with him was his best friend and stood up for us at our wedding."

The memory of the last story Shorty told Tomas about the Navy came alive as he stared at the photograph. His blank stare caught Carol's attention. "Are you alright, Tom?"

"Oh yes, ma'am. Shorty told me a story that last time we worked together." He stopped there and checked his watch. Cliff planned to meet him back at Carol's at three. He had a half-hour left.

Carol showed him all five of the photos in the bag. "Pick out one of these if you'd like. I'd like to keep the rest of them to show his grandkids some day."

Tomas selected the photo of Shorty behind the machine gun in San Francisco. As they prepared to say goodbye, Tomas sheepishly spoke, "I hope the little bit of money we put together from the crew helped some."

She stopped, lowered her head, and twisted her face to the side, "I'm not sure what money you're talking about, Tom. The Superintendent dropped off some groceries, but nobody brought any money."

"Didn't David Sednick bring you the six-hundred fifty dollars the men gave for you and your family?"

"Tom, I don't know any David, whatever you said his last name is. Nobody gave us any money."

Tomas touched his fingers to his lips. "Oh. He probably hasn't had a chance to yet. But he will. I'll talk to him tomorrow morning. He's been pretty busy."

They heard Clifford's car pull up outside. "Thanks Carol for everything. The cake was great, and I'll take good care of this picture of Shorty. Most of all thanks for hearin' what's been on my mind hard for sometime now."

She hugged him and invited him back. From the front seat of the car Tomas waved at Carol as she stood on the doorstep with her arms folded. His mind raced and his temper boiled as he thought of David not bringing Carol the money. "I bet he spent the money drinkin'. He's gonna have to pay her back and soon. I'll see to it."

At the top of the Dam, crews from the graveyard shift gathered at the bus turn around near the cement mixing plant. Their replacements prepared to step down the bus steps to begin the process all over again. Tomas finished telling his dad about his plan to go see David this morning. "Dad, would you do me a favor and take my lunch bucket back to the barracks? I'll see David, and then I'll just walk down the haul road."

Mikhail blew some air through his pursed lips, "What's so big you have to see him right now? You worked all night. He can wait."

"Oh, it's okay Dad. I'll be back down and in bed in an hour. It's important. I need to do it right now."

Mikhail nodded his head, grabbed his son's lunch bucket, and climbed the steps to the bus.

Once the bus cleared the lot, Tomas fast-walked across the walkways covering the entire length of the Dam. He stopped and looked upstream. Small tugboats toted rafts of logs from the west side of the reservoir to the waiting logging trucks on the east end. Tomas couldn't read the words on the side of the tugboat from where he stood. As he made a mental note to find out the name of that boat sometime, he covered the distance to the bosses shack in ten minutes. As drilled into him by his father, Tomas waited until David finished talking to the group of three men before he approached. David caught his eye and nodded he'd be right there by raising his finger.

The three men left. David made a quick note and stuck the pad back into his pocket. He waved Tomas over to him. As Tomas neared, he noticed how haggard and tired David looked. He used to admire how good David always looked. Clean shaved, clean hair, fresh clothes, and he even smelled of after-shave lotion. "What's up Tomas? Didn't you just finish graveyard?"

"Ya I did. But I got to talk to ya. It's real important."

"Let's hear it. I got a ton to do."

"Maybe we could talk over here. It's private." David followed him behind the shack and onto a small wooden landing. "I talked to Shorty Davis' widow the other day and she told me you never gave her that six-hundred fifty dollars from our day's pay."

David jerked his hands in front of him before he said anything, "Oh shit! I totally forgot all about that. I'll get it to her next week or so. She-"

"No David!" She needs the money right away. Their new house costs her a fortune. Carol doesn't start to work at the Columbia Falls Bank for two weeks. She's pert' near broke. You gotta-"

David quickly slid right up to Tomas' face, "Don't ever tell me what I gotta do. Never. I'll get to it when I get the chance. You can go to hell you ungrateful little prick."

Tomas stepped back. Stunned. "Come on, David. She needs it now. Those other men would hang you if they find out."

A patented David Sednick smirk covered his face, "You tellin' em'?

"I don't want to. But it ain't right. They gave their money."

David started to walk away and stopped ten feet away. He turned and wrote a note in his pad. "Meet me here tomorrow morning at the same time and I'll have it then. Then get off my ass. After everything I've done for you. Got you and your old man a job up here. You'd be nowhere without my help."

"David! We're all doin' this for Anna. Have you forgot?"

"Wait right here! I'll be right back! David walked away toward the bosses shack and flipped Tomas the finger over his head with both hands. He slammed the makeshift metal door shut behind him. A few minutes later David walked back out the door and slammed a personal check for six-hundred fifty dollars into Tomas' hand. "Now stay the hell away from me. You're just like your old man."

Tomas turned, jogged across the Dam roadway, and ran down the haul road as fast as he could go. Finally he stopped in the parking lot at the barracks. He bent at the waist and placed the palms of his hands on his knees as he searched for a normal breath of air. Sweat drenched his entire body. His feet stung from the blisters on his feet from the pounding of his work boots and sweaty socks on the gravel road. Tomas Anzich ran his anger deep into the rock bed of the road. But a proud smile filled his sweaty face. Carol Davis would get her money later that afternoon.

CHAPTER TWENTY-TWO

The August 16th afternoon brought the warmest temperature of the summer of 1952. Record breaking heat shot the temperatures into the nineties for the fourth day in a row. The third floor of the Federal Building in Butte roasted the four FBI agents who sat around the turn of the century oak round table. Stacks of photos, notes, and files covered the surface of the table. Agents labored in rolled up white shirtsleeves and loosened ties. Suit jackets hung on the back of the heavy wooden chairs.

Special Agent Moore set his water glass down, wiped his forehead, and tapped the tablet in his hands against the corner of the table. "I feel good about this list of possible victims here. The victims from the other murders were bosses. Each of them had large savings accounts. All three men were in their mid to late thirties. They also hit the bars pretty hard at night. We have two guys here on Hungry Horse who fit that profile."

Agent Ted Hughes looked up from the opened file in front of him. "Who are the two again?"

"Robert Mular and David Sednick."

"Let's take a closer look at both of them. Mular worked at both Coulee and Hoover. You'd think he would have been a target at one of those projects. If Mular was our guy, why wasn't he killed working one of those jobs?"

The elderly gray haired agent sat at the head of the table and cleared his throat before he spoke. He pushed his glasses up on his nose with his index finger and said, "Sednick is our man. He flinched at some of the questions Superintendent Scalf asked him. There's a reason a workingman like him has eight-thousand dollars in his bank account. Mular has ten-thousand but he damn near had that much when he left Coulee City four years ago. It's Sednick all right. He started as a laborer at Hungry Horse and then became a walking boss. We zero in on him. Follow Sednick and we find the killer."

Moore set his paperwork back into his manila folder. "Okay. That settles it. We plant one of us to hide in Sednick's back pocket. Superintendent Scalf will set up the job alongside Sednick. We can begin right away. Who goes in?"

Agent Hughes nodded his head as he convinced himself he was the best person to go undercover. "I think I'd work out. God knows Moore cannot fix a flat tire, let alone work tools on a Dam project." The timely humor lightened the moods and lowered the temperature of the men in the room. "Scalf assured me one of us can work his way in pretty easily with Sednick. Apparently, the guy's shy on friends and men who trust him."

Back in Martin City, the Montana Liberty Bell parade started in front of Mabel's. The ladies in the Care Less Group laughed amongst themselves at the irony of kicking off the U.S. Savings Bond Independence drive in front of a cathouse. The mayor of Columbia Falls didn't share their opinion of starting places, but the truck hauling the copper liberty bell rolled down the hill into the main street of Martin City. Hannah worked her way through the crowd that lined the street on the south side of the gravel road while Lila slid in and out of the men, women, and children on the north side. The ladies distributed pamphlets, which explained the savings bond drive to the adults. They gave small bells to the children. Betty Hansen walked with the sheriff in front of the truck. She tossed small bags of candy to the children standing with their parents. A big smile filled Sheriff Schustrom's face as he waved to the parade watchers. Betty left his bed only an hour earlier and the glow from their passionate love making changed his attitude about another parade in his area. The drum and bugle corps from Kalispell rallied the crowd who clapped as the liberty bell truck crawled by.

Two men stood between the Club Café and Byrd's Grocery. Both men looked ahead as they quietly took care of their business. The shorter older man in the blue suit sipped on a bottle of Pepsi as he uttered his instructions. "Just like Coulee and Hoover, right?"

"Five-thousand. Half up front. The other half when he's dead."

"Agreed. Today is August 16th. Truman dedicates the Dam on October 1st. You're to kill David Sednick on the last day of September. With Truman and secret service people all over the place, the murder will be hushed up."

"I'll come back in five weeks and track your man and pick my spot and time. You can meet with him then so I can see him. Call me in Seattle and tell me when and where you're meeting him. He won't see Truman dedicate the dam."

As the liberty bell passed in front of him, the man in the suit slid his hand into the pocket of his suit coat and retrieved a white envelope. He non-chalantly handed the envelope across to the other man and whispered out of the side of his mouth, "You'll get the other half when I learn Sednick is dead." He smiled and waved to his wife Betty Hansen as she paraded by next to the sheriff. The man's hand paused in the air as he noticed his wife smiling as she looked up at the sheriff. It had been quite awhile since he noticed that happy of a look on her face.

— ·•·· —

Roy Devers slipped the white envelope into his right pant pocket and slowly walked away from the main street. He turned his back on the thousand people that turned out to watch the Liberty Bell Parade. As he rounded the corner to the side street, he yelled at the three teenagers gathered around his 1952 Lincoln Capri,

"Get away from my goddamn car you little punks!"

The boys jumped and stepped back from the luxury sedan parked under a withering cottonwood tree. The taller boy yelled back at the quickly approaching man, "We was just lookin' at her. Go screw yourself you old prick!" They sprinted away, nervously laughing as they disappeared down the alley toward the back of Whitey's Bar.

Roy stood by his two-tone yellow luxury car that looked out of place in the midst of older Chevy trucks and well used cars from the 1930's and 40's. With his bare hand, he rubbed the slightly noticeable mark left by the boys touching his car as they admired the beautiful lines. He mumbled to himself as he noticed dust on the Washington license plates. "Goddamn hick town. Can't wait to get back to Seattle." He brushed the dust from his shoes with the cloth he retrieved from the floor behind the driver's seat. After adjusting his mirror, he started the eight-cylinder engine and drove to the two-lane highway that ran below Martin City.

Once he cleared Columbia Falls he relaxed. He placed the envelope with the twenty-five hundred dollars into the glove compartment. With this payment, he'd pay off the short loan on his two month old Capri. The hot August air brushed his salt and peppered flattop back as he pressured the gas pedal up to sixty-five miles an hour. Soon he'd be racing toward Spokane where he planned to take a hotel room at the Davenport. He liked the way they cared for his car in the underground parking garage.

As he cruised along, Roy flashed on his meeting in Martin City. Seemed like the same day over again when he met and planned to kill that skinny fella in Coulee City. This guy in Hungry Horse will make the third man he eliminated for Slick Hansen as he called his employer. Slick dressed the same most of the time. Blue suit, gray tie, hair perfectly combed. He looked like he just climbed out of the bathtub. But he paid on time and his marks were easy. This one'll be the same. One shot through the head at fifty yards. No problem.

After all, he made head shots in Germany during the war from three-hundred, four-hundred yards and never missed. That was his job for the U.S. Army. Kill Germans. It was more fun to kill them at a distance. He and one of his buddies bet on long distance shots.

He never got to meet any of them before he killed them. These Dam workers were different. He'd actually talked to the other two men several times before he took them down. Roy planned to get real friendly with this Sednick fella before he killed him. It was more interesting that way. He could get closer and the challenge of a night shot also interested him.

On the way back to the contractor's office where he worked, R.T. Hansen loosened his gray tie a little and rolled his neck to relieve the tightness that plagued him whenever he met with Devers. Devers frightened him. He hoped there was another way around killing David. But there wasn't. David knew too much. Once he laundered the money, he wasn't needed any longer. He became a liability. Just like the other two men. It was just the way of things. He suspected that maybe Devers thought the same way about him. Nothing to lose for a man like Devers. Their business ended with Sednick. "I better put a twist to the ending of this story if I plan to stay alive."

CHAPTER TWENTY-THREE

"**O**nly sixteen days ago, Johnny Davis died unnecessarily! Now another one of our vibrators got killed today. It's got to stop!" The anger in Jiggs Quinn's voice roared in the faces of the safety-first committee members. "There's not an excuse in hell that can cover how a crane can fall off a crawler track atop a cliff and land on a man below working a concrete pour covering a water line. No goddamn excuse in hell!"

The other members of the committee sat silently as the words banged against the metal walls of Superintendent Scalf's makeshift office. Two bosses, a member of each union craft, and Scalf conducted their weekly morning meeting. W.R. Scalf started to respond, but Jiggs cut him off with a continuation of his tirade. He slapped down the front-page copy of the *Hungry Horse News*. The grizzly photographs of Shorty's death punctuated Jigg's point. "Too dangerous of work anymore! We got to slow her down some. I don't care if the President of the United States is gonna throw the switch on October 1st. We're pushing too hard, too fast, W.R.

"Whatever happened to safety first for Christ's sake?"

"Hold on there Jiggs! The weather caused Shorty's death. It was an act of God. There was no way we could've seen that short-out with the power. The wet conditions-"

"Bullshit! Act of God, my sweet ass. We should've shut her down for the dayshift. Let things dry out some. We all feel under the gun all the time. That crawler today should've been supported with another bulldozer and more tie down cables. Too many men in too much of a goddamn hurry."

Buck Morris stared at Jiggs. He couldn't rein in his temper and grief for the loss of another good man any longer. "Maybe you been at this too long, Quinn! You can't cut the mustard anymore. You-"

Jiggs Quinn rose out of his gray metal chair with his calloused hands firmly gripped to the edge of the table. He now directed his tirade at Morris. With a trickle of snoose seeping down the side of his mouth he yelled at Morris, "You sayin' I caused Johnny's death. You sayin' that, you dirty son-of-a- bitch!"

The ironworkers superintendent Dick Kearney stepped in, "Knock it off, Jiggs! You too, Buck! This ain't gettin' us nowhere. Let's cool off and meet back here tomorrow. In the meantime, we can all be thinkin' of some ways to prevent accidents for the comin' weeks."

Jiggs pushed away from the table, and stormed out of the office. W.R. sat back in his chair and folded his arms. His blood pressure boiled, and his head pounded. He caught his breath and said, "Dick's right. Back here at 7:30 tomorrow mornin'." The men quietly picked up their note pads, slid back their chairs, and left.

Scalfs' secretary, Mary, hesitated before she entered his office. She opened the door only halfway. "Sorry to interrupt W.R., but there's an agent from the FBI on the telephone. He wants to make an appointment with you in the next two days."

He shook his head back and forth and then signaled her to forward the call to him. "Just what I need now, Mary. The goddamn FBI. What's next, an earthquake that'll take out the Dam?"

She faked a half-hearted smile and returned to her phone.

Mikhail looked out the window of Bill's Texaco Station while he held the black telephone against his ear. He watched Bill wash the windshield of the logging truck while his son pumped gas. His daughter Kat enthusiastically caught him up on the weekly news from Butte. She apparently had finished one too many cups of coffee. "Daddy, the strike settlement was in the paper this morning, and the union agreed to a 3 percent increase on the cost of living increase."

Mikhail switched the phone into his other hand," What was the total wage increase?"

Kat scrolled down the news article with her index finger. "Oh, here it is. Let's see. This brings the total wage increase into the six to six and a half percent range. Is that pretty good, Daddy?"

In his head he calculated what that meant in increase wages for him. "Not too bad. Anything on health insurance?"

Her finger continued to search the *Montana Standard* front-page article, "It says that there isn't any increase in insurance, but there is a good increase in the pension each month. It also says the Company backed off the demand for cross-productivity, whatever that is."

Mikhail swiveled in the worn rocking chair in the gas station, "Ya. I'm happy they got the pension increase. Too bad about nothin' goin' on with the insurance. That was somethin' I was after-" He caught himself as he remembered he wasn't returning to Butte. "Anything new about people sellin' their houses in McQueen?"

She sipped the final drops from her pink plastic coffee cup. "George told me yesterday that the Company's man got close to signing the first deal with the Marinkovichs. The rest of the neighborhood is up in arms with the Marinkovichs maybe sellin' out. We goin' to sell our house before we move up to Columbia Falls in October?"

A few seconds breezed by as Mikhail's stomach flip-flopped with the thought of selling their place. He promised himself to hold out for a while, but he wanted the money from the sale of his house in Butte to buy a nice place in Columbia Falls. He decided not to talk to Katya about it. He would come down in person to deal with the business of selling the family home and dealing with his neighbors and close friends. "We'll just wait and see how this goes, Katya. Don't worry about it now. We'll get you and Anna moved up here before we do anythin'."

"That's a relief. Just movin' away from Butte is goin' to be tough enough without losin' our McQueen friends. They're like part of our family."

Mikhail knew it was time to change the subject. He needed time to make a plan. "How's Anna feelin' this week?"

Her voice changed and her excitement sailed through the phone lines, "Daddy. Your granddaughter took a few steps today. This portable oxygen tank is wonderful. George rigged a harness around her waist that will let her pull the small tank around with her. She's so thrilled."

He licked his lips and swallowed hard. "She walked?"

"Yes, that's what usually happens when you take a few steps." She laughed and rested back in her chair. "She can also go a little longer without the oxygen mask around her mouth. Her eating has improved and everything. We'll be ready to move in October all right."

"Well, someone else wants to use the phone, Honey. When she wakes up from her nap, tell her how proud I am of her." He wiped the tears from his cheek and turned away from the other Dam worker waiting to use the phone. "I'll call you next Sunday, okay?"

"Okay, Daddy. Say hi to Tom and John Nolan. Goodbye now."

Mikhail hung up the phone and walked into the men's room. As he used the urinal, it occurred to him that his daughter never mentioned her husband. He took this as a good sign. His family would be together again in about seven weeks.

CHAPTER TWENTY FOUR

As they drove toward the Going to the Sun Road, Tomas shared the information in the Glacier Park Travel Guide.

The Going To The Sun Road in Glacier National Park stretches across fifty-two miles of alpine heights and connects East and West Glacier. Men armed with shovels, hemp climbing ropes, and several tons of explosives carved a road that followed one of the most difficult and expensive routes in United States road building history. Engineers from the Bureau of Public Roads and the National Park Service designed the road together and laid the foundation for road building in America.

In 1910, transcontinental highway projects sprang up as auto travel became popular throughout the country. Major William Logan looked to build a road through Glacier Park's backcountry. The only road in Glacier at that time was a washed out wagon trail that connected Belton to Apgar near the foot of McDonald Lake. One recommendation for connecting East and West Glacier was to build a road that lead from Belton, along McDonald Lake, over Logan Pass and into St. Mary's Lake on the eastern front of Glacier National Park. The project employed about three-hundred men who moved two-hundred fifty tons of explosives. Men were paid by the cubic yards of material moved. The workers used four three-ton locomotives with dump cars and three-thousand feet of gauged track, portable compressors, a Fortson tractor, two graders, and anassortment of trucks, teams, and wagons. The work season was two-hundred days long, and the men moved snow by hand.

The Garden Wall, a shale rock face from which the Sun Road was carved, is a long steep slope eventually rising to sheer cliffs some one-thousand vertical feet above the road cut. The extreme nature of the surrounding environment often forced survey and construction crews to hang suspended from old hemp ropes. The western leg of the Transmountain Highway reached Logan Pass on October 20, 1928. The new road from the west to Logan Pass opened to car traffic the following June.

Final touches of the completion of the Sun Road were made on July 7, 1933 at a total cost of one-million seven-hundred thousand dollars. With masonry guardrails constructed from the very same rock excavated for the roadbed, the Sun Road stands as a tribute not only to civil engineering, but also to aesthetic beauty. Retaining walls blend into the hill and its contours snake in and out of view, making Going to the Sun one of the least obtrusive paved roads in the country. Opening and dedication ceremonies were held on July 15, 1933. More than four thousand visitors watched the ceremonies including delegates from formerly hostile tribes of Blackfoot, Flathead and Kootenai Indians who gathered for a ceremonial offering of peace and passing of the pipe. The celebration marked twenty years of planning and building.

Tomas stopped reading the travel guide and laid it on his lap. He'd picked up the guide at the visitor center upon entering Glacier Park. As they passed through the first turn after reaching the loop on the Sun Road, he carefully looked out the side window of Clifford's 1949 Ford Sedan. He spoke so quietly that Clifford leaned his right ear toward the middle of the bench seat just to hear, "Pretty hard to believe that them men hung over the sides swingin' on ropes. And we think we work on a scary job."

Without answering, Clifford shifted back into second gear as the road grade climbed. A station wagon stuffed with kids hanging out of the windows crawled by going down the road. Tomas continued with his nervous chatter, "Do you think somebody like us twenty years from now will be lookin' at Hungry Horse Dam and wonder how we did stuff?" He didn't wait for Clifford to answer, "And Clifford, can you imagine workin' that hard for a buck fifteen an hour? Holy smokes."

Clifford pulled his car to a stop in a pull out area where a group of people stood outside of their cars. He shook his head as he watched a little girl feed part of her sandwich to a black bear while her dad took a picture of her. Another bear sat and begged for food from another group of kids about twenty feet away. "They shouldn't do that. Bears aren't meant to be tame. Someone's going to get hurt." Clifford put the car in gear and pulled out back onto the road.

Once they arrived at Logan Pass, the two men walked up the wooden stairs and joined others looking west toward Mt. Reynolds and Mt. Oberlein. It was mid-August and snow still peppered the tops of the mountains. Tomas took a drink from his canteen and marveled at the beauty of the scenery. "I ain't ever seen nothin' like this, Clifford. Thanks a million for bringin' me along. I won't never forget this. Never."

Thunder clouds clapped overhead, and the wind increased its pressure against Clifford's long, black hair as it tossed straight back. He managed a smile before he spoke, "It is beautiful. Too many people now. I like the view better from East Glacier. The Blackfeet call it the Front. It is an important spiritual place for the Blackfeet people. It is known as part of the Backbone of the World, the Rocky Mountains. Peaks have Blackfeet names like Morning Star, Little Plume, Running Crane, Spotted Eagle, Elkcalf Bullshoe, and Curly Bear."

Tomas stared at his friend and waited for more. Clifford turned and walked down the dirt path toward his car. Tomas shrugged his shoulders, took another drink of water, and followed his friend to the parking lot.

As they passed through the tunnel below Logan Pass, Tomas silently reflected on the information about the construction of the four-hundred foot tunnel. The men excavated six-thousand yards of material just to open up a safe bench in order to work. All the supplies were hauled down a hundred foot trail lying at nearly a forty-five degree angle. The men carried fifty pounds of dynamite at a time down this trail and a ladder. Several men looked at the ladder and walked off the job. "Clifford. Do you think you would've climbed down that ladder with fifty pounds of dynamite on your back?"

"No. I don't like working with powder. Some kids in Browning got blown up once from powder. The highway workers used it to blast rock, and the kids got into it at night. One of them was my little cousin."

Tomas felt the mood change in Clifford the closer they got to Browning and the festivities of the North American Indian Days. He wondered if it was going to work out for Clifford bringing a white friend to the Indian celebrations. "Is it okay that I'm along for the Pow Wow Days?"

A few seconds passed before Clifford responded. "It will be okay. I am nervous about seeing a few cousins. That's all. Some people call me an apple."

"Apple? What's that mean?"

"Red on the outside. White on the inside. I get called apple because I left the reservation and live and work with the whites. I am used to it. My cousins are good until they get drunk. Then we will leave before trouble starts."

Clifford made a right turn at the small tourist town of St. Mary's and exited the boundaries of Glacier National Park. Clifford guided the car past two tourists parked in the middle of the road. Tomas compared Clifford's story to his own experience when he returned to McQueen earlier in the summer. He also worried about the reaction of his friends and neighbors once his family moved from Butte. "I think the people in Butte call me banana because I left Butte during the strike."

A welcomed laugh jumped from Clifford, "Banana?"

"Ya. Yellow on the inside and yellow on the outside." They both laughed and greeted the heavy rain and lightning storm that raced across the plains. Through the windshield wipers, Clifford embraced the feelings one knows when the familiar surroundings of a hometown open the memories of childhood. Memories released as the car crossed the bridge outside East Glacier that swept away his parents and uncle. The three white crosses on the guardrail swarmed every corner of his senses.

———•◦•———

Back in Martin City, Hannah joined Mikhail in his Chevy to go out and eat dinner in Whitefish with Bud and his wife Sara. She smiled at him across the front seat before she said anything. "And how was work today, Mr. Mikhail Anzich?"

He returned her smile and visually canvassed her outfit from head to toe. Mikhail engaged the clutch and his car jerked forward. The engine killed. Hannah laughed and managed to say, "Maybe we might get there in better shape if you look ahead instead of at me."

Mikhail turned his head back and let out a weak laugh. "I guess yer right." He restarted the engine and ground the gears as he shifted from first to second gear. As he glanced at her, he wondered what kind of dress she had on. She seemed to wear something new each time they got together. And her hair looked different too. "I like your new hair."

"Oh, it's the same hair. It's not new. I just got it cut real short. I saw it on a lady in the July issue of *Look Magazine*. So I cut out the picture and took it to my friend Judy. She cuts my hair in exchange for going to the movies free of charge. Glad you noticed. That might be worth somethin' later on tonight."

Mikhail glanced straight ahead as he carefully negotiated the hairpin turn through the Berne Park area of Highway 2. What did she mean, later on tonight? "Our hair is about the same amount of long."

"Same amount of long? How about same length." She playfully slapped him on his huge bicep and immediately realized how hard his muscles felt. Her thoughts quickly shifted across the river to the passenger train that zoomed by on the other side. "How about taking a train ride with me sometime?"

Mikhail noticed the Great Northern Streamliner moving smoothly along the tracks toward Whitefish. "Okay."

"There you go again, Mikhail. You're such a blabbermouth. I can't seem to get a word in edgewise."

A predictable short-lived laugh preceded his reply, "Where to?"

Hannah turned and faced him, "How about from Coram to Whitefish?"

"Okay. How'll we get back?"

She turned and looked out her window at the train. "We can take the train back the next morning."

"Where would we stay-" He stopped in the middle of his sentence. They'd need to spend the night together. She continued to surprise him with something new about herself. "Oh, a, that'd be fine."

Hannah smiled and congratulated herself for following through on her plan. It was time to move their relationship along, and she knew she would need to take the lead. "Good. Maybe we can pick sometime in September. The leaves will be changing and everything is so beautiful at that time of year. Besides, it'll give me time to look into a nice hotel in Whitefish."

The drive through Columbia Falls was a blur as Hannah's words about a hotel overwhelmed any other thought that might enter his head. Mikhail stopped in front of Bud and Sara Reynold's house. He noticed a new house across the street with a for sale sign in the front yard. His thoughts roared toward his plans for buying a house in Columbia Falls for his family. He'd talk to Bud about the neighborhood. "What a great place this house would be if it worked out. Big yard, two stories, lots of maple trees, and close to the construction site of the Aluminum Plant. And we'd be neighbors with Bud and his family."

"Mikhail. Are we goin' to sit here all night? Or should we join Bud and Sara standin' outside of their car waitin' for us?"

"Sorry. I, I daydreamed there." He opened his door and walked around the back of his car and opened Hannah's door. She purposefully brushed against him as she walked by, and she playfully raised one eyebrow. Her clean, flowery scent floated by and stayed with him. Thoughts of buying a house became a distant memory. Hannah Holley took over his thoughts for the time being.

———•+•———

Ted Hughes finished his first full week working undercover getting to know David Sednick. Previous summers between college quarters, Hughes worked as a laborer at Grand Coulee Dam. Memories of that experience vividly came back to life. The hard work, long hours, and aching muscles reminded him of why he stayed in college. Little did he realize back in 1942 that after getting his degree and working for the FBI for ten years, he'd be back tearing apart frames and working his tail off on Hungry Horse Dam. His self-pity left as David stopped in front of him. "Good week of work there, Hughes. You been around a little. I can tell."

"Ya. I spent some time on Grand Coulee years ago."

"Probably too tired for a couple of beers, huh?"

Hughes didn't expect to get this close this soon. "I imagine I could stand a couple. Maybe after a shower."

David nodded as his dented hard hat slowly tipped forward on his head. "How about up at Coram at the Dew Drop?"

"Good enough. About 6:00?"

"See ya then."

David walked away and promised himself to go easy with his drinking tonight. Hughes seemed like a guy he could get to know. He chased everybody else away when he got drunk and obnoxious.

After he set his lunch bucket and clipboard in the front seat of his truck, he took off his hard hat and flipped it on the floor. He mumbled as he checked out the inside of his truck. "First chance I get I gotta wash this goddamn thing. It's filthy." On the drive down the haul road, David sauntered back in his mind to some friends he had back in McQueen. It came easy then to keep friends. Nobody had nothin'. Nobody cared. They just had fun and hung around.

Moonshine grappa wine changed all of that. Moonshine grappa and girls. Two of his friends went to Pine Hills in Miles City for burglary. He got away that night, and his friends didn't squeal on him. It wasn't the same after they got out of Miles City. They'd changed. He owed them for not squealing. Twice they beat the shit out of him for not paying them on time. One of them found out about David messing with his girlfriend while he was in Miles City. David started to become a loner. To make his blackmail payments to his ex-friends, he swindled his grandparents out of their savings. This was his biggest mistake. Everybody in McQueen seemed to find out about it. He became a full-time loner. After twenty years, people still never forgave him.

Tonight he'd be different. He needed a friend. The rest of the world around him turned to shit. It was time to turn on the old charm. Hughes might be his last chance. Everyone else wrote him off.

After they ordered their dinners, Bud and Mikhail discussed the technical aspects of one of the highlights of Hungry Horse Dam. Sara and Hannah excused themselves and headed for the restroom in the Cadillac Hotel.

Bud reminisced about his first job on the Dam project as he explained the details of that work to Mikhail. "The first construction activity on Hungry Horse Dam was the work we did on the diversion tunnel. It was during the 1947-48-winter season. The engineers called this shaft-and-tunnel the morning-glory type of spillway. We lined that entire tunnel with concrete. It was supposed to pass a flow of fifty-thousand cubic feet per second."

Mikhail took a long drink of the delicious, dark coffee and set his cup back down in the saucer. "How much rock and dirt did you remove to make room for that size of a tunnel?"

After a short swallow, Bud set his half-empty glass of Pabst Blue Ribbon down on the cloth-lined table. "I think the excavating crews removed just about thirty-thousand cubic yards of material in order to construct the eleven-hundred foot long tunnel."

"How will the tunnel work once we finish up in a month?"

"The way I understand it, the overflow water from the reservoir will plunge over the rest of the spillway and drop about four-hundred feet. It'll discharge through the spillway outlet structure five-hundred fifty feet downstream from the powerhouse."

The women returned to the table, adjusted their cloth napkins back on their laps, and toasted each other's beer glasses.

Bud took a slow glance in their direction and asked, "What's that all about?"

His wife giggled and answered, "I bet Hannah in the bathroom that when we sat down, you two'd still be jawing about that damn old tunnel. And I was right." She toasted Hannah's glass again and laughed.

Bud shook his head, looked over at Mikhail, and continued, "An outlet system provides three ninety-six diameter outlet pipes in order to regulate the flow of water to meet downstream requirements. In addition, these outlet pipes provide a means for rapidly lowering the reservoir in case of an impending flood."

Sara gasped before she spoke, "Stop, Bud Reynolds. Enough of that tunnel talk. Talk about us for a while. Look how good we look tonight." The effects of her second beer allowed her to playfully turn the conversation to include all four of them.

The waitress returned to their table and delivered their garden salads. Bud didn't appreciate being interrupted in his explanation of the Glory Hole to Mikhail. But as he looked at his wife, he noted to himself how nice she did look. "Okay, Sara. Let's talk about you." His sly smile and wink told Sara everything she wanted to hear. She still owned his heart and other important parts of his body. Bud knew what was good for him.

———•◆•———

He sat down on one of the wooden benches in the quonset hut, waited for the bus, and drank his third cup of thermos coffee. From across the room he heard Bob Stebbins yell, "Hey, Nolan. Grab yer gear and come with me." Nolan used his favorite face muscles and mimicked the electrician superintendent to the delight of the men sitting near him. He grabbed his lunch bucket and hardhat and followed the short, stocky boss out to his pickup. He imitated the gorilla-walking gait Stebbins used as he exited the building. Nolan hung his arms low and swayed his body back and forth like a gorilla. Behind him he heard pockets of laughter rise up from various parts of the hut.

Outside, Stebbins motioned John Nolan to his pickup. "I'd like you to ride with me up to the top and give me a hand unloadin' all of this new telephone gear that I picked up at the post office." Nolan flipped the remaining few drops of coffee from his plastic thermos cup into the gravel. Small bursts of dust jumped up at him. The dry weather wore on, and even at 8:00 in the morning, the ground lacked moisture from any kind of dew. Nolan slowly climbed into the packed front seat. He threw a quick glance at the boxes crammed into the pickup bed and the front seat. Nolan looked out the back window as he spoke, "It's a good goddamn thing I got a skinny ass, Bob. Otherwise, I'd be ridin' the runnin' board."

Stebbins grumbled something, spit the dark juice from the chaw in his cheek, and fired up the engine. "We're goin' to replace the whole goddamn setup this week, Nolan. New shit for the Truman press corps and the whole goddamn gang comin' along with the president. I remember the first time I laid eyes on the switchboard we got from a war surplus sale. The equipment must'a been purchased sight unseen because it'd been a part of a multi-position switchboard and somebody took a hacksaw to the interconnecting cable. There it stood with a few hundred wires hanging out of the side, all unlabeled and they didn't know what wire went where because there wasn't no wiring diagram with the piece of junk."

Nolan blinked his eyes and subtly shook his head. To himself he asked, "What the hell he's talking about. I got to bed around five and still got a pretty good load on." He looked in Stebbin's direction, "How in God's good earth did you know where to splice and connect?"

The truck lunged forward as the transmission shifted into third gear. "I worked for a phone company in California installin' every kind of instrument. I took some instruction on how to read a wire diagram and how to repair switchboards."

"It's still pretty damn interestin' you was able to put in the phone system for this here Dam. Christ Almighty, there's phones everywhere!"

"That was just part of it. We put in phones in the town of Hungry Horse and in the small duplexes where the supervisors and engineers live. We wired the bowling alleys, bunkhouse, and chow hall for the workers. Later, I helped put in phones in the company offices and hooked the whole goddamn mess up to the switchboard."

The effect of the coffee and the conversation rallied Nolan from his hangover fog. "Shit. And I thought I knew somethin' about somethin'. You're way ahead of me. Maybe after today I'll go work for the phone company. They might put me in charge of those little operators at the switchboard. I could teach them a thing or two about a thing or two."

Stebbins pulled his pickup to a halt at the cement mixing plant. "Ya. That'd be like puttin' the fox in the henhouse." He allowed himself a deep, robust laugh and then barked out the orders, "We'll unload her here, Nolan. Then we'll signal the hook tenders for a skip and load it to the gunnels." The two men slipped on their leather gloves, and without another word unloaded the truckload of boxes in a matter of minutes.

⌐ CHAPTER TWENTY-FIVE ⌐

W.R. Scalf proofread his September 1st memo to the bosses. He summarized the final weeks of construction of the Dam. Then he outlined the layoff plan and the plan to return the area to its original state. Scalf reminded the bosses that one of the conditions of the construction contract were that the contractor would return the surrounding area to its original condition. This meant that all of the buildings would have to be removed, the power lines, roads, conveyor belts, cableway towers, and anything else that didn't look like a rock or a tree would have to go. All equipment, wire, and motors were to be hauled down by the Forest Service Station in Hungry Horse and sold to contractors or individuals for months after the project was to close. The thirty duplexes were to be sold to individuals and the Forest Service. In his memo, Scalf informed the bosses that a small crew would be needed to tear down and clean up everything left over.

Scalf read the final sentence as he stood over his secretary's desk. She impatiently tapped the side of the desk that held her gray IBM model B electric typewriter. It was five minutes until quitting time and she needed to get home on time to serve dinner to her nagging mother-in-law. Mary felt the soreness in her fingers from the long day of typing the August report.

"Sorry for keepin' you waitin', Mary. Can you get this out by the time you leave today? I'll save you a few steps and run my own copies for my morning meetin'." Scalf walked back into his office and smiled as the whirr of Mary's typewriter heated the all ready toasty office. He knew his faithful secretary would chew his ass tomorrow for waiting until the last minute. The expensive present in his desk would erase all of the last minute typing he gave her to do. He planned to give it to her the day before Truman dedicated the Dam. She didn't know it yet, but she was going to join him with Truman at the dedication ceremony. The four-birthstone mother's ring his wife picked out for Mary would look good on her finger when she shook the President's hand.

———•◦•———

After meeting with Scalf, the bosses talked with their crews about the final plans outlined in the Superintendent's memo. The workers acted just as they did when they were kids during the last week of school before summer vacation. John Nolan sprawled out on an inclined board and rested his head on his empty lunch bucket. He still had fifteen minutes left in his half-hour lunchtime. Nolan mastered the ten-minute nap years ago while working on the Butte Hill. His eyes closed and sleep crawled into his body. The chatter from one of his fellow electricians jolted him awake. "Hey Nolan. What you doin' after?"

Sleepily he opened one eye. "After what?"

The men laughed, Danny Fisher managed to ask another question, "Nolan. Where you gonna work after you leave here in a couple weeks?"

"Pretty tough to get any rest around this cathouse outfit." Nolan sat up and stretched. "I'm takin' a vacation. Maybe Cuba."

Again the men laughed, closed their lunch boxes and prepared to return to work. As they walked back to the electrician's shack, Fisher stopped in front of Nolan. "Seriously, Nolan. What's yer plans?"

"Well seriously, Fish. I'm takin' a few weeks off. Then I'll most likely come back and work the Aluminum Plant with Mikhail. Somebody's got to keep an eye on that Bohunk. He can't fend for himself worth a shit."

Fisher started to walk again and then stopped. "How'd you like to take a trip with me out to Seattle for a week or so. I got a sister out there I plan to visit. We'd have a goddamn good time I imagine."

"Thanks, Fish. But I got some business in Butte I need to take care of first. Then I'm goin' to Frisco for a week or two. Maybe we can go to Seattle some other time."

The two men climbed onto the portable scaffolding platform and lowered themselves down to the base of the Dam.

———•·•———

As he worked the wire, John Nolan silently reviewed his plan for his trip to Butte right after Truman dedicated the Dam. After a wild trip to San Francisco, he'd return to Columbia Falls and buy a small house somewhere near Mikhail and his family. He'd clean out his savings account at the Miners Bank in Butte and open up a savings account for Tomas. Tomas would need the money once he got out of the Navy in two years. For sure he'd need a new car and his own place to start his life.

Tom Fisher startled Nolan's daydreaming, "Hey Nolan, think you might give us a hand with these lines?"

Nolan moved in between Fisher and the wall of the Dam. "Christ Almighty Fish, I was right in the middle of a good tussle with a black Frisco whore and you ruined it."

Fisher shook his head and pulled the electrical wire from the wooden drum. "How much you figure you'll have to give for one of them Frisco women?"

"Don't matter. I'm so good they'll probably pay me once I get done with em."

"Bullshit. You'll most likely throw your hat over it and run."

Nolan clipped the tail off the ground wire and taped it with his black electric tape. "Did I ever tell you about the time I was with a black whore down at the Missoula Rooms? Well I-"

"Only about a thousand times. You need to go somewheres new to get some new stories. We started to number each of your stories like on the jukebox. That there story about the black whore is G-6."

Nolan backhanded Fisher in the chest, "I'll G-6 you. Maybe I'll get married and you'll die of boredom without my stories." He smiled and prepared a hand rolled cigarette. Tiny pieces of tobacco spilled down the front of his bib overalls as he licked the sticky end of the paper. "I almost married once when I was twenty."

Tom Fisher unwrapped a piece of Spearmint Gum and slipped it into his mouth. "Why didn't ya?"

After a long draw of his cigarette, he blew the blue smoke past his squinted eyes. "She was already married to a Butte cop. We snuck around for a year or so until he got wind of it. He and a couple of his buddies waited for me outside of the M & M one night and put the boots to me. That put the skids to that." His eyes searched past the opening to the Canyon to the mountains of the North Fork of the Flathead River. He visualized their picnics together at Basin Creek north of Butte. "She was a beauty, Fish. A once in a lifetime beauty. Too bad a man only gets one of them in his lifetime. Ain't never met one like her since. Most likely won't again either. I think that's why I stick to whores now. No chance of gettin' another broken heart that way."

———·•·———

The next morning at 9:00, W.R. Scalf sat down at a large oak table in the Columbia Falls Library. Two Secret Service men stood in front of the small group and prepared to outline their schedule for the dedication of Hungry Horse Dam by President Truman in a month. Scalf nodded his head to Al Sutter who sat at the table to the right of him. He recognized the mayor of Columbia Falls, the police chief of Kalispell, and a couple of men from the railroad depot in Whitefish. Scalf noticed Betty Hansen as she sat with Mabel and two other women. He wondered how her husband R.T. Hansen would like her sitting with the Madam of the cathouse. As the business manager for the Dam contractor, Hansen seemed to always do the right thing. The women with Betty Hansen giggled as they wrote notes back and forth to one another. Several other people filled the rest of the tables.

The taller Secret Service man distributed a sheet of paper that outlined the time schedule of the President's visit on October 1st.

His partner welcomed the crowd and then spoke in a slow, southern drawl, "On behalf of the President, we want to thank you for meeting with us. The President will arrive here the evening of September 30th. He'll travel by private railroad car and stay near Columbia Falls. His daughter Margaret will be with him."

Once the taller agent returned to the front of the audience, his partner continued, "At nine in the morning of October 1st, we'll move by caravan up to the Dam for an onsite photo session. You will need to provide three vehicles for the President and staff, a large bus for the press corps, and a police escort front and back."

The mayor of Kalispell raised his hand and began to ask his question," Will I-"

"We will have time for questions after we finish, Sir." The Mayor sat down and the agent continued, "The mock dedication will occur in Kalispell in the high school gymnasium at 11:15. You will need to provide a mock electrical switch at the gym that will go at the same time as the switch on the Dam starts the first turbines. You will need to arrange for a telephone setup to do this."

Scalf scribbled notes and regretted not bringing his secretary Mary along with him to take care of note taking. As expected, Mary cleared the air about his last minute requests from the day before. Scalf thought it best to let her cool off while he attended the meeting. So far he needed to plan for the 9:00 Dam visit, a plan for the ceremony, the mock electrical switch, and a worker to operate it at the high school. He needed to arrange for the phone setup at the Dam.

The second Secret Service agent spoke next, "I need to meet with the law enforcement people after this meeting. We'll need to lay out the plan for the caravan to the Dam, to Kalispell, and back to our train in Columbia Falls. I also need to meet with the train personnel in Whitefish for the President's address in Whitefish at 1:00. We'll leave it up to community groups to organize parades or other activities like that."

With that comment, Hannah elbowed Lila and scribbled a note, "That'd be where we come in. Band. Flags. School kids."

Lila nodded and scribbled a note back, "Maybe Betty could get the Sheriff to lead the parade."

Hannah fought to control laughing out loud and covered her

mouth as the speaker continued; "The President's train will pull out of Whitefish toward Spokane at 1:45. All ceremonies and contact with the President in this area will end at that time. Now are there any questions?"

On the drive back to Martin City after the meeting at the library, the Care Less Group chattered at the same time. All four women loudly offered ideas for the October 1st dedication ceremonies of the Hungry Horse Dam by President Truman. "Okay, okay. One at time." Mabel tried to focus her three friends. "Let's start with the trip from the train depot to the Dam. What'll we do there?"

Hannah attempted to speak, but her broken laughter interfered with her words. Finally, she managed a complete sentence, "We can ride in the Sheriff's car. I'm sure Betty can swing that."

Betty Hansen gasped before she answered, "You bitch! At least my boyfriend can fit into a Sheriff's car. That big ox of yours needs to have a school bus just to get his big ass in a seat." In typical Care Less Group fashion, the scene erupted into uncontrollable laughter. Mabel held her stomach and then loudly passed gas. Tears flowed freely from the eyes of her friends as Lila struggled to maintain control of her husband's new 1952 Plymouth.

After she caught her breath and stopped laughing, Hannah retrieved her notepad and listed some possible activities for the group. "Let's see now. How about a parade along the hauling road leading to the bottom of the Dam? Maybe we can get the school kids and the people in both Hungry Horse and Martin City to line the road. Then -"

"Come on Hannah, another damn parade? We just had the Liberty Bell Parade." Lila pushed the gearshift button as she negotiated the turn at Berne Park. "Let's do something different. How about some grandstands at the Dam for people to sit? We could have the high school band play a few songs or something. Then we could have lunch ready too."

The ideas for the dedication filled Hannah's sheet of paper. Lila stopped in front of the Club Café and shut off the engine. One by one the women climbed out of her two-tone black and tan sedan. "Anybody have time for coffee?"

Betty checked her watch and calculated how much time she had left before her husband would walk into their kitchen and expect his lunch. "I, I better not. He'll be home at exactly 11:30. God knows how he'll pout if his lunch isn't sitting there when he hits the door." She wondered how he'd react when he came home in a few weeks and realized she was gone. "It'll serve him right. Let R.T. Hansen get his own damn lunch. Me and the sheriff will be off to Seattle to start our own adventure."

Hannah and Mabel joined Lila in the Club Café, and over three cups of coffee, narrowed down their plans for October 1st. The parade, the grandstands, and then a picnic lunch made their list for their contribution to the big day.

The two Secret Service agents walked along side W.R. Scalf and Al Sutter. They finished a quick walk across the concrete fantail at the base of the Dam. Workers went about their business even though they knew who the well-dressed men were with the Superintendent. Scalf looked upward toward the top of the Dam and thought how time roared by from the first day he stood there after the first footings were poured with cement. He watched as the taller agent wrote some notes in a small notebook. The other man studied the sidewalls of the mountain that contained the canyon in front of the Dam. "Is this the only road into this part of the Dam?"

Scalf looked around and answered, "This haul road is the only way in and out of here."

"Alright then. I think that'll do it for now. We're meeting the Kalispell police chief for lunch and a tour of the route to the high school. So we need to be on our way. If we think of anything before we arrive on September 30th, we'll call. Once you get the ceremonies and small details planned, you can call us. Here's a card with a number to reach us."

Al Sutter made some notes himself. It would be to his advantage to plan his photographs. The big time magazine photographers would need to react on the fly. "Hey W.R., thanks for bringing me along and fixing it for me to ride the press bus. But I have a question for you. How come you didn't tell them about the FBI and the murders at the other Dams?"

Scalf kicked himself for not filling in the Secret service about the FBI involvement. "I batted that around all last night. But I figured it was up to the FBI to talk to them. Now I wished I would've told him. Then they could get a hold of the FBI."

"Where are you on that thing anyway?"

Scalf looked down and shuffled some gravel between his new shoes. "Things are in the hopper. That's all I can tell you now, Al. But I'll get you the scoop as soon as it's safe. I'll make good on my word to you."

≈ CHAPTER TWENTY-SIX ≈

When Columbia Falls was first settled in 1890, the North Fork Valley was a proposed route of rail lines into Canada. The main objective was the North Fork coal beds and the Coal Creek and lignite beds between Big Creek Ranger Station and Polebridge. In 1892, the *Columbia Newspaper* commented that the North Fork held many gallons of oil and that samples had been sent east. These samples were pronounced as best quality. Before 1951, there was a fiftyy-year history of drilling for oil in the region. Iowa corn farmers, Washington and Oregon businessmen, London financiers, and local citizens were among those who helped finance drilling. No commercial quantities of oil resulted.

Extensive road improvements and large timber sales became part of the development of the North Fork Valley. Flathead National Forest sold twenty-six million board feet in 1950 and 1951; much of it was blow-down. The North Fork was slated for an annual log cut of fourteen-million board feet.

The 1952 Labor Day weekend provided the Dam workers with the time off they needed for the final push to complete the work in time for the dedication. Mikhail stowed away the box of groceries behind the backseat of the station wagon he borrowed from his partner Bud Reynolds. Hannah gabbed with Tomas. They waited for John Nolan as he hauled the green metal cooler from her porch. He exaggerated his struggle as he lugged the cooler toward the station wagon. "What the hell you got in here? It must weigh half a ton."

Hannah directed him to the back where Mikhail stood. "Just slide it in next to the box of groceries. And quit whining so much. Half of the weight is your beer." She flirtatiously winked at Mikhail as Nolan wrestled the cooler into place.

Nolan immediately slid open the door handle to the cooler and rescued a bottle of Highlander Beer from the ice-packed container. He produced an opener and snapped the beer lid off of the bottle. Without a slight hesitation, Nolan swallowed his first drink of the day. He gasped a huge sigh, admired the bottle, and spoke, "Now that hits the spot. A man deserves that after all the hell he's put through. Now you, Mik, don't deserve nothin'. Maybe a glass of water. I could've carried that little box with one hand tied behind my back."

Mikhail smiled at him and bluffed a backhand slap. Nolan jumped to an old time boxing stance like John L. Sullivan used and said, "Come on now, Big Boy. Let's see what you got." He pranced around and boxed an imaginary fighter.

This play pleased Tomas as he treasured the time with all of them together. Soon his sister and niece would be part of this fun. Mikhail planned to finish working on September 10th. He then planned to move Anna and Katya to Columbia Falls about September 20th. Tomas battled second thoughts about leaving his family for the Navy. But the papers were signed and his departure date was November 1st. He'd make the best of this weekend and the remaining time together. The ideal September weather made for a perfect day. He watched his dad open the front door of the car for Hannah. He'd hoped to sit in the front seat in order to stretch his long legs. But he'd tough it out in the back with his godfather, John Nolan.

The North Fork Road was in horrible condition. Nolan complained about how difficult it was to take a decent drink from his second and then third beer. "A man would die of thirst drivin' up this road. God himself would walk that there river rather than ride on this bumpy son-of-a-bitch."

Tomas shot him a look and pointed toward Hannah. He signaled by using his thumb. Mikhail looked at him through the rear view mirror. Unfazed, Nolan continued, "Tell me, Hannah, what kind of woman is your ma?"

She pivoted around in the front seat and faced Nolan and Tomas. "Well, she's a character. In fact, you two will get along just fine."

"And will she have a drink or two with me?"

She laughed, "Oh, I think so. In fact, it wouldn't surprise me if she hasn't had a couple already. She does that when she gets a little nervous."

Nolan managed a drink of his beer, "Well then. Maybe I'll tell her a few stories about my favorite Bohunk sittin' up there like a monkey humped over a football."

Tomas howled. He should have expected it. But he thought Nolan might behave with Hannah along. He laughed so loud his father looked in the mirror at him. Mikhail shook his head and said, "See what I mean? He just can't help hisself." To his surprise, Hannah laughed as hard as Tomas. The vision of a monkey humped over a football struck her funny bone. The quick look she snuck at Mikhail with his huge hands draped over the steering wheel strangely fit Nolan's description of Mikhail.

* * *

June Holley sat on a wooden chair on the front porch of the Polebridge Mercantile. The September smells of fading summer filled her nostrils. She completed her baking an hour earlier and managed to fit in a relaxing half-hour in the tub. The ice-cold beer she pulled from the big cooler poured from the bottle and slid smoothly into her Mason jar. She wore her cleanest blue jeans and white blouse. As she often did, she cursed her large chest and shoulders as the buttons pushed the limits of the buttonholes. She envied smaller women without the challenge of tight fitting clothes. When Hannah complained in her younger years about being flat chested, June warned her that down the road she'd be thankful for the body that she had.

Her gray hair gathered easily into the ponytail. June smiled to herself as she dismissed the thought of applying a touch of lipstick. "Hell with em'. They'll take me as I am. No sense in putting on the dog. It'll be fun meeting Hannah's friends." She petted the three-legged dog behind the ear as she enjoyed her second beer. The cloud of dust a mile away caught her attention. Her nerves settled with the effect of the beer and the smell of dying leaves. The colors started earlier this year due to the lack of rain. Brilliant red colors from the red ocher dogwood bushes dotted the facing side hills.

Mikhail guided the dusty station wagon down the half-mile road and stopped in front of the Mercantile. Dust lingered as he turned off the key. June Holley rose from her chair and waved the dust away with her non-beer drinking hand. Mikhail watched as Hannah rushed to her mother and disappeared into her mother's hug.

The backseat car door opened and Nolan emerged with three empty beer bottles in his hands. After he set the bottles on the hood of the station wagon, he interrupted Hannah and her mother, "I need to use your can. I got to pee like a race horse."

June Holley pointed to the back of the mercantile. As Nolan trotted off, he heard June Holley say, "He's too short to be much of a racehorse." In the outhouse, Nolan smiled as he thought of how feisty the old lady must have been as a younger woman. He regretted not knowing her during her heyday.

Warm thoughts of his mother and his aunt flooded Nolan's mind. This lady in jeans and bursting out of her white blouse took him back to days at the Columbia Gardens in East Butte with his mother and aunt Cassie. He treasured the memories of the bantering that went on between the two most important women in his young life. He looked forward to carrying on with Hannah's mother. The outhouse door slammed as he walked out zippering his black work pants. He looked up and saw Hannah introducing Mikhail and Tomas. "Poor bastard," he thought as Mikhail shyly nodded hello to June Holley. "This will be a great place to start," he thought. "He's goin' to get it good today. But first I need a cold beer."

More traffic than normal moved along the highway in Hungry Horse. Ted Hughes waited outside of his small house trailer for David Sednick. They planned to drive around the outside of Glacier Park and back through the Park via the Going To The Sun Highway.

An hour earlier Ted Hughes telephoned his boss in Butte. He planned to push Sednick about his huge bank account. His boss instructed him to approach David Sednick about the source of the money. He also needed to tell Sednick that his life was in danger and his best chance was with the FBI and any deal that they might make for him. He stood up from sitting on the top stair of his trailer home as David's shiny black Chevy pickup stopped in the front. Through the open front window, Hughes welcomed David Sednick, "Looks like you washed her up for the trip."

"Ya. It got away from me. I hate dirty rigs, let alone when it's mine." Hughes smelled the liquor on David's breath and recognized the bewildered hangover stare that followed a night of heavy drinking. It then occurred to Hughes that maybe the way to get Sednick to open up was to get him drunk. Now he had a plan. There'd be lots of stops today at the many bars between Hungry Horse and the town of St. Mary's. David Sednick would tell him what he wanted to know.

In Seattle, Roy Devers dried himself after a long morning shower in his girlfriend's apartment. He mentally organized his day. First thing he'd do after Leslie left was to call Montana and set up a meeting with his contact, R.T. Hansen. The night before, he let Leslie know that he had work in Montana somewhere around the last part of September. Now with his phone call this morning, he'd nail down a time to eyeball his target for the first time. Hansen would arrange a meeting with his victim, and the hunt would be on. Devers figured a couple of days and nights observing Sednick's habits should do it. He told Leslie he'd return around October 1st.

After he hung up the telephone, R.T. Hansen adjusted his tie and neatly rearranged the few bills and envelopes on his desk. He enjoyed the morning solitude in his office due to the Labor Day shut-down of all work on Hungry Horse Dam. The realization of only a few weeks of work left brought some temporary peace and quiet. He shook his head trying to imagine what it would be like to not have to work and carry on his double life. Palm Springs will suit me just fine. My beautiful secret friend is there waiting for me.

His phone conversation with Roy Devers went well. They agreed on September 24th for the meeting with David Sednick. Devers would be at the Club Café while he and Sednick visited over lunch. The thought of being done with the whole ugly business pleased him. It almost pleased him as much as the thought of telling his wife Betty that he had enough. She wouldn't be joining him on his vacation in California and retirement. He reviewed his plan to pay her enough to make her comfortable for the rest of her life. And then he was on his own. She most likely wouldn't care anyway. "Sounds like she and the sheriff are off to the races. Good. I'm sick to death of her. I'm not losing anything."

——•◆•——

June Holley reluctantly climbed into the front seat of the station wagon with Mikhail. She watched her daughter snuggle in the back seat between Tomas and John Nolan. "Well after you cross the bridge, you go through the Park entrance. Then we'll grab a left to get to Bowman Lake. It's about six miles I figure. Or as my friend would say, it's about a six-pack trip."

Nolan perked right up after hearing June's comment, "Well for a lady like yourself, it's more like a tiptoe through the tulips." He smiled across at Tomas. "Yep. Just like a goddamn tiptoe through the proverbial tulips I imagine."

She struggled to turn around to face Nolan. "What in the hell you goin' on about back there. I ain't tiptoed nowhere in my life. I'm not exactly your dainty little dancer, don't you know."

"Oh, but I bet you got around just fine when you were a touch younger." Nolan spilled his beer as Mikhail jerked the station wagon with his sudden slam on the brakes. The second of the four whitetail deer passed quickly in front of them. "Jesus H. Christ. You're one thickheaded Bohunk alright. How am I suppose' to carry on an intelligent conversation with you drivin' like some kind of a ninny?"

Hannah gently elbowed Tomas. Her smile made it plain that she soaked in every bit of the theater unfolding before them. Her mother continued, "So, John Nolan. Anybody ever tell you that you're full of shit?" Hannah's smile broadened into a controlled laugh, and she elbowed Tomas again.

He straightened up his posture in the backseat, took a drink of beer, and twisted his lips in order to answer his new friend. "Well, let's look at it this way. The nun in the first grade at Holy Savior told me that I'd back up the confessional line if I ever decided to tell the priest all of my lies."

"So even the nuns knew you were full of shit."

"Yep. That was right after she took me into the bathroom, pulled down my pants, and took a good long look at my pee wee."

Even June Holley laughed. She snorted in an attempt to catch her laugh. Mikhail momentarily raised his eyes to the roof of the station wagon and shook his head in disbelief. There was no stoppin' Nolan today. He grinned and through the rear view mirror picked up the warm sight of his son and the new love of his life laughing together. John Nolan enriched all of their lives with his powerful sense of timing with his stories. The rough six-mile trip to the picnic grounds at Bowman Lake flew by.

———••••———

After they closed down the Dew Drop Inn, Agent Hughes drove David's pickup back to his trailer. Hughes congratulated himself for pulling off his plan to get Sednick drunk. It worked well. As they drove David continued his slurred bragging about his bank account. "Ya Ted, I got thousands in there. Easiest money I ever made. My partner gave me a good size commission to stash his dirty money in a couple of banks. In a few weeks I'll take it out for him. That's all there's to it."

Hughes pushed the issue, "Where does he get his money?"

After David dropped the empty beer can on the floor of his

truck, he formed an answer, "Don't know. Don't care. I don't ask."

"Who is this guy, Dave?"

David straightened up in his seat, "Oh, can't tell you that Ted. It don't matter anyway. Once the Dam is finished, we go our own way."

Ted Hughes dropped off David in front of his trailer. "That was a hell of a good time. I'll see you tomorrow." He watched David stagger into his trailer. Hughes parked David's truck and walked the half-mile to his own place. As he walked he reviewed his night's work. "With time, the identity of the main man will come out. After that we will close in and possibly prevent another murder." Hughes planned to call Butte on Tuesday morning to receive further instructions.

CHAPTER TWENTY-SEVEN

Mikhail walked to the waiting bus at the end of his afternoon shift. Bud Reynolds strolled beside him. September 10th came to a close as Bud's wristwatch struck midnight. "How does it feel to have your last shift in?"

"Pretty good. This was a good job, Bud. I'm happy we get to work together at the Aluminum Plant."

Bud nodded his agreement and handed Mikhail the keys to his black panel van. "I parked my brother's van near the barracks for you. It's gassed up and ready to go. You still plan on headin' out in the mornin'?"

He stopped and received the keys, "Ya. Probably about six in the morning. I can get to Butte before noon. My daughter Katya promised me lunch."

"When do you plan to come back to Columbia Falls?"

Mikhail cleared his throat before he answered, "They told me we could move in on September 20th. We're gonna rent until I sell my house in McQueen. We can start house payments after that. They been good about it. Katya's excited to see it."

"Well, we're glad to be your neighbors. You can start your new job at the Plant around October 10th or so. Whenever you're ready to go."

Mikhail held out his hand. Bud shook it and smiled. The brief eye contact cemented the new friendship without another word exchanged. Mikhail climbed up the stairs to the bus and took an empty seat near the front. The men on board the bus chattered and made plans to meet at the Dam Town Tavern. Mikhail turned down their offer to join them. He needed to pack and get some sleep before leaving in the morning.

———— •+• ————

As September moved along, the mornings seemed to stay darker a little bit longer. Tomas carried his father's army bag full of his clothes to the panel van. In his white tee shirt and work jeans, he now stood only a couple of inches shorter than his father. He shivered from the cold and the anxiety of his father leaving to move out of their home in McQueen. "Are you sure you don't want me to go with you, Dad?"

Mikhail flipped the heavy army bag onto the floor of the van. "No. I can take care of it. Most of the furniture will go to the Salvation Army."

His voice cracked as he spoke, "Well, I mean you gotta deal with leavin' the neighbors. Maybe I should be there with you."

Mikhail shook his head, "No. You best finish workin' your last couple of weeks. We'll get back here in about ten days. Then I can use your help."

Tomas realized the conversation was just about over. He sighed a sign of relief as he heard Nolan push open the barracks door. He appeared in his underwear. "Hey, Bohunk. Ain't you gonna give me a goodbye kiss?"

Mikhail unzippered his work coat and set it on the front seat. "I'll see you soon enough I expect."

Barefooted, Nolan tiptoed across the gravel, "Ouch, ouch! Holy shit! I better get more than a kiss for this pain I'm goin' through." He wrapped his arms around Mikhail. "I'm gonna miss you so much. Me and my nephew will have to find company with the girls on the hill."

Mikhail pushed him away. "Nolan, you keep my son away from there. It wouldn't hurt you to stay away too."

Tomas managed a smile as he walked close to his father. "Drive careful, Dad. I gotta go down for breakfast before work. See you on the 20th."

Mikhail reached out and hugged his son. He tried to tell him how proud he was of him, but the words stayed inside. He knew a tougher goodbye with Tomas was only a month away. The next few weeks promised to be bittersweet. He dreaded leaving McQueen and his connection with the past. But his family had a new start, a new house, and new friends. Tomas' leaving for the Navy would be hard. But his son would experience the world in a way he couldn't provide. And Hannah. Their goodbye yesterday was special.

"Hey! Snap out of it. You're squeezing the life out of nephew. He won't be worth a shit to any of them lovely ladies of the night." Mikhail released Tomas. He thumped Nolan on the chest with a slight thunderclap. The van door closed and soon disappeared down Sugar Hill.

The next morning at ten, Barnie Harbold entered Mikhail's front porch. The old leather brief case hung by his side as Mikhail opened the door. "Good morning, Mr. Anzich. I'm Barnie Harbold. I got the paperwork in my case here." He extended his hand, but Mikhail turned his back and walked into the kitchen.

Harbold sat down at the kitchen table and opened his briefcase. His fingers struggled to pull out the legal papers needed to buy Mikhail's house and property. He laid the papers on the table and unclipped the paperclip. "Here's how it works, Mr. Anzich. The Anaconda Company will buy your house up in Columbia Falls in exchange for your house here in McQueen. The realtor up in Columbia Falls there puts the price at close to yours here. So no money's exchanged. We pay the realtor, and your house in McQueen belongs to the Company. Any questions?"

Mikhail and Katya sat at the table opposite of Harbold. He paused before he answered, "How long does it all take?"

Harbold stacked the papers in front of him, "It will take about three to four weeks for the papers to clear. Usually-"

"Will I owe anything?"

"No. You'll own your house in Columbia falls free and clear once the Company sends their check to the realtor in Columbia Falls."

Mikhail extended his hand and temporarily released his icy stare, "I'll read the papers now." He and Katya carefully read the terms of the sale agreement. It seemed too easy for Mikhail. Second thoughts plagued him the entire drive to Butte the day before. After a sound night of sleep, all thoughts of doubt left him. His large index finger stopped about halfway down the page at the legal definition of the house and property. He reread the sentence, nodded his head and continued.

Katya finished reading the page and waited for her father to catch up. Inside she vacillated between excitement and nausea. "How in the world would they say goodbye to their friends and neighbors? How would her father face saying goodbye to his life-long friends? And how would Anna stand up to the demands of moving into a new home?" Then the excitement of a new beginning flushed over her. "It will be for the best. Dad knows what he's doin'."

The second page contained lines for signatures. "I'm ready to sign."

Harbold fumbled to hand Mikhail the fountain pen. The other homeowner that sold thought about the terms for a few days. The suddenness and decisiveness surprised him. "Are you sure? You can think about it for a bit if you want. There-"

Mikhail resumed his penetrating stare at the man in front of him, "I'll think on it then. Come by in two days and I'll have my mind made up." Mikhail felt his daughter's hand squeeze his leg. He looked at her and smiled confidently.

Harbold clipped the two papers together, stood up, and extended his hand. Mikhail stood up but didn't shake Harbold's hand. "If I sign, how will I know it's a deal?"

"You'll be contacted by the realtor at Main Street Realty in about two weeks. From there, you work directly with him."

Mikhail nodded his head. He showed Harbold to the door, smiled at his daughter, and walked into the bathroom. He knelt at the toilet, lifted up the toilet seat, and vomited his pancake and eggs breakfast.

Early the next morning, George Maletta knocked on Mikhail's back door. He stood holding a full cup of coffee and a thermos. Katya opened the door and welcomed him inside. "Mornin', George. See you got some of your famous coffee there."

"Would you like a cup, Kat?"

She retrieved a cup from the counter near the sink, "You bet. Dad's coffee isn't very good. Don't tell him that though."

"Where is he anyway?"

The bathroom door opened and Mikhail walked out. His hair stood up from the rough toweling he gave it after the shower. He stopped as he entered the kitchen, "Hello, George."

"Mornin', Mik. I guess that van outside and the visit you had yesterday from Harbold means you're gettin' ready to move."

The moment he dreaded for weeks arrived. Mikhail sat down at the table. "Ya, George. We're movin'."

He opened his thermos and poured Mikhail a cup of coffee and refilled his own. Without looking up, he asked in his gruff voice, "Did you sell out to the Company?"

Katya stood up, "I need to check on Anna. It's about time for her to get up. I'll be right back."

Mikhail took a long drink of coffee, "I told him I'd think on it."

"When'll you move then?"

"I imagine it'll take about a week to load up and give away everything else."

George tapped his fingers on the side of his mug. "Lots of people are upset with ya. But then you already know that, I suppose."

Mikhail recalled times where George and Mikhail's dad sat in the same kitchen and talked about baseball, mining, World War I, the McQueen Club, and how lucky they were to live in McQueen. "I don't want it that way, George. But I don't blame nobody. Someday they'll understand why I'm doin' it. I'd never move if that open pit -"

"Bullshit! You'd move anyway. You ain't like the rest of us. We plan to fight em' to the end. Nobody understands your move now and never will! We'll never see you or your family again. But-"

Mikhail moved his chair away from the table. His voice started to break, "I need to do what's best for my family. Everybody else'll do what's best for themselves. My dad taught me that."

The chair he sat on slid away from the table. He waved his finger at Mikhail, "Don't never bring your father in on this argument. He'd hear nothin' about what you're doin'. You can bet your sweet ass he'd never cut and run."

"George! We're both losing our tempers here. I'm takin' a walk."

"That's it! Walk away! You're gettin' good at it."

Katya walked into the kitchen after she watched her dad slam the front door. "Is everything alright, George?"

He shook his head, picked up his thermos and cup, and went out the back door.

———•◦•———

In the Club Café in Hungry Horse, David ate dinner with Ted Hughes. Outside of work, it was the first time they saw each other since their Labor Day trip around Glacier Park. Hughes now had his new instructions and set up a meeting with David, himself, and the lead FBI agent in the Butte Federal Office.

After they finished their chocolate cake dessert, Hughes approached the subject, "Dave, I got something important to talk to you about. Real important." He praised himself for his selection of a quiet table in the corner near the kitchen away from the rest of the customers.

David wiped the corner of his mouth with the green paper napkin, "What, what'd ya mean?"

"I want you to meet somebody."

With a nervous laugh, David responded, "Who? Is she a beautiful blonde?"

Hughes moved a little closer. "You need to trust me on this one, Dave. It's for your own protection."

He contorted his face and formed a question, "Who do I need protection from?"

The waitress came by with more coffee. Hughes waved her off and then answered, "Let's leave it at that, okay. He wants to meet you at your trailer next Thursday after work. "Again, trust me Dave."

"Okay. Will you be there too?"

He waved his hand, "Oh ya. I'll be there too."

———

As it had done for the past ten years, the siren in the McQueen Firehall sounded the noon signal. The workers in the nearby Leonard Mine opened their lunch buckets by the sound of the siren. Some of the older men automatically matched the siren against their worn pocket watches as they sat down to eat their lunches. Kids raced home from playing in order to get their peanut butter and jam lunch.

Mikhail walked back into the living room of his house. Anna slowly turned in her chair at the kitchen table. She greeted him with a big smile as she set her glass of milk down in front of her. Her smile momentarily chased away the heavy burden of his angry words with George.

"Did ya save any food for me, Anna?"

"Yes, Papa. Mom made two big sandwiches for you." He washed his hands in the kitchen sink before he sat down next to her. "You have big hands, Papa."

"Big hands to eat big sandwiches." She smiled again and took a drink of milk. A milk moustache topped her lip as she carefully returned the glass. Mikhail laughed and said, "When did ya grow a moustache?"

"I don't have a moustache, Papa." He reached behind him and picked up a hand mirror from the counter near the sink. Anna giggled as she saw her image in the mirror. "Oh that's milk, Silly." She handed him the glass of milk. "Your turn, Papa. Make a moustache." He looked around to make sure that no one else was watching. Slowly he brought the glass up to his mouth and created a huge white moustache. Anna clapped her hands together and laughed.

The happy noise in the kitchen brought Katya out from her

bedroom. She hauled a load of freshly folded clothes with her. "What in the world is goin' on out here?"

Mikhail wiped his mouth with his shirt sleeve but not before his daughter enjoyed the white moustache too. What a change of mood from his early morning visit with George Maletta.

"I can't leave you two alone for a minute without you gettin' into some kind of trouble." Anna laughed again and then secured her oxygen mask to help her breathing. Mikhail picked up one of his salami sandwiches and took a bite.

— • ‹ • —

After lunch, Anna laid down in her bedroom for her required afternoon nap. She got stronger each day, and the naps revitalized her strength. Her walking improved with the use of a walker, but the effort sapped her energy. Each walk got a little longer, and she stopped less frequently.

In the kitchen, Katya and Mikhail sat at the table and listed the household items that would make the trip to Columbia Falls, which items went to the dump, and which items went to the Salvation Army or neighbors. "I think we can get new furniture in Columbia Falls. I got enough put away to pay for what we need to get started. Our stuff here is pretty old anyways."

"What about the beds and dressers and those things?"

"Same thing. We'll replace em'."

Katya sipped on her black tea, "How about the dishes, pots and pans, and kitchen stuff?"

"I think we pack all that and take it with us."

The black wall telephone rang and interrupted them. Katya listened and then handed the phone to her father. "Hello."

"Hello, Mik. This is Jim Bugni. A few of us would like to try and talk you out' a movin'. Can you come down to the McQueen Club later today?"

Mikhail paused before answering, "Ya, I'll see yous at 2:30." He hung up the telephone and looked across the table at his daughter. "I'm goin' to visit with my friends at the McQueen Club. I'm sure it'll be more of what we had with George this mornin'."

"Oh Daddy, I'm so sorry you have to go through this. We can

still get out of it if you want."

His face contorted into a scowl, "Don't you wanna go to Columbia Falls?"

"All I want is for us to be together. I was just tryin' to take the easy way."

"There ain't no easy way! We jump in with both feet. Only way I know how." He took a deep breath. "Sorry, Katya. I'm just nervous about-"

"It'll be for the best. I'll work on the list some more, and tomorrow we can start gettin' ready to move." She got up and walked over and hugged him. "We'll do it together, Daddy."

Mikhail checked out the cars parked outside of the McQueen Club. Four of the cars belonged to long-time friends and neighbors. He didn't recognize the new two-toned beige Desoto. After he sucked in some fresh air, he stood as tall as he could and walked in. Five older men and one well-dressed man in his late twenties sat at a table drinking coffee. He nodded to each one of them and headed for the only vacant wooden seat. Jim Bugni smiled and said, "Want some coffee, Mik?"

"Ya."

The younger man stood and introduced himself, "Mr. Anzich, you might not remember me, but I'm Frank Micholotti. I used to deliver papers to your house as a kid. My dad is that old geezer sitting over there." The rest of the men laughed, and some of the tension snapped from the room.

Mikhail firmly shook his hand and forced a weak smile. "Sure I remember you, Frankie. It's been a long time. Where you livin' now a days?"

The younger man released Mikhail's hand and took a step back, "I moved back to Butte this summer after I finished medical school. I opened up a new clinic up on West Broadway. My wife and I and baby live in my in-laws' old house. They moved to Nevada and gave us the family home."

"Your dad told me you become a doctor. Good for you, Frankie. Butte can use good doctors." He nodded his head and slowly took his seat. Jim Bugni set the coffee cup down in front of Mikhail and took his own seat across the table.

Mikhail envisioned a meeting something like this for months. The time to face the music arrived. He set his coffee cup back down after a sip of the freshly made coffee.

His neighbor George Maletta sat with his arms folded and his eyes glued to the table. It was obvious George filled in the rest of the men about their argument from the morning. Jim Bugni spoke first, "Mik, we're all old friends here. How about tellin' us about your plan to sell your place and move to Columbia Falls?"

Mikhail felt the perspiration drip down the sides of his body below his armpits. The task at hand outweighed any of his visualizations. His mouth went dry. He took another drink of coffee. Talking wasn't his strong suit. "Relax, Mikhail, relax. Take your time; you've practiced it a thousand times."

"I need to move my family to Columbia Falls. There's a good job waitin' for me there. Should last for ten or fifteen years. I put money down on a new house. My daughter and granddaughter will live with me. After my son gets back from the Navy, he might join us. I need to sell my house to pay for-"

George Maletta interrupted him, "You got that here, too! You don't need to go to no goddamn Columbia Falls."

Bugni stepped in, "Come on, George. Take it easy. Let's hear him out."

After a deep breath and some needed self-talk, Mikhail continued, "If I sell my house now, I can pay for my house outright. Then I can put money away for my granddaughter to go to college like young Frankie over there."

The older Micholotti cleared his throat and spoke in a low-tone husky voice, "Did you already sell to the Company?"

George Maletta pushed his chair closer to the table and leaned toward Mikhail, "Of course he sold out. He don't give a shit about us no more." His red face and neck stood out beneath his silver hair. His whole body shook as he waved his finger at Mikhail.

Again Bugni attempted to calm down Maletta, "Jesus, George. Let him answer the questions. Maybe this is too much for you to handle. You look like you're gonna have a stroke."

"Ya, well maybe it's too much for me. I'm not goin' sit here and listen to his bullshit!" He pushed his chair away from the table and left.

Bugni brought the focus back to Mikhail, "Go ahead and finish Mik. Mitch asked you if you already sold to the Company."

Sweat soaked his back and his stomach flipped over. He gulped and gathered himself, "Not yet. I got the papers. Harbold's comin' back tomorrow."

Bugni shook his head, "How can you leave us here Mik? If we stick together, the Company can't buy us out. We need to stay solid. Besides, that open-pit might be just talk anyways. Even if it went through, it would be years before it ever reached McQueen."

Mikhail lost composure. He stood up and raised his voice, "It's comin', Jimmy! No stoppin' it! Meaderville, McQueen, East Butte, Dublin Gulch, Anaconda Road are all goin'. I can't wait to see what's gonna happen. Maybe it'll be fifteen years. Maybe ten. Nobody knows. I hate to leave McQueen. But I gotta look out for my own. Now and down the road."

Frank Micholotti stood up and buttoned his tweed sport coat, "Mr. Anzich, would you sell your house to me?"

The room went silent. The men looked back and forth at each other. Mikhail sat back down in his undersized chair, "You'd buy my house, Frankie?"

The dark, good looking young man smiled as he spoke, "My wife and I've always loved your house. We've driven and walked by a dozen times since we got back in July. We've driven through your alley. You've taken such great care of your house."

Mikhail nervously tapped the table with his fingers, "Do you want to live in McQueen?"

"We love McQueen. We want our kids to go to Holy Savior School. We want them to play baseball on the Eastern Little League Field. We want them to go watch McQueen play in the Copper League at Clark Park. Our kids need to play on Sunflower Hill. And finally we want our kids to grow up next to their grandparents and become McQueen kids. Just like all of us got to do. We're family here. We take care of each other. Even if it's only for ten or fifteen years." Tears slowly rolled down his cheeks as he cast a look toward his father. "We have someone who wants to buy our house up on Excelsior right now. It'll bring more than you'll need to buy your house up in Columbia Falls."

His large knuckles rubbed the tears and snot from his nose and cheeks. Mikhail Anzich felt small compared to the young man who just brought tears to a salty group of men. He stood up, extended his hand to Frank Micholotti, and said, "I'd sell my house to you, Frankie. To hell with the Company."

CHAPTER TWENTY-EIGHT

His birthday rolled in unannounced and passed without any celebration. September 21st went down as just another day in September for David Sednick. Quick memories of birthdays past flashed before him. His mother used to make his favorite dinner and birthday cake. Just three years earlier, his wife Kat surprised him with a babysitter and plans to go out for the night.

David set his dirty work clothes on the floor in his bathroom. He stepped into the tub, slid down into the hot water that he drew for himself, and closed his eyes. *Time for me to soak and relax.* It was time to clean up, go have a couple of drinks at the Dew Drop, and meet Ted Hughes back at his trailer at six. His mind wandered back to his conversation with Hughes at the Club Café. Ted's serious words and face appeared in David's mind. "I want you to meet someone. Trust me."

David continued to soak and think. "What's with all the mystery? For my own protection? What the hell's he talkin' about?" He checked his alarm clock and figured he had an hour and a half before meeting Ted. "I'll feel better after talking to Jackie. She's my kind of woman. Sexy, listens to me, and she likes to drink. She doesn't pressure me. Never wants anything from me. She only wants to have fun."

At the Glacier Inn in Columbia Falls, Ted Hughes sat in the easy chair in Agent Moore's motel room. He proudly briefed his partner of his progress with David Sednick. "I think he'll roll today if we do it right. The tough part will be for me to break the news that I work for the Bureau."

"You're right there, Ted. I thought about that on the drive up from Butte. Sednick most likely will spook after he sees you in that suit. We might have to block the door so he doesn't try and run."

Hughes ran his hand back and forth through his short crew cut and adjusted his black horned-rim glasses, "I think I'll tell him that his life's in danger and that we're his only chance to stay alive. I don't think we have to go into too much detail about the past murders or that."

Moore adjusted the papers carefully placed on the round table. He moved the table lamp closer to see the papers. "What's the best way to get him talking about his large bank account? How do we get him to talk about the man in charge? We need to find that out if we're going to find out who killed the other two walking bosses. I'm pretty sure the head man hired the men killed."

Ted Hughes unfolded the bank statements and copies of Sednick's income tax forms from the previous three years, "We might just as well show him the copies of his bank statements and income tax forms. He'll have to explain that somehow. Might be a good place to start. That should shake him up some."

Moore stood up and looked out the window. The top of Columbia Mountain showed some sign of light snow from the night before. Still looking out the window he spoke, "It might be too much too fast. We don't want to lose him."

"Maybe you're right. But we can't waste too much time. Hungry Horse Dam will be finished in a couple of weeks. Something tells me we need to get it done in the next couple of days."

She smiled in her favorite sexy way as David sidled up to the barstool at the Dew Drop. Jackie set him up with the usual. She inhaled the scent of his Old Spice aftershave. "So, you lookin' to get yourself screwed tonight or something?"

He tossed back the shot of Jim Beam and shook his head as the taste burned his throat. David moved closer to her and whispered, "I might be. You offerin'?"

She leaned her large chest forward, raised her eyebrows, and whispered back, "Bet your sweet ass I am, honey. I'm off in about fifteen minutes. You interested?"

Thoughts of his prior commitment with Ted Hughes shot to the front of his brain. The back of his right hand felt the weight of her soft chest as she pressed against the surface of the bar. "Oh ya. I'm very interested. Fifteen minutes ya say."

Jackie stood up, winked and mouthed the words, "Fifteen minutes."

"He's not going to show, Ted. You said 6:00 and it's 7:15. Something's wrong. I hope we're not too late. I don't have a good feeling about this."

Ted Hughes looked at his wristwatch, "Let's give him twenty more minutes. Maybe he just forgot about it."

"Hey, you reminded him at work today."

The two agents stretched in the front seat of the blue 1951 Ford sedan like they had done many times before in waiting for one person or another. Both men drifted away in their own thoughts. Ted Hughes stole a quick memory where he sat in his own living room and enjoyed a pleasant conversation with his wife. She found a way to switch his attention away from work. Her peaceful view of life allowed him to drift away to pleasant topics of discussion. Somehow she managed to take him away from criminals and sadness to places where he thrived. More than once she allowed him to become his real self. With her, his sense of humor came out of the closet. He craved her and the security blanket she wrapped around him in their small little home with the great view of the Highlands south of Butte.

Twenty minutes later his partner dropped him off in front of his trailer. "Well, Ted. How about calling me around noon tomorrow after you talk to Sednick? We can set up something again. I have to return to the Butte office in two days. So we're under the gun a little bit here.

"Okay. I'll find out what happened and call you at noon." He hurried into his trailer and called his wife.

———·—·———

She rolled over in bed and crossed her right leg over his middle. He woke from a restless sleep. David grumbled something and moved her bare leg from his thigh. He realized he had to pee. After he hustled into the bathroom, he closed the door and flipped on the light switch. He cast a blurry look into her sink mirror. The bags under his eyes forced him to blink. He looked again. "Who was this worn out drunk looking back at him?" He finished peeing, put the toilet seat back down, and stepped over to the sink. After he splashed some cold water on his face, the thought of the missed meeting with his friend Ted popped into his sluggish mind. "Hell with it," he thought and returned to bed. Jackie welcomed him back to her bed and snuggled him close. Before falling back to sleep, he told himself, "I'll deal with Ted tomorrow. Can't be that important anyway."

≈ Chapter Twenty-Nine ≈

As Mikhail steered the loaded van into downtown Columbia Falls, he savored the goodbye events as he prepared to leave McQueen five hours earlier. His neighbors showed up and quietly helped him load the items needed to begin his family's new life in Columbia Falls. He planned to return to McQueen in October to pick up the remainder of personal items stored in George Maletta's garage. The last person to say goodbye was Maletta. He handed Mikhail a new thermos full of his best coffee for the trip. They didn't exchange any words. The gesture, handshake, and brief eye contact said it all. One neighbor at a time kissed and hugged Anna and Katya. They shook hands with Mikhail and wished him well. As he glanced in the side view mirror of the panel van, he saw Frank Micholotti move his first box of belongings into the only home Mikhail had ever known. The neighbors joined the young doctor and his wife as they moved into a spotless house with freshly painted walls. Life moved on in McQueen. The Anaconda Company needed to wait awhile for the Anzich home.

Mikhail rounded the corner and entered Columbia Drive. He drove the two blocks to their new home. Immediately he noticed the small gathering of people in his driveway. As he neared his new house, he spotted Hannah and a few other women talking and laughing with John Nolan and Tomas. He drew the van to a stop. Nolan sauntered toward him. As usual he cupped a can of beer. "Did you carry the goddamn thing on your back? I could've pushed that van here faster than you drove. I knew I should've gone. You'd queer trade in a post office." Nolan looked around and appreciated the laughter that followed his verbal punishment of his favorite target.

The last thing in the world Mikhail wanted was a big scene when they moved in. He wasn't going to be allowed to quietly move in his daughter and Anna. He pushed open the heavy door and walked around the back to help unload Anna and her equipment.

Tomas beat him to the back of the van and opened the twin doors. Anna smiled as Tomas gently lifted her from her cocoon formed from pillows and blankets. "Hi, Butterfly. Welcome to your new house."

"Where's my room, Uncle?"

Tomas carried her up the sidewalk and talked as they neared the front door. "I'll show you. I decorated it special for you. You wanted snakes and bugs on the wall didn't you?"

She prepared to scream and noticed the broad smile break over his unshaven face. "Uncle, I'm scared of snakes."

After he entered the living room, he set her down and softly reached for her tiny hand. With the use of her walker, they walked into her room. Wallpaper with yellow butterflies covered one wall of her bedroom. "What do you think?"

Her smile answered his question. She pushed her walker over to the wall and touched one of the butterflies. Tomas knelt down near the door and watched her slowly examine her new bed, dresser, table and lamp, and a red box for her dolls. Thoughts of leaving to go to the Navy tugged hard at him as he saw her place her tiny fingers on the new record player. She looked back at him and giggled. How could he ever leave her? How would he leave this new life they all were about to begin?

Nolan broke his painful line of thought. "I painted them butterflies on the wall for you, little girl."

Tomas rolled his eyes and pointed up at Nolan. She laughed before she said, "Uncle did it."

"The only thing he can paint is his toe nails. Did he show em' to ya?"

She gasped and looked toward Tomas before she asked, "You painted your toenails?"

Tomas smirked, "No. But I did paint his toenails before he put on his dress last night."

"I'm rubbin' off on you Kid. Too bad you ain't as good-lookin' as me. That Bohunk nose is gonna grow with all them lies."

They heard Katya noisily take the tour of their new home. "Oh this kitchen is so big! Look at the room in the cabinets! And the counter tops. I've died and gone to heaven." Mikhail followed and proudly pointed out the new stove and sink. He snuck a glace at Hannah as she hovered in the background. She and her friends cleaned the house before Mikhail arrived.

Bud and Sara Reynolds joined them in the kitchen and announced that dinner was ready across the street. Mikhail nodded his approval even though he and Katya finished the last of the McQueen prepared food about an hour earlier.

———•••———

Across town, Roy Devers checked into the Glacier Inn. He looked at the Burma Shave calendar behind the clerk's desk. September 22nd. The next day, Hansen planned to point out David Sednick. They scheduled their meeting for 11:00 at the Club Café in Martin City. He'd get there early and order his lunch before Slick Hansen and Sednick sat down at their table. Devers unloaded his suitcase and rifle in the motel room and moved his car across from the parking spaces. No sense in taking any chances of somebody opening their door against his car. From his motel window he'd watch his car and keep nosy kids from poking around. He checked his gold watch and noted the sun sunk below the mountains. Later he'd walk to the Paul Bunyon and eat a steak. The waitress bragged a few weeks ago about their steaks. I'd rather be sitting down to a decent meal in Seattle. These people don't know anything about good food.

Before they went to sleep that night, Mikhail and Katya made plans to go into Kalispell the next day to shop for more furniture and beds. The borrowed bed from Bud barely held Mikhail's weight. Somehow he knew it wouldn't matter. He and his daughter worked non-stop for six days getting ready to move. Countless trips to the dump and the Salvation Army stripped him of his energy. He'd sleep regardless.

Katya slept on an air mattress on the floor in Anna's room. The comforting sound of her daughter sleeping allowed peaceful thoughts to sneak into her tired brain. She dismissed earlier thoughts she had of David sleeping somewhere nearby. These upsetting thoughts fleeted in and out of her consciousness. In a few days, they'd meet and figure out the details of their upcoming divorce. She wanted custody and child support and that's it. She worried more about custody and visits. Faces of all the old neighbors in McQueen and the new friends that helped them move in shoved thoughts of David to the back of her mind. Soon she joined Anna in restful, delicious sleep.

The next day, he arrived at the Club Café at exactly 11:00. David rose early that morning and cleaned up better than he had for weeks. He enjoyed the feeling of his new blue dress shirt and black slacks. The beautiful morning encouraged him to enjoy the fresh start to the September 23rd morning. He stayed sober the night before and got to bed early. Today promised to put the nasty business behind him. After today, he'd be free to move about the day without worrying about getting caught. He waited for the well-dressed man and held the door for him. "Morning, David. You look good today."

As they made their way to a corner table, David responded to the unexpected compliment, "Thanks. I feel good today. Can't beat the weather, that's for sure."

The waitress poured coffee and told them she'd be back short-ly for their order. She sauntered across the room and stopped in front of Roy Devers. "Are you ready to order there, honey?"

Devers frowned at her and ordered the bacon and scrambled eggs. He held his cup up in front of her. She splashed some coffee as she poured, "Sorry, honey. I been up for awhile. I'll get a dishrag."

David sipped his luke-warm coffee and waited for the instruc-tions from Hansen. "Now David, today is the day you withdraw all of our cleaned money from those five savings accounts. Are you ready to wrap up this venture?"

He sighed a deep breath, "I'm ready. Just tell me how I'm to do it."

The waitress came back and took their breakfast orders. After she left, he leaned toward David and spoke in a low voice, "Here is how I need you to do this. Have each bank draft a cashier's check made out to me. Then you go to the post office in Columbia Falls and mail the checks in this envelope. It's all addressed and every-thing. So far so good?"

After he rubbed the side of his face he said, "What do I tell them about why yer name is on the checks?"

"That's a very good question, David. I knew you were a sharp guy the first time I talked to you. Tell them that you are sending the money to Palm Springs to your investor. Tell them you are going to be a partner in a new hotel down there. I am your investor."

"That's all there is to it?"

He straightened his dark blue tie and checked out his appear-ance in the reflection of the window that faced the street, "That's all there is to it. You have your commission in your own bank account, right?"

His stomach turned as he thought about the additional money he faked during June, July, and August, "Ya, I do. I got plans for it too."

"Knowing you, David, I just bet you do. Stop by my office this afternoon after you've mailed my letter. Be sure and bring me the receipt for the certified mail."

He knew it was close to being over. Relief from the pressure allowed David to front a real smile before he spoke, "I will. Should be around 2:00 or so. And thanks for lettin' me in on this deal. I squirreled away lots of money."

"That's good, David. Keep it all to yourself. Money laundering is a pretty serious crime. We could-"

"Oh, you don't have to tell me. I been worried for two years now. I'm leavin' the second week of October. Nobody'll ever see me again."

In a feminine sort of way, the man set his paper napkin on his lap and thought, "Yes, David. You are going away. And nobody will ever see you alive again."

Roy Devers stood at the cashier's desk. He looked around the café and gave a very subtle head nod to his employer. Now he knew his next victim. He'd drive back to Seattle in three days with the $2,500 from Hansen locked away in his glove box. The waitress accepted his money and flashed a painted smile as he turned away. Under her breath she whispered to a waiting customer, "Cheap bastard didn't leave me a tip."

Across the street, the two FBI agents sat in the blue Ford sedan. They followed David from his mobile home. The café door opened and David walked out. He walked down the boardwalk to his pickup and looked at an envelope. A big smile broke over his clean-shaven face. A few seconds later, David's breakfast partner emerged from the café and walked in the opposite direction. Hughes cursed himself for only bringing one car, "I knew we'd need both cars. One of us should follow the suit and the other stay with Sednick."

"Wait for that guy to come by. I'll get his license plate number. Sednick doesn't seem to be in any big hurry. You watch him, and I'll get the plate number." After the new green Dodge Coronet drove by, Moore jotted down his plate number. "I'll call this in to the office later and get them to put a trace on it. Sednick just pulled out, time to go."

From his viewpoint in the front seat of his car, Roy Devers watched the blue Ford follow Sednick. The passengers wore suits.

Devers slipped his Lincoln Capri into gear and followed a ways behind the Ford. "Everybody likes a parade," Devers thought. "Who are those guys anyway? Suits in this hick town? I better see what's what. If they get in my way, they'll get it too."

———·•·———

David felt giddy with relief when he walked out of the post office. He finished his work. "I'll drop off this mail receipt and then head straight up to the Dew Drop to celebrate. Five more days on the job and then I'm headin' out. I'll pay off what I owe on the property and then live the good life for a long time. The realtor told me I'd be able to sell the whole works for quite a profit." He placed his hand on his truck door handle. Agent Ted Hughes covered his hand before he opened his door. "What? What you doin', Ted?"

"You didn't show up for our meeting the other day. Let's go talk for a minute."

David shrugged free from Hughes, "I'm not goin' anywhere with you. I got plans. What you doin' in that suit, anyway?'

Moore joined them. "You best hear us out, Mr. Sednick."

"Who the hell are you? I don't know you! What's goin' on, Ted?"

Agent Moore put up his hands in front of his chest, "Mr. Sednick, we are FBI agents. Your life is in danger. We can protect you. But you need to cooperate with us."

"I ain't in no danger. What the hell you talkin' about?"

"Let's go someplace private. How about we follow you over to your trailer?"

David searched his brain for the right answer. He had to drop off the receipt for the certified mail. "I'll meet you there in twenty minutes. I gotta take care of something important first. I'll be there in twenty."

Ted Hughes moved closer to David Sednick, "Don't skip out on us again. Your life is in danger. We know what we're talking about."

———·•·———

The Lincoln Capri idled quietly as Roy Devers watched the encounter between the two men in suits and Sednick. He shook his head as the men argued. "They gotta be dicks. Something's up. I better give Hansen a heads up. Maybe I hit Sednick sooner than later." He watched his target drive away in his pickup. After a few minutes of talking it over the men drove away in their Ford in a different direction. "Now what the hell are they doin'? Maybe they got him mixed up with somebody else. I'll keep an eye on them. I can always find Sednick."

* * *

After he accepted the certified mail receipt, Hansen calmly spoke to David Sednick, "You look a little rough there, David. What's going on?"

The encounter with the two FBI agents rattled him to the core. "Oh, nothin'. I just been runnin' around hard for a few weeks and it's catchin' up to me."

"Now you'd tell me if there was something wrong, wouldn't you David? I mean, after all we're in this together. Be honest, what's bothering you?"

Nothing in his life experience prepared him for this moment. He felt trapped. More trapped than any other time in his life. Maybe the man in front of him was the one the FBI talked about. "Would he really kill me?" He cracked his knuckles a couple of times and rolled his head. Another bad headache started. He knew one thing for sure; he'd have to go it alone. "Like I said. I'm all in. I'll most likely take a couple of aspirin and take five."

David Sednick read like a dime store novel. Something happened from the time he left him at the café until now. "Okay David. You best go lie down for a while. I'm sure you'll feel better." They shook hands, and David hustled down the sidewalk and jumped into his truck. He pulled things out of his glove box until he found a bottle of aspirin. Without anything to wash them down, he swallowed four aspirin and drove away.

The blue Ford waited for him outside of his mobile home. He closed his eyes for a few seconds, closed his truck door, and walked to his trailer. The car door closed. David never turned to watch them follow him in. He left the front door opened, walked to the kitchen, and drained a large glass of water. When he turned around, the two FBI agents stood in his doorway. "Come on in. I'm all ears."

CHAPTER THIRTY

The next afternoon, Hannah knocked on Mikhail's door. Katya answered and invited her inside. "Come on in, Hannah. We're just finished puttin' the knickknacks here and there. We most likely threw away some good stuff and hung onto junk. Dad's hangin' the curtains in the living room. It's nice having somebody tall for jobs like that." She moved closer and whispered, "But he's all thumbs. Do me a favor. Take him away for a few days. He's drivin' me nuts. We been together entirely too much." After a good laugh together, they joined Mikhail in the living room.

Hannah walked in with her arms folded. Katya just gave her the opening she needed for their overnight trip to Whitefish. She quietly slipped up next to him. "I think tomorrow night will be fine for our trip to Whitefish."

The hammer banged his left thumb as he missed the bracket nail. He shook his throbbing thumb and set the hammer on the couch. "Did you say tomorrow?"

"Yes. What'd you think about that?"

"Well, I, I think so." The redness in his face matched the glow in his left thumb. "We're pert' near done here. Sure."

She unfolded her arms and smiled at the effect she had on him. "Pick me up around three, and we'll drive up to West Glacier and meet the 3:30 train for Whitefish. I'll call and make reservations at the Cadillac."

The flow of blood raced around his body like a racecar around the Butana Speedway in Butte. "Ah, I'll be there at three o'clock. It kinda snuck up on us didn't it?"

"Not really. It seems like it took forever to get here. I packed two weeks ago." She turned and slowly left the living room. On her way by Katya, she whispered, "Kat, you owe me one. I'm gettin' him out of your hair for at least twenty-four hours. He'll tell you all about it."

Katya hugged her and raised her arms in celebration. "Thank you," she whispered back.

Ted Hughes donned his carpenter's belt and walked to the carpenter's shack at the northwest corner of the Dam complex. Operation scaled down to dayshift and afternoon shift. With the downsizing, workers totaled less than two-hundred. The walk across the Dam roadway only lasted about ten minutes. Two days earlier, the day shift removed the footings for the roadway. The final concrete pours included the viewing walls and the elevator towers. Workers already dismantled the last footings and cleanup hit fast-forward. David met Hughes as he reached for the shack door handle. "Oh, hi Ted. We're gonna set the frames for tower two."

As the two men walked back across the Dam roadway, Ted spoke to a crew of electricians as they rolled up cable and excess wire. He moved closer to David, "Did you think over what we talked about last night?"

"Ya. I did. I'll talk to ya, but I need a good deal."

"If you tell us who's involved, the Bureau will guarantee a plea bargain agreement and your safety."

"Will I have to testify at court?"

Ted rearranged his heavy belt as they walked, "You'll have to testify. The money laundering is one thing, but the murder of those other two men is serious. You're our first lead. We'll make sure you're safe."

They reached the second tower and assessed the work to be done. "Ted, when will all of this take place?"

"My partner is in Kalispell right now. Our boss will arrive there in about an hour. We'll meet with you tomorrow at nine to take your statements. We'll have to get a judge to sign warrants for arrests. That might take a day. We most likely will pick up those involved in two days. I'll transport you to Butte right after that and put you up until the trial. We're only guessing but we think a pro has been hired to kill you. And if so, he's still out there with a contract."

He licked his chapped lips before he spoke, "That means today is my last shift on the Dam."

"That's right. I won't leave your sight until we meet them at nine."

"Well, I gotta meet my wife tomorrow afternoon to settle up with our divorce. Especially since I'll be most likely leavin' the next day."

Ted unloaded the two by fours from the truck and stacked them near the tower door, "Good idea. Maybe you can do that while we make the arrests. After that you'll be safe anyway. You'll need to square away your trailer."

The 25 X 52 Lieberman Gortz Spy Binoculars hung from his neck as Roy Devers pretended to observe the final stages of the completion of Hungry Horse Dam. A few minutes earlier, he zoomed in his binoculars on Hughes and David Sednick. Devers followed David the night before and witnessed the two FBI agents enter and exit David's mobile home. He followed Sednick to work and studied the conversation with Ted Hughes. His adrenaline flowed generously as he realized time drew near for him to perform. No doubt about it, Sednick talked to the police. Slick Hansen wanted the timetable moved up by one day. They argued. Devers convinced his employer that you can't hurry a safe kill. Too risky. They agreed to do Sednick in two days. In the meantime he'd get close to his target while Slick made a road trip to Spokane. After he killed Sednick, they'd meet at the Davenport in Spokane. "I might even buy Slick a drink or two before I sight him in too. Too many loose ends. We'll split company, but only one of us will eat dinner that night." He laughed and placed his treasured binoculars back into their brown leather case.

The twenty-five minute drive into Kalispell went by quickly. Neither man said much as Ted Hughes sped down Highway 2 West. As they neared the outskirts of Kalispell, David nervously reached for a couple of aspirin that he stashed in his shirt pocket. He swiveled his neck and searched for relief from his headache. The aspirin stuck in his throat and came back up. Agent Hughes looked over at him and said, "You might try and wash those down with some coffee. Help yourself to my thermos."

David swallowed the aspirin and coffee and struggled to compose himself, "Who all will be there this mornin'?"

"My boss, partner, and us. Most likely we'll have a tape recorder running. That's about it, David."

"I'll get immunity for my part, right?"

"That's what we promised. You'll have to give back any money you received as a commission."

David reveled in the fact that he'd get off without going to jail. But the thought of losing his stash sickened him. He congratulated himself for withdrawing the money from his bogas accounts. David squirreled that foxy money in the safe in the Dew Drop Inn with his friend Jackie. At least he had that to show for his trouble.

The meeting in the courtroom at the Flathead Court House in Kalispell took about an hour. After sworn in by the court recorder, David described in detail how he deposited the money into the bank accounts in Whitefish, Kalispell, and Columbia Falls. He carefully relayed the details of the most recent days with mailing the checks in an envelope to Palm Springs. He named the bank in Palm Springs and listed R.J. Hansen as the owner of that account. Finally David listed which banks and which savings accounts he just cleaned out. Agent Moore pushed the stop button on the tape recorder and the meeting ended.

As agreed, Katya met David in her lawyer's office on Main Street in Columbia Falls. David still wore the dress slacks and white shirt and tie that he wore with his business with the FBI. Agent Hughes waited outside the building in David's truck. Katya sat next to her lawyer and greeted David as he entered, "Hi David. How're you doin'?" She wondered about his attire and for a moment regretted going through with the divorce. "Was there anything more I could have done to save our marriage? Was it my fault for giving so much of myself to Anna?"

He sat down across the table and quietly spoke, "Hi, Kat. You look good. How's the new house doin'?"

"We're gettin' moved in alright. Lots more little things to take care of. But it's comin' along."

"How's Anna feelin'?"

She straightened up in her chair. She prayed David would not push for joint custody. She didn't want to have to drag up his terrible side in order to prevent him from seeing Anna on a regular basis. But she promised herself that she would if she had to. "Anna's doin' a whole lot better. We like her doctor up here."

Katya's lawyer cleared his throat, "Hmm, we best be getting down to it. First of all, Mr. Sednick, I'm John Longheart. Your wife wants to make this as easy as possible on everybody. She is asking for child support only. Everything else you own is yours. In return she is asking for full custody of your daughter. That is the long and short of it."

Hearing Kat referred to as his wife seemed so distant to him. Time took care of that. They hadn't been husband and wife for nearly a year, and before that things were very tenuous at best.

"I want it to be easy on all of us too. Especially for Anna. I think Kat should have complete custody for Anna. She's all the parent Anna has and will need."

Katya's heart nearly jumped out of her chest. "Thank you, David. Thank you so much."

"What is child support to cost? My job at the Dam ends

tomorrow, and I plan to leave the area."

The lawyer shuffled the papers in front of his desk and retrieved a pad that contained monthly figures of Anna's expenses. "According to the figures your wife finished for me, looks like your daughter will need just a little over a hundred dollars a month."

"What?" What expenses could she have? She'll live and eat free with her grandfather. I mean what costs are there?"

He cleared his throat again, "Medical costs will take the big bite of the cost. Your wife also wants to start putting away money for college. Then there is-"

"College? She's only five years old. I can't be in charge of her goin' to college! Her mother might think about gettin' a job if she wants Anna to go to college!"

Katya promised herself and her lawyer she'd keep quiet and contain herself. She tried, but her emotions won out. "David, I need to be home with her. I can't be off workin'. Maybe in a couple of years when she gets stronger, but not now. I'm only askin' for your help until she turns eighteen."

He stood up, slapped the table hard with his right hand, and yelled, "Eighteen! You expect me to pay a hundred bucks a month for the next thirteen years. Yer crazier than I thought."

This wasn't the first time an angry husband blew his top in one of these meetings. Longheart took control, "Mr. Sednick, I've been around awhile, and I'm pretty damn sure a judge would take a look at what your daughter and wife have gone through the last half a year and demand a whole lot more than what's being asked. You could have your monthly check sent directly to your wife. Or any savings or other accounts you might have could go to her. You're getting off easy."

David visualized his stash of money going up in flames. He sat back down and drummed his fingers on the table. "Okay. Okay. Hmmm. When would this start?"

"If we filed the papers tomorrow, we could most likely get a judge to decree within a couple of weeks. My best guess would be around the first of November."

He blinked his eyes as the headache blurred his vision and his thoughts. "Fine! I'll sign your paper there and be done with it!"

Katya battled hard to not give in and tell him to go to hell. Her lawyer warned her that many women do that and later learn to regret it. She bit her lip and fought back tears of anger and frustration. It would be over soon. Too many good things lie ahead for she and her family. David Sednick no longer existed. He didn't even ask to see Anna. His own flesh and blood. "Screw him," she screamed inside of her head. "Screw him!"

———•—•—•———

That night David attempted to play poker with the two FBI agents. The motel room they rented smelled of cigar smoke and onions from the hamburgers Agent Moore picked up for the three of them for dinner. From time to time, David craved a drink. He promised himself that tomorrow while they made their arrests, he'd make a break for Columbia Falls and get loaded. He already lied and told the agents he'd pack his trailer and that he'd be ready to leave the following day.

After the lights went out, David reviewed his meeting with the FBI and later with Kat and her big-mouthed lawyer. The terms of the child support ate at him. His plans to vacation for a few months just went out the window. Now he most likely needed to work just to pay the monthly child support. "If Kat'd get off her fat ass and work, I wouldn't have to pay so much. College? Who's she kidding? Anna would be lucky to graduate from high school." His stomach tossed as the heavy dose of aspirin nauseated him. The shitty burger and greasy fries didn't help either. It promised to be a long night for David Sednick.

☞ CHAPTER THIRTY-ONE ☜

At 3:15 the next afternoon, Hannah and Mikhail anxiously waited for the arrival of the Great Northern Streamliner. The depot agent informed the dozen or so waiting passengers that it would be only a few more minutes before the train arrived. Hannah identified events in her life as good or bad omens, and when the picture perfect autumn day showed such beautiful cooperation, she sensed that this planned adventure would be more than satisfactory. Wondering what Mikhail thought wasted time and energy.

Mikhail tried to enjoy the gentle breeze and peace offered by the weather, but feelings of doubt and inadequacy haunted him. His thoughts ticked off one by one when he imagined how the events of the next twenty-four hours would unfold. Wait for the train, get on the train, make small talk, get off the train in Whitefish, and eat a nice dinner at the Cadillac Hotel. This followed by feeling foolish as he approached what he wanted so badly to happen. He just didn't know how. At this juncture in his thoughts, he quickly returned to just get on the train.

Hannah's thoughts brought her back to recent conversations she shared with her mother. With lots of hugs, tears, and emotional overload, her mother helped Hannah come to grips with the fact that she suitably grieved for her deceased husband, and it was time to begin again. Her mother stated that however it played out, meeting a man and becoming happily involved was nothing to feel guilty about. "Hell," thought Hannah, "she even gave me her favorite sweater twin set to wear when the occasion presented itself."

And this was the occasion. The sound of the train engine interrupted each of them as the required triple horn blasts sounded as it crossed the intersection. They glanced at each other as if to say, "No turning back now."

Mikhail reached for Hannah's well-worn canvas satchel to assist her with boarding. This gentlemanly gesture was not lost on Hannah as she made direct eye contact, smiled, and said, "Thanks, Mikhail. Good move." Why did she always have to use the smile that caused him to melt when he felt most uncomfortable or out of place? It didn't help matters.

The weight of the satchel briefly caused Mikhail to speculate on the contents, but he knew better than to make any guesses and he certainly didn't ask. What he knew about women and overnight packing could fit into a small shot glass. He already felt embarrassed. He hadn't packed a thing. Not even clean shorts or socks. At least he had his wallet and felt somewhat manly with money to spend on this intriguing and very fascinating woman. The rendezvous in Whitefish had been her idea. He remembered that he agreed fairly quickly as long as she understood he paid.

Mikhail followed Hannah up the grated, metal steps and caught more than just glimpses of her behind as it swayed from side to side with each step. Why hadn't he noticed that before? As she proceeded down the narrow aisle way looking for two seats together, he observed that the sway was hidden when Hannah simply walked. He decided that they needed to find more steps in the future. Hannah located two seats and immediately claimed the window. "I get the window," she pronounced with her typically assertive tone when argument was out of the question.

Mikhail give Hannah her way when she used that particular voice because her requests were usually no big deal and simply part of her personality. He figured out, too, that if she looked out the window, he'd more easily take her into the safety of his own thoughts and not converse. He promptly did just that as Hannah sat back and gazed out the large glassed area. Quietly, Mikhail started with her attire, clothes he never saw before. Hannah wore a well cared for, pale pink sweater twin set that included a dainty silver fox fur collar and gray pearl buttons. Mikhail knew little of women's sweaters, but it crossed his mind that it might be cashmere.

Again, it was safe to wonder about Hannah. Flat out asking was dangerous. To match the twin set, Hannah chose a neatly pressed lightweight gray pleated wool skirt. He noticed the shear nylons and quickly averted his eyes from her legs and made the assumption that she surely had shoes on of some kind. He decided to check that out later.

As his gaze returned to above the little fur collar, he saw that face. The face that stopped him in his tracks several months ago. The face that seldom appeared confused or without thought. It was the face that for today showed hints of blush and perhaps a little mascara. She covered her lips with a peachy pink color. Right now that face looked more deeply in thought than he ever observed before. "What's on her mind? Is she having second thoughts? Did I already do something wrong just a few miles into the trip? Did I need my own satchel? Hell, I haven't done anything yet! How can she be having second thoughts? Take it easy you big mope!"

Hannah continued to take in the landscape as the train slowly picked up speed winding to Whitefish and the eventual shit canning of her past celibate-like life. She smiled to herself thinking about how much she loved this time of year. There was just a tinge of color coming to the trees, and the river rolled ever so low on its banks. From experience, she knew that one good frost and the trees would be the vibrant gold, red, and yellow shades of fall. Hannah never tired of the change in the larch trees, a species of evergreen that turned the most beautiful golden yellow in autumn and dropped its needles to cushion and protect the forest floor in winter.

She likened this change in the evergreen to a change in herself. Hannah planned to shed her needles of worn out grief and take on different hues of happiness. With Mikhail, she hoped to cushion her heart from the pain of loneliness and find protection from future winters. She'd do this with class and knew that Mikhail required mental patience, physical guidance, and verbal instructions from her. Hannah grinned slightly and had long ago concluded that if characters in her romance novels and those from her theater's silver screen could find pure, unadulterated pleasure in the body of the opposite sex, so could she. She promised herself to not let history repeat itself in this department. Hannah quit looking out the window and faced Mikhail as best she could while sitting side by side.

"Hey, Mikhail Anzich. What's goin' on in that genius mind of yours? For your sake, I hope it's nothin' to do with pulleys, cement, or big buckets that have no business being suspended hundreds of feet above the earth."

"No."

"Do your thoughts have anything to do with your crews, emergencies, and whether the proper people are on shift to handle them?"

"No."

"Okay, Mr. Open Book, what are you thinkin' about?" quipped Hannah.

"Shoes and socks."

"What?" Hannah questioned a bit too loudly.

"I wondered if your shoes were gray like your skirt or pink like your sweater. I think I gotta buy socks when we get to Whitefish."

"And shorts," he silently said to himself.

"We're finally going away to be alone and learn more about each other and you're thinkin' about my shoes and your own under clothing. You know, Mikhail, you just might be the most romantic man I know," joked Hannah.

Mikhail sort of liked the shoes and socks routine. Two could play at her very fun and stimulating games. He thought maybe he was one up but then Hannah removed the cardigan sweater from the twin set to reveal toned, tanned, and soft looking arms. Her Lion Lake fishing trips and physically encouraging, unsavory patrons from her theater left their mark leaving her upper torso muscular in a feminine sort of way. She tucked in the matching, pale pink sleeveless camisole showing her waist, the waist Mikhail craved to put his hands on.

The Great Northern Streamliner continued on course to

Whitefish. The sound of the engine and the clikety-clack of movement across the tracks put many passengers to sleep. Once again, Mikhail and Hannah seemed lost in their own thoughts, but the tension between them was apparent and exciting. As the train whistle sounded three times near the Christmas tree farm that Hannah recognized, she knew they would soon be coming into town. As if willed by her thoughts, she felt the train lose speed and she glanced over at Mikhail. They smiled simultaneously and instinctually reached for each other's hand. His hand nearly swallowed hers, but he gently gave it a squeeze. She immediately felt safe and cared for. The train came to a slow and calculated, brakes screeching halt. Mikhail reached for Hannah's satchel, glad to be useful, and gestured that he would follow her to the exit. At the exit, he asked her to wait while he went down the stairs first. At the bottom, he turned and reached up to offer his hand to guide her safe descent.

As she took the second step, he boldly stated, "Pink suits you."

"Funny you should say that. That's kind of what my mother said when she loaned me her favorite cashmere sweater duo."

"Kind of, what's that mean?".

"Well, ya," answered Hannah. "Actually my mother told me that it was the color that made my dad's heart flutter and his putter stutter."

"Hannah, you make me nervous like I've never known before. That there smile of yours most likely melts glaciers in Glacier Park."

Mikhail's soft voice and utter vulnerability gave Hannah pause. Right then and there, she knew she didn't make a mistake. This would be the night of all nights for her. She'd let up on him, but only some.

"Mikhail, let's check in and take a walk. It's too early to eat."

"Okay."

Hannah and Mikhail casually made their way the few blocks to the Cadillac Hotel and Restaurant. It was easy to look down Whitefish's main street and see that this was a quaint western town with a history to tell. The Cadillac stood out from the other buildings because it had multiple floors unlike the other weathered storefronts that lined the pot-holed street.

Initially, people called Whitefish by the name of Stumptown. Before the arrival of the railroad and people, the area around Whitefish was heavily wooded. To make room for a town site, a huge number of trees had to be cut down, all of which left stumps behind. These stumps created problems almost immediately in the form of creating traffic problems and making it a pain for new additional construction as all of the stumps had to be removed.

The name of Stumptown didn't stick. The first buildings were all built around the railroad. The railroad became one of the towns' biggest employers. Once the railroad came, Whitefish grew quickly. The influx of railroad workers, loggers, and trappers combined to give Whitefish a solid foundation that was unlike the boom and bust mining towns that died off once the gold ran out.

Mikhail and Hannah entered the main doors of the Cadillac and shyly made their way to the check-in desk.

The desk clerk greeted them with a big smile as they approached, "Good afternoon, folks. Beautiful day, isn't it? Need to appreciate days like these; snow could come anytime now. May I help you?"

Mikhail swallowed hard hearing the word, folks. Did they already look like a couple to everybody else?

"Yes," answered Hannah in an uncharacteristically timid voice. "We have a reservation for tonight and just wanted to check in and drop off this satchel."

"What's the name on the reservation?" The clerk sensed a bit of uneasiness with his current customers and then asked Hannah, "Do I know you?"

"Mikhail Anzich," stated Hannah more boldly while deliberately ignoring the clerk's question. Her volunteer work in Hungry Horse often made her face more recognizable than her name. She generally didn't enjoy this.

It pleased Mikhail that she had made the reservation in his name. It seemed more appropriate even though he felt pretty certain that his mother wouldn't be proud of this rendezvous that he found himself as an actor. To become part of the conversation and not just a giant fixture, Mikhail inquired if they needed dinner reservations for tonight. The friendly clerk indicated that he thought that would be a good idea, and he would oblige as soon as he finished up with the paper work.

"Check out is at 11:00 AM. Did you want to pay now or then? We prefer now so no one skips out on us, but you two look as honest as the day is long so it's up to you." The clerk chuckled a little sensing that Mikhail and Hannah weren't legally bound by a wedding license. The hotel owner already warned him to keep his jokes and jabs to himself, so he left it at that.

"I'll pay now," answered Mikhail with a firm tone. "Now about those dinner reservations. We're celebratin' a special event. We'd like a table for two in a quiet section of the dinin' room. Can ya do that?"

"Oh, yes sir! I'll let the hostess know right away. Would you like to look at a menu?"

"Not really," they answered in unison.

"We'd like the table ready at 6:00 PM," ordered Mikhail.

"However," added Hannah, "We'd like to store our satchel behind your counter while we stretch our legs in your fair town. The train ride is short, but we'd love to take a walk. The key, please."

The clerk quickly handed over the key and gestured to the staircase leading up to the rooms. Now, that's a staircase to appreciate thought Mikhail. I will definitely let her walk up first! They exited through the heavy, dark, oak doors and headed south into town. The laughter exploded from them as they reviewed their encounter with the clerk who demonstrated such haughty self-importance.

"And," voiced Hannah, "what is the special event we are celebratin'?"

"It's my mother's birthday in a couple of weeks, Hannah. She'd like it that I celebrated early with you!"

"She must be a lot more easy goin' than you, Mikhail Anzich. I'll be sure and let her know what a great time we had."

It pleased Mikhail that Hannah used the words, great time. Little by little, he relaxed and knew that Hannah showed kindness as they both maneuvered through this rather awkward interlude in their private get-away.

They casually walked down the rest of Main Street. Mikhail stopped outside of the barbershop and straddled the penny horse ride outside of the front door. Hannah slipped in a penny and laughed as the horse rocked back and forth under Mikhail. His legs cleared the machine as he mocked the action of a rodeo rider. They agreed that more than one parent bribed their young son with a ride on the horse after he braved the first haircut activity.

The outing did both of them good. With the fresh early evening air and a fine walk, each felt a renewed calm and self-assurance for the evening ahead. The clerk helped another customer as they returned from window-shopping and the numerous informal encounters they ran into with the well-meaning townspeople. Mikhail's size generally drew attention and strangers naturally looked at him. Mikhail knew exactly how to be genuinely friendly while communicating the message that he didn't want to share his life's story. Hannah took the opportunity to observe a new side of him. She liked this side a lot.

Hannah watched as Mikhail assertively reached behind the hotel counter and hefted her satchel like it weighed nothing at all. She pulled the key from her purse while Mikhail gestured that he would follow her up the stairs. Mikhail began to eagerly realize that she didn't intimidate him as she slowly ascended the stairs. Hannah didn't know how much he savored the naturally feminine sway from right to left. He enjoyed that there were so many stairs to the second floor where they would find the room waiting.

At the top, Hannah glanced back and caught Mikhail with his eyes rather low on her body. She then deliberately looked forward and noted the brass plaque showing that room numbers two through eight were down the hall to the right. She held the key to room number six and headed in the correct direction. Boldly she inserted the key into the ornate lock and entered first. She opened the door wider, and Mikhail followed. The rather little bed loomed before them with a nightstand and lamp on one side and an oak rocker opposite. Near the window that faced the main street, she noticed a sitting area with a round three-legged table and two straight back chairs. The bedspread, window curtains, wallpaper, and any other available surface were covered in various flowered prints of pastel hues.

"Glad you didn't give me flowers to celebrate our special event," stated Hannah in her deadpan voice. "I think we have plenty."

In an uncharacteristic move, Mikhail slowly made his way across the room to stand directly in front of her. He gently laid his hands on her waist and pulled her towards him. Mikhail lowered his face. Hannah looked up and raised herself on tiptoes. Their eyes locked briefly and then closed as mouths met with a long and passionate kiss. The easy and natural meeting of their bodies that were so different in stature surprised them. He felt her soft breasts through her sweater and she noted an emerging hardness through his jeans. They remained embraced for several minutes after the kiss ended.

"Let's eat. I'm starved." Those were the first words out of Mikhail's mouth after the kiss. "I can't make proper love to you on an empty stomach."

It slightly disappointed Hannah that the kiss didn't lead to more, but she quieted her feelings knowing that the whole night was ahead of them. Besides, she could use a bite to eat as well, and the restaurant had such a great local reputation.

"Great. Let me freshen up some. I'll just be a minute." Hannah went to the water closet that was part of the room. She congratulated herself on selecting the reservations based on not having to use a community facility down the hall. She came out smiling from ear to ear, grabbed Mikhail by the arm, and pulled him towards the door.

"We walk down the stairs together, Mikhail Anzich. No ogling my bum on the way down!"

<hr />

The afternoon light roared through her dining room window. With less than a week left of September, signs of the coming sunlight changes warmed the window plants she cherished. Betty Hansen intently listened to the telephone conversation with her husband. She jumped as the knock on her door resonated off the hardwood floor in her living room. "I got to go, there's someone at the door."

The voice on the other end finished his message abruptly, "Well, that's it then. You can draw money from that account as needed. My lawyer will mail you the divorce papers next week.

Goodbye, Betty. Good luck to you."

She gently set the phone receiver back on the wall hook. His unexpected words lingered in the air as she shook her head. Another loud knock on her front door broke the stunned stare at the telephone. Betty Hansen walked to the front door. Still dazed, she opened the door and greeted the three men standing in her doorway. Her eyes moved up and down the men wearing the pressed suits in front of her. "Yes, may I help you?"

He looked her straight in the eyes, "We are FBI agents. My name is Ted Hughes and these are Agents Moore and Taylor. We have an arrest warrant for your husband, R.J. Hansen. We also have a search warrant for your house. Is your husband here?"

Betty Hansen backed into her living room and sat down on the flower-patterned couch. "He isn't here right now. What's going on?" She reeled from the phone message her husband just delivered, and now the FBI stood in her living room. "I don't understand, what-"

Moore and Taylor strolled by her while Hughes spoke, "Where is your husband, Mrs. Hansen?"

She fidgeted with her fingers near her mouth, "He's gone."

"Apparently so. But where is he?"

Tears burst from her eyes as she struggled to answer, "Can't you tell me what's going on?"

The other agents opened desk drawers, cabinets, and looked under beds and in the closets. Agent Hughes moved and stood directly in front of her. "Mrs. Hansen, I can't tell you what's going on. Now where is he?"

She lowered her cupped hands from her mouth, "I, I just hung up the phone. He told me he filed for divorce. He's driving somewhere. He said goodbye and good luck."

Hughes determined he needed to turn up the heat. "If you shield him, or lie to us, we will arrest you. One last chance. Where is your husband?"

Betty Hansen stood up and raised her voice, "I don't know where he is! I'm in shock that he left. He went to work as usual this morning, and then-"

"We went to his office at the contractors. He never showed for work today. His assistant said he stayed home with a cold."

Moore joined them in the living room, "Nothing in the bedroom or kitchen, Ted. I'll check with Taylor."

She sat back down and wiped her nose with a used Kleenex, "I think I'm entitled to know what kind of trouble he's in."

He unbuttoned his suit jacket, "No. No you're not." He wrote down his name and the phone number at the Glacier Inn. "When you hear from him, call this number and ask for me. If you interfere in any way, you will be arrested."

His partners returned from searching the other rooms. "Nothing as far as records here. Let's go back to his business office at the contractors."

She watched the three men through the corner of her lace curtain. After they drove away from her curb, she picked up the phone and called Sheriff Patrick Schustrom.

———•••———

Agent Taylor drove Hughes back to the Glacier Inn Motel to check in on David Sednick. In the meantime, the other two agents planned to search Hansen's accounting files in his office. Taylor slowly pulled the blue Ford away from the motel parking lot but stopped suddenly as Hughes rushed out of their motel room and waved his arms. He ran to the back seat door and climbed in, "Sednick's gone! He took his bag with him and his truck isn't out in back where he parked it. That idiot! How the hell we suppose' to protect him? Now what do we do?"

Taylor spun the tires and shot gravel into the motel shrubs, "We go find him is what we do. I'll bet you he's headed for a bar back up the canyon. He isn't the smartest guy in the world. We'll find his truck."

———•••———

In Columbia Falls, David Sednick sat in the Stockman Bar and enjoyed the Jim Beam glow that he missed over the past few days. He flicked the long ash from his Pall Mall into the glass ashtray. He squinted as the smoke rolled past his eyes. From her barstool, the older blond lady used her eyes to flirt with him as her husband and his friend racked the pool balls for another game. Sednick flashed his patented barroom smile and seductively sipped his high-ball. Over the years he perfected the knack of seeing the eyes of husbands and communicating with the wives or girlfriends at the same time. She pushed her chair from the table and signaled to her husband she needed to pee. He ignored her and fired the cue ball into the tightly racked pool balls. On her way by Sednick, she lifted her eyebrows and tilted her head in the direction of the restrooms. David put out his cigarette, took a look at the pool players, and nonchalantly walked back to the restrooms.

Roy Devers sat in his car and took in the view of the alley behind the Stockman Bar. He watched the backdoor and David's black pickup. He praised Sednick for leaving the safety of the motel and the protection of the cops. This uncomplicated things. Now all he had to do was wait for dark and the perfect time to get his work done. Only a few hours now remained. Then on to Spokane and his final meeting with Slick Hansen.

The bright light in the hallway by the women's restroom became unkind to the blond lady. Her age and hard lifestyle gave away her true looks. She combed her hair with her long fingernails as David approached her. After a good look behind him, she sidled up to him and pressed her sagging chest against him. "I can meet back here at ten thirty when he goes to work. What do you say?"

"Sure, I'll be here. See you then." He walked into the bath-room and talked to the smoke-damaged mirror, "You bet old lady. I'll be here at ten." He laughed and relieved himself at the ciga-rette-filled urinal. After another Jim Beam highball, Sednick entered the dark alley and climbed into his truck. His watch read nine o'clock. The engine fired up and David adjusted his rear view mirror. Thoughts of his current life worked their way into drunken thoughts. "Maybe I'll run by and see my daughter. I gotta right to do that. Give her grandpa somethin' to think about. I'll be long gone tomorrow anyway. Ya, I'll go see my little girl."

Katya opened the front door, "David. What you doin' here? You're, you're drunk! You can't be here."

He slurred his words as he spoke, "Katt, I want to say goodbye to my little baby girl."

She blocked the doorway and stuttered as she searched for the right words, "Anna's been asleep for an hour. There's no-"

He forced his way into the front room, "I gotta right to see her. Let me see her." He elevated his voice, "Anna! Baby girl! It's your daddy."

With all her strength, Katya pushed him toward the opened door. "Get out, David! Come back tomorrow when you're sober. She can't remember you like this! Get out!" She continued to shove him. He tripped and fell awkwardly into the new table lamp and end table. The lamp crashed to the floor and the table collapsed under his weight. He struggled to stand up but fell back down on the splintered wood.

From the back bedroom Anna's sleepy voice penetrated the mayhem. "Mom, is that Daddy?"

Katya streaked toward her daughter's bedroom and stopped in the doorway; she gathered herself and breathlessly spoke, "No. Go back to sleep, sweetie. Everything's okay."

The wall near the door allowed David to regain his feet. He staggered toward Anna's bedroom and knocked over another new table lamp. David slurred his words as he spoke, "It's me. I'm here for you little girl. I love you so much. It's Daddy."

She closed the door to her daughter's bedroom. With three quick steps, Katya met David in the middle of the front room. "You ain't seein' her. Get out!"

He swung his right fist as hard as he could and punched her directly in the nose. Blood exploded from her broken and now disfigured nose. She went down hard on her left side and narrowly missed the edge of the coffee table.

The bedroom door squeaked opened. Anna stood in the doorway and clung to her Raggedy Ann doll. She started to breathe deeply as she looked at her mother lying unconscious on the floor. David swayed back and forth as he attempted to stand still. He slowly glanced back and forth between his daughter and his motionless wife lying on the floor.

From the open doorway to the outside, a booming voice broke the ugly scene, "What the hell's goin' on in here?" Bud Reynolds stood and held the dog leash in his hands. His playful golden retriever puppy pounced into the room. Bud stepped toward Katya as David brushed by him and fell down the step that led to the sidewalk. He managed to get to his feet and staggered to his truck. Bud used the wall phone and called the operator, "Get the ambulance over here right now. A woman is hurt bad." He waited for the operator's question and then answered, "1800 Columbia Drive. Send Doc Green too." He hung up the phone and went into the bathroom. Bud talked calmly to the crying and wheezing Anna as he returned with two towels, "It's going to be okay, honey! I'll take care of your mom. The doctor'll be here in just a minute. You best go put on your oxygen mask."

In the distance, he heard a faint siren. Katya moaned as Bud gently applied the corner of the towel to the front of her bleeding nose. Her eyes rolled as she felt the firm hand cradle her neck. Bud squeezed her nostril in an attempt to stop the flow of blood.

He looked up as he heard Anna crumble to the floor. Bud placed Katya's hand on the towel. He rushed to Anna, picked her up, and hurried into her bedroom. The night-light revealed the portable oxygen mask and tank. He gently laid her down on the bed and propped her pillow to support her head. The oxygen mask slipped on easily over her head. Bud pushed the white button on the tank and thanked God once the sound of air pushed through the tube into her mask. "Come on, honey. Breathe. Breathe." Anna coughed. Her face lost its blue hue. She coughed again and started to breathe. "Good girl. Easy does it now. Easy does it."

The siren roared louder. Through the bedroom window, Bud saw the blinking red lights. The siren stopped, and he heard the medics out in the living room. He smiled at Anna, patted her arm, and went to the living room. "This lady here most likely has a broken nose. The little girl back here is upset and back on the oxygen. Go slow with her. Her name is Anna. She's scared."

One of the medics knelt over Katya with his open first aid kit. He stuffed both of Katya's nostrils with cotton pads. With his support, she sat up and leaned against the front of the couch and laid her head back. Bud and the other medic went into the bedroom with Anna. Both of her hands squeezed her doll. Bud introduced the medic. "Honey, this man is kind of like a doctor. He's here to help. Okay."

After Dr. Green and the police left, Sara and Bud made coffee and prepared to stay the night. Dr. Green reset Katya's nose and gave her something for her pain. Bud called the quonset hut at the

Dam, "Ya Jack. Bud Reynolds."

"Hey Bud, what's goin' on?"

"Do me a favor. Tom Anzich is up top workin'. Probably near one of the towers. Will you get him to come home early? Just tell him to come to his sister's house. We had some trouble down here."

After Bud's friend Jack dropped him off at his dad's car at the quonset hut, Tomas drove to Columbia Falls and sprinted up the driveway and burst into the living room. Out of breath he spoke, "What happened? What's goin' on?" Bud and Sara sat on the couch with coffee cups in their hands.

"Take it easy. Everybody's okay, now. Sit down and I'll fill you in." Bud set his coffee cup down on the coffee table. "We had some trouble here a while ago. Your sister got a broken nose. And little Anna got pretty upset, but she's good now. Your-"

Tomas stood up again and started for the bedroom, "How did it happen? What-"

"Your brother-in-law came in here drunk and punched Kat. He-"

Tomas peeked in and saw the large bandage that covered his sister's nose. The front door opened and slammed in one swift movement. Tomas gunned the engine and spun the tires as he roared away from the curb. The 1949 Chevy peeled around the corner and into the main street of Columbia Falls. The words of the policeman in Butte after his fight at Clark Park jumped into his mind, "Be careful of that temper. You could hurt somebody sometime. You don't know your own strength." Tomas ground the gears as he hit third gear. He ran the red light near the Catholic Church and passed two cars a block later. He yelled as he swerved to miss a third car, "You're right. I'll hurt somebody sometime. Tonight! I'll hurt him real bad for what he did to Kat and Anna."

Roy Devers watched David park his pickup in the small pullout in the trees behind the Dew Drop Inn. A big smile came over his face as he watched his target stumble and fall as he walked the seventy-five yards to the back door of the Dew Drop Inn. "This is going to be so easy. I'll set up and drop him when he comes back to his truck. Drunken bastard." Devers found a small abandoned road in the trees. He parked his car and gloated over locating such a clear view of his target. The trunk opened with a solid click. He flapped the blanket back. The leather rifle case housed his rifle. From a wooden box he pulled out a small tripod and a box of 30/30 shells. Devers placed the tripod on a stump near the front of his car. He laid down the blanket and assumed the killing position. The scope focused on the front of David's pickup. "Now I'll wait. No wind. Nobody around. This will be like taking candy from a baby."

As Tomas roared through Berne Park on his way to Martin City, the FBI agents passed him going the opposite direction toward Columbia Falls. Agent Hughes commented on the speed of Tomas' car. "That guy's really flying. Probably doin' sixty miles per hour. I wonder if Sednick passed us too. We better find him in Columbia Falls or he won't see morning."

Moore agreed and increased his own speed. "He sure isn't in the Canyon anywhere. We checked every bar and Mabel's. He has to be back in Columbia Falls. We'll find him. For his sake I hope so."

After a quick sweep of the bars in Hungry Horse, Tomas continued up the Canyon to Martin City. He drove by all thirteen bars and slowly searched through the alleys behind each one. From there he roared up Sugar Hill and checked out the area near Mabel's. No sign of David's black pickup. And then Tomas remembered. "He's going to the Dew Drop to see his girlfriend." The five-mile drive seemed to take forever. His blind anger grew with each passing mile. The red lights of the Dew Drop sign came into view. Tomas slowed and turned into the parking lot. No sign of David's pickup. He circled around the front of the bar. Still no sign of the black Chevy truck. He impatiently tapped on the steering wheel.

His peripheral vision caught the sight of a man staggering

toward the trees. In the trees he spotted David's pickup. Tomas popped the clutch and fishtailed toward David. Gravel splashed up against a parked car. He slammed on the brakes in front of the Black Chevy pickup and jumped out. His brother-in-law attempted to stop as he neared Tomas. Tomas never said a word; he unleashed a powerful right hand that caught David on the side of his head. His feet stayed glued to the gravel while his dead weight sent him crashing face first toward the ground. The front of his head slammed the front bumper with a deafening thud. His neck snapped back and then in slow motion, his body crumbled to the gravel. His hands hung near his sides as his face met the ground and bounced twice.

Roy Devers rose up from his sitting shooting position. He scratched his head as he attempted to figure out what he just witnessed. What the hell? You just killed my target. Now what do you expect me to do? Devers returned to his sitting position and refocused his scope on the young man kneeling over his victim. The crosshairs lined up perfectly. He moved his index finger closer to the trigger and took a deep breath.

———•—•———

As requested, Mikhail and Hannah sat at a private table on the north wall of the restaurant. A convenient window provided them with a view of Big Mountain, an up and coming ski area for the adventurous of heart. Cloth napkins, real silverware, delicate wine glasses, and very fine china table settings covered the table.

Within minutes a waitress appeared and asked, "What can I get you folks to drink?" Folks again, thought Mikhail.

"Please, I'd like a draft beer, very cold, a glass of water without ice, and coffee, very hot with cream," answered Hannah.

"All at the same time?" came back a very puzzled waitress. Uh-huh."

"And you sir, what assortment of beverages would you like?"

"Just coffee."

The waitress left to fill the order and barely shook her head and muttered under her breath, "It takes all kinds."

He broke with a short laugh, "Do you usually order that many drinks at once?"

"Not usually, but then I usually don't have a handsome man, warm bed, and wild sex waiting for me after dinner either. Just trying to save time."

"O.K. then, you've got thirty seconds to decide. Here she comes."

After she shuffled the table decoration, salt, pepper, and the unnecessary wine glasses, the waitress found six places to set down the drinks. She was about to ask if they were ready to order or if they needed more time. "Can I -"

"We've decided. Can we order now?" interjected Mikhail before Hannah could even look at the menu. She shook her head yes and reached for her pad and pencil.

"What will it be, then?"

"I'd like grilled shrimp with wild rice," stated Hannah as she assumed every fancy food establishment had shrimp. "If I get a salad with that, please put bleu cheese dressing on the side. You have bleu cheese, right?"

Mikhail cleared his throat, "The chicken fried steak dinner is fine for me. Same on the salad."

Hannah and Mikhail struggled to disguise their laughter as the waitress looked at them more oddly than before. At this rate, drinks, dinner, and coffee will be concluded within an hour thought the waitress. She wondered what the tip would be, if any. They didn't look like the high rollers who frequently ate at the Cadillac.

They made the necessary small talk, appropriately commented on the good food, and anxiously anticipated the evening before them. Mikhail paid the bill and left a generous tip. He needed change but just didn't want to waste any more time in this environment when he really wanted the one upstairs.

The waitress reappeared and met them on the way out stating the obvious, "I guess you don't want dessert, huh?" They grinned knowing what was mentally planned for their desserts.

———•◆•———

After he returned his tripod and rifle to the trunk of his car,

Roy Devers walked over to the motionless body in the trees. A few minutes earlier, he watched the man who hit Sednick drag him into the trees. He saw no point in killing the young man. Sednick probably deserved it. Besides, no fee promised for killing anybody else. Devers checked the man's pulse and breathing. Accustomed to testing downed men for signs of life, he made a definite decision that the man on the ground was dead. The powerful punch probably knocked him out, but the pickup bumper broke his neck and made sure of the work. Devers calmly walked back to his car and prepared to drive away. What a beautiful night for a drive. In a matter of a few hours, I'll wait in the restaurant of the Davenport Hotel in Spokane. I'll enjoy a wonderful breakfast with Old Slick. He turned on the radio and once again cursed the static from the local station.

John Nolan sat at the bar in the Bucket of Blood. He munched on some beer nuts while he listened to the disjointed story his best new drinking buddy told him. Tomas walked the length of the bar and stopped behind Nolan. The image of Tomas in the bar mirror snapped Nolan from his mindless attention to the story about some lost dog. Nolan spun around and detected the apparent torture in Tomas' whitened face. "What's wrong, Kid? You look like shit."

His red and tear-swollen eyes bulged out from his colorless face. "I, I need your help. I, I-"

The sound of a silver dollar slapped on the bar top. "Good night lads. I'm off." Nolan slipped his arm under the elbow of his godson and they walked out of the bar. Once outside, he poised his face in front of Tomas and asked, "Tell me. What happened?"

"I killed David," he sobbed and walked around in small circles. He tore his hands through his sweat-soaked hair. "I killed David!"

"You what?"

Tomas leaned against his father's Chevy, "I hit him and he fell against the bumper. He's dead! I murdered him."

Nolan held out his hand, "Give me the keys, Tommy. He ain't dead. Most likely he's just knocked out. Take me to 'em."

On the drive back to the Dew Drop Inn, Tomas attempted to explain what happened. His incoherent words showed the cloudiness of his thoughts. Nolan screamed as he drove, "Goddamn it! I told you to stay away from him. You wouldn't listen would you? I hope you did kill the son of a bitch. Because if you didn't, I will. I should of done it years ago. Dirty bastard!"

Tomas guided Nolan across the abandoned parking lot into the trees where he laid David's body. "There. In the trees behind his truck."

Nolan bent down and checked David for any signs of life. He slowly returned to the car and paused before he spoke. He handed the keys to Tomas and calmly said, "Drive back to the barracks and stay there. I'll take care of him."

"But I should tell the police."

With both hands, Nolan grabbed Tomas firmly by the shirt, "Goddamn it! Do as I tell you! I'll take care of it. Don't say nothin' to nobody! Nobody. Not never. No matter what happens. Nobody, you follow!"

"What, what'll ya do with him? We gotta call the police! I killed him."

John Nolan closed his fist and slammed it into Tomas' chest. "Get in that fuckin' car and drive back to the barracks. Don't talk about it. Don't do nothin'!"

He cupped his hands on the unshaven face of his godson, Tommy. "You do as I tell you. I'll take care of all of this. Understand?"

Tomas hugged him and walked around to the driver's side of his father's car. His shaky fingers fumbled as he stuck the keys into the ignition. "Oh my God, what've I done? Oh God, please help me." The engine killed as he attempted to pull away from David's pickup. He opened the front door and vomited on the gravel. Tomas restarted the car and drove toward Martin City. His better sense told him to go to the sheriff, but the look in Nolan's eyes and his words drew him to follow his instructions. He parked the car behind the barracks and walked into his room and sat on the hard chair in the darkness.

CHAPTER THIRTY-TWO

"Thanks for dinner, Mikhail. You can trail me up the stairs, if you want. Have the time of your life. Then I get to do what I want."

The stirring in his groin revved up again. They quietly entered the room that felt a bit too warm. Hannah lifted the window a few inches. She gestured for Mikhail to join her at the round table even though the chairs were somewhat too little for someone of Mikhail's size. Hannah reached across the table to secure both of his hands and clung rather tightly. "Mikhail Anzich" she began, "I am not very experienced when it comes to sex. My fourteen-year marriage was pleasant enough but never what I would call exciting. For many years I imagined lovin' and bein' loved with a passion as deep as the reservoir you and your crews dammed up. I know it's possible. My romance novels and movie love stories tell me so."

Mikhail squirmed in his uncomfortable chair as Hannah continued talking about her sexual experience.

"Now's the time I would love for us to experiment and fully discover what our bodies are capable of givin' this time and this place. We'll love each other with abandon, but please be patient with your own body's need. Let's play with each other, enjoy our bodies, and imagine we are explorin' sex for the first time. Are you game, dear Mikhail?"

"Just tell me what to do, when to do it, and for how long, Hannah."

She breathed deeply, stood, and made her way over to her satchel. Hannah lifted it almost as easily as Mikhail had and put it on the bed. She reached in and pulled out a sleeveless, white, cotton nightie with pink lace trim. She rummaged a bit more and found a bottle filled with a liquid. Several candles also appeared from the satchel with a decorative box of matches. Hannah draped the nightie over the rocking chair and set the bottle, candles, and matches on the nightstand. Mikhail's curiosity peeked beyond belief, but he kept his mouth shut even though he wanted to voice his opinion that she could repack the nightgown. He had no idea what the little bottle had in it.

"Mikhail, I'm going to remove my clothes and think maybe you should do the same. The lighting seems pleasant but would you light a couple of the candles please? I like the mood they'll give to our evenin' together. I don't wish to cover myself. I've been modest all my life. It's time to try somethin' new. When you're ready, come and join me in bed."

He quickly put fire to the candles and worked to disguise his desire to rip off his clothes and leap across the room to the bed. He knew his below-the-belt buddy would physically give him away, but apparently Hannah was prepared for this. After he tossed his clothes in the chair where he sat, Mikhail gathered his courage and moved toward Hannah and the inviting bed. There was no way to camouflage his physical excitement. Hannah looked unfazed. She climbed onto the bed, plumped up the pillows, and left an obvious spot for Mikhail to join her. As he laid down next to her, she shifted her weight so that she was sitting Indian-style on his left side. Reaching back to the nightstand, Hannah grabbed the mysterious bottle, removed the lid, and poured several drops of an oil into her cupped, left palm. After she returned the opened bottle to its safe place, she vigorously rubbed her hands together and then gently rubbed the exotic smelling oil into his skin. Mikhail felt his body relax, but he couldn't close his eyes. What he imagined she would look like paled in comparison to the real thing. In his eyes, she was perfect.

Her hands continued to roam free, and with the silence, beautiful aromas, and sensual calm, Mikhail willed some of the blood to return to his brain. He knew his timing was an important issue on this special evening, and he most of all did not want to disappoint her.

"This is what I want you to do to me so try and pay attention, Mikhail," Hannah whispered. "I'm not done yet, though." He had no suitable reply.

Hannah secured another small palm of oil and moved to the foot of the bed. She shared the oil from her left hand with her right and touched his feet gently. Little by little, she moved her entire body up his strong, muscular legs into the insides of his thighs and lingered briefly with her hands. He felt her breasts skim the tops of his legs. Mikhail could no longer keep his eyes open and uttered, "I think I've died and gone to heaven."

Hannah whispered, "Our trip has just begun. Don't leave without me."

The blood flow went out of his control and Mikhail felt the hardness return with a vengeance. At the sight of his pleasure, she slowly took him into her hand and slid up and down. Simultaneously, she moved up and down on him alternating soft and deep pressure. She gently kissed the inside of his thighs. Hannah felt him respond uncontrollably but stopped short of his explosion. She let go and began retreating slowly to the foot of the bed repeating the massage on his legs as she went. "We sure have a big boy on our hands now don't we?"

"Long Steel."

Hannah stopped her hand motion and gasped, "Long Steel?"

"That's what Nolan calls it."

She laughed and shook her head before she said, "You guys from Butte got names for everything. You even name your thing."

"Is it my turn, Hannah? Can I do that to you? I want to touch your body like you done to me. Teach me."

"That would be the plan, Mikhail. Anything you want to do will please me. But Mikhail, you need to know that a woman can go more than once."

"Okay," uttered Mikhail with a voice full of concern. "Where do I start?"

"Just like I did. The oil's for both of us," encouraged Hannah.

Candlelight gave the room an interesting glow. Making untiring love and stimulating each other to the ends of the earth gave Hannah and Mikhail's bodies an even more interesting glow. Mikhail proved to be an attentive student turned lover who wanted to please her over and over and over again. With guidance he found the parts of her with his sensual mouth, tongue, and gentle fingers that resulted in the pleasure she sought for a lifetime. Mikhail was stunned to learn that giving her enjoyment was far more pleasurable in the short term than focusing on his own needs.

— • • —

John Nolan struggled as he wrestled David's limp and bloodied body into the passenger side of his pickup. Nolan managed to position the body forward and below the view of the windshield. After he closed the door from the inside, he climbed over to the driver's side with David's truck keys in his hands. "Shit!" he yelled as he noticed the dead man's coat stuck in the door. He reached across the front seat and attempted to open the door. After the door refused to open, he stepped outside and mumbled as he stomped around and opened the door. "Suffering bald-headed Christ! Nothing works around this cathouse outfit!" Nolan started the engine and pulled away from the trees and crossed the Dew Drop Inn parking lot. His pocket watch read five minutes after one in the morning.

David's limp arm dropped to the floor and startled Nolan. "Holy shit! What the hell was that?" He nervously squirted out a weak laugh. The empty highway greeted Nolan as he shifted into second gear. He reviewed the plan in his mind as he drove the six miles to the road that led to the Dam. The thought of using a blinker on the deserted highway amused him as the truck began the ascent up the now paved road. "No cars in sight," he thought. "Good. I'll get up pretty high before I turn around."

The headlights of a boss' pickup rounded the corner and pulled up behind him. Nolan pulled off and let him by. He raised his left arm and shielded his face as he looked down at David. For the first time since seeing him dead, Nolan realized the seriousness of what happened. Tomas killed him and now he'd cover it up or take the blame for his godson. "No way in hell the person I love most in the world will go down for this. I'm glad the son-of-a-bitch is dead. Just wished I did it. They'll never know the difference."

He stepped out and walked around to the passenger side and peed. As he looked up the road he identified his spot. "Perfect," he thought. "No guardrail and a straight drop off." Nolan got back in and drove past his spot and turned the pickup around. He wished for a drink to bolster his courage. His hand searched behind the seat. Nothing. Then he checked under the seat. His fingernails clanged on a half-empty bottle of Jim Beam. Nolan took a large swig and poured the rest all over David's body. He placed the empty bottle on the floor in front of him.

After a long look up and down the road, he turned off the headlights and the ignition. Nolan pulled David's body to the center of the front seat. He then walked around in front of the pickup and opened the passenger side. David's body slid easily on the red nylon seat covers. Nolan positioned the body directly in front of the steering wheel and closed his own door. With his left foot he stepped on the clutch pedal. He slammed his right foot on the brake pedal. Out loud he talked himself through the next steps, "Okay, Johnny Boy, all you got to do now is shift into neutral, release the emergency brake, slowly let go of the brake, and steer this dirty bastard toward the open space. And then jump like a deer before it leaves the road."

Another car rounded the corner and sped by as Nolan ducked out of sight. His heart pumped, his head throbbed, and his mind raced. "It's time, Johnny Boy; coast is clear." He took a deep breath and shifted the gearshift into neutral. One more look. The emergency brake released easily. His foot eased off the brake pedal and the truck began to coast. Nolan loosened his fingers on the steering wheel. He lined up the truck perfectly as it picked up speed. He switched his left foot over to work the brake and slid over toward the passenger door. His left hand barely guided the steering wheel as the truck picked up speed. Fifteen feet from the road's edge, he let go and reached for the doorknob.

The door didn't open. Ten feet. Faster. Five feet. He grabbed the window handle and furiously wound it downward. "Oh good Christ Almighty." The front wheels left the pavement. The cold

September air rushed into his face as the back wheels of the pickup left the pavement. In slow motion action, the shiny, black Chevy pickup sailed quietly into the night.

Mikhail sat up in bed. His quick movement started Hannah. "Are you alright, Mikhail?"

"Ya. Ya. Fine. Thought I heard somethin'." He looked over at the black alarm clock on the table near their bed. One fifteen.

She snuggled up against him. "Hold me, Mikhail. I'm cold." They wrapped each other with their bodies. "How about some more of that yummy stuff we did earlier right after coffee in the morning? You animal!"

"Great, as long as I go get it for us. Very hot with cream, right?"

Hannah turned over and nuzzled in the curves of his chest. Mikhail wrapped his arms around her and found a way to watch and smell her as she fell asleep. Several thoughts swirled around his mind as his body gave way to sleep. Number one, what else was in that satchel? Number two, why did she bring the nightgown? Number three, this room number, his new lucky number? They barely moved the rest of the night.

The longest night of his young life came to an end. Tomas sat in the hard wooden chair and stared at the bed in John Nolan's bunkhouse room. The bed remained untouched. Nolan didn't return right away like he said he would. So many times throughout the night, Tomas prayed that it all had been a bad dream. A nightmare. The swelling on the knuckle on his right hand ruined the dream. He killed David Sednick. Nolan said he'd take care of it. Morning light poured under the closed door. Tomas told himself he'd wait until eight in the morning. Then he'd go find the Sheriff and turn himself in. Throughout the long night, he emptied his stomach from the onslaught of shattered nerves. Several times dry heaves shook his body. He'd be sent to prison for sure. His life was over.

The hallway door opened and at least two men stopped outside of his room down the hall from where he sat. One of the men knocked on the door. After no one answered, Tomas heard the door open. "His sister said he stayed here and he'd want to know. Nobody around." Once outside, Ted Hughes continued, "We better get back over to the wreck site. We've got a lot of explaining to do, and we'll need every detail. That dumbshit Sednick anyway."

Al Sutter snapped photos of the area where David's pickup left the pavement. He paused as he focused on the branches off to the side of the opening. "Hey Sheriff. Come on over here a second."

Sheriff Schustrom stood up from his kneeling position of checking the tire tracks and meandered over to Sutter. "What you got there, Al?"

Sutter rubbed his fingers together with the red liquid he gathered from the fir tree branch. "Looks and feels like blood."

After a closer look, Schustrom walked over to the branch, held on, and took a few steps down the embankment. "I got more blood down here Al. Lots of it."

Sutter reloaded film into his camera. "Do you think he tried to get out of the window before it left the road?"

"Possibly. I'll walk down as far as I can. Maybe there was somebody else in the truck. I'll see what's what."

Hannah cupped the steaming hot cup of coffee Mikhail brought to her as she lazed about in their hotel bed. He sat on the bed and faced her. The morning light pierced the window through the partially drawn curtain. "I thought you looked beautiful last night. The mornin' suits you fine, too."

She held the cup near her mouth and sleepily looked over the rim of the cup at him, "You're really a smooth talker Mikhail

Anzich. But the words aren't necessary. After I finish this coffee, you're gonna get it again. And you'll like the view too. And you won't have to walk up the stairs behind me to get it."

Ten minutes later Hannah laid on her left side and guided Mikhail into position behind her. Slowly and with a newfound confidence, Mikhail entered Hannah from behind and moved in and out with a gentleness that left her in awe. Due to the arch and curve in the small of Hannah's back, Mikhail watched his own movements briefly, rather struck by the waning and waxing of blood in his penis. He cupped her right breast with his right hand and reminded himself to let go with his own climax.

"Tell me when, Mikhail. I want to make that trip with you at the right moment." Again, Hannah laughed with pure joy and release at what her body provided her. "You are gorgeous, Mikhail Anzich. Absolutely gorgeous."

— · · —

FBI agents Moore and Hughes stood near the hearse as the men loaded David's mangled body into the back of the vehicle. Moore shook his head, "Sednick must've been pretty drunk. The inside of the truck smells of whiskey. You wonder what he was doin' up on that road at night anyway. The headlights weren't even on in his pickup." He examined what remained of the inside of the pickup. His hands and eyes focused on the key plugged into the ignition in the off position. Next he wiggled the gearshift. It remained locked securely in neutral. Agent Moore jotted down some notes and closed his small notebook.

The tow truck driver pushed the boom handle and lifted the front end of the truck into the air. The back tires stayed on the ground for the trip to the junkyard in Columbia Falls. He jawed to the small crowd as he worked, "Shame. Hell of a rig. There ain't nothing left of her to salvage. Musta flew three hundred feet before it hit the rocks. Hard to believe it didn't burn up. Damn shame is all."

— · · —

The Davenport Hotel in downtown Spokane first opened in 1914. This historic thirteen-story hotel featured amenities unlike any other hotel in the region. All of the furniture was hand-carved mahogany. Imported Irish linens and crosscut travertine marble showers and bathrooms decorated the spacious guest rooms.

Roy Devers sat in the one-hundred year old chair near his ornate feather bed and read the letter handed to him by the night clerk as he registered. Devers set the twenty-five hundred dollars on the table as he reread the brief note clipped to the money. "Goodbye, Mr. Devers. This ends our business together."

He flipped the note over and stared at the blank page. "Son-of-a-bitch," he mumbled. "Hansen must of known what I planned for him." Devers returned the note to the white envelope and looked at the postal marking on the outside of the envelope. "Kalispell, Montana."

Roy Devers laid down on his bed. He shook his head as he thought, "Old Slick mailed it a week ago. Son-of-a-bitch."

Tomas closed the door to Nolan's room behind him. Time to call the sheriff. His foggy mind searched for answers. The long night of searching his soul didn't produce any answers. "I'm all-alone when I need somebody most of all. I wish Dad didn't go to Whitefish. I don't even know where to get a hold of him. I could sure use him now to go with me to the sheriff. I can't wait any longer for John Nolan." As he headed for the front door, he slowly turned around as the back door hinges creaked. Through the dim light he saw Nolan crawl in and crumble in a pile on the floor. With ten long steps, Tomas knelt down and reached him. "Oh my God! What happened? I'll get Dr. Green."

The bloody right hand of John Nolan weakly grabbed Tomas' arm. "No. My room." He gasped and passed out.

Another man came out of the shower room a few feet away. Tomas yelled at him, "Help me get him into his room. Help me, please! He's hurt bad!"

The two men lifted Nolan and walked him into Nolan's room and gently placed him on his bed. The man rubbed the blood off his hands to the towel wrapped around his waist. "Hey, fella. This guy's bleedin' real bad. Looks like to me we best get the doctor. He might die if we don't get him help."

"Okay! Okay! Call for the doctor? I'll stay here with him." The man raced back to his room, dressed, and ran across the street to use the phone.

Tomas cried as he patted Nolan's chest and applied pressure to his bleeding right arm. His white skin contrasted with the blood-covered clothes and deep scratches across his face. John Nolan weakly opened his eyes. They blinked and battled the need to close. Through the tears and runny nose, Tomas whispered, "Uncle. What happened? What did you do with David?"

Nolan lifted his finger and motioned Tomas closer. "It's okay, Kid. His truck crashed."

With his shirt sleeve, Tomas brushed the tears from his eyes and the snot from his nose, "What? I killed him."

He attempted to grab Tomas, but all of his energy left him on the walk and crawl back to the barracks. In a barely audible voice Nolan mumbled, "Kid, he died in his truck. Follow." His hands went limp and his eyes closed.

Tomas listened to Nolan's shallow, rapid breathing. He covered him with the green army blanket from the end of the bed. "Okay Uncle John. Okay. I follow. Doctor'll be here soon. Don't die. It's all my fault. Please don't die."

---·•·---

Nolan's blood trail followed the road down from the Dam. Sheriff Schustrom tracked the trail in and out of the trees that paralleled the road. Al Sutter followed in the Sheriff's car and stopped next to the Sheriff. "Guy's bleeding pretty good, huh Sheriff."

"Ya. He's lost a lot of blood. I expect we'll find him along the road. Let's drive ahead and check from time to time. Looks like he's trying to make it to town. Wonder why he didn't flag somebody down? Most likely didn't know what he was doin'. That happens sometimes after losin' this kind of blood."

Sutter nodded his agreement. They slowly drove down the road a half-mile or so and stopped. Schustrom checked the side of the road and found traces of blood. "Let's go down to the bottom of the road and see if we still find trace. If not, we'll double back up here and start again." At the junction of the road and Highway 2, they found a pool of blood. The trail headed toward Martin City. Schustrom got back in the car and said, "Whoever he is, he's one tough bastard. I can't imagine he has much blood left in him."

The Columbia Falls ambulance raced by and turned for Martin City. Al Sutter waved his index finger and said, "Let's take a chance here and follow the ambulance. Maybe the guy works on the Dam and lives at the barracks."

Schustrom slid into the driver's seat, turned on the siren, and followed the ambulance into Martin City. As they passed Bill's Texaco, they saw the ambulance turn into the parking lot at the worker's barracks. "Nice guess, Al. Let's hope they came for our guy."

The nine o'clock morning train ride from Whitefish back to Coram went by quickly. Earlier Hannah and Mikhail leisurely ate their breakfast at the Cadillac. Hannah enjoyed the freshly squeezed orange juice along with her soft-boiled eggs and toast. She marveled at Mikhail's large appetite as he devoured ham and eggs, toast, hash browns, and several cups of coffee. As the train made the bend in the river across from Berne Park, Hannah turned to him and said, "Do you always eat that much in the morning?"

A big smile crossed his face, "Yes. If I can get it."

"And you did get it, didn't you?" She playfully elbowed him in the ribs and turned back to enjoy the scenery.

Mikhail watched the ambulance on the highway speed toward Columbia Falls. The lights on the ambulance flashed and the siren blared. The weird feeling from the night before returned to Mikhail. He couldn't put his finger on it. Hannah snapped him from his thoughts as she smoothly slid her arm inside of his when the train entered the dark tunnel.

CHAPTER THIRTY-THREE

The Great Northern Streamliner train pulled into Coram with a smooth stop. Mikhail and Hannah joined three other people and stepped on to the gangplank. They took their time and walked toward the gravel parking lot. "I told Tomas to leave my Chevy. I don't see it."

"We did get in a little early. He'll show up."

"Maybe. Hope somethin' ain't wrong with the car."

She playfully swatted him on the rump and said, "If he doesn't show up in a few minutes, I'll give you a ride home. That way I get you to myself a little bit longer."

Mikhail forced a weak smile, but his gut told him something wasn't right. "I'd appreciate a ride, Hannah. He ain't comin'. He'd be here by now. Somethin' ain't right."

"Okay, Mr. Worry Wart. Let's go." Hannah sensed his concern and thought it better to hold back on the joking around. The drive back to Columbia Falls took twenty minutes. Mikhail barely said five words as he stared out the window and fiddled with the spare set of car keys. He answered with one-word sentences or not at all. How quickly his mood changed she thought. I hope this isn't a side of him I need to worry about.

Outside of his house, Hannah turned to him, "Mikhail, did I do somethin' wrong?"

He turned quickly toward her as he released his right hand from the door handle, "No. No, Hannah. Everything was swell. I'm worried somethin' happened." He wrapped his hands around hers, "No, you were wonderful. Best time of my life. I mean it. I-"

"Mikhail Anzich, it was the best time of my life too. You need to go see to your family. Can you call me later?"

He reached over and softly kissed her lips. He moved back and opened the car door, "Ya. I'll call you later." The door gently closed. He quickly covered the distance of the driveway while his stomach flip-flopped and his heart thumped heavily in his chest.

Mikhail stood in the living room doorway and stared at his daughter's bandaged and swollen nose. Anna sat on the couch with Sara Reynolds reading a comic book. Bud Reynolds entered from the kitchen with a bowl of soup in his hand. He set it down on the dining room table and walked over to Mikhail. "You best sit down, Mik. A lot happened while you was gone."

Mikhail's legs rubberized, but he managed to get to his rocker in front of the bay window. Not wanting the answer he feared, he asked, "Is Tomas alright?"

Bud pulled the footstool over next to him and sat down. Bud stayed with Katya and Anna all night. Sleep called his name, but Katya asked him to break the news to her father. He struggled as he searched to present the news in the best words he knew, and then he belted out, "Ya. He's fine. Let me fill you in. It's a long story."

After Bud related everything that happened, Mikhail silently rose up, walked over to his daughter, and knelt in front of her. Before he could say a word, Anna spoke, "Papa. Daddy hit mommy. But he died."

Mikhail gulped and wrestled with the flood of emotions that engulfed him, "I'm sorry, honey. Everything will be fine. Just you wait and see." His time with Hannah seemed like a lifetime ago. Guilt roared into his mind for being gone when his family needed him most. The precious moments with Hannah blurred as the thought of David hitting Katya overwhelmed him. And Nolan. His best friend. Nolan always seemed to be there when Mikhail needed him. But when Nolan needed him most, he wasn't there.

Bud placed his hand on Mikhail's shoulder, "You best get up

to the hospital my friend. Nolan's in a bad way. Your son needs you too. He rode in the ambulance to the hospital. The Kid's pretty upset."

Mikhail braced his huge hands against the hardwood floor and stood up. He placed his right hand on her cheek and kissed Katya on the forehead. From across the room he heard Anna, "Papa. Hugs."

He leaned over and gently lifted Anna into his arms and softly caressed her. "Papa's proud of you. You're very brave." He kissed her and lumbered out to Bud's car. The storm of emotions attacked his broken heart. How'll I ever make it up to em'? I should've been there. I thought things was gonna be better. Nothing's ever gonna change. Things just keep goin' haywire.

The makeshift Sheriff's office in Hungry Horse squeezed in between the two-cell jail and the post office. Sheriff Schustrom sat at his tiny wooden desk and rewrote his notes from the truck accident. He planned to visit with the coroner later that afternoon after he visited with Nolan at the hospital. The rusty spring on the screen door squeaked as the FBI agents entered his office. Ted Hughes looked disheveled after a long night of absolutely no sleep and nothing to eat. He flashed his wallet badge and introduced himself to the Sheriff. "I'm Agent Hughes, and my partner is Agent Moore. We need everything you have on that truck accident last night."

Schustrom managed little sleep himself. He responded to the accident after a call from the station tender at the base of the Dam at four in the morning. He took his time as he stood up, "Well Agent Hughes, we all need somethin' now don't we. I need a good night's sleep, a bath, and a warm meal. But it don't look like I'm gonna get any of 'em anytime soon." He stretched his six-foot-three frame across his desk, leaned his weight on his desk, and glared at Hughes, "So you're gonna have to wait!"

Agent Hughes rolled his neck and wrinkled his nose to adjust his glasses. He edged closer to the desk and laid down his own glare before he responded, "The victim was in our care and was a key witness in two outstanding homicide investigations."

The Sheriff stood tall and looked down at the pen in his hand, "By the looks of things, you did a piss-poor job of takin' care of him." He smirked as he sat down in his creaky wooden chair.

Hughes heard enough, "Listen, you small town Roy Rogers, we-"

His partner interrupted him, "Hey men. Let's settle down. All of us can use some sleep. How about I buy lunch across the street? We can go over there and work together on this thing."

His Irish temper seethed as he swiveled his head and shot Moore his best dirty look. "Fine. Let's go eat." Hughes turned his back and walked out. The screen door slammed.

Schustrom gathered up his notes and notepad. "Well since the FBI is buyin', I'm eatin'. Let's go."

Mikhail entered the lobby of North Valley Hospital and approached the information table. A high school candy striper cheerfully greeted him. "Good afternoon. May I help you?"

"Yes. The room for John Nolan."

She paged through the patient roster and stopped at Nolan's name, "Are you family, sir?"

"He's my first cousin."

"Oh good. Mr. Nolan's in room 320. The elevator is-"

Mikhail stepped away and walked toward the elevator. The ebb and flow of guilt flowed freely now as he pushed the third floor button. "What the hell was Nolan doin' ridin' with David anyway? They hated each other. And what should I say to Tomas? He got stuck dealin' with all of it." The bell sounded the arrival of the elevator as it reached the third floor. He ducked his head as he stepped out into the hall. The nurse at the station looked over the counter of her station and asked, "Which room you looking for mister?"

"John Nolan. Room 320, I think."

She pointed her hand and arm as she spoke, "To the right, about half-ways down. He's been in and out, so don't stay long."

The overpowering smell of purex immediately attacked his nostrils. He hated the smell. There were just too many sad memories of ill or seriously injured friends or relatives in the hospital in Butte. But nothing in the past tortured him like seeing John Nolan. He paused in the doorway of Nolan's room. Tubes filled with blood flowed into Nolan's arm. His face showed only his eyes and mouth through the wrapped bandages.

Tomas rose from his seat at the foot of Nolan's bed. Mikhail immediately noticed how tired he looked. So worn out. His pale skin bleached out next to his dark hair, red eyes from crying, and his dirty, bloodstained white shirt. Tomas attempted to say something, but his lips trembled. Mikhail walked over to him and embraced him. Tomas broke away first and managed to speak, "He's so weak. Doctor said he's lost a ton of blood."

"He's tough. He'll make it. Seen him look worse."

"I, I needed you Dad. A lot happened. You always been there before. I didn't know what to do." Tomas moved back a few steps. His hands trembled as he fought back tears. "He punched Kat."

"You mean, David."

"Ya. I got so mad when I saw her face I lost control. I-"

Nolan knocked the water glass from the table. Tomas rushed to his side. Nolan's lips moved, but words didn't come out. Tomas clearly recognized the word "no" and the message attached to the slight wave of his finger back and forth. Nolan blinked his eyes a couple of times and drifted in and out of sleep.

Mikhail came closer, "Nolan. It's me, Mik. You know, the Bohunk. Wake up. It's gonna be fine. Don't quit!" His large hands gently shook Nolan's shoulder. "Hang tough, Partner. Hang tough." He moved back, turned away, and looked out the window into the gravel parking lot.

Tomas watched his father wipe his tears with the back of his right hand. Nolan's subtle message to him came out loud and clear. He remembered the last thing Nolan told him the night before about telling nobody about what happened. Tomas told himself he'd try his best, but it would be hard. The guilt of killing David haunted him, and not even twenty-four hours had passed. Now Nolan's life hung in the balance. It's all my fault. How would he keep the secret? For now, he'd do it for Nolan. But if somehow Nolan were blamed for David's death, he'd confess. He silently prayed, "God please don't take John Nolan. Please. We all need em."

After lunch, Sheriff Schustrom stood outside the Club Café with Hughes and Moore. He put in a plug of chew, straightened his black cowboy hat, and rubbed the fresh coffee stain on his wrinkled western shirt. After he shook their hands, he spoke in a hoarse, deep voice, "I'll follow up with that Nolan fella if he pulls thorough. Looks like he jumped from the truck alright. I'll send you whatever I find."

Hughes knocked off a couple of sandwich breadcrumbs from his suit coat, "Thanks. Our Butte office talked with the Los Angeles office. Looks like they will have a couple of agents sitting on Hansen's bank accounts in Palm Springs. I look forward to bringing him back to Montana. I don't know if we can pin those two homicides on him, but the money laundering will be easy. We have Sednick's signed statements. We'll get Hansen and anybody else connected with him."

Once Schustrom pulled away in his pickup, Hughes turned and faced his partner. "Maybe we should've been straight with him. You and I both know that was no car accident. The damn car was in neutral and the key was in the off position."

Agent Moore loosened his tie, nodded his head forward and said, "I know. Sednick crossed a lot of people. Who knows what went on in that truck. No need for us to pursue it though."

"I agree. Besides, I don't think we want a big homicide investigation going on while Truman and half of the country's press are here. Pretty tough for us to pin it on Nolan anyway. Too little evidence to build a case against him."

Hughes started the car engine and shifted out of neutral, "That's good enough with me. We need to get back to Butte and pack for California. I can't wait to close the book on Hansen."

CHAPTER THIRTY-FOUR

Three days later, the October 1st early morning sun greeted Al Sutter when his wife shook him awake at 5:30. "Rise and shine, Al. Big day. You get to meet the President of the United States."

The restless night of sleep already informed him of what the day had in store for him. His stomach burned. He made a mental note to have his high school assistant run and get him some Rolaids. Sutter sponsored a writing contest at Columbia Falls High School, and a with a flip of the coin, Will Talbott became his assistant for one day.

He munched down some corn flakes and dry toast. His wife helped him load his cameras, cases, and other photography equipment into the trunk of his car. "I'm picking up young Will at 7:00, so I better hit the road." Sutter received a kiss from his wife and drove across Columbia Falls to pick up the young man that would never forget today. One by one, Al mentally checked off each of his planned activities for the Hungry Horse dedication ceremonies.

Will Talbott sat on the top step of his front porch. He leaped off the porch when he saw Sutter's car pull up the street. The car barely stopped when Will opened the door and crashed down into the front seat opposite the famed newspaperman. "Holy smokes, Will! Take it easy. Thank God I didn't have my camera on the seat."

Al Sutter wore a white tee shirt underneath his long sleeve white shirt. The light-colored tan sport coat covered the shoulders that supported the camera bag, light meter, and camera. His white hat with the colorful band tipped to the side of his head. The black-rimmed glasses hung out of his coat pocket.

They arrived at the train depot in Columbia Falls. The Pennsylvania Railroad provided the presidential train for Harry Truman. Al coasted to a stop across from the train. "Let's go snap some photos. Maybe we'll be lucky enough to get a shot of the President." Will lugged the pack supplied with film, flash bulbs, and assorted camera equipment. Al led them across the tracks and up to the single secret service guard at the caboose end of the train. He started to introduce himself when the back door of the caboose opened. President Harry Truman and his daughter Margaret stepped out and climbed down the temporary medal steps.

Truman smiled and stepped over to Sutter and the stunned high school boy, Will Talbott. "Good morning. How about joining me on my morning constitutional?" He shook Al Sutter's hand and then Talbott's. The secret service man, Margaret, and the President strode down the gravel road toward the North Fork. The camera buzzed with action, and equipment bounced as the two jogged to stay up with the President. Al's hat drooped well below his right eye. His stomach blazed from the stomach acid fire as he looked at Will, "First chance you get, buy me some antacid, lots of it. Here's a silver dollar."

At ten o'clock that morning, a crowd of one-thousand cheering people stood around the back of the train and listened to the high school band bang out patriotic songs. President Truman stepped out and held a microphone. Montana Senator Mike Mansfield stood beside him on the porch of the caboose. Three large black speakers attached to the caboose belted out the President's words, "The Republicans have nominated a great general to run for President. I am very fond of that great general, but his whole life has been spent as a military man. He has a military mind, which is a very peculiar one. He did a wonderful job as commanding general of allied forces in Europe. But that in no way fits him to be President of the United States." Sutter snapped photos while Will wrote every word the President said.

The President and his five secret service men climbed into loaned cars. They joined the police and highway patrol caravan toward Hungry Horse. As they approached the bridge over the South Fork of the Flathead River, the President viewed the crowd that lined the haul road leading to the base of the Dam.

The Care Less Group ladies walked the sides of the dusty road and distributed miniature flags to the school kids and locals that waited for a chance to see the President up close. Hannah paused as she came by Mikhail and his family. Anna sat high on Tomas' shoulders. She smiled at Hannah as she accepted the flag. Mikhail handed her his flag, and Anna waved both of the flags on the wooden sticks. Hannah raised her eyebrows and smiled at Mikhail as she continued along the parade route.

President Truman waved as the motorcade passed by the impressive tunnel of canyon residents. His eyes temporarily stopped ahead on Anna with her two flags and the oxygen tank in her uncle's hand. "Stop a second, driver. Pull up by that little girl with the walker in front of her." The car paused in front of Anna. Truman smiled at her and winked. Anna wrinkled her face in a vain attempt to form her best wink. After no success, she blew him a kiss. Truman waved and instructed the driver to continue. The press bus marked the end of the parade. Inside, Al Sutter and his assistant sat with pressmen from national magazines and newspapers. Al nervously fumbled with his film cartridges as he spoke, "You'll never forget today, Will. Nether will I. Just think, we shook the President's hand. The spotlight of the nation's press, radio, newsreel and television is on the Flathead today. One million dollars worth of publicity is spent for the thirty-thousand people of Flathead County." Will shook his head and nodded his agreement with what Sutter said.

At the base of the Dam, Superintendent W.R. Scalf introduced President Truman. He stepped back and stood next to his friend Al Sutter and his secretary Mary Metcalf. As the President made his way to the set of microphones, Scalf gazed up at the completed structure. He vividly recalled the day the first concrete poured from the massive bucket onto the pad where they now stood. Quick visions of men working in all kinds of conditions roared by. Mammoth challenges faced and met marched quickly through his mind's eye. Stomach-turning accidents that claimed lives and destroyed families sent faces racing across in front of him. The crowd's loud applause welcomed the President of the United States. W.R. Scalf refocused his attention. Harry Truman stood only five feet away from him.

A white hard hat covered the President's head as he spoke to the crowd of dignitaries and politicians. "One brand new heavy industry plant, a chemical plant at Silver Bow, has already been built to operate on Hungry Horse electrical power. A major aluminum plant is to be built near here, and it too will use Hungry Horse electricity. New industry is coming in, in other words, before the dam is even finished. There isn't the slightest doubt that this electricity will be used, that you people will get new production and new jobs and new prosperity out of it, and that your government will be repaid every cent the dam has cost, with interest."

At 11:15 later that morning, the President pulled a switch that acknowledged the start of the first of four 71,250-kilowatt generators at Hungry Horse Dam. Five-thousand people listened to his fiery speech at Flathead High School in Kalispell. The twenty-minute speech blasted the Republicans and the Montana Power for dragging their feet about building Hungry Horse Dam. "The Republicans are tools of the special interests. Public power is as much a part of the country today as the public school and the forest service. If the Republicans win this election, it will be a long time before you will see another dam like Hungry Horse."

Al Sutter chewed the antacid pills and shot rolls of film while his assistant continued taking notes. The press passes allowed him to stand on the floor of the gym right below the stage. Twenty minutes later, the president drove back to Columbia Falls and boarded his train for the final stop at the Whitefish train depot. And then Truman departed west.

Chapter Thirty-Five

A month later, Tomas sat on a bench in the Whitefish Train Depot and held Anna in his lap. The first snow of the season appeared two days earlier and the temperature read 18 degrees on the thermometer outside of the train station. Anna toyed with the zipper on Tomas' winter coat. She stared at his zipper as she quietly spoke, "Where's Seattle, Uncle?"

He rubbed her knee, "It's near the ocean. Remember I showed you on the map. Not too far away."

"I wanna go too."

The last few weeks sped by as Tomas helped Katya around the house and babysat Anna whenever his sister needed to do something away from the house. The time with Anna was bittersweet. Their relationship took a turn upward. He turned all of his attention to the family and fought the reoccurring thoughts of what happened with David and with Nolan. He questioned himself over and over about whether or not he should turn himself in. But as John Nolan slowly recovered, Tomas renewed his promise to not expose the truth. His stomach flipped as the clerk at the counter announced that the westbound train entered the yard and would leave in about ten minutes.

Mikhail and Hannah stood arm in arm a few feet away. She

flashbacked to their wonderful train trip weeks ago. John Nolan nervously entertained Katya near the front door. Small band-aids replaced the mummy wrap bandages on his right arm. The stitches on his forehead and cheek sealed the worst cuts. He kept the serious wound on his thigh covered with a heavy bandage. "Now listen to me, Kat. It ain't no lie, if you honest to God believe it's true. That woman flirted with me first. I never started it. Her husband had no right."

Katya faked a laugh. Her nervous attention focused on her daughter and her brother. "John Nolan. You're a Butte cur. A loveable one for sure. But still a cur." She kissed his unscarred cheek and walked over and sat down on the bench next to Tomas.

"Mommy. Uncle's going to Seattle."

She snuggled closer. "Yes, honey. He is. And we get to see him at Christmas right here at this train depot."

"Will I get a present?"

Tomas grinned, "Butterfly. I'll bring you the biggest present they have in Seattle." He spread his arms to show how big the present would be."

"No. Bigger Uncle. Bigger."

He sat her down on the bench next to him and stood up. His arms spread across in front of him and made a six-foot span. "How about this here big?"

Anna jumped into his arms. "Yes! That big."

Other train passengers picked up their bags and walked toward the door to the train. The clerk bellered out, "We're now loadin' for Spokane, Pasco, and Seattle."

Katya took Anna from Tomas. He'd cried enough the past few months, and he wouldn't cry today. Not today. He promised himself to be strong. The promise didn't expect the words from his father as they sauntered together to board the train. Once outside, Mikhail motioned Tomas to the side. In a very clear voice Mikhail said, "Proud of you son. Real proud." They embraced after Tomas dropped his green suitcase. Through his tears Mikhail spoke as he kissed Tomas on the cheek, "I love you, Tom."

His promise not to cry broke. Tomas never heard those words from his father until now. Nor did he ever speak those words himself. "I love you too, Dad." The sight of the two men embracing caused an avalanche of emotions from the rest of the family.

John Nolan picked up Tomas' suitcase and smirked as he spoke, "Holy Shit! Two big ugly bears hugging the shit out of each other. Wait 'til I tell the boys at the Aluminum Plant about this. A perfectly good woman there to hug and the big Bohunk hugs his boy. Christ, haven't learned him nothin'. Not one goddamn thing."

The group laughed and his timely humor broke the stomach-churning scene. Nolan handed Tomas his bag and limped toward the last train car. As they neared the steps, Nolan stopped, focusing his eyes on Tomas' red eyes. "Remember Kid. It's our secret. Never tell nobody. And one more thing. While you're in the Navy, nail one of them China girls for me. I heard their snappers go sideways. I gotta know for myself. Follow?"

Tomas shook his head, laughed, and rolled his eyes. "Give me a hug, Uncle John. Our secret, I promise. Thank you. I love you very much, and that's one more secret."

Katya interrupted their moment, "My turn Little Brother. Get over here." After one more emotional embrace with his sister, he walked over to his dad one more time. He reached up and kissed Anna who draped her arm around her grandfather's neck. The conductor yelled, "All aboard." Tomas stretched his arms to show Anna how big her present would be and boarded the train to Seattle to begin his great adventure in Shorty Davis' Navy.

⁀ Chapter Thirty-Six ⁀

September 10, 2007
Montana Veterans Home
Columbia Falls, Montana

Columbia Falls police detectives Danford and Raiman walked with the personal care attendant Steve toward the picnic area of the Montana Veterans Home. As they walked, Detective Danford spoke to the young man, "You say this man wants to confess to a crime from way back in the 50's?"

Steve clipped the pencil to the snap on his clipboard, "Yes, Sir. That's all he told me. That's him over there sleeping in his wheelchair by the birch tree." He led the detectives and stood in front of the man slouched over in his wheelchair. "Mr. A. I got the police for you like you asked." Steve gently shook the man's arm, "Mr. A., Mr. A. It's me, Steve."

Detective Raiman placed his fingers on the man's neck and searched for a pulse. He checked his wrist. No pulse. His eyes turned and faced Steve. "Sorry son, this man's dead."

Steve knelt in front of the chair, "No. Not Mr. A. It can't be." He covered his mouth, and the tears streamed down his face.

"What was his name, son?"

After he gained some composure, Steve mumbled, "Thomas John Anzich."

"Does he have living relatives nearby?"

"Yes. His niece and her kids and husband come by often. She

was just here earlier this morning to visit him."

Detective Danford wrote the name on his notepad. "Are you sure you don't know what he wanted to confess? Not that it makes any difference now."

"No. He only talked to me about his wonderful travels in the Navy. Mr. A. traveled all over the world. He retired from the Navy after twenty-five years before he started to work at the Aluminum Plant. He's lived in Columbia Falls for the past thirty years or so before he got cancer last year.

Detective Raiman moved closer to Tomas and touched the faded tattoo of an orange butterfly on Tomas' forearm. "Neat tat. Don't expect to see a butterfly on a Navy man's arm. Usually a snake or woman or something."

Steve sobbed again as he pulled the blanket up over Tomas' body, "He told me it was for his niece. I guess he called her Butterfly."

"So he never married?"

"Oh ya, he was happily married for a long time. His wife died a few years back. She couldn't have kids, but it didn't matter. His niece's kids were like their kids, I guess. They sure love him anyway."

Steve wheeled Tomas' body inside to the infirmary. As he removed the blanket, a faded photograph drifted to the floor. Steve picked up the photo and smiled as he looked at two older men, two women, and a smiling, young man. The other men and women in the photo also smiled. This must have been one of his favorite days. He read the aged inscription on the back, "Polebridge, North Fork, August 1952. Dad, Uncle John, Hannah, her mother, and me."